LOOKING BACKWARD

2000–1887

LOOKING BACKWARD

2000–1887

Edward Bellamy

edited by Alex MacDonald

broadview literary texts

National Library of Canada Cataloguing in Publication

Bellamy, Edward, 1850-1898
    Looking backward, 2000-1887 / Edward Bellamy; edited by Alex MacDonald.

(Broadview literary texts)
Includes bibliographical references.
ISBN 1-55111-406-2

1. Utopias—Fiction. I. MacDonald, Alex, 1948- II. Title. III. Series.

HX811.1887 B33 2002   813'.4   C2002-904421-9

Broadview Press Ltd. is an independent, international publishing house, incorporated in 1985. Broadview believes in shared ownership, both with its employees and with the general public; since the year 2000 Broadview shares have traded publicly on the Toronto Venture Exchange under the symbol BDP.

We welcome comments and suggestions regarding any aspect of our publications—please feel free to contact us at the addresses below or at broadview@broadviewpress.com.

North America
PO Box 1243, Peterborough, Ontario, Canada K9J 7H5
3576 California Road, Orchard Park, NY, USA 14127
Tel: (705) 743-8990; Fax: (705) 743-8353
email: customerservice@broadviewpress.com

UK, Ireland, and continental Europe
Thomas Lyster Ltd., Units 3 & 4a, Old Boundary Way
Burscough Road, Ormskirk
Lancashire, L39 2YW
Tel: (01695) 575112; Fax: (01695) 570120
email: books@tlyster.co.uk

Australia and New Zealand
UNIREPS, University of New South Wales
Sydney, NSW, 2052
Tel: 61 2 9664 0999; Fax: 61 2 9664 5420
email: info.press@unsw.edu.au
www.broadviewpress.com

Broadview Press Ltd. gratefully acknowledges the financial support of the Government of Canada through the Book Publishing Industry Development Program for our publishing activities.

This book is printed on acid-free paper containing 100% post-consumer fibre.

Series editor: Professor L.W. Conolly
Advisory editor for this volume: Michel Pharand

PRINTED IN CANADA

Recycled
Supporting responsible use
of forest resources
FSC www.fsc.org Cert no. SGS-COC-003153
© 1996 Forest Stewardship Council

Contents

Acknowledgements

I would like to acknowledge and thank the following for their help: Cathy Kroll of Sonoma State University, colleague and friend, for conversations out of which came the idea for this book; Julia Gaunce, Don LePan, Leonard Conolly, Barbara Conolly, Michel Pharand and Judith Earnshaw of Broadview Press for encouragement and editorial support; Rod MacDonald for legal advice; Stacey Sallenback of Campion College, for expertly typing and preparing the manuscript and for reminding me—notwithstanding Edith Leete (Chapter X)—that perfection is not an option; Campion College for a sabbatical leave in which to do the necessary research; Myfanwy Truscott, Librarian at Campion College, for help with copyright questions; staff of the University of Regina Library for help with research, especially the Inter-Library Loans office; staff of the Regina Public Library for reference help; staff of the Houghton Library at Harvard University for help with research and for permission to quote from the unpublished Bellamy papers; the Boston Public Library for permission to examine microfilm records; Jeffrey Martin of the Cleveland Public Library for help with a reference; Stephen R. Jendrysik, President of the Edward Bellamy Memorial Association, for help exploring the materials at Bellamy House in Chicopee, for permission to use photographs from the collection to illustrate this edition and for suggestions; my sister-in-law, Kim A. Pruden, for encouragement; my mother Helen Fraser MacDonald, for information on the bustle, and to my father-in-law, the late John E. Arthur Jr., for information about Francis Bellamy; Kim Korby Fraser of *Ladies' Home Journal* and Scott Sanders of Antioch College for help with copyright questions; Jack Boan, Stuart Wilson and Rick Kleer (Economics, University of Regina) for helpful suggestions; William Howard (English, University of Regina) for help with a Wordsworth quotation; Tim Lilburn, of St. Peter's at Muenster, for information about Duns Scotus; Bryan Alexander, Rob Vaughn, Ed Kunin, Phil Wegner, Toby Widdicombe, Peter Sands of the H-Net List for Utopian Studies, Larry Ashley, Jean-Louis

Margolin and other colleagues in and around the Society for Utopian Studies for suggestions and especially to Ken Roemer and Lyman Tower Sargent for comments on the draft; Mike Bellamy, great-grandson of Edward Bellamy, for helpful suggestions; students in Humanities 260 (Utopian Literature, Thought and Experiment) who have repeatedly confirmed my belief that a good utopian book is a blessing to the world, for even if we don't agree, it challenges us to think beyond to what could be.

EDWARD BELLAMY
Courtesy of the Edward Bellamy Memorial Association

EMMA SANDERSON BELLAMY
Courtesy of the Edward Bellamy Memorial Association

Introduction

Edward Bellamy's *Looking Backward: 2000–1887* is one of the great utopian novels. It tells the story of Julian West, a wealthy young Bostonian who goes into a hypnotic sleep in 1887 and is wakened in the year 2000. His hosts show him the world of the future and explain the wonderful changes which have occurred: the nineteenth-century society of cut-throat economic competition has been replaced by a world of harmonious co-operation and abundance for all. Before the end, West goes back to the nineteenth century in a dream and is horrified at the poverty and the inequality. When he wakes he is deeply grateful to be in a future where poverty and inequality have disappeared, though feeling guilty because he has done nothing to bring this future about. He is also overjoyed to be in love with the beautiful Edith, a descendant of his nineteenth-century sweetheart. Such is the tale. When it appeared in 1888 it catapulted Bellamy from relative obscurity to fame and it had a huge impact.

Edward Bellamy was born in 1850 in the Western Massachusetts mill town of Chicopee Falls. His father was the Reverend Rufus King Bellamy, a Baptist minister. His mother was also a deeply religious person and this family background was evident in *Looking Backward* in two ways. One was the oppressive sense which Julian West feels at one point and which he relates to his experience, and no doubt Edward Bellamy's, of Calvinist Sundays as a youth. But a more important way was the joyous and exalted sense that the happy future of humanity was a fulfillment of the Divine evolutionary plan. There are many biblical references in *Looking Backward*, and even a radio sermon by the utopian preacher Mr. Barton. Although Bellamy's central concern was the economic arrangement of society, there is also a sense in which *Looking Backward* may be accurately described as a religious novel.

In his youth Bellamy observed the mills of Chicopee Falls and the lives of the laborers who worked in them, and his journals of an early age reflect his interest in social arrangements, stimulated by a trip to Europe on which he saw examples of extreme poverty (Appendix A). Another strong interest was the military life. When he was ten he wrote about the character of the soldier as demonstrating "Self control...Obedience to orders...Love for his profession."[1] The next year the Civil War began and brought daily stories from the front. Bellamy applied to the famous military academy, West Point, in 1867, but his dream of a soldier's life ended when he was refused due to his health (the tubercular tendencies which eventually killed him). These elements of his early life—the mills of Chicopee Falls and the battlefields of the Civil War—were clearly reflected in the great economic idea of *Looking Backward*, the industrial army.

He qualified to practise law but turned instead to newspaper journalism and the authorship of novels. His first novel in 1878 was *Six to One*, the light romantic story of a bachelor and six girls on Nantucket Island for the summer. Next came *The Duke of Stockbridge*, an historical novel about the Revolutionary episode of Shays' Rebellion, and *Dr. Heidenhoff's Process*, which involved the science fiction notion of erasing unpleasant memories.

Bellamy married Emma Sanderson in 1882 (she had grown up in the Bellamy household as his adopted sister) and their children Paul and Marion were born in 1884 and 1886. Although they had to live very frugally, the family appears to have been a happy one, and for Bellamy the children were profoundly important in turning his thoughts to the future, to the kind of world they could expect to live in, and therefore to *Looking Backward*. In the excerpt in Appendix A, Bellamy explains how he moved from planning to write a mere fantasy to writing a serious social prophecy.

After the publication of *Looking Backward*, his passion and his life's work became working for his ideas in the Nationalist Movement as editor, writer and sometime public speaker, and expanding them in the sequel *Equality*, published in 1897. But his tubercular condition began to get the better of him and according to those who knew him he was a sick man by 1894. However:

He did not have the appearance of an invalid upon the streets and in the fields where he often wandered, for his

---

[1] Mason A. Green. "Edward Bellamy Biography." Bellamy Papers in the Houghton Library at Harvard University, bMs Am 1181.10, 10.

bright, grey penetrating eye and steady step were about as they had always appeared to his neighbors; but he had a perfect knowledge of his impending dissolution.[1]

After a trip to Denver in hopes of improvement, he died at home in Chicopee Falls in 1898.

Looking Backward is a utopia and the first task of this introduction must be to define and describe Bellamy's place in this ancient tradition of social thought. The second section focuses on Bellamy's time and describes the background to this particular utopian novel: its writing, publication, reception and influence. The third task, of course, is to make some suggestions about the text itself. Any utopian projection invites us to ask how it came about and what are its important features. While commenting on the transition to utopia, and such matters as economics, government, education, relations of men and women, and the arts, I will trace a theme which is important both to the background of the novel and to its content: the tension between the conventional and the radical. *Looking Backward* makes a number of important concessions to what Bellamy saw as practical demands of the real world, but it remains at its heart a profoundly radical work of social prophecy.

Bellamy In the Utopian Tradition

Although St. Thomas More did not invent the idea of a better place, he certainly named it when he published his *Utopia* in 1516. The word involves a clever pun on its Greek roots, so that it means both good place (eu-topos) and no place (ou-topos). A "utopia" by this etymological definition is a good place which is no place, an imaginary commonwealth which is better than the real world of our experience. The commonly accepted antonym of utopia is "dystopia," a place which is worse than the real world of our experience. Utopian literature is that tradition of imagining better (and worse) places which began with ancient myths and is as contemporary as the most recent science fiction

---

[1]   Green, 183.

novel (or movie) about an alternate world. Utopias can be in fictional form, with characters and dialogue, or presented as documents, such as constitutions. Because these books set out to describe entire societies or worlds, they overlap with travel and time-travel stories, with political and sociological theorizing (a book like E.F. Schumacher's *Small is Beautiful* (1973) is a sort of utopian economics) and with fields like city planning (which also has to make assumptions about how social and spatial features relate). An area of study related to utopian writing is the study of "intentional communities"—colonies or communes in which people actually try to put utopian ideas into practice.

Most histories of utopia begin with the ancient account of the Golden Age given in Hesiod's *Works and Days*, in the eighth century BC, or with the story of Adam and Eve in the Garden in the Book of Genesis. A feature common to both these ancient stories is a better place which existed before time began, but a better place which was lost due to fate or human transgression. In the Greek myth the age of gold declined to an age of iron, and in Genesis Adam and Eve were expelled into the harsh world of pain and sweat. In this context, the search for utopia is the search to regain the lost paradise. Some have translated the myth into psychological terms and see human life as a search for the peace, harmony and security we enjoyed within our mothers' wombs. In this regard it is fascinating how the many independent accounts of near-death experiences involve passing through a tunnel into another world.

Utopia as a literary tradition begins with classical Greece, especially with Plato's *Republic* (c. 375 BC) and Aristotle's *Politics* (c. 350 BC). The familiar dictionary definition of utopia as a "perfect" state comes from Plato, whose Republic was presented frankly as a philosophical ideal rather than a blueprint for a real state. The Republic is a state characterized by justice, because it is ruled by Philosopher–Kings able to distinguish between appearances and reality. It is a hierarchical state, one of the standard patterns in the genre, the other being the egalitarian or democratic. Aristotle's *Politics* is more "practical" in a sense; it gives, for example, instructions for the best way to design city streets to achieve efficiency of movement yet confound invaders.

Over and over, elements of these classical utopias appear in the works which followed them, including *Looking Backward*: one thinks of the wise "philosophers" in Bellamy's America who vote for the President or the design of city streets with one efficient covering to replace many individual umbrellas.

The Renaissance has traditionally been described as a re-birth of classical ideas, including the idea of utopia. But contemporary features, such as the voyages of discovery and the birth of modern science, were also influential upon writers such as Thomas More and Francis Bacon. More's *Utopia* presented a country of hard-working citizens who yet didn't work too much, in fact only six hours per day, so that they could devote their time to the highest pleasure of all—the cultivation of the mind. Bellamy's citizens retire at 45 for a very similar reason. Bacon's *New Atlantis* (1626) described an island where scholars engaged in all manner of scientific studies, and where inventions included refrigeration and flying machines, a clear precursor of Bellamy's technological imagination in such features as the pneumatic tubes to distribute goods or the musical telephone.

In the eighteenth century the utopian impulse went in two directions: into conservative satires of utopianism such as Jonathan Swift's *Gulliver's Travels* (1726) or Samuel Johnson's *Rasselas* (1759) and into hopes for transformation of the real world in the American and French Revolutions:

> Not in Utopia, subterraneous Fields,
> Or some secreted Island, Heaven knows where,
> But in the very world which is the world
> Of all of us, the place on which, in the end,
> We find our happiness, or not at all.

Thus did William Wordsworth put it in *The Prelude* (X, 140-44) in 1805, at the start of the great industrial century which produced all manner of utopian dreaming, including the co-operative vision of Robert Owen, the time when the state shall wither away hinted at in *The Communist Manifesto* (1848) of Karl Marx and Friedrich Engels, the Transcendentalist communitarians of Brook Farm described in Nathaniel Hawthorne's *The*

Blithedale Romance (1852) and, at the end of the century, Bellamy's *Looking Backward* (1888), Morris's *News from Nowhere* (1890), Howells's *A Traveller from Altruria* (1894) as well as, in the new century, H.G. Wells's *A Modern Utopia* (1905) and Charlotte Perkins Gilman's feminist utopia *Herland* (1915). These famous works are only representative, for in the nineteenth century the bibliography of utopian works expanded enormously, an expansion which became an explosion in the twentieth century.

Several important currents of thought were running in the late nineteenth century and into the twentieth. Darwin had demonstrated with immense research the struggle for survival in the natural world. Freud had laid bare the unconscious primal drives in the human psyche. And World War I showed the terrible destructive power of science. All of it together meant human beings were not the rational creatures dreamed by some utopians, but that we had within us the seeds of our own annihilation.[1] The most famous utopias in the first half of the twentieth century were in fact dystopias: the inhuman mechanization of a world of total state domination in Yvgeni Zamiatin's *We* (1924), the ironic coldness of Aldous Huxley's *Brave New World* (1932) of mindless pleasures, and the nightmare of Thought Police and tortures in George Orwell's *Nineteen Eighty-Four* (1948). There is an interesting parallel between a recent embodiment of this dystopian vision and *Looking Backward*. In Bellamy's novel Julian West awakens to find a world which has achieved true equality and human happiness. In the film "The Matrix" (1999) Neo awakens to discover that the world he lives in is a simulation and the reality is a grotesque horror of domination by intelligent machines.

There have also been positive worlds depicted in twentieth-century utopias, for example in Aldous Huxley's *Island* (1962), Ursula K. Le Guin's *The Dispossessed* (1974) or Starhawk's *The Fifth Sacred Thing* (1993). But they are positive worlds with various kinds of serious problems to solve, and perhaps therefore it is possible to see Bellamy's *Looking Backward* as the crest of a wave of positive utopianism which began during the Renaissance with modern science and the idea of progress, reached its peak at the end of the

---

[1] See Chad Walsh. *From Utopia to Nightmare*. London: Geoffrey Bles, 1962.

nineteenth century, and thereafter broke into the contradictory currents of the twentieth century. The future of utopian writing is not known yet, of course, although it seems likely the dialectic between utopia and dystopia will continue and more "critical utopias"—worlds with serious problems—will be produced.[1]

The Writing And Influence Of *Looking Backward*

There are many references to contemporary conditions in *Looking Backward* which show that a good deal of Bellamy's motivation was his reaction to the society he lived in. It was a period of fierce business competition, competition in which some of the winners amassed enormous personal fortunes. Some of these fortunes were spent in lavish display, as evidenced by the A & E television series "America's Castles." The "barons" of oil and railways were among the most vigorous proponents of laissez-faire, which was raised to the status of dogma by the publication of such works as Spencer's *Social Statics* (1865).[2] The argument was reinforced by passage of the Fourteenth Amendment in 1868, which provided that no state should make law abridging the privileges or immunities of United States citizens, later becoming a "shield for business interests" in the courts.[3] At the same time there were many signs of government intervention in economic affairs, such as establishment of tax-supported municipal services. Repeated swings of boom and depression contributed to a situation in which strikes and violent disturbances of public order were increasingly common, a fact noted several times by Julian West, the narrator of *Looking Backward*. The affair of the Chicago Anarchists, seven men executed for alleged complicity in a bomb-throwing incident at a rally in 1886, became a symbol of the unrest. It is evident from *Looking Backward* that Bellamy was deeply moved by what he saw as

---

[1] See Lyman Tower Sargent, "Utopia and the Late Twentieth Century: A View From North America" in Sargent et al. *Utopia. The Search for the Ideal Society in the Western World.* New York, Oxford: Oxford University Press, 2000, 333-43.

[2] Samuel Eliot Morison. *The Oxford History of the American People.* New York: Oxford University Press, 1965, 770.

[3] Harry N. Scheiber et al. *American Economic History.* New York: Harper & Row, 1976 [1960] 297.

evidences of the failure of his society, and the general climate of contradictory economic beliefs and harsh contrasts of rich and poor are an important part of the background to the novel.

Looking Backward was first conceived, however, merely as a fantastic tale of the future rather than as a serious contribution to social and economic literature. Bellamy's notebooks of the late seventies and early eighties contain outlines for stories of the future of various kinds, including utopias based on eugenics and the raising of children by the state, and one intended to show the impossibility of communist and socialist ideas. It was principally his "discovery" of the concept of an industrial army which convinced him such ideas were not impossible of realization and led him to drop the more fantastic sections of *Looking Backward* to concentrate on social and economic matters.[1] Although still to be "in the form of a story," he resolved to "sacrifice all other effects" to explaining his solution for pressing social problems. This resolve taken, he began in earnest to write the novel late in 1886. It was completed within six or eight months and went to the printer in August of 1887. (See Appendix A for Bellamy's own accounts.)

Looking Backward was first published by Benjamin Ticknor of Boston in January 1888. In the first year it sold only 10,000 copies, but by December of 1889, after the Houghton Mifflin second edition, it was selling that number every week. Within a decade over a million copies had been sold in America and England, and as late as 1938 it was still selling 5,000 copies per year in the United States.[2] Its popularity was enormous, in part because it "tapped into a widespread sentiment."[3] The book was helped into the

---

1   However, it is probably more exact to say that Bellamy was of two minds on the matter, as there is considerable evidence of utopian idealism in his youthful writings, such as a speech of about 1870 which spoke of "faith in the good time coming." "Autobiographical Sketch." Bellamy Papers Binder 3-B, bMs Am 1181.6.

2   James D. Hart. *The Popular Book*. Berkeley and Los Angeles: University of California Press, 1961 [1950] 170-71.

3   One of the critical sequels to *Looking Backward*, Arthur Dudley Vinton's *Looking Further Backward* (Albany, N.Y.: Albany Book Co., 1890; reprinted by Arno Press 1971) admitted that it was "one of the wonders of the age" because "the majority of the thinking portion of the community found in this book an echo of their own thought," 5. However, in Vinton's sequel Bellamy's Nationalist system has fallen, the Chinese have taken over, individualism is again honored, and women have again become the "handmaiden" of male humanity, 188.

public eye by favorable notices from influential figures like William Dean Howells and Mark Twain; Twain read it in 1889 and found it a "fascinating book," and called Bellamy a "man who has made the accepted heaven paltry by inventing a better one on earth."[1] (An excerpt from Howells's own utopia appears in Appendix H.)

Looking Backward provoked a flood of utopian novels and pamphlets which reflected Bellamy's ideas, extended them in some fashion, or enthusiastically debated or opposed them. From as far away as New Zealand one earnest pamphleteer wrote: "I merely wish to show *how* we are to reach the state pictured by Bellamy, and also to show that we *must* go on in that direction, or back to barbarism."[2] In a French edition of 1891 the translator cautioned: "de tous les livres communistes que j'ai eus sous les yeux, c'est le plus dangereux," and he attached twenty pages of criticisms to the end of the novel.[3] Chief among these, and one noted by many critics, was the feared loss of individual freedoms in a bureaucratic state. In Richard Michaelis's satirical sequel, Dr. Leete becomes an advocate of paternalistic and authoritarian mind control, making such sarcastic remarks as "ideas are little sparks. They may easily cause a conflagration if not watched."[4] Many critics deplored the loss of competition: at the end of another sequel, showing how Bellamy's utopia would destroy itself, J.W. Roberts rejoiced that "business proper was born again," and concluded triumphantly that "PATERNALISM WAS DEAD."[5] George Sanders of Cleveland dedicated his reply "To Law and Order," confusing Bellamy with the anarchist dynamiters; his message was that "GOD HIMSELF RECOGNIZED THE RIGHT TO HOLD PRIVATE PROPERTY."[6]

---

1   *Mark Twain—Howells Letters,* ed. Henry Nash Smith et al. Cambridge, Mass.: Harvard University Press, 1960, 579.

2   Robinson Crusoe [Arthur William Sanford] *Looking Upwards,* Auckland, N.Z.: H. Brett, 1892, 7.

3   *Seul de Son Siècle.* Translation of *Looking Backward* by Le Vte Combes de Lestrade. Paris, 1891 np: "of all the communist books I have read, this is the most dangerous."

4   Richard Michaelis. *Looking Further Forward.* Chicago and New York: Rand, McNally & Co, 1890, 27. Reprinted by Arno Press in 1971.

5   J.W. Roberts. *Looking Within.* New York: A. S. Barnes & Co., 1893, 273 and 279. Reprinted by Arno Press in 1971.

6   George A. Sanders. *Reality ... A Reply to Edward Bellamy's "Looking Backward" and "Equality."* Cleveland: Burrows Brothers Co., 1898, 24.

Other reactions came in letters which Bellamy received after the publication of his utopian novel. A.L. McWhorter, who lived in "a little sod shanty on the arid and poverty stricken plains of South Dakota," wrote: "at one reading I have finished Looking Backward... I have never stood in reverential awe of any man. To You I bow in humble adoration. Your goodness and great abilities inspire in me a reverential feeling I never before possessed for any being."[1] E.D. Cooke of Santa Anna wrote: "I have just finished the perusal of 'Looking Backward' and tho' a stranger I cannot refrain from writing you. Your book has the stamp of Immortality. I had rather have written it than to be Author of *any* work, contemporaneous with, or preceding it."[2] From Europe came requests to translate the book: "After having perused a few chapters of your work *'Looking Backward'* I was so struck with the truth and beauty of the ideas in it that I instantly took the resolution of translating it into Hungarian."[3] Another wrote seeking permission to translate the work into Italian.[4] E. Lewis was an Ohio preacher who edited *Plain Talk*, a "newspaper for the people" which had as its motto "Do Right, Fear God and Make Money": Lewis wrote hailing *Looking Backward* as a "new gospel."[5] Another correspondent sent for Bellamy's edification a clipping from an unidentified newspaper, which takes a rather different approach:

Mr. Manhattan—Have you read that very extraordinary work by Bellamy, called 'Looking Backward'?

Miss Beacon Hill—Oh, yes: all Boston is raving about it.

Mr. M.—What do you think of it?

Miss B.H. (polishing her glasses)—I consider it a philosophical, encyclopedial histoury [sic],

---

1   A.L. McWhorter to E.B. (Dec. 6, 1889) bMs Am 1181 (280).
2   E.D. Cooke to E.B. (Aug. 29, 1889) bMs Am 1181 (167).
3   Julius Csernyci to E.B. (Budapest, Oct. 31, 1891) bMs Am 1181 (168).
4   P. Mazzoni to E.B. (London, July 21, 1890) bMs Am 1181 (283).
5   E. Lewis to E.B. (June 16, 1889) bMs Am 1181 (272).

reaching searchingly to the core of sociological
problems, astutely analyzing and disintegrating
the paradoxical relations by which
constitutional government is seemingly
opposed by impracticable demagogism,
ultimately to be moulded by masterminds and
colossal genius into an unity of peaceful
purpose, concatenated continuation, and an
almost inconceivably felicitous and
harmonious relations.[1]

One result of all this attention was that Bellamy himself became
a public figure for the first time. Although he pushed himself to
speak out on issues that concerned him, he remained deeply
attached to the privacy of his home. His wife later recalled his
habit of asking her to pull down the window shades in case
anyone called, yet spending hours chatting with tramps who
knocked at the back door, giving away his clothing or her baking
in return for their stories.[2] He worked mostly at home and was
often so preoccupied with a current project that he would dash
off to his study, crying "I've got a thought." According to his wife
"he had no system of writing at all. He wrote when he felt like
it, taking great pains with it all."[3] He was by nature something
of a hermit, and one visitor to his home remembered that when
a photograph was suggested Bellamy said "dearly beloved friend,
I'll be damned if I do."[4] Despite this taste for seclusion he played
an important role in the Nationalist movement, which was a
direct outgrowth of the popularity of *Looking Backward*.

The Nationalist movement, which flourished between 1889
and 1896, was a movement for nationalization of the means of
production, distribution and communication. Bellamy defined

---

1   Albert Hardy to E.B. (Springfield, Aug. 10, 1889) bMs Am 1181 (208).
2   Transcript of interview with Bellamy's wife. bMs Am 1182 (523). Not long before
     Looking Backward appeared Bellamy wrote to his wife: "Dear Emma, It occurs to me
     that you forgot to kiss me when I came away. I'll excuse you this time but don't let
     it happen again. Love, Ed." (19 May 1887) bMs Am 1181 (46).
3   bMs Am 1182 (523).
4   Henry Holiday. *Reminiscences of My Life.* London: William Heinemann, 1914, 356.

Nationalism as "the doctrine of those who hold that the principle of popular government by the equal voice of all for the equal benefit of all, which, in advanced nations, is already recognized as the law of the political organization, should be extended to the economical organization as well...." He saw "fragmentary anticipations" of the movement in various anti-monopoly and reform parties, in the rise of the Knights of Labor and in "the Henry George agitation" (see Appendix G) and he felt that the "particular service" of *Looking Backward* was "to interpret the purport and direction of the conditions and forces which were tending towards Nationalism, and thereby to make the evolution henceforth a conscious, and not, as previously, an unconscious, one."[1]

From its inception Nationalism was a middle-class movement. In an article on "Nationalism in California" in 1890, F.I. Vassault wrote that "the class of the people from which the strength of the Nationalist movement has been drawn is its most striking feature... For the most part, they are people connected with...the professions."[2] The First Nationalist Club of Boston was a collaboration between the Theosophical Society and a group of retired military men attracted by Bellamy's conception of an "industrial army."[3] In June of 1888 Cyrus Willard, a Boston journalist and a Theosophist, wrote to Bellamy with a proposal to establish a club to spread the message of *Looking Backward*. Bellamy had already

---

[1] Edward Bellamy. "The Progress of Nationalism in the United States." *North American Review* 154 (June, 1892) 742, 746.

[2] Quoted in Arthur E. Morgan. *Edward Bellamy*. New York: Columbia University Press, 1944, 266. At the October 1997 meeting of the Society for Utopian Studies, Ronald Howe of the American University of Washington, D. C., provided data to show that some 21 per cent of male Nationalist leaders, as located in the census of 1900, held blue-collar occupations, a somewhat higher proportion than has traditionally been thought. Thanks to Ken Roemer for this information. Roemer is currently preparing a new book entitled *Utopian Audiences* which will include an extensive account of reader response to *Looking Backward*. Ronald Howe's "Reconsidering Edward Bellamy in the Year 2000" will appear in *Edward Bellamy: His Legacy for a New Millennium*, edited by Toby Widdicombe and Hank Preiser.

[3] The Theosophical Society was founded in the United States in 1875 by Helen Blavatsky, a Russian immigrant. Its positive message was based on a belief in divine immanence and a process of upward evolution by reincarnation. Theosophists were attracted to Bellamy by the theme of universal brotherhood in his thinking but were interested exclusively in moral reform, while Bellamy wanted to see Nationalism develop as a practical political movement. Morgan, 260ff.

received a similar proposal from Sylvester Baxter, and he replied to Willard in July: "I heartily wish you and Mr. Baxter success in organizing in Boston the first Nationalist Club or association... I thoroughly approve what you say as to directing your efforts more particularly to the conversion of the cultured and conservative class. That was precisely the special end for which *Looking Backward* was written."[1] In a speech given on the first anniversary of the Boston Club, Willard noted that the organizers had made it an "unwritten law" that membership be limited as much as possible "to men who had been successful in the present fierce competitive struggle" and not open to the "crank and uneducated foreigner" with "exotic" ideas.[2] One critic has judged that "Nationalists feared coarseness more than capitalism," and his remark is paralleled by the club's journal, *The Nationalist*, which claimed proudly that members were "men of position, educated, conservative in speech, and of the oldest New England families."[3] But to balance this somewhat incongruous snobbery, it can be noted that Bellamy himself sought a more rational basis for the movement's class orientation, which he found partly in a new definition of conservatism. He saw this conservatism as vested in the middle-class, and he suspected both capitalist "barons" and working class radicals who might precipitate social calamity with extreme actions. He himself had none of some Nationalist members' concern for association with the "right people."

By September of 1888 the "Boston Bellamy Club" had been formed with twenty-seven charter members; in December the club adopted a constitution and elected Bellamy its first vice-president. In the spring of 1889 the "Nationalist Education Association" was incorporated, with Bellamy as president, and publication of *The Nationalist* began in May. The paper continued until April of 1891, and during the two years of its existence the Boston Club also distributed over 25,000 pamphlets to spread the

---

1 Morgan, 249.

2 Howard H. Quint. *The Forging of American Socialism*. Indianapolis, New York, Kansas City: Bobbs-Merrill, 1964 [1953] 85.

3 Quoted in Henry F. Bedford. *Socialism and the Workers in Massachusetts, 1886-1912*. Amherst, Mass.: University of Massachusetts Press, 1966, 13.

message of *Looking Backward*. A second Boston group was formed in October of 1889, which was "to some extent a reaction from the exclusiveness and the theoretical and literary detachment" of the first club.[1] The second club was more practical, more political, and it was the second that Bellamy came to prefer. Much of the orientation of the first club came of the fact that, the retired army men having faded out, it was dominated by the Theosophists. All those on the committee which had drafted the club's statement of principles were Theosophists, except Bellamy himself.

The wide acceptance of these principles, by many groups in America and abroad, is further evidence of the enthusiasm created by *Looking Backward*. The statement is worth quoting in full:

The principle of the Brotherhood of Humanity is one of the eternal truths that govern the world's progress on lines which distinguish human nature from brute nature.

The principle of competition is simply the application of the brutal law of the survival of the strongest and the most cunning.

Therefore, so long as competition continues to be the ruling factor in our industrial system, the highest development of the individual cannot be reached, the loftiest aims of humanity cannot be realized.

No truth can avail unless practically applied. Therefore, those who seek the welfare of man must endeavor to suppress the system founded on the brute principle of competition and put in its place another based on the nobler principle of association.

But in striving to apply this nobler and wiser principle to the complex conditions of modern life, we advocate no sudden or ill considered changes; we make no war upon individuals; we do not censure those who have accumulated immense fortunes simply by carrying to a logical end the false principles upon which business is now based.

The combinations, trusts, and syndicates of which the people at present complain demonstrate the practicability

---

[1] Morgan, 252.

of our basic principle of association. We merely seek to push this principle a little further and have all industries operated in the interest of all the nation—the people organized—the organic unity of the whole people.

The present industrial system proves itself wrong by the immense wrongs it produces; it proves itself absurd by the immense waste of energy and material which is admitted to be its concomitant. Against this system we raise our protest: for the abolition of the slavery it has wrought and would perpetuate, we pledge our best efforts.[1]

The ethical basis of these principles, and the absence of any hint of violent social change, assured support from conservative thinkers and reformers as well as from the more enthusiastic sort. One such supporter was economist Richard J. Ely of Baltimore, who wrote: "I do not accept the full program of Nationalism but I am glad to see Nationalism encouraged because I think it is the direction in which we in this country at least ought to move."[2] Many others shared this view; a reception by San Francisco Nationalists attracted nearly 2000 people.[3]

It would be surprising if such a movement did not also have its critics. One writer felt that reports of the movement were greatly exaggerated: "the size of this party is altogether unknown. We read one day of a hundred and fifty, and another day of a hundred and eighty Nationalist Clubs; but the word club has a highly elastic meaning."[4] Another observer criticized the movement for "its sentimental rather than literal character," which was indicated "by the number of ladies associated with it," and its "failure to enlist practical men of affairs."[5] There was undoubtedly some basis in

---

1   Quoted in Sylvia E. Bowman. *Edward Bellamy*. Boston: Twayne Publishers, 1986, 111.
2   Richard J. Ely to Alfred Russell Wallace (Oct. 9, 1890) British Museum Additional Manuscript 46440 f 124. Ely was the author of *The Labor Movement in America* (London, 1890).
3   Morgan, 266.
4   Francis A. Walker. "Mr. Bellamy and the New Nationalist Party." *Atlantic Monthly* 65:388 (Feb. 1890) 259-60.
5   Nicholas P. Gilman. "Nationalism in the United States.". *Quarterly Journal of Economics* IV (1889-90) 67 & 73. Kraus Reprint Corporation, 1961.

fact for these objections and they provide a useful balance for the enthusiasm of some accounts.

Although Bellamy did not approve the establishment of utopian colonies, many groups of pioneers found encouragement in Nationalism. California was particularly suited for such experiments and one historian has noted the "dominant influence" of Nationalism in many colonies in the state.[1] The best known was the Kaweah colony, to which "the Bellamy movement directed a steady stream of members...even from as far away as England."[2] Although Kaweah began in 1887, before the publication of *Looking Backward*, the colonists were often later referred to in the press as Bellamists."[3] Bellamy himself argued that these efforts were escapes from social problems rather than solutions. He turned his own energies to local politics, in particular to campaign for a bill to permit municipal ownership of public utilities. The bill was finally passed by the Massachusetts legislature in 1891. Bellamy felt this kind of development to be significant because it would educate people to the advantages of public over private ownership; that habit being established, he wrote in a *North American Review* article, "Nationalism is inevitable."[4]

He kept track of victories won in the battle of "gas and water socialism" in his new periodical *The New Nation*.[5]

In 1891 Bellamy announced his support of the People's Party, or Populists, as the vehicle by which Nationalist policies could be transformed into federal legislation. When the party held its founding convention in Cincinnati in May of 1891, the platform adopted most of the "first steps" of the Nationalist program, which included the nationalization of railway and telegraph

---

[1] Robert V. Hine. *California's Utopian Colonies.* Berkley: University of California Press, 1983 [1953] 162.

[2] Hine, 85.

[3] Ruth R. Lewis. "Kaweah: An Experiment in Coöperative Colonization." *Pacific Historical Review* 12:4 (November 1948) 436.

[4] "The Progress of Nationalism in the United States," 752.

[5] He began *The New Nation* so that he could deal more directly with political and economic issues than the Theosophist-dominated *Nationalist* had done. This provoked some Theosophical members, one of whom later wrote that Bellamy had given up his "proper sphere" of "essay editorship" to "play at politics." Morgan, 269-70.

companies.[1] Populism showed its greatest strength in those areas of the country where *Looking Backward* was most popular, especially in the Mid-West and among farmers. As the months passed the two movements merged into each other more and more.

Bellamy's personal involvement in Populism was limited by his health, but he gave some speeches and in March of 1892 was selected as a delegate to the Omaha convention of the party. At the convention a separate meeting of Nationalist delegates was held to form a national committee to circulate petitions demanding nationalization of industries. This plan was eventually abandoned, but from 1893 until 1898 the Bureau of Nationalist Literature, with headquarters in Philadelphia, distributed Nationalist propaganda, including *Looking Backward* and Bellamy's speeches.

In the presidential election of 1892 the Populist candidate polled over one million votes and twenty-two electoral college votes, making the Populists the first third party since the Civil War to win electoral votes. Republicans and Democrats were perturbed even more by the Populist election of three governors, three state senators, and seventeen representatives. Their fears were needless; although in the Congressional election of 1894 the Populist vote increased by 40 per cent, the movement was suffering from a lack of attention in the national press and from a decline in subscriptions, and in 1896 the Populists threw in their lot with the Democrats. During these years many Nationalists "gave Populism such whole-hearted support that Nationalism lost its identity in the People's Party," and after the election of 1896 both movements had virtually disappeared.[2]

In addition to American consequences of *Looking Backward,* there was also a considerable international impact. For example, Ebenezer Howard, the author of *Garden Cities of Tomorrow* (1898), was deeply influenced by Bellamy and instrumental in getting the British edition of *Looking Backward* published, and Nationalist

---

[1] Morgan, 275. A major figure at the Cincinnati convention was Ignatius Donnelly, who was the author of another famous utopia called *Caesar's Column* (1889). See Martin Ridge. *Ignatius Donnelly. The Portrait of a Politician.* St. Paul: Minnesota Historical Society Press, 1991 [1962].

[2] Chester M. Destler. *American Radicalism 1865-1901.* New York: Octagon Books, 1965 [1946] 14.

Clubs were formed in England too. The Appendices include another British response by William Morris (Appendix B). Sylvia Bowman's *Edward Bellamy Abroad* describes responses in other countries such as Germany, Japan and New Zealand. In the Canadian North West Territories two young men wrote the constitution for a co-operative colony which was strongly influenced by Bellamy's ideas.[1] And there were many more responses, in the years following 1888 and during a major Bellamy revival in the 1930s.[2]

Since the 1930s *Looking Backward* has been constantly in print and has continued to generate critical debate. Daphne Patais's 1988 collection of centenary articles on Bellamy reflects the diversity of responses, from those who read him as a paternalistic reactionary to those who read him as a genuine American radical. A selection of articles since 1988 is included in the list of further reading at the end.

Looking Backward As Radical Social Prophecy

In the Postscript, Bellamy states that *Looking Backward* "was written in the belief that the Golden Age lies before us and not behind us, and is not far away." This is an affirmation that Bellamy sees his utopia as "kinetic" rather than "static" (the terms are H.G. Wells's, from the first chapter of his 1905 book *A Modern Utopia*), as a stage in human history rather than as a society existing in an ideal Platonic realm or on some undiscovered island or planet. He sees the process leading to his utopia as a political and economic evolution rather than a revolution, although the moral change to solidarity from individualism is indeed revolutionary. The practical direction of the change is an increasing centralization of economic control.

The research which Bellamy did for his historical novel *The Duke of Stockbridge* was undoubtedly important in shaping his

---

[1] Alex MacDonald. "Practical Utopians: Ed and Will Paynter and the Harmony Industrial Association." *Saskatchewan History* 47:1 (Spring 1995) 13-26.

[2] See Elizabeth Sadler. "One Book's Influence: Edward Bellamy's *Looking Backward.*" *New England Quarterly* 17 (Dec. 1944) 530-55.

thought about the transition to utopia. Poor economic conditions among Massachusetts debtor-farmers in 1786 provide opportunity for the landowning "squires" to sell them out, and the rebellion consists of the clashes between the two groups. The skirmishes, involving a number of violent acts, result in a partial victory for the squires, but some reforms of law and taxation are instituted. More importantly, the rebellion brings to the fore the idea of equality, as one of the Squires says: "I think none can deny seeing in these late troubles the first fruits of those pestilent notions of equality, whereof we heard so much from certain quarters, during the late war of independence."[1] The rebellion of the oppressed farmers and the beginnings of the notion of equality, anticipate two important features of Bellamy's description of his own society: the labor troubles and the social misery of a world based on inequality.

As William Morris allowed in his review, Bellamy's criticisms of the inequalities of his day are certainly "forcible and fervid." The famous metaphor of the coach in Chapter I, the fortunate few riding while the great mass pulls, is one example; another is Mr. Barton's sermon, in chapter 26, on the contrasts between the age of misery and the age of solidarity. Perhaps most powerful is the final chapter which describes Julian's return to the Boston of 1887 to find a nightmare world of poverty and human degradation. Given such conditions in 1887, how did so tremendous a change come about?

Bellamy felt that if *Looking Backward* had gone into "details of means the result would have been largely to concentrate attention and criticism upon them, when it was the design of the book to concentrate attention upon ends."[2] As a result we get only hints about the transition. In this same period as the labor troubles, there is also occurring a concentration of capital in greater masses than had ever been known before. Small business waned and giant corporations assumed control of every significant enterprise. The process of the aggregation of capital and the growth of

[1]   *The Duke of Stockbridge.* Ed. Joseph Schiffman, Cambridge, Mass.: Harvard University Press, 1962 [1879] 304.
[2]   "Notes on Looking Backward." n.d., bMs Am 1181.6, Binder No. 3-B, 1.

monopolies "was recognized at last, in its true significance, as a process which only needed to complete its logical evolution to open a golden future to humanity." This evolution was completed by the "final consolidation of the entire capital of the nation" in the hands of the nation itself, which became "the one capitalist in the place of all other capitalists, the sole employer, the final monopoly in which all previous and lesser monopolies were swallowed up, a monopoly in the profits and economies of which all citizens shared" (Chapter V). The change, in other words, involved the intellectual and moral act of recognizing and accepting what was occurring. Later in the novel Bellamy underlines this when he says the change to a "higher ethical system" was "recognized as the interest, not of one class, but equally of all classes." Once this recognition occurred, he adds, "the national party arose to carry it out by political methods" (Chapter XXIV).

Bellamy's analysis of the Stockbridge situation and of the situation of society in Julian West's day is a class analysis, and this much he certainly shares with Marx. But his remedy explicitly rejects class struggle as the means to social change, and emphasizes instead a moral leap of consciousness shared by all people. Perhaps one reason for this is Bellamy's belief that there is in every human being a soul common in nature with all other souls (his "Religion Of Solidarity"—Appendix C) and this tends to exclude a theory of social change based on struggle of individuals and classes. It has also been suggested that Marxism in the Boston of 1887 was considered foreign and exotic and that the relative prosperity of workers in America encouraged a bourgeois rather than a proletarian mentality, or that American Socialism suffered shipwreck on "the reefs of roast beef."[1] In *Looking Backward* Mrs. Bartlett remarks that the working class seems to be going crazy, but "in Europe it is far worse even than here" (Chapter II). The transition, then, is a rapid, apparently inevitable and non-violent evolutionary process, characterized by a moral and ethical leap of consciousness which signalled the beginning of the age of solidarity. While it might be suggested

---

[1] Werner Sombart, quoted in David Herreshof. *The Origins of American Marxism.* New York: Monad Press, 1973 [1967] 16.

that this view of social change is less radical than it should be, because of the rejection of class struggle, it might also be suggested that Bellamy's bold assertion that humans are capable of such a change is even more radical in a deeper sense.[1]

Let us turn now to some of the features of Bellamy's utopian world, beginning with its economic arrangements. The system of production and distribution described in *Looking Backward* is a vast social pyramid. At the apex is the President and below him the heads of the various industries. There is a central administration which fixes the price of goods according to the hours of work taken to produce them and in general regulates demand and supply like the governor on an engine (Chapter XXII). Dr. Leete observes of the administrators that "the machine which they direct is indeed a vast one, but so logical in its principles and direct and simple in its workings, that it all but runs itself" (Chapter XVII). The machine produces goods which are available to all, everywhere in the nation, by means of a series of sample stores and warehouses connected by the pneumatic tubes mentioned above, an innovation of Bellamy's day. The underlying assumption that bigness is better because more efficient is precisely the assumption made by nineteenth-century monopolists to whom Bellamy looked for confirmation of the power of concentrated capital. For example, in a letter to a Senate Transportation Committee in 1874, George Pullman wrote that the "aim of the Pullman Company is...to do work in connection with the railroad companies which they separately could not so well perform...so as to enable the public to use the different railway lines as though they all were under the same management."[2] It is interesting indeed that Bellamy's radical utopia should share with great capitalists the view that consolidation of power and centralization of management would lead to the most efficient form of society. It is also important to note his positive use of the image of the machine, setting him quite clearly apart

---

[1]   See Roemer's *The Obsolete Necessity* (87ff) for a discussion of how many of the late nineteenth-century utopias, including Bellamy's, were religious works in their imagery and moralistic fervor.

[2]   Quoted in Stanley Buder. *Pullman...* New York: Oxford University Press, 1967, 19.

from the nineteenth-century anti-mechanical tradition beginning with Blake's "Satanic mills" and encompassing sages such as Carlyle and Dickens, Emerson and Thoreau.

The idea of the industrial army which is at the heart of Bellamy's economic system, with all its grades and ranks and insignia, and all its strategies to motivate workers by lower motives (such as emulation) or higher motives (such as love of the work itself), was one of the most controversial features of the utopia. Some responded with alarm or scorn at the regimentation. M. D. O'Brien said of the army's decorations and badges, "Glory! Bits of bronze! *Esprit de corps!* Rather should we not say 'Fudge'?... So brilliant an idea deserves the whole lot of them, strung on a bit of ribbon and thrown over the writer's neck."[1] Compare this with a response by A. J. Duganne in a London religious periodical:

> Following close these conquering armies—
> Dancing on with twinkling feet—
> White-armed maids and flower-crowned children
> Haste those warrior-men to greet—
> Hands are clasped in holiest union,
> Joy, like incense, soars above,
> Hail! thrice hail! the Industrial Armies!
> Hail the immortal strife of Love.[2]

Duganne's positive response was echoed by many, as was O'Brien's criticism. Following this theme, there is one aspect of the industrial army which needs particular comment because it is one of the cruxes of the book:

> As for actual neglect of work, positively bad work, or other overt remissness on the part of men incapable of generous motives, the discipline of the industrial army is far too strict to allow anything whatever of the sort. A man able to do duty, and persistently refusing, is sentenced to solitary imprisonment on bread and water till he consents. (Chapter XII)

[1] *Socialism Tested By Facts.* London: Liberty and Property Defence League, 1892, 38-39.
[2] *Brotherhood* VI, 7 (Feb. 1892) np.

There can be no doubt that Bellamy intended this to be as harsh as it sounds—in the first edition the penalty of solitary imprisonment was not stated but merely the more general comment that a lazy or bad workman is "cut off from all human society." When Bellamy wrote to his publishers about the revisions to the first edition, he said the second would "involve no changes in ideas but merely some improvements in statement and some slight emendations, the whole amounting to very little."[1] Here is the iron hand in the velvet glove and pretty clear evidence that Bellamy was capitulating to the conventional notion of efficiency. Some have found the system, which gives government far greater power over the individual than anything we would accept today, evidence that *Looking Backward* is tinged with the dystopian. For example, W. W. Satterlee's *Looking Backward And What I Saw* (1890), one of the many sequels, names the capital city of North America "Bellamy" and the head of the Great United Army "General Dick Tator." The editors of a standard utopian anthology see the coercion as "vicious," but allow that Bellamy was probably carried away by enthusiasm for the positive elements of his scheme.[2] In response to this it could be noted that a bit later in the novel Bellamy provides that a man in his thirty-third year may retire from the army on half pay, as though perhaps realizing that some escape hatch was needed for the determined individualist (such as he was himself). And by the time of *Equality* (see Appendix D), this had changed again so that people could refuse service if they were willing to go live on a special reservation. However, this remains one of the conflicted issues of *Looking Backward* and there are divergent opinions.

Another controversial point is the role of women in *Looking Backward*. To the modern feminist who reads the book, it may be objectionable that women, although they receive the same annual income as men do, are employed in a separate women's division of the industrial army, under an "exclusively feminine régime." And what may be highly objectionable is the language used by Dr. Leete to express the situation:

---

[1] Bellamy to Houghton Mifflin & Co. (21 July 1889) bMs Am 1181 (59).
[2] Glenn Negley and J. Max Patrick. *The Quest for Utopia*. New York: Henry Schuman, 1952, 78.

The men of this day so well appreciate that they owe to the beauty and grace of women the chief zest of their lives and their main incentive to effort, that they permit them to work at all only because it is fully understood that a certain regular requirement of labor, of a sort adapted to their powers, is well for body and mind, during the period of maximum physical vigor. (Chapter XXV)

That men will "permit" women to work may well be thought superior and patronizing in tone, and does not the passage actually belittle the powers of women in the world of work? Further, is it not the case that Dr. Leete invokes a regressive form of sexual selection when he suggests, in relation to motivating men to work, "of all the whips, and spurs, and baits, and prizes, there is none like the thought of the radiant faces which the laggards will find averted"? Women, he says, are regarded as "wardens of the world to come" and this is a "cult" in which women "educate their daughters from childhood" (Chapter XXV). All of this sounds suspiciously like the familiar Victorian strategy of placing women on a pedestal and thereby removing them from the real world of work, business and professions (see Appendix E).

In response to this it can fairly be said that Bellamy was both a man of his time in history and one who was extremely idealistic about women, and it may be that in *Looking Backward* he, in effect, ghettoizes women because he is so determined to do them honour. His thinking changed on this by the time he wrote *Equality*, as may clearly be seen from the passage in Appendix D, in which women follow all occupations in perfect equality with men. Bellamy's sincerity about this is very clear from his editorials in *The New Nation*, on the frequent occasions when the subject of women in the world to come arose. A good example is his favourable review of George N. Miller's fantasy novel called *The Strike of a Sex*, a story in which women discontinue relations with men and retire to a colony of their own. It is not property rights or voting rights they claim, for they already have those. What they claim is the right to their own bodies. Bellamy says:

Mr. Miller's book is a needed and valuable contribution to the literature of nationalism, of which it is a distinguishing characteristic that it claims all for woman that it claims for man, and not only that, but claims it for her in her own right and not by or through the favor of man.[1]

A few months later Bellamy congratulated the English Methodists for striking the word "obey" out of the marriage ritual, but Nationalism will do more, he said: "it will strike the necessity of obedience out of the married state, and put an end to sexual servility in or out of matrimony."[2] This is absolutely clear and it places Bellamy in the very forefront of progressive thought about the role of women. Thus, it is important to recognize the distinction between Bellamy's first utopian novel, *Looking Backward*, and his vision of utopia; the latter encompasses not only *Equality* but also the many columns and reviews which he wrote on the same subjects. At the same time, it should be noted that there are many statements in Chapter XXV which express the radical position that women are no longer dependents upon men in any way. (See Appendix F for a poetic response by feminist writer Charlotte Perkins Gilman.)

Two other evolutions in Bellamy's thought are reflected in Appendix D: in *Looking Backward* utopia was imagined as a great city (although—as is often not noticed—it is a very green city with many parks and fountains), whereas by *Equality* population had become more evenly spread around the countryside, anticipating Frank Lloyd Wright's Broadacre City;[3] and in *Looking Backward* there was said to be absolutely no violence in the transition to utopia, whereas in *Equality* it is allowed that although the change was peaceful on the whole there was "considerable" violence. Perhaps Bellamy listened here to William Morris, who criticized this aspect of *Looking Backward* in his review (Appendix B).

---

1   "The Strike of a Sex." *The New Nation.* 1, 43 (Nov. 21, 1891) 683.
2   "The Word 'Obey' In The Marriage Service." *The New Nation* 2, 25 (18 June 1892) 387.
3   See Ruth Eaton, "Architecture and Urbanism: The Faces of Utopia" in *Utopia. The Search For The Ideal Society In the Western World*, 308, cited above.

There are some subjects which appear over and over again in utopias through the ages; one of these is education, for the obvious reason that education is often the mechanism for bringing utopia about and it is almost always the means of maintaining a utopia once it is established. Not only do children learn skills and acquire knowledge for careers, but they absorb the worldview and the values of their utopian society. In this there is, of course, a very close parallel with the real world, in which we expect education to do the same things. In a number of ways the educational system of *Looking Backward* is a very conventional one and it reflects the trends of the day toward universal compulsory schooling which could serve as a filtering mechanism to sort people out for their future lives. For example, there are clearly different educational paths for those who go on to serve in the industrial army and those who go on to work in the professions.

Although one purpose of education is to produce the educated voter, in *Looking Backward* the members of the industrial army are not allowed to vote for the President because that would be "perilous" to the army's discipline, while members of the professions do vote for the President. Here Bellamy applies the military model to civilian life and the result is surely undemocratic, another of the cruxes of the novel. Dr. Leete makes it clear that the utopians do not believe all people are created equal and the differences between people "as to natural endowments" is as "marked as in a state of nature." But because of the universal education enjoyed by the utopians the "level of the lowest [people] is vastly raised" (Chapter XXI). However, although the utopians do not see all people as equal, it is clear that they believe strongly in accessibility and equality of opportunity; Dr. Leete tells Julian that "the schools of technology, of medicine, of art, of music, of histrionics, and of higher liberal learning are always open to aspirants without condition" (Chapter VII). Bellamy's compromise position here is as old as the Western utopia: in Plato's *Republic* classes of people are separated according to their abilities yet provision is made for upward mobility of children into higher classes (see Appendix I for Morris on education).

Plato's *Republic* is also famous for its ban on dramatic poets, thus introducing into the genre the feature of uncomfortable relations between the utopian state and the creative artist. The basic idea is that: the utopian state is rational, planned, orderly while artistic creation is irrational, serendipitous, disorderly, and the content of art is often subversive of established values. Bellamy solves this problem in an ingenious way. Dr. Leete describes his age as a great one for artistic productivity, a new Renaissance, but the novels of the day leave out all "contrasts of wealth and poverty, education and ignorance, coarseness and refinement, high and low…together with sordid anxieties of any sort for one's self or others" (Chapter XV). Here seems to be a reflection of the Edward Bellamy who wrote that as a literary man he was a "goner," since he could think or write of nothing else but the great change in society for which he longed,[1] for he was willing to sacrifice so much of the content of literature for the coherence of the utopian culture. Both Bellamy and William Morris, for all their marked differences on the subject of art, imagined utopias in which the role of dramatic art, especially the novel, would be attenuated or shrunken in some regard. Their enthusiasm for utopia carried them to this conclusion. That enthusiasm was an element of the late nineteenth-century mix which tended to evaporate in the twentieth century, especially as one of the important paradigms became dystopia rather than utopia, and writers in the twentieth century have been suspicious that trading art for utopia could be a good bargain for human beings.

However, if Bellamy is a man of his times, he is also a man who transcends those times and offers us a radical and prophetic vision too. The universal idea which speaks to us over a century later, and which will continue to speak to our descendants in centuries to come, is simply the idea that we should be concerned to relieve the sufferings of our fellow human beings. In his description of Julian West's return to the old Boston in a dream Bellamy might well have quoted the prophet Ezekiel: "I will take out of your flesh the heart of stone and give you a heart of flesh" (36:26). Julian finds the wealthy diners to have hearts of stone, unresponsive to his plea, and he is driven to say: "Do you not know that close to your doors a great multitude of men and

---

[1]   Bellamy to Horace Scudder, (Aug. 25, 1890) bMs Am 1181 (73).

women, flesh of your flesh, live lives that are one agony from birth to death? Listen! their dwellings are so near that if you hush your laughter you will hear their grievous voices... With what have you stopped your ears that you do not hear these doleful sounds?" (Chapter XXVIII) Their response is to have Julian thrown out and to dismiss his plea for empathy with the poor as an unwanted intrusion into their comfortable lives.

Bellamy is challenging us not to do the same. Even if our hearts are not stone, but we are merely too busy or too preoccupied with life's demands, Bellamy is challenging us to care, just as he challenged the readers of 1888. Despite the differences in our worlds he still invites us men and women to help bring a new and more compassionate society into being "by our faith and by our works." And if we do that, he says, we may be optimistic rather than pessimistic about the prospects for humanity. We need not accept the idea that human beings are incapable of building a better world. It is this Bellamy, the radical utopian, who speaks at the end of Mr. Barton's sermon:

> With a tear for the dark past, turn we then to the dazzling future, and, veiling our eyes, press forward. The long and weary winter of the race has ended. Its summer has begun. Humanity has burst the chrysalis. The heavens are before it. (Chapter XXVI)

A Note on the Text

Looking Backward: 2000–1887 was first published by Ticknor and Co. of Boston in January of 1888. Bellamy revised the text for a German translation by Boston Rabbi Solomon Schindler (who was also the author of one of the many sequels). The changes were incorporated into the next English edition published by Houghton Mifflin in 1889. This text is the basis for the present edition. Substantive changes from the first to the second edition are given in John L. Thomas's critical edition (Harvard University Press, 1967). Many of these, as Bellamy himself suggested, are merely expansions or amplifications. But it is interesting that about half of them (a dozen out of two dozen) deal with the issue of individual freedom in the utopia. A couple add more options and flexibility for individuals, but the majority tighten up the discipline or add to the power of the state. This tends to confirm the suggestion in the Introduction that on this issue the novel is conflicted. These passages are indicated in the explanatory notes. A few silent editorial changes have been made where spelling, capitalization or punctuation seemed incorrect, or where the first edition seemed preferable.

Illustration from *Anarchy and Anarchists*
by Michael J. Schaak. Chicago: F.J. Schulte, 1889, 142.

Edward Bellamy: A Brief Chronology

1850   Edward Bellamy is born on March 26th to Rev. Rufus Bellamy (a Baptist Minister) and Maria Putnam Bellamy, in Chicopee Falls, Massachusetts

1867   Does not pass physical examination for West Point, a dream since childhood. Studies at Union College, Schenectady, New York

1868   Travels to Germany and studies there; begins legal studies in Springfield

1871   Passes the Bar examination with distinction; opens law office in Chicopee but closes it after one case— the eviction of a widow for failure to pay rent (he told Mason Green he could not recall which side he was on)

1872   Goes to New York City, works for six months as a journalist; begins working as editorial writer and book reviewer for the *Springfield Union*; notebooks and speeches of the 1870s explore concepts which later appear in *Looking Backward*

1874   "The Religion of Solidarity"

1877   Leaves *Springfield Union*; travels to Hawaii with his brother Frederick

1878   *Six To One: A Nantucket Idyl* (first novel); between 1875-89 Bellamy writes 25 short stories

1879   *The Duke of Stockbridge* appears as a serial in the *Berkshire Courier*. Bellamy's brother Charles publishes an industrial novel called *The Breton Mills*

1880   With his brother Charles establishes the *Penny News* in Springfield, which becomes the *Daily News*; *Dr. Heidenhoff's Process*

1882   Marries Emma Sanderson

1884   Their son Paul is born; Bellamy leaves the *Daily News; Miss Ludington's Sister*

1886   Their daughter Marion is born; Bellamy begins writing *Looking Backward*

1888   First edition of *Looking Backward* in January; revised edition based on changes made for a German translation

1889   The first and second Bellamy Clubs of Boston begin meeting; monthly magazine *The Nationalist* begins publication, with Bellamy contributing articles

1891   *The Nationalist* ceases publication shortly after Bellamy begins *The New Nation* as editor; follows the cause of "gas and water socialism"; Nationalists support the Populist movement

1894   *New Nation* ceases publication

1897   *Equality*; Bellamy family moves to Denver because of Edward's tuberculosis

1898   Returns to Chicopee Falls; dies on May 22nd

1900   Bellamy's cousin Francis Bellamy (author of the "Pledge of Allegiance" to the flag) edits *The Duke of Stockbridge* for book publication

1935   Emma Bellamy appears before a Congressional committee to support a bill for unemployment, old age and social insurance. This was the time of Roosevelt's "New Deal" and a major revival of interest in Bellamy's ideas

1956   Emma Sanderson Bellamy dies September 4th

1972   The Bellamy House declared a national landmark; maintained and restored (1974) by the Edward Bellamy Memorial Association

LOOKING BACKWARD

2000—1887

BY

EDWARD BELLAMY

AUTHOR OF "MISS LUDINGTON'S SISTER," "DR. HEIDENHOFF'S PROCESS,"
"A NANTUCKET IDYL," ETC., ETC.

TWO HUNDRED AND SIXTY-FOURTH THOUSAND

BOSTON AND NEW YORK
HOUGHTON, MIFFLIN AND COMPANY
The Riverside Press, Cambridge
1890

Title Page from the text of *Looking Backward*
used for the present edition.

PREFACE.

HISTORICAL SECTION
SHAWMUT COLLEGE, BOSTON,
DECEMBER 26, 2000.[1]

LIVING as we do in the closing year of the twentieth century, enjoying the blessings of a social order at once so simple and logical that it seems but the triumph of common sense, it is no doubt difficult for those whose studies have not been largely historical to realize that the present organization of society is, in its completeness, less than a century old. No historical fact is, however, better established than that till nearly the end of the nineteenth century it was the general belief that the ancient industrial system, with all its shocking social consequences, was destined to last, with possibly a little patching, to the end of time. How strange and well-nigh incredible does it seem that so prodigious a moral and material transformation as has taken place since then could have been accomplished in so brief an interval! The readiness with which men accustom themselves, as matters of course, to improvements in their condition, which, when anticipated, seemed to leave nothing more to be desired, could not be more strikingly illustrated. What reflection could be better calculated to moderate the enthusiasm of reformers who count for their reward on the lively gratitude of future ages!

The object of this volume is to assist persons who, while desiring to gain a more definite idea of the social contrasts between the nineteenth and twentieth centuries, are daunted by the formal aspect of the histories which treat the subject. Warned by a teacher's experience that learning is accounted a weariness to the

---

[1] An imaginary college. Boston is built on the Shawmut Peninsula. Today Shawmut is a stop on Boston's Red Line subway.

flesh, the author has sought to alleviate the instructive quality of the book by casting it in the form of a romantic narrative, which he would be glad to fancy not wholly devoid of interest on its own account.

The reader, to whom modern social institutions and their underlying principles are matters of course, may at times find Dr. Leete's explanations of them rather trite, —but it must be remembered that to Dr. Leete's guest they were not matters of course, and that this book is written for the express purpose of inducing the reader to forget for the nonce that they are so to him. One word more. The almost universal theme of the writers and orators who have celebrated this bi-millennial epoch has been the future rather than the past, not the advance that has been made, but the progress that shall be made, ever onward and upward, till the race shall achieve its ineffable destiny. This is well, wholly well, but it seems to me that nowhere can we find more solid ground for daring anticipations of human development during the next one thousand years, than by "Looking Backward" upon the progress of the last one hundred.

That this volume may be so fortunate as to find readers whose interest in the subject shall incline them to overlook the deficiencies of the treatment is the hope in which the author steps aside and leaves Mr. Julian West to speak for himself.

CHAPTER I.

I FIRST saw the light in the city of Boston in the year 1857. "What!" you say, "eighteen fifty-seven? That is an odd slip. He means nineteen fifty-seven, of course." I beg pardon, but there is no mistake. It was about four in the afternoon of December the 26th, one day after Christmas, in the year 1857 not 1957, that I first breathed the east wind of Boston, which, I assure the reader, was at that remote period marked by the same penetrating quality characterizing it in the present year of grace, 2000.

These statements seem so absurd on their face, especially when I add that I am a young man apparently of about thirty years of age, that no person can be blamed for refusing to read another word of what promises to be a mere imposition upon his credulity. Nevertheless I earnestly assure the reader that no imposition is intended, and will undertake, if he shall follow me a few pages, to entirely convince him of this. If I may, then, provisionally assume, with the pledge of justifying the assumption, that I know better than the reader when I was born, I will go on with my narrative. As every schoolboy knows, in the latter part of the nineteenth century the civilization of to-day, or anything like it, did not exist, although the elements which were to develop it were already in ferment. Nothing had, however, occurred to modify the immemorial division of society into the four classes, or nations, as they may be more fitly called, since the differences between them were far greater than those between any nations nowadays, of the rich and the poor, the educated and the ignorant.[1] I myself was rich and also educated, and possessed, therefore, all the elements of happiness enjoyed by the most fortunate in that age. Living in luxury, and occupied only with the pursuit of the pleasures and refinements of life, I derived the means of

---

[1]   One of the best-known expressions of the idea that rich and poor form two "nations" is Benjamin Disraeli's *Sybil* (1845).

my support from the labor of others, rendering no sort of service in return. My parents and grand-parents had lived in the same way, and I expected that my descendants, if I had any, would enjoy a like easy existence.

But how could I live without service to the world? you ask. Why should the world have supported in utter idleness one who was able to render service? The answer is that my great-grandfather had accumulated a sum of money on which his descendants had ever since lived. The sum, you will naturally infer, must have been very large not to have been exhausted in supporting three generations in idleness. This, however, was not the fact. The sum had been originally by no means large. It was, in fact, much larger now that three generations had been supported upon it in idleness, than it was at first. This mystery of use without consumption, of warmth without combustion, seems like magic, but was merely an ingenious application of the art now happily lost but carried to great perfection by your ancestors, of shifting the burden of one's support on the shoulders of others. The man who had accomplished this, and it was the end all sought, was said to live on the income of his investments. To explain at this point how the ancient methods of industry made this possible would delay us too much. I shall only stop now to say that interest on investments was a species of tax in perpetuity upon the product of those engaged in industry which a person possessing or inheriting money was able to levy. It must not be supposed that an arrangement which seems so unnatural and preposterous according to modern notions was never criticised by your ancestors. It had been the effort of law-givers and prophets from the earliest ages to abolish interest, or at least to limit it to the smallest possible rate. All these efforts had, however, failed, as they necessarily must so long as the ancient social organizations prevailed. At the time of which I write, the latter part of the nineteenth century, governments had generally given up trying to regulate the subject at all.

By way of attempting to give the reader some general impression of the way people lived together in those days, and especially of the relations of the rich and poor to one another, perhaps I cannot do better than to compare society as it then was to a prodigious coach which the masses of humanity were harnessed to and dragged toilsomely along a very hilly and sandy road. The driver was hunger, and permitted no lagging, though the pace was necessarily very slow. Despite the difficulty of drawing the coach at all along so hard a road, the top was covered with passengers who never got down, even at the steepest ascents. These seats on top were very breezy and comfortable. Well up out of the dust, their occupants could enjoy the scenery at their leisure, or critically discuss the merits of the straining team. Naturally such places were in great demand and the competition for them was keen, every one seeking as the first end in life to secure a seat on the coach for himself and to leave it to his child after him. By the rule of the coach a man could leave his seat to whom he wished, but on the other hand there were many accidents by which it might at any time be wholly lost. For all that they were so easy, the seats were very insecure, and at every sudden jolt of the coach persons were slipping out of them and falling to the ground, where they were instantly compelled to take hold of the rope and help to drag the coach on which they had before ridden so pleasantly. It was naturally regarded as a terrible misfortune to lose one's seat, and the apprehension that this might happen to them or their friends was a constant cloud upon the happiness of those who rode.

But did they think only of themselves? you ask. Was not their very luxury rendered intolerable to them by comparison with the lot of their brothers and sisters in the harness, and the knowledge that their own weight added to their toil? Had they no compassion for fellow beings from whom fortune only distinguished them? Oh, yes; commiseration was frequently expressed by those who rode for those who had to pull the coach, especially when the vehicle came to a bad place in the road, as it was constantly doing, or to a particularly steep hill. At such times, the desperate straining of the team, their agonized leaping and plunging under the pitiless lashing of hunger, the many who fainted at the rope and were trampled in the mire, made a very distressing spectacle, which often called forth highly creditable displays of feeling on the top of the coach. At such times the passengers would call down encouragingly to the toilers of the rope, exhorting them to patience, and holding out hopes of possible compensation in another world for the hardness of their lot, while others contributed to buy salves and liniments for the crippled and injured. It was agreed that it was a great pity that the coach should be so hard to pull, and there was a sense of general relief when the specially bad piece of road was gotten over. This relief was not, indeed, wholly on account of the team, for there was always some danger at these bad places of a general overturn in which all would lose their seats.

It must in truth be admitted that the main effect of the spectacle of the misery of the toilers at the rope was to enhance the passengers' sense of the value of their seats upon the coach, and to cause them to hold on to them more desperately than before. If the passengers could only have felt assured that neither they nor their friends would ever fall from the top, it is probable that, beyond contributing to the funds for liniments and bandages, they would have troubled themselves extremely little about those who dragged the coach.

I am well aware that this will appear to the men and women of the twentieth century an incredible inhumanity, but there are two facts, both very curious, which partly explain it. In the first place, it was firmly and sincerely believed that there was no other way in which Society could get along, except the many pulled at the rope and the few rode, and not only this, but that no very radical improvement even was possible, either in the harness, the coach, the roadway, or the distribution of the toil. It had always been as it was, and it always would be so. It was a pity, but it could not be helped, and philosophy forbade wasting compassion on what was beyond remedy.

The other fact is yet more curious, consisting in a singular hallucination which those on the top of the coach generally shared, that they were not exactly like their brothers and sisters who pulled at the rope, but of finer clay, in some way belonging to a higher order of beings who might justly expect to be drawn. This seems unaccountable, but, as I once rode on this very coach and shared that very hallucination, I ought to be believed. The strangest thing about the hallucination was that those who had but just climbed up from the ground, before they had outgrown the marks of the rope upon their hands, began to fall under its influence. As for those whose parents and grandparents before them had been so fortunate as to keep their seats on the top, the conviction they cherished of the essential difference between their sort of humanity and the common article was absolute. The effect of such a delusion in moderating fellow feeling for the sufferings of the mass of men into a distant and philosophical compassion is obvious. To it I refer as the only extenuation I can offer for the indifference which, at the period I write of, marked my own attitude toward the misery of my brothers.

In 1887 I came to my thirtieth year. Although still unmarried, I was engaged to wed Edith Bartlett. She, like myself, rode on the top of the coach. That is to say, not to encumber ourselves further with an illustration which has, I hope, served its purpose of giving the reader some general impression of how we lived then, her family was wealthy. In that age, when money alone commanded all that was agreeable and refined in life, it was enough for a woman to be rich to have suitors; but Edith Bartlett was beautiful and graceful also.

My lady readers, I am aware, will protest at this. "Handsome she might have been," I hear them saying, "but graceful never, in the costumes which were the fashion at that period, when the head covering was a dizzy structure a foot tall, and the almost incredible extension of the skirt behind by means of artificial contrivances more thoroughly dehumanized the form than any former device of dressmakers. Fancy any one graceful in such a costume!"[1] The point is certainly well taken, and I can only reply that while the ladies of the twentieth century are lovely demonstrations of the effect of appropriate drapery in accenting feminine graces, my recollection of their great grandmothers enables me to maintain that no deformity of costume can wholly disguise them.

Our marriage only waited on the completion of the house which I was building for our occupancy in one of the most desirable parts of the city, that is to say, a part chiefly inhabited by the rich. For it must be understood that the comparative desirability of different parts of Boston for residence depended

---

[1] Bellamy refers to the "bustle": padding, or a metal frame worn under the skirt to accentuate the posterior, in some exaggerated styles of the 1880s extending more than a foot behind. See J. Anderson Black and Madge Garland. *A History of Fashion*. London: Orbis, 1978 [1975] 288.

then, not on natural features, but on the character of the neighboring population. Each class or nation lived by itself, in quarters of its own. A rich man living among the poor, an educated man among the uneducated, was like one living in isolation among a jealous and alien race. When the house had been begun, its completion by the winter of 1886 had been expected. The spring of the following year found it, however, yet incomplete, and my marriage still a thing of the future. The cause of a delay calculated to be particularly exasperating to an ardent lover was a series of strikes, that is to say, concerted refusals to work on the part of the bricklayers, masons, carpenters, painters, plumbers, and other trades concerned in house building. What the specific causes of these strikes were I do not remember. Strikes had become so common at that period that people had ceased to inquire into their particular grounds. In one department of industry or another, they had been nearly incessant ever since the great business crisis of 1873. In fact it had come to be the exceptional thing to see any class of laborers pursue their avocation steadily for more than a few months at a time.

The reader who observes the dates alluded to will of course recognize in these disturbances of industry the first and incoherent phase of the great movement which ended in the establishment of the modern industrial system with all its social consequences. This is all so plain in the retrospect that a child can understand it, but not being prophets, we of that day had no clear idea what was happening to us. What we did see was that industrially the country was in a very queer way. The relation between the workingman and the employer, between labor and capital, appeared in some unaccountable manner to have become dislocated. The working classes had quite suddenly and very generally become infected with a profound discontent with their condition, and an idea that it could be greatly bettered if they only knew how to go about it. On every side, with one accord, they preferred demands for higher pay, shorter hours, better dwellings, better educational advantages, and a share in the refinements and luxuries of life, demands which it was impossible to see the way to granting unless the world were to become a great deal richer than it then was. Though they knew something of what they wanted, they knew nothing of how to accomplish it, and the eager enthusiasm with which they thronged about any one who seemed likely to give them any light on the subject lent sudden reputation to many would-be leaders, some of whom had little enough light to give. However chimerical the aspirations of the laboring classes might be deemed, the devotion with which they supported one another in the strikes, which were their chief weapon, and the sacrifices which they underwent to carry them out left no doubt of their dead earnestness.

As to the final outcome of the labor troubles, which was the phrase by which the movement I have described was most commonly referred to, the opinions of the people of my class differed according to individual temperament. The sanguine argued very forcibly that it was in the very nature of things impossible that the new hopes of the workingmen could be satisfied, simply because the world had not the wherewithal to satisfy them. It was only because the masses worked very hard and lived on short commons[1] that the race did not starve outright, and no considerable improvement in their condition was possible while the world, as a whole, remained so poor. It was not the capitalists whom the laboring men were contending with, these maintained, but the ironbound environment of humanity, and it was merely a question of the thickness of their skulls when they would discover the fact and make up their minds to endure what they could not cure.

The less sanguine admitted all this. Of course the workingmen's aspirations were impossible of fulfillment for natural reasons, but there were grounds to fear that they would not discover this fact until they had made a sad mess of society. They had the votes and the power to do so if they pleased, and their leaders meant they should. Some of these desponding observers went so far as to predict an impending social cataclysm. Humanity, they argued, having climbed to the top round of the ladder of civilization, was about to take a header into chaos, after which it would doubtless pick itself up, turn round, and begin to climb again. Repeated experiences of this sort in historic and prehistoric times possibly accounted for the puzzling bumps on the human cranium. Human

---

[1]   Short commons: meals consisting of little food.

history, like all great movements, was cyclical, and returned to the point of beginning. The idea of indefinite progress in a right line was a chimera of the imagination, with no analogue in nature. The parabola of a comet was perhaps a yet better illustration of the career of humanity. Tending upward and sunward from the aphelion of barbarism, the race attained the perihelion of civilization only to plunge downward once more to its nether goal in the regions of chaos.

This, of course, was an extreme opinion, but I remember serious men among my acquaintances who, in discussing the signs of the times, adopted a very similar tone. It was no doubt the common opinion of thoughtful men that society was approaching a critical period which might result in great changes. The labor troubles, their causes, course, and cure, took lead of all other topics in the public prints, and in serious conversation.

The nervous tension of the public mind could not have been more strikingly illustrated than it was by the alarm resulting from the talk of a small band of men who called themselves anarchists, and proposed to terrify the American people into adopting their ideas by threats of violence, as if a mighty nation which had but just put down a rebellion of half its own numbers, in order to maintain its political system, were likely to adopt a new social system out of fear.

As one of the wealthy, with a large stake in the existing order of things, I naturally shared the apprehensions of my class. The particular grievance I had against the working classes at the time of which I write, on account of the effect of their strikes in postponing my wedded bliss, no doubt lent a special animosity to my feeling toward them.

CHAPTER II.

THE thirtieth day of May, 1887, fell on a Monday. It was one of the annual holidays of the nation in the latter third of the nineteenth century, being set apart under the name of Decoration Day, for doing honor to the memory of the soldiers of the North who took part in the war for the preservation of the union of the States. The survivors of the war, escorted by military and civic processions and bands of music, were wont on this occasion to visit the cemeteries and lay wreaths of flowers upon the graves of their dead comrades, the ceremony being a very solemn and touching one. The eldest brother of Edith Bartlett had fallen in the war, and on Decoration Day the family was in the habit of making a visit to Mount Auburn, where he lay.[1]

I had asked permission to make one of the party, and, on our return to the city at nightfall, remained to dine with the family of my betrothed. In the drawing-room, after dinner, I picked up an evening paper and read of a fresh strike in the building trades, which would probably still further delay the completion of my unlucky house. I remember distinctly how exasperated I was at this, and the objurgations, as forcible as the presence of the ladies permitted, which I lavished upon workmen in general, and these strikers in particular. I had abundant sympathy from those about me, and the remarks made in the desultory conversation which followed, upon the unprincipled conduct of the labor agitators, were calculated to make those gentlemen's ears tingle. It was agreed that affairs were going from bad to worse very fast, and that there was no telling what we should come to soon. "The worst of it," I remember Mrs. Bartlett's saying, "is that the working classes all over the world seem to be going crazy at once. In Europe it is far worse even than here. I'm sure I should not dare to live there at all. I asked Mr. Bartlett the other day where we should emigrate to if all the terrible things took place which those socialists threaten. He said he did not know any place now where society could be called stable except Greenland, Patagonia, and the Chinese Empire." "Those Chinamen knew what they were about," somebody added, "when they refused to let in our western civilization. They knew what it would lead to better than we did. They saw it was nothing but dynamite in disguise."

After this, I remember drawing Edith apart and trying to persuade her that it would be better to be married at once without waiting for the completion of the house, spending the time

---

[1] Today the holiday is called Memorial Day.

in travel till our home was ready for us. She was remarkably handsome that evening, the mourning costume that she wore in recognition of the day setting off to great advantage the purity of her complexion. I can see her even now with my mind's eye just as she looked that night. When I took my leave she followed me into the hall and I kissed her goodby as usual. There was no circumstance out of the common to distinguish this parting from previous occasions when we had bade each other goodby for a night or a day. There was absolutely no premonition in my mind, or I am sure in hers, that this was more than an ordinary separation.

Ah, well!

The hour at which I had left my betrothed was a rather early one for a lover, but the fact was no reflection on my devotion. I was a confirmed sufferer from insomnia, and although otherwise perfectly well had been completely fagged out that day, from having slept scarcely at all the two previous nights. Edith knew this and had insisted on sending me home by nine o'clock, with strict orders to go to bed at once.

The house in which I lived had been occupied by three generations of the family of which I was the only living representative in the direct line. It was a large, ancient wooden mansion, very elegant in an old-fashioned way within, but situated in a quarter that had long since become undesirable for residence, from its invasion by tenement houses and manufactories. It was not a house to which I could think of bringing a bride, much less so dainty a one as Edith Bartlett. I had advertised it for sale, and meanwhile merely used it for sleeping purposes, dining at my club. One servant, a faithful colored man by the name of Sawyer, lived with me and attended to my few wants. One feature of the house I expected to miss greatly when I should leave it, and this was the sleeping chamber which I had built under the foundations. I could not have slept in the city at all, with its never ceasing nightly noises, if I had been obliged to use an upstairs chamber. But to this subterranean room no murmur from the upper world ever penetrated. When I had entered it and closed the door, I was surrounded by the silence of the tomb. In order to prevent the dampness of the subsoil from penetrating the chamber, the walls had been laid in hydraulic cement and were very thick, and the floor was likewise protected. In order that the room might serve also as a vault equally proof against violence and flames, for the storage of valuables, I had roofed it with stone slabs hermetically sealed, and the outer door was of iron with a thick coating of asbestos. A small pipe, communicating with a windmill on the top of the house, insured the renewal of air.

It might seem that the tenant of such a chamber ought to be able to command slumber, but it was rare that I slept well, even there, two nights in succession. So accustomed was I to wakefulness that I minded little the loss of one night's rest. A second night, however, spent in my reading chair instead of my bed, tired me out, and I never allowed myself to go longer than that without slumber, from fear of nervous disorder. From this statement it will be inferred that I had at my command some artificial means for inducing sleep in the last resort, and so in fact I had. If after two sleepless nights I found myself on the approach of the third without sensations of drowsiness, I called in Dr. Pillsbury.

He was a doctor by courtesy only, what was called in those days an "irregular" or "quack" doctor. He called himself a "Professor of Animal Magnetism." I had come across him in the course of some amateur investigations into the phenomena of animal magnetism. I don't think he knew anything about medicine, but he was certainly a remarkable mesmerist.[1] It was for the purpose of being put to sleep by his manipulations that I used to send for him when I found a third night of sleeplessness impending. Let my nervous excitement or mental preoccupation be however great, Dr. Pillsbury never failed, after a short time, to leave me in a deep slumber, which continued till I was aroused by a reversal of the mesmerizing process. The process for awaking the sleeper was much simpler than that for putting him to sleep, and for convenience I had made Dr. Pillsbury teach Sawyer how to do it.

My faithful servant alone knew for what purpose Dr. Pillsbury visited me, or that he did so at all. Of course, when Edith became my wife I should have to tell her my secrets. I had not hitherto told her this, because there was unquestionably a slight risk in the

---

[1] Mesmerism: an early version of hypnosis. Mesmerism or "animal magnetism" was introduced in Paris in 1778 and had a vogue in the mid-nineteenth century.

mesmeric sleep, and I know she would set her face against my practice. The risk, of course, was that it might become too profound and pass into a trance beyond the mesmerizer's power to break, ending in death. Repeated experiments had fully convinced me that the risk was next to nothing if reasonable precautions were exercised, and of this I hoped, though doubtingly, to convince Edith. I went directly home after leaving her, and at once sent Sawyer to fetch Dr. Pillsbury. Meanwhile I sought my subterranean sleeping chamber, and exchanging my costume for a comfortable dressing-gown, sat down to read the letters by the evening mail which Sawyer had laid on my reading table.

One of them was from the builder of my new house, and confirmed what I had inferred from the newspaper item. The new strikes, he said, had postponed indefinitely the completion of the contract, as neither masters nor workmen would concede the point at issue without a long struggle. Caligula[1] wished that the Roman people had but one neck that he might cut it off, and as I read this letter I am afraid that for a moment I was capable of wishing the same thing concerning the laboring classes of America. The return of Sawyer with the doctor interrupted my gloomy meditations.

It appeared that he had with difficulty been able to secure his services, as he was preparing to leave the city that very night. The doctor explained that since he had seen me last he had learned of a fine professional opening in a distant city, and decided to take prompt advantage of it. On my asking, in some panic, what I was to do for some one to put me to sleep, he gave me the names of several mesmerizers in Boston who, he averred, had quite as great powers as he.

Somewhat relieved on this point, I instructed Sawyer to rouse me at nine o'clock next morning, and, lying down on the bed in my dressing-gown, assumed a comfortable attitude, and surrendered myself to the manipulations of the mesmerizer. Owing, perhaps, to my unusually nervous state, I was slower than common in losing consciousness, but at length a delicious drowsiness stole over me.

---

[1] Caligula: Roman emperor known for cruel excesses, 37-41 AD.

CHAPTER III.

"HE is going to open his eyes. He had better see but one of us at first."

"Promise me, then, that you will not tell him."

The first voice was a man's, the second a woman's, and both spoke in whispers.

"I will see how he seems," replied the man.

"No, no, promise me," persisted the other.

"Let her have her way," whispered a third voice, also a woman.

"Well, well, I promise, then," answered the man. "Quick, go! He is coming out of it."

There was a rustle of garments and I opened my eyes. A fine looking man of perhaps sixty was bending over me, an expression of much benevolence mingled with great curiosity upon his features. He was an utter stranger. I raised myself on an elbow and looked around. The room was empty. I certainly had never been in it before, or one furnished like it. I looked back at my companion. He smiled.

"How do you feel?" he inquired.

"Where am I?" I demanded.

"You are in my house," was the reply.

"How came I here?"

"We will talk about that when you are stronger. Meanwhile, I beg you will feel no anxiety. You are among friends and in good hands. How do you feel?"

"A bit queerly," I replied, "but I am well, I suppose. Will you tell me how I came to be indebted to your hospitality? What has happened to me? How came I here? It was in my own house that I went to sleep."

"There will be time enough for explanations later," my unknown host replied, with a reassuring smile. "It will be better to avoid agitating talk until you are a little more yourself. Will you oblige me by taking a couple of swallows of this mixture? It will do you good. I am a physician."

I repelled the glass with my hand and sat up on the couch, although with an effort, for my head was strangely light.

"I insist upon knowing at once where I am and what you have been doing with me," I said.

"My dear sir," responded my companion, "let me beg that you will not agitate yourself. I would rather you did not insist upon explanations so soon, but if you do, I will try to satisfy you, provided you will first take this draught, which will strengthen you somewhat."

I thereupon drank what he offered me. Then he said, "It is not so simple a matter as you evidently suppose to tell you how you came here. You can tell me quite as much on that point as I can tell you. You have just been roused from a deep sleep, or, more properly, trance. So much I can tell you. You say you were in your own house when you fell into that sleep. May I ask you when that was?"

"When?" I replied, "when? Why, last evening, of course, at about ten o'clock. I left my man Sawyer orders to call me at nine o'clock. What has become of Sawyer?"

"I can't precisely tell you that," replied my companion, regarding me with a curious expression, "but I am sure that he is excusable for not being here. And now can you tell me a little more explicitly when it was that you fell into that sleep, the date, I mean?"

"Why, last night, of course; I said so, didn't I? that is, unless I have overslept an entire day. Great heavens! that cannot be possible; and yet I have an odd sensation of having slept a long time. It was Decoration Day that I went to sleep."

"Decoration Day?"

"Yes, Monday, the 30th."

"Pardon me, the 30th of what?"

"Why, of this month, of course, unless I have slept into June, but that can't be."

"This month is September."

"September! You don't mean that I've slept since May! God in heaven! Why, it is incredible."

"We shall see," replied my companion; "you say that it was May 30th when you went to sleep?"

"Yes."

"May I ask of what year?"

I stared blankly at him, incapable of speech, for some moments.

"Of what year?" I feebly echoed at last.

"Yes, of what year, if you please? After you have told me that I shall be able to tell you how long you have slept."

"It was the year 1887," I said.

My companion insisted that I should take another draught from the glass, and felt my pulse.

"My dear sir," he said, "your manner indicates that you are a man of culture, which I am aware was by no means the matter of course in your day it now is. No doubt, then, you have yourself made the observation that nothing in this world can be truly said to be more wonderful than anything else. The causes of all phenomena are equally adequate, and the results equally matters of course. That you should be startled by what I shall tell you is to be expected; but I am confident that you will not permit it to affect your equanimity unduly. Your appearance is that of a young man of barely thirty, and your bodily condition seems not greatly different from that of one just roused from a somewhat too long and profound sleep, and yet this is the tenth day of September in the year 2000, and you have slept exactly one hundred and thirteen years, three months, and eleven days."

Feeling partially dazed, I drank a cup of some sort of broth at my companion's suggestion, and, immediately afterward becoming very drowsy, went off into a deep sleep.

When I awoke it was broad daylight in the room, which had been lighted artificially when I was awake before. My mysterious host was sitting near. He was not looking at me when I opened my eyes, and I had a good opportunity to study him and meditate upon my extraordinary situation, before he observed that I was awake.

My giddiness was all gone, and my mind perfectly clear. The story that I had been asleep one hundred and thirteen years, which, in my former weak and bewildered condition, I had accepted without question, recurred to me now only to be rejected as a preposterous attempt at an imposture, the motive of which it was impossible remotely to surmise.

Something extraordinary had certainly happened to account for my waking up in this strange house with this unknown companion, but my fancy was utterly impotent to suggest more than the wildest guess as to what that something might have been. Could it be that I was the victim of some sort of conspiracy? It looked so, certainly; and yet, if human lineaments ever gave true evidence, it was certain that this man by my side, with a face so refined and ingenuous, was no party to any scheme of crime or outrage. Then it occurred to me to question if I might not be the butt of some elaborate practical joke on the part of friends who had somehow learned the secret of my underground chamber and taken this means of impressing me with the peril of mesmeric experiments. There were great difficulties in the way of this theory; Sawyer would never have betrayed me, nor had I any friends at all likely to undertake such an enterprise; nevertheless the supposition that I was the victim of a practical joke seemed on the whole the only one tenable. Half expecting to catch a glimpse of some familiar face grinning from behind a chair or curtain, I looked carefully about the room. When my eyes next rested on my companion, he was looking at me.

"You have had a fine nap of twelve hours," he said briskly, "and I can see that it has done you good. You look much better. Your color is good and your eyes are bright. How do you feel?"

"I never felt better," I said, sitting up.

"You remember your first waking, no doubt," he pursued, "and your surprise when I told you how long you had been asleep?"

"You said, I believe, that I had slept one hundred and thirteen years."

"Exactly."

"You will admit," I said, with an ironical smile, "that the story was rather an improbable one."

"Extraordinary, I admit," he responded, "but given the proper conditions, not improbable nor inconsistent with what we know of the trance state. When complete, as in your case, the vital functions are absolutely suspended, and there is no waste of the tissues. No limit can be set to the possible duration of a trance when the external conditions protect the body from physical injury. This trance of yours is indeed the longest of which there is any positive record, but there is no known reason wherefore, had you not been discovered and had the chamber in which we found you continued intact, you might not have remained in a state of suspended animation till, at the end of indefinite ages, the gradual refrigeration of the earth had destroyed the bodily tissues and set the spirit free."

I had to admit that, if I were indeed the victim of a practical joke, its authors had chosen an admirable agent for carrying out their imposition. The impressive and even eloquent manner of this man would have lent dignity to an argument that the moon was made of cheese. The smile with which I had regarded him as he advanced his trance hypothesis did not appear to confuse him in the slightest degree.

"Perhaps," I said, "you will go on and favor me with some particulars as to the circumstances under which you discovered this chamber of which you speak, and its contents. I enjoy good fiction."

"In this case," was the grave reply, "no fiction could be so strange as the truth. You must know that these many years I have been cherishing the idea of building a laboratory in the large garden beside this house, for the purpose of chemical experiments for which I have a taste. Last Thursday the excavation for the cellar was at last begun. It was completed by that night, and Friday the masons were to have come. Thursday night we had a tremendous deluge of rain, and Friday morning I found my cellar a frogpond and the walls quite washed down. My daughter, who had come out to view the disaster with me, called my attention to a corner of masonry laid bare by the crumbling away of one of the walls. I cleared a little earth from it, and, finding that it seemed part of a large mass, determined to investigate it. The workmen I sent for unearthed an oblong vault some eight feet below the surface, and set in the corner of what had evidently been the foundation walls of an ancient house. A layer of ashes and charcoal on the top of the vault showed that the house above had perished by fire. The vault itself was perfectly intact, the cement being as good as when first applied. It had a door, but this we could not force, and found entrance by removing one of the flagstones which formed the roof. The air which came up was stagnant but pure, dry and not cold. Descending with a lantern, I found myself in an apartment fitted up as a bedroom, in the style of the nineteenth century. On the bed lay a young man. That he was dead and must have been dead a century was of course to be taken for granted; but the extraordinary state of preservation of the body struck me and the medical colleagues whom I had summoned with amazement. That the art of such embalming as this had ever been known we should not have believed, yet here seemed conclusive testimony that our immediate ancestors had possessed it. My medical colleagues, whose curiosity was highly excited, were at once for undertaking experiments to test the nature of the process employed, but I withheld them. My motive in so doing, at least the only motive I now need speak of, was the recollection of something I once had read about the extent to which your contemporaries had cultivated the subject of animal magnetism. It had occurred to me as just conceivable that you might be in a trance, and that the secret of your bodily integrity after so long a time was not the craft of an embalmer, but life. So extremely fanciful did this idea seem, even to me, that I did not risk the ridicule of my fellow physicians by mentioning it, but gave some other reason for postponing their experiments.

"No sooner, however, had they left me, than I set on foot a systematic attempt at resuscitation, of which you know the result."

Had its theme been yet more incredible, the circumstantiality of this narrative, as well as the impressive manner and personality of the narrator, might have staggered a listener, and I had begun to feel very strangely, when, as he closed, I chanced to catch a glimpse of my reflection in a mirror hanging on the wall of the room. I rose and went up to it. The face I saw was the face to a hair and a line and not a day older than the one I had looked at as I tied my cravat before going to Edith that Decoration Day, which, as this man would have me believe, was celebrated one hundred and thirteen years before. At this, the colossal character of the fraud which was being attempted on me, came over me afresh. Indignation mastered my mind as I realized the outrageous liberty that had been taken.

"You are probably surprised," said my companion, "to see that, although you are a century older than when you lay down to sleep in that underground chamber, your appearance is unchanged. That should not amaze you. It is by virtue of the total arrest of the vital functions that you have survived this great period of time. If your body could have undergone any change during your trance, it would long ago have suffered dissolution."

"Sir," I replied, turning to him, "what your motive can be in reciting to me with a serious face this remarkable farrago, I am utterly unable to guess; but you are surely yourself too intelligent to suppose that anybody but an imbecile could be deceived by it. Spare me any more of this elaborate nonsense and once for all tell me whether you refuse to give me an intelligible account of where I am and how I came here. If so, I shall proceed to ascertain my whereabouts for myself, whoever may hinder."

"You do not, then, believe that this is the year 2000?"

"Do you really think it necessary to ask me that?" I returned.

"Very well," replied my extraordinary host. "Since I cannot convince you, you shall convince yourself. Are you strong enough to follow me upstairs?"

"I am as strong as I ever was," I replied angrily, "as I may have to prove if this jest is carried much farther."

"I beg, sir," was my companion's response, "that you will not allow yourself to be too fully persuaded that you are the victim of a trick, lest the reaction, when you are convinced of the truth of my statements, should be too great."

The tone of concern, mingled with commiseration, with which he said this, and the entire absence of any sign of resentment at my hot words, strangely daunted me, and I followed him from the room with an extraordinary mixture of emotions. He led the way up two flights of stairs and then up a shorter one, which landed us upon a belvedere on the housetop. "Be pleased to look around you," he said, as we reached the platform, "and tell me if this is the Boston of the nineteenth century."

At my feet lay a great city. Miles of broad streets, shaded by trees and lined with fine buildings, for the most part not in continuous blocks but set in larger or smaller inclosures, stretched in every direction. Every quarter contained large open squares filled with trees, among which statues glistened and fountains flashed in the late afternoon sun. Public buildings of a colossal size and an architectural grandeur unparalleled in my day raised their stately piles on every side. Surely I had never seen this city nor one comparable to it before. Raising my eyes at last towards the horizon, I looked westward. That blue ribbon winding away to the sunset, was it not the sinuous Charles? I looked east; Boston harbor stretched before me within its headlands, not one of its green islets missing.

I knew then that I had been told the truth concerning the prodigious thing which had befallen me.

CHAPTER IV.

I DID not faint, but the effort to realize my position made me very giddy, and I remember that my companion had to give me a strong arm as he conducted me from the roof to a roomy apartment on the upper floor of the house, where he insisted on my drinking a glass or two of good wine and partaking of a light repast.

"I think you are going to be all right now," he said cheerily. "I should not have taken so abrupt a means to convince you of your position if your course, while perfectly excusable under the circumstances, had not rather obliged me to do so. I confess," he added laughing, "I was a little apprehensive at one time that I should undergo what I believe you used to call a knockdown in the nineteenth century, if I did not act rather promptly. I remembered that the Bostonians of your day were famous pugilists, and thought best to lose no time. I take it you are now ready to acquit me of the charge of hoaxing you."

"If you had told me," I replied, profoundly awed, "that a thousand years instead of a hundred had elapsed since I last looked on this city, I should now believe you."

"Only a century has passed," he answered, "but many a millennium in the world's history has seen changes less extraordinary."

"And now," he added, extending his hand with an air of irresistible cordiality, "let me give you a hearty welcome to the Boston of the twentieth century and to this house. My name is Leete, Dr. Leete they call me."

"My name," I said as I shook his hand, "is Julian West."

"I am most happy in making your acquaintance, Mr. West," he responded. "Seeing that this house is built on the site of your own, I hope you will find it easy to make yourself at home in it."

After my refreshment Dr. Leete offered me a bath and a change of clothing, of which I gladly availed myself.

It did not appear that any very startling revolution in men's attire had been among the great changes my host had spoken of, for, barring a few details, my new habiliments did not puzzle me at all.

Physically, I was now myself again. But mentally, how was it with me, the reader will doubtless wonder. What were my intellectual sensations, he may wish to know, on finding myself so suddenly dropped as it were into a new world. In reply let me ask him to suppose himself suddenly, in the twinkling of an eye, transported from earth, say, to Paradise or Hades. What does he fancy would be his own experience? Would his thoughts return at once to the earth he had just left, or would he, after the first shock, wellnigh forget his former life for a while, albeit to be remembered later, in the interest excited by his new surroundings? All I can say is, that if his experience were at all like mine in the transition I am describing, the latter hypothesis would prove the correct one. The impressions of amazement and curiosity which my new surroundings produced occupied my mind, after the first shock, to the exclusion of all other thoughts. For the time [being] the memory of my former life was, as it were, in abeyance.

No sooner did I find myself physically rehabilitated through the kind offices of my host, than I became eager to return to the house-top; and presently we were comfortably established there in easy-chairs, with the city beneath and around us. After Dr. Leete had responded to numerous questions on my part, as to the ancient landmarks I missed and the new ones which had replaced them, he asked me what point of the contrast between the new and the old city struck me most forcibly.

"To speak of small things before great," I responded, "I really think that the complete absence of chimneys and their smoke is the detail that first impressed me."

"Ah!" ejaculated my companion with an air of much interest, "I had forgotten the chimneys, it is so long since they went out of use. It is nearly a century since the crude method of combustion on which you depended for heat became obsolete."

"In general," I said, "what impresses me most about the city is the material prosperity on the part of the people which its magnificence implies."

"I would give a great deal for just one glimpse of the Boston ,of your day," replied Dr. Leete. "No doubt, as you imply, the cities of that period were rather shabby affairs. If you had the taste to make them splendid, which I would not be so rude as to question, the general poverty resulting from your extraordinary industrial system would not have given you the means. Moreover, the excessive individualism which then prevailed was inconsistent with much public spirit. What little wealth you had seems almost wholly to have been lavished in private luxury. Nowadays, on the contrary, there is no destination of the surplus wealth so popular as the adornment of the city, which all enjoy in equal degree."

The sun had been setting as we returned to the house-top, and as we talked night descended upon the city.

"It is growing dark," said Dr. Leete. "Let us descend into the house; I want to introduce my wife and daughter to you."

His words recalled to me the feminine voices which I had heard whispering about me as I was coming back to conscious life; and, most curious to learn what the ladies of the year 2000 were like, I assented with alacrity to the proposition. The apartment in which we found the wife and daughter of my host, as well as the entire interior of the house, was filled with a mellow light, which I knew must be artificial, although I could not discover the source from which it was diffused. Mrs. Leete was an exceptionally fine looking and well preserved woman of about her husband's age, while the daughter, who was in the first blush of womanhood, was the most beautiful girl I had ever seen. Her face was as bewitching as deep blue eyes, delicately tinted complexion, and perfect features could make it, but even had her countenance lacked special charms, the faultless luxuriance of her figure would have given her place as a beauty among the women of the nineteenth century. Feminine softness and delicacy were in this lovely creature deliciously combined with an appearance of health and abounding physical vitality too often lacking in the maidens with whom alone I could compare her. It was a coincidence trifling in comparison with the general strangeness of the situation, but still striking, that her name should be Edith.

The evening that followed was certainly unique in the history of social intercourse, but to suppose that our conversation was peculiarly strained or difficult would be a great mistake. I believe indeed that it is under what may be called unnatural, in the sense of extraordinary, circumstances that people behave most naturally, for the reason, no doubt, that such circumstances banish artificiality. I know at any rate that my intercourse that evening with these representatives of another age and world was marked by an ingenuous sincerity and frankness such as but rarely crown long acquaintance. No doubt the exquisite tact of my entertainers had much to do with this. Of course there was nothing we could talk of but the strange experience by virtue of which I was there, but they talked of it with an interest so naive and direct in its expression as to relieve the subject to a great degree of the element of the weird and the uncanny which might so easily have been overpowering. One would have supposed that they were quite in the habit of entertaining waifs from another century, so perfect was their tact.

For my own part, never do I remember the operations of my mind to have been more alert and acute than that evening, or my intellectual sensibilities more keen. Of course I do not mean that the consciousness of my amazing situation was for a moment out of mind, but its chief effect thus far was to produce a feverish elation, a sort of mental intoxication.[1]

Edith Leete took little part in the conversation, but when several times the magnetism of her beauty drew my glance to her face, I found her eyes fixed on me with an absorbed intensity, almost like fascination. It was evident that I had excited her interest to an extraordinary degree, as was not astonishing, supposing her to be a girl of imagination. Though I supposed curiosity was

---

[1] In accounting for this state of mind it must be remembered that, except for the topic of our conversations, there was in my surroundings next to nothing to suggest what had befallen me. Within a block of my home in the old Boston I could have found social circles vastly more foreign to me. The speech of the Bostonians of the twentieth century differs even less from that of their cultured ancestors of the nineteenth than did that of the latter from the language of Washington and Franklin, while the differences between the style of dress and furniture of the two epochs are not more marked than I have known fashion to make in the time of one generation. [Bellamy's note]

the chief motive of her interest, it could but affect me as it would not have done had she been less beautiful.

Dr. Leete, as well as the ladies, seemed greatly interested in my account of the circumstances under which I had gone to sleep in the underground chamber. All had suggestions to offer to account for my having been forgotten there, and the theory which we finally agreed on offers at least a plausible explanation, although whether it be in its details the true one, nobody, of course, will ever know. The layer of ashes found above the chamber indicated that the house had been burned down. Let it be supposed that the conflagration had taken place the night I fell asleep. It only remains to assume that Sawyer lost his life in the fire or by some accident connected with it, and the rest follows naturally enough. No one but he and Dr. Pillsbury either knew of the existence of the chamber or that I was in it, and Dr. Pillsbury, who had gone that night to New Orleans, had probably never heard of the fire at all. The conclusion of my friends, and of the public, must have been that I had perished in the flames. An excavation of the ruins, unless thorough, would not have disclosed the recess in the foundation walls connecting with my chamber. To be sure, if the site had been again built upon, at least immediately, such an excavation would have been necessary, but the troublous times and the undesirable character of the locality might well have prevented rebuilding. The size of the trees in the garden now occupying the site indicated, Dr. Leete said, that for more than half a century at least it had been open ground.

CHAPTER V.

WHEN, in the course of the evening the ladies retired, leaving Dr. Leete and myself alone, he sounded me as to my disposition for sleep, saying that if I felt like it my bed was ready for me; but if I was inclined to wakefulness nothing would please him better than to bear me company. "I am a late bird, myself," he said, "and, without suspicion of flattery, I may say that a companion more interesting than yourself could scarcely be imagined. It is decidedly not often that one has a chance to converse with a man of the nine-teenth century."

Now I had been looking forward all the evening with some dread to the time when I should be alone, on retiring for the night. Surrounded by these most friendly strangers, stimulated and supported by their sympathetic interest, I had been able to keep my mental balance. Even then, however, in pauses of the conversation I had had glimpses, vivid as lightning flashes, of the horror of strangeness that was waiting to be faced when I could no longer command diversion. I knew I could not sleep that night, and as for lying awake and thinking, it argues no cowardice, I am sure, to confess that I was afraid of it. When, in reply to my host's question, I frankly told him this, he replied that it would be strange if I did not feel just so, but that I need have no anxiety about sleeping; whenever I wanted to go to bed, he would give me a dose which would insure me a sound night's sleep without fail. Next morning, no doubt, I would awake with the feeling of an old citizen.

"Before I acquire that," I replied, "I must know a little more about the sort of Boston I have come back to. You told me when we were upon the house-top that though a century only had elapsed since I fell asleep, it had been marked by greater changes in the conditions of humanity than many a previous millennium. With the city before me I could well believe that, but I am very curious to know what some of the changes have been. To make a beginning somewhere, for the subject is doubtless a large one, what solution, if any, have you found for the labor question? It was the Sphinx's riddle of the nineteenth century, and when I dropped out the Sphinx was threatening to devour society, because the answer was not forthcoming. It is well worth sleeping a hundred years to learn what the right answer was, if, indeed, you have found it yet."[1]

"As no such thing as the labor question is known nowadays," replied Dr. Leete, "and there is no way in which it could arise, I

---

[1] Sphinx's riddle: this is the Sphinx of Greek mythology rather than the famous Egyptian Sphinx. The riddle is: "What goes on four feet, on two feet, and three/But the more feet it goes on the weaker it be?" Oedipus solved the riddle: a man, who crawls as a baby, then walks, then uses a staff in old age. Source: *Brewer's Dictionary of Phrase and Fable.*

suppose we may claim to have solved it. Society would indeed have fully deserved being devoured if it had failed to answer a riddle so entirely simple. In fact, to speak by the book, it was not necessary for society to solve the riddle at all. It may be said to have solved itself. The solution came as the result of a process of industrial evolution which could not have terminated otherwise. All that society had to do was to recognize and cooperate with that evolution, when its tendency had become unmistakable."

"I can only say," I answered, "that at the time I fell asleep no such evolution had been recognized."

"It was in 1887 that you fell into this sleep, I think you said."

"Yes, May 30th, 1887."

My companion regarded me musingly for some moments. Then he observed, "And you tell me that even then there was no general recognition of the nature of the crisis which society was nearing? Of course, I fully credit your statement. The singular blindness of your contemporaries to the signs of the times is a phenomenon commented on by many of our historians, but few facts of history are more difficult for us to realize, so obvious and unmistakable as we look back seem the indications, which must also have come under your eyes, of the transformation about to come to pass. I should be interested, Mr. West, if you would give me a little more definite idea of the view which you and men of your grade of intellect took of the state and prospects of society in 1887. You must, at least, have realized that the widespread industrial and social troubles, and the underlying dissatisfaction of all classes with the inequalities of society, and the general misery of mankind, were portents of great changes of some sort."

"We did, indeed, fully realize that," I replied.

"We felt that society was dragging anchor and in danger of going adrift. Whither it would drift nobody could say, but all feared the rocks."

"Nevertheless," said Dr. Leete, "the set of the current was perfectly perceptible if you had but taken pains to observe it, and it was not toward the rocks, but toward a deeper channel."

"We had a popular proverb," I replied, "that 'hindsight is better than foresight,' the force of which I shall now, no doubt, appreciate more fully than ever. All I can say is, that the prospect was such when I went into that long sleep that I should not have been surprised had I looked down from your house-top today on a heap of charred and moss-grown ruins instead of this glorious city."

Dr. Leete had listened to me with close attention and nodded thoughtfully as I finished speaking. "What you have said," he observed, "will be regarded as a most valuable vindication of Storiot, whose account of your era has been generally thought exaggerated in its picture of the gloom and confusion of men's minds. That a period of transition like that should be full of excitement and agitation was indeed to be looked for; but seeing how plain was the tendency of the forces in operation, it was natural to believe that hope rather than fear would have been the prevailing temper of the popular mind."

"You have not yet told me what was the answer to the riddle which you found," I said. "I am impatient to know by what contradiction of natural sequence the peace and prosperity which you now seem to enjoy could have been the outcome of an era like my own."

"Excuse me," replied my host, "but do you smoke?" It was not till our cigars were lighted and drawing well that he resumed. "Since you are in the humor to talk rather than to sleep, as I certainly am, perhaps I cannot do better than to try to give you enough idea of our modern industrial system to dissipate at least the impression that there is any mystery about the process of its evolution. The Bostonians of your day had the reputation of being great askers of questions, and I am going to show my descent by asking you one to begin with. What should you name as the most prominent feature of the labor troubles of your day?"

"Why, the strikes, of course," I replied.

"Exactly; but what made the strikes so formidable?"

"The great labor organizations."

"And what was the motive of these great organizations?"

"The workmen claimed they had to organize to get their rights from the big corporations," I replied.

"That is just it," said Dr. Leete; "the organization of labor and the strikes were an effect, merely, of the concentration of capital in greater masses than had ever been known before. Before this concentration began, while as yet commerce and industry were conducted by innumerable petty concerns with small capital, instead of a small number of great concerns with vast capital, the individual workman was relatively important and independent in his relations to the employer. Moreover, when a little capital or a new idea was enough to start a man in business for himself, workingmen were constantly becoming employers and there was no hard and fast line between the two classes. Labor unions were needless then, and general strikes out of the question. But when the era of small concerns with small capital was succeeded by that of the great aggregations of capital, all this was changed. The individual laborer, who had been relatively important to the small employer, was reduced to insignificance and powerlessness over against the great corporation, while at the same time the way upward to the grade of employer was closed to him. Self-defense drove him to union with his fellows.[1]

"The records of the period show that the outcry against the concentration of capital was furious. Men believed that it threatened society with a form of tyranny more abhorrent than it had ever endured. They believed that the great corporations were preparing for them the yoke of a baser servitude than had ever been imposed on the race, servitude not to men but to soulless machines incapable of any motive but insatiable greed. Looking back, we cannot wonder at their desperation, for certainly humanity was never confronted with a fate more sordid and hideous than would have been the era of corporate tyranny which they anticipated.

"Meanwhile, without being in the smallest degree checked by the clamor against it, the absorption of business by ever larger monopolies continued. In the United States there was not, after the beginning of the last quarter of the century, any opportunity whatever for individual enterprise in any important field

---

[1] Historians Charles and Mary Beard have described four stages in the evolution of unions, from the Philadelphia shoemakers who formed a local union in 1792, to unions of single trades in more than one city, to federation of local unions in national associations by the 1830s, and finally to attempts to establish a national union of unions such as the National Labor Union (1866), the Knights of Labor (1875) and the American Federation of Labor (1886). This amalgamation paralleled the amalgamation of industries into the great monopolies which Bellamy describes. The Beards' *New Basic History of the United States*. Revised William Beard. Garden City, N.Y.: Doubleday, 1968, 196-7 and 295-7.

of industry, unless backed by a great capital. During the last decade of the century, such small businesses as still remained were fast-failing survivals of a past epoch, or mere parasites on the great corporations, or else existed in fields too small to attract the great capitalists. Small businesses, as far as they still remained, were reduced to the condition of rats and mice, living in holes and corners, and counting on evading notice for the enjoyment of existence. The railroads had gone on combining till a few great syndicates controlled every rail in the land. In manufactories, every important staple was controlled by a syndicate. These syndicates, pools, trusts, or whatever their name, fixed prices and crushed all competition except when combinations as vast as themselves arose. Then a struggle, resulting in a still greater consolidation, ensued. The great city bazaar crushed its country rivals with branch stores, and in the city itself absorbed its smaller rivals till the business of a whole quarter was concentrated under one roof, with a hundred former proprietors of shops serving as clerks. Having no business of his own to put his money in, the small capitalist, at the same time that he took service under the corporation, found no other investment for his money but its stocks and bonds, thus becoming doubly dependent upon it.

"The fact that the desperate popular opposition to the consolidation of business in a few powerful hands had no effect to check it proves that there must have been a strong economical reason for it. The small capitalists, with their innumerable petty concerns, had in fact yielded the field to the great aggregations of capital, because they belonged to a day of small things and were totally incompetent to the demands of an age of steam and telegraphs and the gigantic scale of its enterprises. To restore the former order of things, even if possible, would have involved returning to the day of stagecoaches. Oppressive and intolerable as was the régime of the great consolidations of capital, even its victims, while they cursed it, were forced to admit the prodigious increase of efficiency which had been imparted to the national industries, the vast economies effected by concentration of management and unity of organization, and to confess that since the new system had taken the place of the old the wealth of the world had increased at a rate before undreamed of. To be sure this vast increase had gone chiefly to make the rich richer, increasing the gap between them and the poor; but the fact remained that, as a means merely of producing wealth, capital had been proved efficient in proportion to its consolidation. The restoration of the old system with the subdivision of capital, if it were possible, might indeed bring back a greater equality of conditions, with more individual dignity and freedom, but it would be at the price of general poverty and the arrest of material progress.

"Was there, then, no way of commanding the services of the mighty wealth-producing principle of consolidated capital without bowing down to a plutocracy like that of Carthage?[1] As soon as men began to ask themselves these questions, they found the answer ready for them. The movement toward the conduct of business by larger and larger aggregations of capital, the tendency toward monopolies, which had been so desperately and vainly resisted, was recognized at last, in its true significance, as a process which only needed to complete its logical evolution to open a golden future to humanity.

"Early in the last century the evolution was completed by the final consolidation of the entire capital of the nation. The industry and commerce of the country, ceasing to be conducted by a set of irresponsible corporations and syndicates of private persons at their caprice and for their profit, were intrusted to a single syndicate representing the people, to be conducted in the common interest for the common profit. The nation, that is to say, organized as the one great business corporation in which all other corporations were absorbed; it became the one capitalist in the place of all other capitalists, the sole employer, the final monopoly in which all previous and lesser monopolies were swallowed up, a monopoly in the profits and economies of which all citizens shared. The epoch of trusts had ended in The Great Trust. In a word, the people of the United States concluded to assume the conduct of their own business, just as one hundred odd years before they had assumed the conduct of their own government, organizing now for industrial purposes on

---

[1]   Carthage: one of the great cities of the ancient world, founded around 800 BC. It is now a suburb of Tunis.

precisely the same grounds that they had then organized for political purposes. At last, strangely late in the world's history, the obvious fact was perceived that no business is so essentially the public business as the industry and commerce on which the people's livelihood depends, and that to entrust it to private persons to be managed for private profit is a folly similar in kind, though vastly greater in magnitude, to that of surrendering the functions of political government to kings and nobles to be conducted for their personal glorification."

"Such a stupendous change as you describe," said I, "did not, of course, take place without great bloodshed and terrible convulsions."

"On the contrary," replied Dr. Leete, "there was absolutely no violence. The change had been long foreseen. Public opinion had become fully ripe for it, and the whole mass of the people was behind it. There was no more possibility of opposing it by force than by argument. On the other hand the popular sentiment toward the great corporations and those identified with them had ceased to be one of bitterness, as they came to realize their necessity as a link, a transition phase, in the evolution of the true industrial system. The most violent foes of the great private monopolies were now forced to recognize how invaluable and indispensable had been their office in educating the people up to the point of assuming control of their own business. Fifty years before, the consolidation of the industries of the country under national control would have seemed a very daring experiment to the most sanguine. But by a series of object lessons, seen and studied by all men, the great corporations had taught the people an entirely new set of ideas on this subject. They had seen for many years syndicates handling revenues greater than those of states, and directing the labors of hundreds of thousands of men with an efficiency and economy unattainable in smaller operations. It had come to be recognized as an axiom that the larger the business the simpler the principles that can be applied to it; that, as the machine is truer than the hand, so the system, which in a great concern does the work of the master's eye in a small business, turns out more accurate results. Thus it came about that, thanks to the corporations themselves, when it was proposed that the nation should assume their functions, the suggestion implied nothing which seemed impracticable even to the timid. To be sure it was a step beyond any yet taken, a broader generalization, but the very fact that the nation would be the sole corporation in the field would, it was seen, relieve the undertaking of many difficulties with which the partial monopolies had contended."

CHAPTER VI.

DR. Leete ceased speaking, and I remained silent, endeavoring to form some general conception of the changes in the arrangements of society implied in the tremendous revolution which he had described.

Finally I said, "The idea of such an extension of the functions of government is, to say the least, rather overwhelming."

"Extension!" he repeated, "where is the extension?"

"In my day," I replied, "it was considered that the proper functions of government, strictly speaking, were limited to keeping the peace and defending the people against the public enemy, that is, to the military and police powers."

"And, in heaven's name, who are the public enemies?" exclaimed Dr. Leete. "Are they France, England, Germany, or hunger, cold, and nakedness? In your day governments were accustomed, on the slightest international misunderstanding, to seize upon the bodies of citizens and deliver them over by hundreds of thousands to death and mutilation, wasting their treasures the while like water; and all this oftenest for no imaginable profit to the victims. We have no wars now, and our governments no war powers, but in order to protect every citizen against hunger, cold, and nakedness, and provide for all his physical and mental needs, the function is assumed of directing his industry for a term of years. No, Mr. West, I am sure on reflection you will perceive that it was in your age, not in ours, that the extension of the functions of governments was extraordinary. Not even for the best ends would men now allow their governments such powers as were then used for the most maleficent."

"Leaving comparisons aside," I said, "the demagoguery and corruption of our public men would have been considered, in my day, insuperable objections to any assumption by government of the charge of the national industries. We should have thought that no arrangement could be worse than to entrust the politicians with control of the wealth-producing machinery of the country. Its material interests were quite too much the football of parties as it was."

"No doubt you were right," rejoined Dr. Leete, "but all that is changed now. We have no parties or politicians, and as for demagoguery and corruption, they are words having only an historical significance."

"Human nature itself must have changed very much," I said.

"Not at all," was Dr. Leete's reply, "but the conditions of human life have changed, and with them the motives of human action.[1] The organization of society with you was such that officials were under a constant temptation to misuse their power for the private profit of themselves or others. Under such circumstances it seems almost strange that you dared entrust them with any of your affairs. Nowadays, on the contrary, society is so constituted that there is absolutely no way in which an official, however ill-disposed, could possibly make any profit for himself or any one else by a misuse of his power. Let him be as bad an official as you please, he cannot be a corrupt one. There is no motive to be. The social system no longer offers a premium on dishonesty. But these are matters which you can only understand as you come, with time, to know us better."

"But you have not yet told me how you have settled the labor problem. It is the problem of capital which we have been discussing," I said. "After the nation had assumed conduct of the mills, machinery, railroads, farms, mines, and capital in general of

---

[1] Human nature: one of the great debates within utopian thought is whether human nature is intrinsically flawed (in religious terms the idea of "original sin") or whether human nature is the product of external influences—the heredity/environment or nature/nurture debate. Bellamy here is a typical utopian in opting for the environment side and presuming that if we change the conditions human nature will rise to the challenge. However, note that the discussion of motivation in Chapter 12 suggests some men have "inferior natures" and need the motive of emulation or competition, so the novel is slightly conflicted on the issue.

the country, the labor question still remained. In assuming the responsibilities of capital the nation had assumed the difficulties of the capitalist's position."

"The moment the nation assumed the responsibilities of capital those difficulties vanished," replied Dr. Leete. "The national organization of labor under one direction was the complete solution of what was, in your day and under your system, justly regarded as the insoluble labor problem. When the nation became the sole employer, all the citizens, by virtue of their citizenship, became employees, to be distributed according to the needs of industry."

"That is," I suggested, "you have simply applied the principle of universal military service, as it was understood in our day, to the labor question."

"Yes," said Dr. Leete, "that was something which followed as a matter of course as soon as the nation had become the sole capitalist. The people were already accustomed to the idea that the obligation of every citizen, not physically disabled, to contribute his military services to the defense of the nation was· equal and absolute. That it was equally the duty of every citizen to contribute his quota of industrial or intellectual services to the maintenance of the nation was equally evident, though it was not until the nation became the employer of labor that citizens were able to render this sort of service with any pretense either of universality or equity. No organization of labor was possible when the employing power was divided among hundreds or thousands of individuals and corporations, between which concert of any kind was neither desired, nor indeed feasible. It constantly happened then that vast numbers who desired to labor could find no opportunity, and on the other hand, those who desired to evade a part or all of their debt could easily do so."

"Service, now, I suppose, is compulsory upon all," I suggested.

"It is rather a matter of course than of compulsion," replied Dr. Leete. "It is regarded as so absolutely natural and reasonable that the idea of its being compulsory has ceased to be thought of. He would be thought to be an incredibly contemptible person who should need compulsion in such a case. Nevertheless, to speak of service being compulsory would be a weak way to state its absolute inevitableness. Our entire social order is so wholly based upon and deduced from it that if it were conceivable that a man could escape it, he would be left with no possible way to provide for his existence. He would have excluded himself from the world, cut himself off from his kind, in a word, committed suicide."

"Is the term of service in this industrial army for life?"

"Oh, no; it both begins later and ends earlier than the average working period in your day. Your workshops were filled with children and old men, but we hold the period of youth sacred to education, and the period of maturity, when the physical forces begin to flag, equally sacred to ease and agreeable relaxation. The period of industrial service is twenty-four years, beginning at the close of the course of education at twenty-one and terminating at forty-five. After forty-five, while discharged from labor, the citizen still remains liable to special calls, in case of emergencies causing a sudden great increase in the demand for labor, till he reaches the age of fifty-five, but such calls are rarely, in fact almost never, made. The fifteenth day of October of every year is what we call Muster Day, because those who have reached the age of twenty-one are then mustered into the industrial service, and at the same time those who, after twenty-four years' service, have reached the age of forty-five, are honorably mustered out. It is the great day of the year with us, whence we reckon all other events, our Olympiad, save that it is annual."

CHAPTER VII.

"IT is after you have mustered your industrial army into service," I said, "that I should expect the chief difficulty to arise, for there its analogy with a military army must cease. Soldiers have all the same thing, and a very simple thing, to do, namely, to practice the manual of arms, to march and stand guard. But the industrial army must learn and follow two or three hundred diverse trades and avocations. What administrative talent can be equal to determining wisely what trade or business every individual in a great nation shall pursue?"

"The administration has nothing to do with determining that point."

"Who does determine it, then?" I asked.

"Every man for himself in accordance with his natural aptitude, the utmost pains being taken to enable him to find out what his natural aptitude really is. The principle on which our industrial army is organized is that a man's natural endowments, mental and physical, determine what he can work at most profitably to the nation and most satisfactorily to himself. While the obligation of service in some form is not to be evaded, voluntary election, subject only to necessary regulation, is depended on to determine the particular sort of service every man is to render. As an individual's satisfaction during his term of service depends on his having an occupation to his taste, parents and teachers watch from early years for indications of special aptitudes in children. A thorough study of the National industrial system, with the history and rudiments of all the great trades, is an essential part of our educational system. While manual training is not allowed to encroach on the general intellectual culture to which our schools are devoted, it is carried far enough to give our youth, in addition to their theoretical knowledge of the national industries, mechanical and agricultural, a certain familiarity with their tools and methods. Our schools are constantly visiting our workshops, and often are taken on long excursions to inspect particular industrial enterprises. In your day a man was not ashamed to be grossly ignorant of all trades except his own, but such ignorance would not be consistent with our idea of placing every one in a position to select intelligently the occupation for which he has most taste. Usually long before he is mustered into service a young man has found out the pursuit he wants to follow, has acquired a great deal of knowledge about it, and is waiting impatiently the time when he can enlist in its ranks."

"Surely," I said, "it can hardly be that the number of volunteers for any trade is exactly the number needed in that trade. It must be generally either under or over the demand."

"The supply of volunteers is always expected to fully equal the demand," replied Dr. Leete. "It is the business of the administration to see that this is the case. The rate of volunteering for each trade is closely watched. If there be a noticeably greater excess of volunteers over men needed in any trade, it is inferred that the trade offers greater attractions than others. On the other hand, if the number of volunteers for a trade tends to drop below the demand, it is inferred that it is thought more arduous. It is the business of the administration to seek constantly to equalize the attractions of the trades, so far as the conditions of labor in them are concerned, so that all trades shall be equally attractive to persons having natural tastes for them. This is done by making the hours of labor in different trades to differ according to their arduousness. The lighter trades, prosecuted under the most agreeable circumstances, have in this way the longest hours, while an arduous trade, such as mining, has very short hours. There is no theory, no *a priori* rule, by which the respective attractiveness of industries is determined. The administration, in taking burdens off one class of workers and adding them to other classes, simply follows the fluctuations of opinion among the workers themselves as indicated by the rate of volunteering. The principle is that no man's work ought to be, on the whole, harder for him than any other man's for him, the workers themselves to be the judges. There are no limits to the application of this rule. If any particular occupation is in itself so arduous or so oppressive that, in order to induce volunteers, the day's work in it had to be reduced to ten minutes, it would be done. If, even then, no man was willing to do it, it would remain undone. But of course, in point of fact, a moderate reduction in the hours of labor, or addition of other privileges, suffices to secure all needed volunteers for any occupation necessary to men. If, indeed, the unavoidable difficulties and dangers of such a necessary pursuit were so great that no inducement of compensating advantages would overcome men's repugnance to it, the administration would only need to take it out of the common order of occupations by declaring it 'extra hazardous,' and those who pursued it especially worthy of the national gratitude, to be overrun with volunteers. Our young men are very greedy of honor, and do not let slip such opportunities. Of course you will see that dependence on the purely voluntary choice of avocations involves the abolition in all of anything like unhygienic conditions or special peril to life and limb. Health and safety are conditions common to all industries. The nation does not maim and slaughter its workmen by thousands, as did the private capitalists and corporations of your day."

"When there are more who want to enter a particular trade than there is room for, how do you decide between the applicants?" I inquired.

"Preference is given to those who have acquired the most knowledge of the trade they wish to follow. No man, however, who through successive years remains persistent in his desire to show what he can do at any particular trade, is in the end denied an opportunity. Meanwhile, if a man cannot at first win entrance into the business he prefers, he has usually one or more alternative preferences, pursuits for which he has some degree of aptitude, although not the highest. Every one, indeed, is expected to study his aptitudes so as to have not only a first choice as to occupation, but a second or third, so that if, either at the outset of his career or subsequently, owing to the progress of invention or changes in demand, he is unable to follow his first vocation, he can still find reasonably congenial employment. This principle of secondary choices as to occupation is quite important in our system. I should add, in reference to the counterpossibility of some sudden failure of volunteers in a particular trade, or some sudden necessity of an increased force, that the administration, while depending on the voluntary system for filling up the trades as a rule, holds always in reserve the power to call for special volunteers, or draft any force needed from any quarter. Generally, however, all needs of this sort can be met by details from the class of unskilled or common laborers."

"How is this class of common laborers recruited?" I asked. "Surely nobody voluntarily enters that."

"It is the grade to which all new recruits belong for the first three years of their service. It is not till after this period, during which he is assignable to any work at the discretion of his superiors, that the young man is allowed to elect a special avocation. These three years of stringent discipline none are exempt from, and very glad our young men are to pass from this severe school into the comparative liberty of the trades. If a man were so stupid as to have no choice as to occupation, he would simply remain a common laborer; but such cases, as you may suppose, are not common."

"Having once elected and entered on a trade or occupation," I remarked, "I suppose he has to stick to it the rest of his life."

"Not necessarily," replied Dr. Leete: "while frequent and merely capricious changes of occupation are not encouraged or even permitted, every worker is allowed, of course, under certain regulations and in accordance with the exigencies of the service, to volunteer for another industry which he thinks would suit him better than his first choice. In this case his application is received just as if he were volunteering for the first time, and on the same terms. Not only this, but a worker may likewise, under suitable regulations and not too frequently, obtain a transfer to an establishment of the same industry in another part of the country which for any reason he may prefer. Under your system a discontented man could indeed leave his work at will, but he left his means of support at the same time, and took his chances as to future livelihood. We find that the number of men who wish to abandon an accustomed occupation for a new one, and old friends and associations for strange ones, is small. It is only the poorer sort of workmen who desire to change even as frequently as our regulations permit. Of course transfers or discharges, when health demands them, are always given."[1]

"As an industrial system, I should think this might be extremely efficient," I said, "but I don't see that it makes any provision for the professional classes, the men who serve the nation with brains instead of hands. Of course you can't get along without the brain-workers. How, then, are they selected from those who are to serve as farmers and mechanics? That must require a very delicate sort of sifting process, I should say."

"So it does," replied Dr. Leete; "the most delicate possible test is needed here, and so we leave the question whether a man shall be a brain or hand worker entirely to him to settle. At the end of the term of three years as a common laborer, which every man must serve, it is for him to choose, in accordance to his natural tastes, whether he will fit himself for an art or profession, or be a farmer or mechanic. If he feels that he can do better work with his brains than his muscles, he finds every facility provided for

---

[1]   The two and one half paragraphs from "These three years of stringent discipline" to "are always given" were added in the second edition. These provisions add some flexibility for the individual, although the many qualifications should be noted.

testing the reality of his supposed bent, of cultivating it, and if fit, of pursuing it as his avocation. The schools of technology, of medicine, of art, of music, of histrionics, and of higher liberal learning are always open to aspirants without condition."

"Are not the schools flooded with young men whose only motive is to avoid work?"

Dr. Leete smiled a little grimly.

"No one is at all likely to enter the professional schools for the purpose of avoiding work, I assure you," he said. "They are intended for those with special aptitude for the branches they teach, and any one without it would find it easier to do double hours at his trade than try to keep up with the classes. Of course many honestly mistake their vocation, and, finding themselves unequal to the requirements of the schools, drop out and return to the industrial service; no discredit attaches to such persons, for the public policy is to encourage all to develop suspected talents which only actual tests can prove the reality of. The professional and scientific schools of your day depended on the patronage of their pupils for support, and the practice appears to have been common of giving diplomas to unfit persons, who afterwards found their way into the professions. Our schools are national institutions, and to have passed their tests is a proof of special abilities not to be questioned.

"This opportunity for a professional training," the doctor continued, "remains open to every man till the age of thirty is reached, after which students are not received, as there would remain too brief a period before the age of discharge in which to serve the nation in their professions. In your day young men had to choose their professions very young, and therefore, in a large proportion of instances, wholly mistook their vocations. It is recognized nowadays that the natural aptitudes of some are later than those of others in developing, and therefore, while the choice of profession may be made as early as twenty-four, it remains open for six years longer."[1]

---

[1]   In the first edition options remained open until age thirty-five, so the changes in this paragraph decrease individual flexibility. In this emphasis upon professions Bellamy was reflecting a contemporary trend toward professionalization—the establishment of professions with set training courses and qualifying exams. In 1825 there were 35 professional schools in the country and this had grown to 283 by the end of the century. Burton J. Bledstein. *The Culture of Professionalism*. New York: Norton, 1976, 84.

A question which had a dozen times before been on my lips now found utterance, a question which touched upon what, in my time, had been regarded the most vital difficulty in the way of any final settlement of the industrial problem. "It is an extraordinary thing," I said, "that you should not yet have said a word about the method of adjusting wages. Since the nation is the sole employer, the government must fix the rate of wages and determine just how much everybody shall earn, from the doctors to the diggers. All I can say is that this plan would never have worked with us, and I don't see how it can now unless human nature has changed. In my day, nobody was satisfied with his wages or salary. Even if he felt he received enough, he was sure his neighbor had too much, which was as bad. If the universal discontent on this subject, instead of being dissipated in curses and strikes directed against innumerable employers, could have been concentrated upon one, and that the government, the strongest ever devised would not have seen two pay days."

Dr. Leete laughed heartily.

"Very true, very true," he said, "a general strike would most probably have followed the first pay day, and a strike directed against a government is a revolution."

"How, then, do you avoid a revolution every pay day?" I demanded. "Has some prodigious philosopher devised a new system of calculus satisfactory to all for determining the exact and comparative value of all sorts of service, whether by brawn or brain, by hand or voice, by ear or eye? Or has human nature itself changed, so that no man looks upon his own things but 'every man on the things of his neighbor?' One or the other of these events must be the explanation."

"Neither one nor the other, however, is," was my host's laughing response. "And now, Mr. West," he continued, "you must remember that you are my patient as well as my guest, and permit me to prescribe sleep for you before we have any more conversation. It is after three o'clock."

"The prescription is, no doubt, a wise one," I said; "I only hope it can be filled."

"I will see to that," the doctor replied, and he did, for he gave me a wineglass of something or other which sent me to sleep as soon as my head touched the pillow.

CHAPTER VIII.

WHEN I awoke I felt greatly refreshed, and lay a considerable time in a dozing state, enjoying the sensation of bodily comfort. The experiences of the day previous, my waking to find myself in the year 2000, the sight of the new Boston, my host and his family, and the wonderful things I had heard, were a blank in my memory. I thought I was in my bed-chamber at home, and the half-dreaming, half-waking fancies which passed before my mind related to the incidents and experiences of my former life. Dreamily I reviewed the incidents of Decoration Day, my trip in company with Edith and her parents to Mount Auburn, and my dining with them on our return to the city. I recalled how extremely well Edith had looked, and from that fell to thinking of our marriage; but scarcely had my imagination begun to develop this delightful theme than my waking dream was cut short by the recollection of the letter I had received the night before from the builder announcing that the new strikes might postpone indefinitely the completion of the new house. The chagrin which this recollection brought with it effectually roused me. I remembered that I had an appointment with the builder at eleven o'clock, to discuss the strike, and opening my eyes, looked up at the clock at the foot of my bed to see what time it was. But no clock met my glance, and what was more, I instantly perceived that I was not in my room. Starting up on my couch, I stared wildly round the strange apartment.

I think it must have been many seconds that I sat up thus in bed staring about, without being able to regain the clew to my personal identity. I was no more able to distinguish myself from pure being during those moments than we may suppose a soul in the rough to be before it has received the earmarks, the individualizing touches which make it a person. Strange that the sense of this inability should be such anguish! but so we are constituted. There are no words for the mental torture I endured during this helpless, eyeless groping for myself in a boundless void. No other experience of the mind gives probably anything like the sense of absolute intellectual arrest from the loss of a mental fulcrum, a starting point of thought, which comes during such a momentary obscuration of the sense of one's identity. I trust I may never know what it is again.

I do not know how long this condition had lasted,— it seemed an interminable time, —when, like a flash, the recollection of everything came back to me. I remembered who and where I was, and how I had come here, and that these scenes as of the life of yesterday which had been passing before my mind concerned a generation long, long ago mouldered to dust. Leaping from bed, I stood in the middle of the room clasping my temples with all my might between my hands to keep them from bursting. Then I fell prone on the couch, and, burying my face in the pillow, lay without motion. The reaction which was inevitable, from the mental elation, the fever of the intellect that had been the first effect of my tremendous experience, had arrived. The emotional crisis which had awaited the full realization of my actual position, and all that it implied, was upon me, and with set teeth and laboring chest, gripping the bedstead with frenzied strength, I lay there and fought for my sanity. In my mind, all had broken loose, habits of feeling, associations of thought, ideas of persons and things, all had dissolved and lost coherence and were seething together in apparently irretrievable chaos. There were no rallying points, nothing was left stable. There only remained the will, and was any human will strong enough to say to such a weltering sea, "Peace, be still"?[1] I dared not think. Every effort to reason upon what had befallen me, and realize what it implied, set up an intolerable swimming of the brain. The idea that I was two persons, that my identity was double, began to fascinate me with its simple solution of my experience.

I knew that I was on the verge of losing my mental balance. If I lay there thinking, I was doomed. Diversion of some sort I must have, at least the diversion of physical exertion. I sprang up, and, hastily dressing, opened the door of my room and went downstairs. The hour was very early, it being not yet fairly light, and I found no one in the lower part of the house. There was a hat in the hall, and, opening the front door, which was fastened with a

---

[1] The idea of stilling the sea is an allusion to Jesus in the Gospels, e.g., Matthew 8:23-27.

slightness indicating that burglary was not among the perils of the modern Boston, I found myself on the street. For two hours I walked or ran through the streets of the city, visiting most quarters of the peninsular part of the town. None but an antiquarian who knows something of the contrast which the Boston of today offers to the Boston of the nineteenth century can begin to appreciate what a series of bewildering surprises I underwent during that time. Viewed from the housetop the day before, the city had indeed appeared strange to me, but that was only in its general aspect. How complete the change had been I first realized now that I walked the streets. The few old landmarks which still remained only intensified this effect, for without them I might have imagined myself in a foreign town. A man may leave his native city in childhood, and return fifty years later, perhaps, to find it transformed in many features. He is astonished, but he is not bewildered. He is aware of a great lapse of time, and of changes likewise occurring in himself meanwhile. He but dimly recalls the city as he knew it when a child. But remember that there was no sense of any lapse of time with me. So far as my consciousness was concerned, it was but yesterday, but a few hours, since I had walked these streets in which scarcely a feature had escaped a complete metamorphosis. The mental image of the old city was so fresh and strong that it did not yield to the impression of the actual city, but contended with it, so that it was first one and then the other which seemed the more unreal. There was nothing I saw which was not blurred in this way, like the faces of a composite photograph.

Finally, I stood again at the door of the house from which I had come out. My feet must have instinctively brought me back to the site of my old home, for I had no clear idea of returning thither. It was no more homelike to me than any other spot in this city of a strange generation, nor were its inmates less utterly and necessarily strangers than all the other men and women now on the earth. Had the door of the house been locked, I should have been reminded by its resistance that I had no object in entering, and turned away, but it yielded to my hand, and advancing with uncertain steps through the hall, I entered one of the apartments opening from it. Throwing myself into a chair, I covered my burning eyeballs with my hands to shut out the horror of strangeness. My mental confusion was so intense as to produce actual nausea. The anguish of those moments, during which my brain seemed melting, or the abjectness of my sense of helplessness, how can I describe? In my despair I groaned aloud. I began to feel that unless some help should come I was about to lose my mind. And just then it did come. I heard the rustle of drapery, and looked up. Edith Leete was standing before me. Her beautiful face was full of the most poignant sympathy.

"Oh, what is the matter, Mr. West?" she said. "I was here when you came in. I saw how dreadfully distressed you looked, and when I heard you groan, I could not keep silent. What has happened to you? Where have you been? Can't I do something for you?"

Perhaps she involuntarily held out her hands in a gesture of compassion as she spoke. At any rate I had caught them in my own and was clinging to them with an impulse as instinctive as that which prompts the drowning man to seize upon and cling to the rope which is thrown him as he sinks for the last time. As I looked up into her compassionate face and her eyes moist with pity, my brain ceased to whirl. The tender human sympathy which thrilled in the soft pressure of her fingers had brought me the support I needed. Its effect to calm and soothe was like that of some wonder-working elixir.

"God bless you," I said, after a few moments. "He must have sent you to me just now. I think I was in danger of going crazy if you had not come." At this the tears came into her eyes.

"Oh, Mr. West!" she cried. "How heartless you must have thought us! How could we leave you to yourself so long! But it is over now, is it not? You are better, surely."

"Yes," I said, "thanks to you. If you will not go away quite yet, I shall be myself soon."

"Indeed I will not go away," she said, with a little quiver of her face, more expressive of her sympathy than a volume of words. "You must not think us so heartless as we seemed in leaving you so by yourself. I scarcely slept last night, for thinking how strange your waking would be this morning; but father said you would sleep till late. He said that it would be better not to show too much sympathy with you at first, but to try to divert your thoughts and make you feel that you were among friends."

"You have indeed made me feel that," I answered. "But you see it is a good deal of a jolt to drop a hundred years, and although I did not seem to feel it so much last night, I have had very odd sensations this morning." While I held her hands and kept my eyes on her face, I could already even jest a little at my plight.

"No one thought of such a thing as your going out in the city alone so early in the morning," she went on. "Oh, Mr. West, where have you been?"

Then I told her of my morning's experience, from my first waking till the moment I had looked up to see her before me, just as I have told it here. She was overcome by distressful pity during the recital, and, though I had released one of her hands, did not try to take from me the other, seeing, no doubt, how much good it did me to hold it. "I can think a little what this feeling must been like," she said. "It must have been terrible. And to think you were left alone to struggle with it! Can you ever forgive us?"

"But it is gone now. You have driven it quite away for the present," I said.

"You will not let it return again," she queried anxiously.

"I can't quite say that," I replied. " It might be too early to say that, considering how strange everything will still be to me."

"But you will not try to contend with it alone again, at least," she persisted. "Promise that you will come to us, and let us sympathize with you, and try to help you. Perhaps we can't do much, but it will surely be better than to try to bear such feelings alone."

"I will come to you if you will let me," I said.

"Oh yes, yes, I beg you will," she said eagerly. "I would do anything to help you that I could."

"All you need do is to be sorry for me, as you seem to be now," I replied.

"It is understood, then," she said, smiling with wet eyes, "that you are to come and tell me next time, and not run all over Boston among strangers."

This assumption that we were not strangers seemed scarcely strange, so near within these few minutes had my trouble and her sympathetic tears brought us.

"I will promise, when you come to me," she added, with an expression of charming archness, passing, as she continued, into one of enthusiasm, "to seem as sorry for you as you wish, but you must not for a moment suppose that I am really sorry for you at all, or that I think you will long be sorry for yourself. I know, as well as I know that the world now is heaven compared with what it was in your day, that the only feeling you will have after a little while will be one of thankfulness to God that your life in that age was so strangely cut off, to be returned to you in this."

CHAPTER IX.

DR. and Mrs. Leete were evidently not a little startled to learn, when they presently appeared, that I had been all over the city alone that morning, and it was apparent that they were agreeably surprised to see that I seemed so little agitated after the experience.

"Your stroll could scarcely have failed to be a very interesting one," said Mrs. Leete, as we sat down to table soon after. "You must have seen a good many new things."

"I saw very little that was not new," I replied. "But I think what surprised me as much as anything was not to find any stores on Washington Street, or any banks on State. What have you done with the merchants and bankers? Hung them all, perhaps, as the anarchists wanted to do in my day?"

"Not so bad as that," replied Dr. Leete. "We have simply dispensed with them. Their functions are obsolete in the modern world."

"Who sells you things when you want to buy them?" I inquired.

"There is neither selling nor buying nowadays; the distribution of goods is effected in another way. As to the bankers, having no money we have no use for those gentry."

"Miss Leete," said I, turning to Edith, "I am afraid that your father is making sport of me. I don't blame him, for the temptation my innocence offers must be extraordinary. But, really, there are limits to my credulity as to possible alterations in the social system."

"Father has no idea of jesting, I am sure," she replied, with a reassuring smile.

The conversation took another turn then, the point of ladies' fashions in the nineteenth century being raised, if I remember rightly, by Mrs. Leete, and it was not till after breakfast, when the doctor had invited me up to the housetop, which appeared to be a favorite resort of his, that he recurred to the subject.

"You were surprised," he said, "at my saying that we got along without money or trade, but a moment's reflection will show that trade existed and money was needed in your day simply because the business of production was left in private hands, and that, consequently, they are superfluous now."

"I do not at once see how that follows," I replied.

"It is very simple," said Dr. Leete. "When innumerable different and independent persons produced the various things needful to life and comfort, endless exchanges between individuals were requisite in order that they might supply themselves with what they desired. These exchanges constituted trade, and money was essential as their medium. But as soon as the nation became the sole producer of all sorts of commodities, there was no need of exchanges between individuals that they might get what they required. Everything was procurable from one source, and nothing could be procured anywhere else. A system of direct distribution from the national storehouses took the place of trade, and for this money was unnecessary."

"How is this distribution managed?" I asked.

"On the simplest possible plan," replied Dr. Leete. "A credit corresponding to his share of the annual product of the nation is given to every citizen on the public books at the beginning of each year, and a credit card issued him with which he procures at the public storehouses, found in every community, whatever he desires whenever he desires it. This arrangement, you will see, totally obviates the necessity for business transactions of any sort between individuals and consumers. Perhaps you would like to see what our credit cards are like.

"You observe," he pursued as I was curiously examining the piece of pasteboard he gave me, "that this card is issued for a certain number of dollars. We have kept the old word, but not the substance. The term, as we use it, answers to no real thing, but merely serves as an algebraical symbol for comparing the values of products with one another. For this purpose they are all priced in dollars and cents, just as in your day. The value of what I procure on this card is checked off by the clerk, who pricks out of these tiers of squares the price of what I order."

"If you wanted to buy something of your neighbor, could you transfer part of your credit to him as consideration?" I inquired.

"In the first place," replied Dr. Leete, "our neighbors have nothing to sell us, but in any event our credit would not be transferable, being strictly personal. Before the nation could even think of honoring any such transfer as you speak of, it would be bound to inquire into all the circumstances of the transaction, so as to be able to guarantee its absolute equity. It would have been reason enough, had there been no other, for abolishing money, that its possession was no indication of rightful title to it. In the hands of the man who had stolen it or murdered for it, it was as good as in those which had earned it by industry. People nowadays interchange gifts and favors out of friendship, but buying and selling is considered absolutely inconsistent with the mutual benevolence and disinterestedness which should prevail between citizens and the sense of community of interest which supports our social system. According to our ideas, buying and selling is essentially antisocial in all its tendencies.[1] It is an education in self-seeking at the expense of others, and no society whose citizens are trained in such a school can possibly rise above a very low grade of civilization."

"What if you have to spend more than your card in any one year?" I asked.

"The provision is so ample that we are more likely not to spend it all," replied Dr. Leete. "But if extraordinary expenses should exhaust it, we can obtain a limited advance on the next year's credit, though this practice is not encouraged, and a heavy discount is charged to check it. Of course if a man showed himself a reckless spendthrift he would receive his allowance monthly or weekly instead of yearly, or if necessary not be permitted to handle it all."[2]

"If you don't spend your allowance, I suppose it accumulates?"

---

[1] The rejection of buying and selling echoes Christ's expulsion of trade from the temple in John 1:13-16.

[2] The sentence "Of course if a man…" was added in the second edition. It reinforces the power of the state.

"That is also permitted to a certain extent when a special outlay is anticipated. But unless notice to the contrary is given, it is presumed that the citizen who does not fully expend his credit did not have occasion to do so, and the balance is turned into the general surplus."

"Such a system does not encourage saving habits on the part of citizens," I said.

"It is not intended to," was the reply. "The nation is rich and does not wish the people to deprive themselves of any good thing. In your day, men were bound to lay up goods and money against coming failure of the means of support and for their children. This necessity made parsimony a virtue. But now it would have no such laudable object, and, having lost its utility, it has ceased to be regarded as a virtue. No man any more has any care for the morrow, either for himself or his children, for the nation guarantees the nurture, education, and comfortable maintenance of every citizen from the cradle to the grave."[1]

"That is a sweeping guarantee!" I said. "What certainty can there be that the value of a man's labor will recompense the nation for its outlay on him? On the whole, society may be able to support all its members, but some must earn less than enough for their support, and others more; and that brings us back once more to the wages question, on which you have hitherto said nothing. It was at just this point, if you remember, that our talk ended last evening; and I say again, as I did then, that here I should suppose a national industrial system like yours would find its main difficulty. How, I ask once more, can you adjust satisfactorily the comparative wages or remuneration of the multitude of avocations, so unlike and so incommensurable, which are necessary for the service of society? In our day the market rate determined the price of labor of all sorts, as well as of goods. The employer paid as little as he could, and the worker got as much. It was not a pretty system ethically, I admit; but it did, at least, furnish us a rough and ready formula for settling a question which must be settled ten

---

[1]   In "Grongar Hill" (1726) John Dyer wrote: "A little rule, a little sway/A sunbeam in a winter's day,/Is all the proud and mighty have/Between the cradle and the grave." Shelley also uses the expression in Prometheus Unbound (1819).

thousand times a day if the world was ever going to get forward. There seemed to us no other practicable way of doing it."

"Yes," replied Dr. Leete, "it was the only practicable way under a system which made the interests of every individual antagonistic to those of every other; but it would have been a pity if humanity could never have devised a better plan, for yours was simply the application to the mutual relations of men of the devil's maxim, 'Your necessity is my opportunity.' The reward of any service depended not upon its difficulty, danger, or hardship, for throughout the world it seems that the most perilous, severe, and repulsive labor was done by the worst paid classes; but solely upon the strait of those who needed the service."

"All that is conceded," I said. "But, with all its defects, the plan of settling prices by the market rate was a practical plan; and I cannot conceive what satisfactory substitute you can have devised for it. The government being the only possible employer, there is of course no labor market, or market rate. Wages of all sorts must be arbitrarily fixed by the government. I cannot imagine a more complex and delicate function than that must be, or one, however performed, more certain to breed universal dissatisfaction."

"I beg your pardon," replied Dr. Leete, "but I think you exaggerate the difficulty. Suppose a board of fairly sensible men were charged with settling the wages for all sorts of trades under a system which, like ours, guaranteed employment to all, while permitting the choice of avocations. Don't you see that, however unsatisfactory the first adjustment might be, the mistakes would soon correct themselves? The favored trades would have too many volunteers, and those discriminated against would lack them till the errors were set right. But this is aside from the purpose, for, though this plan would, I fancy, be practicable enough, it is no part of our system."

"How, then, do you regulate wages?" I once more asked.

Dr. Leete did not reply till after several moments of meditative silence. "I know, of course," he finally said, "enough of the old order of things to understand just what you mean by that question; and yet the present order is so utterly different at this point that I am a little at loss how to answer you best. You ask me how we regulate wages; I can only reply that there is no idea in the modern social economy which at all corresponds with what was meant by wages in your day."

"I suppose you mean that you have no money to pay wages in," said I. "But the credit given the worker at the government storehouse answers to his wages with us. How is the amount of the credit given respectively to the workers in different lines determined? By what title does the individual claim his particular share? What is the basis of allotment?"

"His title," replied Dr. Leete, "is his humanity. The basis of his claim is the fact that he is a man."

"The fact that he is a man!" I repeated, incredulously. "Do you possibly mean that all have the same share?"

"Most assuredly."

The readers of this book never having practically known any other arrangement, or perhaps very carefully considered the historical accounts of former epochs in which a very different system prevailed, cannot be expected to appreciate the stupor of amazement into which Dr. Leete's simple statement plunged me.

"You see," he said, smiling, "that it is not merely that we have no money to pay wages in, but, as I said, we have nothing at all answering to your idea of wages."

By this time I had pulled myself together sufficiently to voice some of the criticisms which, man of the nineteenth century as I was, came uppermost in my mind, upon this to me astounding arrangement. "Some men do twice the work of others!" I exclaimed. "Are the clever workmen content with a plan that ranks them with the indifferent?"

"We leave no possible ground for any complaint of injustice," replied Dr. Leete, " by requiring precisely the same measure of service from all."

"How can you do that, I should like to know, when no two men's powers are the same?"

"Nothing could be simpler," was Dr. Leete's reply. "We require of each that he shall make the same effort; that is, we demand of him the best service it is in his power to give."

"And supposing all do the best they can," I answered, "the amount of the product resulting is twice greater from one man than from another."

"Very true," replied Dr. Leete; "but the amount of the resulting product has nothing whatever to do with the question, which is one of desert. Desert is a moral question, and the amount of the product a material quantity. It would be an extraordinary sort of logic which should try to determine a moral question by a material standard. The amount of the effort alone is pertinent to the question of desert. All men who do their best, do the same. A man's endowments, however godlike, merely fix the measure of his duty. The man of great endowments who does not do all he might, though he may do more than a man of small endowments who does his best, is deemed a less deserving worker than the latter, and dies a debtor to his fellows. The Creator sets men's tasks for them by the faculties he gives them; we simply exact their fulfillment."

"No doubt that is very fine philosophy," I said; "nevertheless it seems hard that the man who produces twice as much as another, even if both do their best, should have only the same share."

"Does it, indeed, seem so to you?" responded Dr. Leete. "Now, do you know, that seems very curious to me? The way it strikes people nowadays is, that a man who can produce twice as much as another with the same effort, instead of being rewarded for doing so, ought to be punished if he does not do so. In the nineteenth century, when a horse pulled a heavier load than a goat, I suppose you rewarded him. Now, we should have whipped him soundly if he had not, on the ground that, being much stronger, he ought to. It is singular how ethical standards change." The doctor said this with such a twinkle in his eye that I was obliged to laugh.

"I suppose," I said, "that the real reason that we rewarded men for their endowments, while we considered those of horses and goats merely as fixing the service to be severally required of them, was that the animals, not being reasoning beings, naturally did the best they could, whereas men could only be induced to do so by rewarding them according to the amount of their product. That brings me to ask why, unless human nature has mightily changed in a hundred years, you are not under the same necessity."

"We are," replied Dr. Leete. "I don't think there has been any change in human nature in that respect since your day. It is still so constituted that special incentives in the form of prizes, and advantages to be gained, are requisite to call out the best endeavors of the average man in any direction."

"But what inducement," I asked, "can a man have to put forth his best endeavors when, however much or little he accomplishes, his income remains the same? High characters may be moved by devotion to the common welfare under such a system, but does not the average man tend to rest back on his oar, reasoning that it is of no use to make a special effort, since the effort will not increase his income, nor its withholding diminish it?"

"Does it then really seem to you," answered my companion, "that human nature is insensible to any motives save fear of want and love of luxury, that you should expect security and equality of livelihood to leave them without possible incentives to effort? Your contemporaries did not really think so, though they might fancy they did. When it was a question of the grandest class of efforts, the most absolute self-devotion, they depended on quite other incentives. Not higher wages, but honor and the hope of men's gratitude, patriotism and the inspiration of duty, were the motives which they set before their soldiers when it was a question of dying for the nation, and never was there an age of the world when those motives did not call out what is best and noblest in men. And not only this, but when you come to analyze the love of money which was the general impulse to effort in your day, you find that the dread of want and desire of luxury was but one of several motives which the pursuit of money represented; the others, and with many the more influential, being desire of power, of social position, and reputation for ability and success. So you see that though we have abolished poverty and the fear of it, and inordinate luxury with the hope of it, we have not touched the greater part of the motives which underlay the love of money in former times, or any of those which prompted the supremer sorts of effort. The coarser motives, which no longer move us, have been replaced by higher motives wholly unknown to the mere wage earners of your age. Now that industry of whatever sort is no longer self-service, but service of the nation, patriotism, passion for humanity, impel the worker as in your day they did the soldier. The army of industry is an army, not alone by virtue of its perfect organization, but by reason also of the ardor of self-devotion which animates its members.

"But as you used to supplement the motives of patriotism with the love of glory, in order to stimulate the valor of your soldiers, so do we. Based as our industrial system is on the principle of requiring the same unit of effort from every man, that is, the best he can do, you will see that the means by which we spur the workers to do their best must be a very essential part of our scheme. With us, diligence in the national service is the sole and certain way to public repute, social distinction, and official power. The value of a man's services to society fixes his rank in it. Compared with the effect of our social arrangements in impelling men to be zealous in business, we deem the object-lessons of biting poverty and wanton luxury on which you depended a device as weak and uncertain as it was barbaric. The lust of honor even in your sordid day notoriously impelled men to more desperate effort than the love of money could."

"I should be extremely interested," I said, "to learn something of what these social arrangements are."

"The scheme in its details," replied the doctor, "is of course very elaborate, for it underlies the entire organization of our industrial army; but a few words will give you a general idea of it."

At this moment our talk was charmingly interrupted by the emergence upon the aerial platform where we sat of Edith Leete. She was dressed for the street, and had come to speak to her father about some commission she was to do for him.

"By the way, Edith," he exclaimed, as she was about to leave us to ourselves, "I wonder if Mr. West would not be interested in visiting the store with you? I have been telling him something about our system of distribution, and perhaps he might like to see it in practical operation."

"My daughter," he added, turning to me, "is an indefatigable shopper, and can tell you more about the stores than I can."

The proposition was naturally very agreeable to me, and Edith being good enough to say that she should be glad to have my company, we left the house together.

CHAPTER X.

"IF I am going to explain our way of shopping to you," said my companion, as we walked along the street, "you must explain your way to me. I have never been able to understand it from all I have read on the subject. For example, when you had such a vast number of shops, each with its different assortment, how could a lady ever settle upon any purchase till she had visited all the shops? For, until she had, she could not know what there was to choose from."

"It was as you suppose; that was the only way she could know," I replied.

"Father calls me an indefatigable shopper, but I should soon be a very fatigued one if I had to do as they did," was Edith's laughing comment.

"The loss of time in going from shop to shop was indeed a waste which the busy bitterly complained of," I said; "but as for the ladies of the idle class, though they complained also, I think the system was really a godsend by furnishing a device to kill time."

"But say there were a thousand shops in a city, hundreds, perhaps, of the same sort, how could even the idlest find time to make their rounds?"

"They really could not visit all, of course," I replied. "Those who did a great deal of buying, learned in time where they might expect to find what they wanted. This class had made a science of the specialties of the shops, and bought at advantage, always getting the most and best for the least money. It required, however, long experience to acquire this knowledge. Those who were too busy, or bought too little to gain it, took their chances and were generally unfortunate, getting the least and worst for the most money. It was the merest chance if persons not experienced in shopping received the value of their money."

"But why did you put up with such a shockingly inconvenient arrangement when you saw its faults so plainly?" Edith asked me.

"It was like all our social arrangements," I replied. "You can see their faults scarcely more plainly than we did, but we saw no remedy for them."

"Here we are at the store of our ward," said Edith, as we turned in at the great portal of one of the magnificent public buildings I had observed in my morning walk. There was nothing in the exterior aspect of the edifice to suggest a store to a representative of the nineteenth century. There was no display of goods in the great windows, or any device to advertise wares, or attract custom. Nor was there any sort of sign or legend on the front of the building to indicate the character of the business carried on there; but instead, above the portal, standing out from the front of the building, a majestic life-size group of statuary, the central figure of which was a female ideal of Plenty, with her cornucopia. Judging from the composition of the throng passing in and out, about the same proportion of the sexes among shoppers obtained as in the nineteenth century. As we entered, Edith said that there was one of these great distributing establishments in each ward of the city, so that no residence was more than five or ten minutes' walk from one of them. It was the first interior of a twentieth-century public building that I had ever beheld, and the spectacle naturally impressed me deeply. I was in a vast hall full of light, received not alone from the windows on all sides, but from the dome, the point of which was a hundred feet above. Beneath it, in the centre of the hall, a magnificent fountain played, cooling the atmosphere to a delicious freshness with its spray. The walls and ceiling were frescoed in mellow tints, calculated to soften without absorbing the light which flooded the interior. Around the fountain was a space occupied with chairs and sofas, on which many persons were seated conversing. Legends on the walls all about the hall indicated to what classes of commodities the counters below were devoted. Edith directed her steps towards one of these, where samples of muslin of a bewildering variety were displayed, and proceeded to inspect them.

"Where is the clerk?" I asked, for there was no one behind the counter, and no one seemed coming to attend to the customer.

"I have no need of the clerk yet," said Edith; "I have not made my selection."

"It was the principal business of clerks to help people to make their selections in my day," I replied.

"What! To tell people what they wanted?"

"Yes; and oftener to induce them to buy what they didn't want."

"But did not ladies find that very impertinent?" Edith asked, wonderingly. "What concern could it possibly be to the clerks whether people bought or not?"

"It was their sole concern," I answered. "They were hired for the purpose of getting rid of the goods, and were expected to do their utmost, short of the use of force, to compass that end."

"Ah, yes! How stupid I am to forget!" said Edith. "The storekeeper and his clerks depended for their livelihood on selling the goods in your day. Of course that is all different now. The goods are the nation's. They are here for those who want them, and it is the business of the clerks to wait on people and take their orders; but it is not the interest of the clerk or the nation to dispose of a yard or a pound of anything to anybody who does not want it." She smiled as she added, "How exceedingly odd it must have seemed to have clerks trying to induce one to take what one did not want, or was doubtful about!"

"But even a twentieth-century clerk might make himself useful in giving you information about the goods, though he did not tease you to buy them," I suggested.

"No," said Edith, "that is not the business of the clerk. These printed cards, for which the government authorities are responsible, give us all the information we can possibly need."

I saw then that there was fastened to each sample a card containing in succinct form a complete statement of the make and materials of the goods and all its qualities, as well as price, leaving absolutely no point to hang a question on.

"The clerk has, then, nothing to say about the goods he sells?" I said.

"Nothing at all. It is not necessary that he should know or profess to know anything about them. Courtesy and accuracy in taking orders are all that are required of him."

"What a prodigious amount of lying that simple arrangement saves!" I ejaculated.

"Do you mean that all the clerks misrepresented their goods in your day?" Edith asked.

"God forbid that I should say so!" I replied, "for there were many who did not, and they were entitled to especial credit, for when one's livelihood and that of his wife and babies depended on the amount of goods he could dispose of, the temptation to deceive the customer—or let him deceive himself—was well-nigh overwhelming. But, Miss Leete, I am distracting you from your task with my talk."

"Not at all. I have made my selections." With that she touched a button, and in a moment a clerk appeared. He took down her order on a tablet with a pencil which made two copies, of which he gave one to her, and enclosing the counterpart in a small receptacle, dropped it into a transmitting tube.

"The duplicate of the order," said Edith as she turned away from the counter, after the clerk had punched the value of her purchase out of the credit card she gave him, "is given to the purchaser, so that any mistakes in filling it can be easily traced and rectified."

"You were very quick about your selections," I said. "May I ask how you knew that you might not have found something to suit you better in some of the other stores? But probably you are required to buy in your own district."

"Oh, no," she replied. "We buy where we please, though naturally most often near home. But I should have gained nothing by visiting other stores. The assortment in all is exactly the same, representing as it does in each case samples of all the varieties produced or imported by the United States. That is why one can decide quickly, and never need visit two stores."

"And is this merely a sample store? I see no clerks cutting off goods or marking bundles."

"All our stores are sample stores, except as to a few classes of articles. The goods, with these exceptions, are all at the great central warehouse of the city, to which they are shipped directly from the producers. We order from the sample and the printed statement of texture, make, and qualities. The orders are sent to the warehouse, and the goods distributed from there."

"That must be a tremendous saving of handling," I said. "By our system, the manufacturer sold to the wholesaler, the wholesaler to the retailer, and the retailer to the consumer, and the goods had to be handled each time. You avoid one handling of the goods, and eliminate the retailer altogether, with his big profit and the army of clerks it goes to support. Why, Miss Leete, this store is merely the order department of a wholesale house, with no more than a wholesaler's complement of clerks. Under our system of handling the goods, persuading the customer to buy them, cutting them off, and packing them, ten clerks would not do what one does here. The saving must be enormous."

"I suppose so," said Edith, "but of course we have never known any other way. But, Mr. West, you must not fail to ask father to take you to the central warehouse some day, where they receive the orders from the different sample houses all over the city and parcel out and send the goods to their destinations. He took me there not long ago, and it was a wonderful sight. The system is certainly perfect; for example, over yonder in that sort of cage is the dispatching clerk. The orders, as they are taken by the different departments in the store, are sent by transmitters to him. His assistants sort them and enclose each class in a carrier-box by itself. The dispatching clerk has a dozen pneumatic transmitters before him answering to the general classes of goods, each communicating with the corresponding department at the warehouse. He drops the box of orders into the tube it calls for, and in a few moments later it drops on the proper desk in the warehouse, together with all the orders of the same sort from the other sample stores. The orders are read off, recorded, and sent to be filled, like lightning. The filling I thought the most interesting part. Bales of cloth are placed on spindles and turned by machinery, and the cutter, who also has a machine, works right through one bale after another till exhausted, when another man takes his place; and it is the same with those who fill the orders in any other staple. The packages are then delivered by larger tubes to the city districts, and thence distributed to the houses. You may understand how quickly it is all done when I tell you that my order will probably be at home sooner than I could have carried it from here."

"How do you manage in the thinly settled rural districts?" I asked.

"The system is the same," Edith explained, "the village sample shops are connected by transmitters with the central county warehouse, which may be twenty miles away. The transmission is so swift, though, that the time lost on the way is trifling. But, to save expense, in many counties one set of tubes connect several villages with the warehouse, and then there is time lost waiting for one another. Sometimes it is two or three hours before goods ordered are received. It was so where I was staying last summer, and I found it quite inconvenient."[1]

"There must be many other respects also, no doubt, in which the country stores are inferior to the city stores," I suggested.

"No," Edith answered, "they are otherwise precisely as good. The sample shop of the smallest village, just like this one, gives you your choice of all the varieties of goods the nation has, for the county warehouse draws on the same source as the city warehouse."

As we walked home I commented on the great variety in the size and cost of the houses. "How is it," I asked, "that this difference is consistent with the fact that all citizens have the same income?"

"Because," Edith explained, " although the income is the same, personal taste determines how the individual shall spend it. Some like fine horses; others, like myself, prefer pretty clothes; and still others want an elaborate table. The rents which the nation receives for these houses vary, according to size, elegance, and location, so that everybody can find something to suit. The larger houses are usually occupied by large families, in which there are several to contribute to the rent; while small families, like ours, find smaller houses more convenient and economical. It is a matter of taste and convenience wholly. I have read that in old times people often kept up establishments and did other things which they could not afford for ostentation, to make people think them richer than they were. Was it really so, Mr. West?"

"I shall have to admit that it was," I replied.

"Well, you see, it could not be so nowadays; for everybody's income is known, and it is known that what is spent one way must be saved another."

---

[1] I am informed since the above is in type that this lack of perfection in the distributing service of some of the country districts is to be remedied, and that soon every village will have its own set of tubes. [Bellamy's note]

CHAPTER XI.

WHEN we arrived home, Dr. Leete had not yet returned, and Mrs. Leete was not visible. "Are you fond of music, Mr. West?" Edith asked.

I assured her that it was half of life, according to my notion.

"I ought to apologize for inquiring," she said. "It is not a question that we ask one another nowadays; but I have read that in your day, even among the cultured class, there were some who did not care for music."

"You must remember, in excuse," I said, "that we had some rather absurd kinds of music."

"Yes," she said, "I know that; I am afraid I should not have fancied it all myself. Would you like to hear some of ours now, Mr. West?"

"Nothing would delight me so much as to listen to you," I said.

"To me!" she exclaimed, laughing. " Did you think I was going to play or sing to you?"

"I hoped so, certainly," I replied.

Seeing that I was a little abashed, she subdued her merriment and explained. "Of course, we all sing nowadays as a matter of course in the training of the voice, and some learn to play instruments for their private amusement; but the professional music is so much grander and more perfect than any performance of ours, and so easily commanded when we wish to hear it, that we don't think of calling our singing or playing music at all. All the really fine singers and players are in the musical service, and the rest of us hold our peace for the main part. But would you really like to hear some music?"

I assured her once more that I would.

"Come, then, into the music room," she said, and I followed her into an apartment finished, without hangings, in wood, with a floor of polished wood. I was prepared for new devices in musical instruments, but I saw nothing in the room which by any stretch of imagination could be conceived as such. It was evident that my puzzled appearance was affording intense amusement to Edith.

"Please look at today's music," she said, handing me a card, "and tell me what you would prefer. It is now five o'clock, you will remember."

The card bore the date "September 12, 2000," and contained the longest programme of music I had ever seen. It was as various as it was long, including a most extraordinary range of vocal and instrumental solos, duets, quartettes, and various orchestral combinations. I remained bewildered by the prodigious list until Edith's pink fingertip indicated a particular section of it, where several selections were bracketed, with the words "5 P.M." against them; then I observed that this prodigious programme was an allday one, divided into twenty-four sections answering to the hours. There were but a few pieces of music in the "5 p.m." section, and I indicated an organ piece as my preference.

"I am so glad you like the organ," said she. "I think there is scarcely any music that suits my mood oftener."

She made me sit down comfortably, and, crossing the room, so far as I could see, merely touched one or two screws, and at once the room was filled with the music of a grand organ anthem; filled, not flooded, for, by some means, the volume of melody had been perfectly graduated to the size of the apartment. I listened, scarcely breathing, to the close. Such music, so perfectly rendered, I had never expected to hear.

"Grand!" I cried, as the last great wave of sound broke and ebbed away into silence. "Bach must be at the keys of that organ; but where is the organ?"

"Wait a moment, please," said Edith; "I want to have you listen to this waltz before you ask any questions. I think it is perfectly charming;" and as she spoke the sound of violins filled the room with the witchery of a summer night. When this had also ceased, she said: "There is nothing in the least mysterious about the music, as you seem to imagine. It is not made by fairies or genii, but by good, honest, and exceedingly clever human hands. We have simply carried the idea of labor-saving by cooperation into our musical service as into everything else. There are a number of music rooms in the city, perfectly adapted acoustically to the different sorts of music. These halls are connected by telephone with all the houses of the city whose people care to pay the small fee, and there are none, you may be sure, who do not.[1] The corps of musicians attached to each hall is so large that, although no individual performer, or group of performers, has more than a brief part, each day's programme lasts through the twenty-four hours. There are on that card for today, as you will see if you observe closely, distinct programmes of four of these concerts, each of a different order of music from the others, being now simultaneously performed, and any one of the four pieces now going on that you prefer, you can hear by merely pressing the button which will connect your housewire with the hall where it is being rendered. The programmes are so coördinated that the pieces at any one time simultaneously proceeding in the different halls usually offer a choice, not only between instrumental and vocal, and between different sorts of instruments; but also between different motives from grave to gay, so that all tastes and moods can be suited."

"It appears to me, Miss Leete," I said, "that if we could have devised an arrangement for providing everybody with music in their homes, perfect in quality, unlimited in quantity, suited to every mood, and beginning and ceasing at will, we should have considered the limit of human felicity already attained, and ceased to strive for further improvements."

"I am sure I never could imagine how those among you who depended at all on music managed to endure the old-fashioned system for providing it," replied Edith. "Music really worth hearing must have been, I suppose, wholly out of the reach of the masses, and attainable by the most favored only occasionally, at great trouble, prodigious expense, and then for brief periods, arbitrarily fixed by somebody else, and in connection with all sorts of undesirable circumstances. Your concerts, for instance, and operas! How perfectly exasperating it must have been, for the sake of a piece or two of music that suited you, to have to sit for hours listening to what you did not care for! Now, at a dinner one can skip the courses one does not care for. Who would ever dine, however hungry, if required to eat everything brought on the

---

[1] Alexander Graham Bell patented the telephone in 1876 and in 1901 Marconi sent the first wireless radio message across the Atlantic. Radio broadcasts for entertainment became widespread in the 1920s.

table? and I am sure one's hearing is quite as sensitive as one's taste. I suppose it was these difficulties in the way of commanding really good music which made you endure so much playing and singing in your homes by people who had only the rudiments of the art."

"Yes," I replied, "it was that sort of music or none for most of us."

"Ah, well," Edith sighed, "when one really considers, it is not so strange that people in those days so often did not care for music. I dare say I should have detested it, too."

"Did I understand you rightly," I inquired, "that this musical programme covers the entire twenty-four hours? It seems to on this card, certainly; but who is there to listen to music between say midnight and morning?"

"Oh, many," Edith replied. "Our people keep all hours; but if the music were provided from midnight to morning for no others, it still would be for the sleepless, the sick, and the dying. All our bedchambers have a telephone attachment at the head of the bed by which any person who may be sleepless can command music at pleasure, of the sort suited to the mood."

"Is there such an arrangement in the room assigned to me?"

"Why, certainly; and how stupid, how very stupid, of me not to think to tell you of that last night! Father will show you about the adjustment before you go to bed tonight, however; and with the receiver at your ear, I am quite sure you will be able to snap your fingers at all sorts of uncanny feelings if they trouble you again."

That evening Dr. Leete asked us about our visit to the store, and in the course of the desultory comparison of the ways of the nineteenth century and the twentieth, which followed, something raised the question of inheritance. "I suppose," I said, "the inheritance of property is not now allowed."

"On the contrary," replied Dr. Leete, "there is no interference with it. In fact, you will find, Mr. West, as you come to know us, that there is far less interference of any sort with personal liberty nowadays than you were accustomed to. We require, indeed, by law that every man shall serve the nation for a fixed period, instead of leaving him his choice, as you did, between working, stealing, or starving. With the exception of this fundamental law, which is, indeed, merely a codification of the law of nature—the edict of Eden—by which it is made equal in its pressure on men, our system depends in no particular upon legislation, but is entirely voluntary, the logical outcome of the operation of human nature under rational conditions.[1] This question of inheritance illustrates just that point. The fact that the nation is the sole capitalist and landowner of course restricts the individual's possessions to his annual credit, and what personal and household belongings he may have procured with it. His credit, like an annuity in your day, ceases on his death, with the allowance of a fixed sum for funeral expenses. His other possessions he leaves as he pleases."

"What is to prevent, in course of time, such accumulations of valuable goods and chattels in the hands of individuals as might seriously interfere with equality in the circumstances of citizens?" I asked.

"That matter arranges itself very simply," was the reply. "Under the present organization of society, accumulations of personal property are merely burdensome the moment they exceed what adds to the real comfort. In your day, if a man had a house crammed full with gold and silver plate, rare china, expensive furniture, and such things, he was considered rich, for these things represented money, and could at any time be turned into it. Nowadays a man whom the legacies of a hundred relatives, simultaneously dying, should place in a similar position, would be considered very unlucky. The articles, not being salable, would be of no value to him except for their actual use or the enjoyment of their beauty. On the other hand, his income remaining the same, he would have to deplete his credit to hire houses to store the goods in, and still further to pay for the service of those who took care of them. You may be very sure that such a man would lose no time in scattering among his friends possessions which only made him the poorer, and that none of those friends would accept more of them than they could easily spare room for and time to attend to. You see, then, that to prohibit the inheritance of personal property with a view to prevent great accumulations would be a superfluous precaution for the nation. The individual citizen can be trusted to see that he is not overburdened. So careful is he in this

---

[1]   See Genesis 3:19 for the "edict of Eden" or the law that humans would have to work after they were expelled from the garden.

respect, that the relatives usually waive claim to most of the effects of deceased friends, reserving only particular objects. The nation takes charge of the resigned chattels, and turns such as are of value into the common stock once more."

"You spoke of paying for service to take care of your houses," said I; "that suggests a question I have several times been on the point of asking. How have you disposed of the problem of domestic service? Who are willing to be domestic servants in a community where all are social equals? Our ladies found it hard enough to find such even when there was little pretense of social equality."

"It is precisely because we are all social equals whose equality nothing can compromise, and because service is honorable, in a society whose fundamental principle is that all in turn shall serve the rest, that we could easily provide a corps of domestic servants such as you never dreamed of, if we needed them," replied Dr. Leete. "But we do not need them."

"Who does your housework, then?" I asked.

"There is none to do," said Mrs. Leete, to whom I had addressed this question. "Our washing is all done at public laundries at excessively cheap rates, and our cooking at public kitchens. The making and repairing of all we wear are done outside in public shops. Electricity, of course, takes the place of all fires and lighting.[1] We choose houses no larger than we need, and furnish them so as to involve the minimum of trouble to keep them in order. We have no use for domestic servants."

"The fact," said Dr. Leete, "that you had in the poorer classes a boundless supply of serfs on whom you could impose all sorts of painful and disagreeable tasks, made you indifferent to devices to avoid the necessity for them. But now that we all have to do in turn whatever work is done for society, every individual in the nation has the same interest, and a personal one, in devices for lightening the burden. This fact has given a prodigious impulse to labor-saving inventions in all sorts of industry, of which the combination of the maximum of comfort and minimum of trouble in household arrangements was one of the earliest results.

---

[1] Thomas Edison invented an electric filament lamp in 1879 and the new technology of electricity spread rapidly in the 1880s and 90s.

"In case of special emergencies in the household," pursued Dr. Leete, "such as extensive cleaning or renovation, or sickness in the family, we can always secure assistance from the industrial force."

"But how do you recompense these assistants, since you have no money?"

"We do not pay them, of course, but the nation for them. Their services can be obtained by application at the proper bureau, and their value is pricked off the credit card of the applicant."

"What a paradise for womankind the world must be now!" I exclaimed. "In my day, even wealth and unlimited servants did not enfranchise their possessors from household cares, while the women of the merely well-to-do and poorer classes lived and died martyrs to them."

"Yes," said Mrs. Leete, "I have read something of that; enough to convince me that, badly off as the men, too, were in your day, they were more fortunate than their mothers and wives."

"The broad shoulders of the nation," said Dr. Leete, "bear now like a feather the burden that broke the backs of the women of your day. Their misery came, with all your other miseries, from that incapacity for cooperation which followed from the individualism on which your social system was founded, from your inability to perceive that you could make ten times more profit out of your fellow men by uniting with them than by contending with them. The wonder is, not that you did not live more comfortably, but that you were able to live together at all, who were all confessedly bent on making one another your servants, and securing possession of one another's goods."

"There, there, father, if you are so vehement, Mr. West will think you are scolding him," laughingly interposed Edith.

"When you want a doctor," I asked, "do you simply apply to the proper bureau and take any one that may be sent?"

"That rule would not work well in the case of physicians," replied Dr. Leete. "The good a physician can do a patient depends largely on his acquaintance with his constitutional tendencies and condition. The patient must be able, therefore, to call in a particular doctor, and he does so just as patients did in your day. The only difference is that, instead of collecting his fee for himself, the doctor collects it for the nation by pricking off the amount, according to a regular scale for medical attendance, from the patient's credit card."

"I can imagine," I said, "that if the fee is always the same, and a doctor may not turn away patients, as I suppose he may not, the good doctors are called constantly and the poor doctors left in idleness."

"In the first place, if you will overlook the apparent conceit of the remark from a retired physician," replied Dr. Leete, with a smile, "we have no poor doctors. Anybody who pleases to get a little smattering of medical terms is not now at liberty to practice on the bodies of citizens, as in your day. None but students who have passed the severe tests of the schools, and clearly proved their vocation, are permitted to practice. Then, too, you will observe that there is nowadays no attempt of doctors to build up their practice at the expense of other doctors. There would be no motive for that. For the rest, the doctor has to render regular reports of his work to the medical bureau, and if he is not reasonably well employed, work is found for him."

CHAPTER XII.

THE questions which I needed to ask before I could acquire even an outline acquaintance with the institutions of the twentieth century being endless, and Dr. Leete's good-nature appearing equally so, we sat up talking for several hours after the ladies left us. Reminding my host of the point at which our talk had broken off that morning, I expressed my curiosity to learn how the organization of the industrial army was made to afford a sufficient stimulus to diligence in the lack of any anxiety on the worker's part as to his livelihood.

"You must understand in the first place," replied the doctor, "that the supply of incentives to effort is but one of the objects sought in the organization we have adopted for the army. The other, and equally important, is to secure for the file-leaders and captains of the force, and the great officers of the nation, men of proven abilities, who are pledged by their own careers to hold their followers up to their highest standard of performance and permit no lagging. With a view to these two ends the industrial army is organized. First comes the unclassified grade of common laborers, men of all work, to which all recruits during their first three years belong. This grade is a sort of school, and a very strict one, in which the young men are taught habits of obedience, subordination, and devotion to duty. While the miscellaneous nature of the work done by this force prevents the systematic grading of the workers which is afterwards possible, yet individual records are kept, and excellence receives distinction corresponding with the penalties that negligence incurs. It is not, however, policy with us to permit youthful recklessness or indiscretion, when not deeply culpable, to handicap the future careers of young men, and all who have passed through the unclassified grade without serious disgrace have an equal opportunity to choose the life employment they have most liking for. Having selected this, they enter upon it as apprentices. The length of the apprenticeship naturally differs in different occupations. At the end of it the apprentice becomes a full workman, and a member of his trade or guild. Now not only are the individual records of the apprentices for ability and industry strictly kept, and excellence distinguished by suitable distinctions, but upon the average of his record during apprenticeship the standing given the apprentice among the full workmen depends.

"While the internal organizations of different industries, mechanical and agricultural, differ according to their peculiar conditions, they agree in a general division of their workers into first, second, and third grades, according to ability, and these grades are in many cases subdivided into first and second classes. According to his standing, as an apprentice a young man is assigned his place as a first, second, or third grade worker. Of course only young men of unusual ability pass directly from apprenticeship into the first grade of the workers. The most fall into the lower grades, working up as they grow more experienced, at the periodical regradings. These regradings take place in each industry at intervals corresponding with the length of the apprenticeship to that industry, so that merit never need wait long to rise, nor can any rest on past achievements unless they would drop into a lower rank. One of the notable advantages of a high grading is the privilege it gives the worker in electing which of the various branches or processes of his industry he will follow as his specialty. Of course it is not intended that any of these processes shall be disproportionately arduous, but there is often much difference between them, and the privilege of election is accordingly highly prized. So far as possible, indeed, the preferences even of the poorest workmen are considered in assigning them their line of work, because not only their happiness but their usefulness is thus enhanced. While, however, the wish of the lower grade man is consulted so far as the exigencies of the service permit, he is considered only after the upper grade men have been provided for, and often he has to put up with second or third choice, or even with an arbitrary assignment when help is needed. This privilege of election attends every regrading, and when a man loses his grade he also risks having to exchange the sort of work he likes for some other less to his taste. The results of each regrading, giving the standing of every man in his industry, are gazetted in the public prints, and those who have won promotion since the last regrading receive the nation's thanks and are publicly invested with the badge of their new rank."

"What may this badge be?" I asked.

"Every industry has its emblematic device," replied Dr. Leete, "and this, in the shape of a metallic badge so small that you might not see it unless you knew where to look, is all the insignia which the men of the army wear, except where public convenience demands a distinctive uniform. This badge is the same in form for all grades of industry, but while the badge of the third grade is iron, that of the second grade is silver, and that of the first is gilt.[1]

"Apart from the grand incentive to endeavor afforded by the fact that the high places in the nation are open only to the highest class men, and that rank in the army constitutes the only mode of social distinction for the vast majority who are not aspirants in art, literature, and the professions, various incitements of a minor, but perhaps equally effective, sort are provided in the

---

[1]   An allusion to the utopian tradition. In Hesiod's *Works and Days* is the story of the world's decline from an age of gold through silver and bronze to iron. Plato uses the metals in *The Republic* to indicate different qualities of human beings.

form of special privileges and immunities in the way of discipline, which the superior class men enjoy. These, while intended to be as little as possible invidious to the less successful, have the effect of keeping constantly before every man's mind the great desirability of attaining the grade next above his own.

"It is obviously important that not only the good but also the indifferent and poor workmen should be able to cherish the ambition of rising. Indeed, the number of the latter being so much greater, it is even more essential that the ranking system should not operate to discourage them than that it should stimulate the others. It is to this end that the grades are divided into classes. The grades as well as the classes being made numerically equal at each regrading, there is not at any time, counting out the officers and the unclassified and apprentice grades, over one-ninth of the industrial army in the lowest class, and most of this number are recent apprentices, all of whom expect to rise. Those who remain during the entire term of service in the lowest class are but a trifling fraction of the industrial army, and likely to be as deficient in sensibility to their position as in ability to better it.

"It is not even necessary that a worker should win promotion to a higher grade to have at least a taste of glory. While promotion requires a general excellence of record as a worker, honorable mention and various sorts of prizes are awarded for excellence less than sufficient for promotion, and also for special feats and single performances in the various industries. There are many minor distinctions of standing, not only within the grades but within the classes, each of which acts as a spur to the efforts of a group. It is intended that no form of merit shall wholly fail of recognition.

"As for actual neglect of work, positively bad work, or other overt remissness on the part of men incapable of generous motives, the discipline of the industrial army is far too strict to allow anything whatever of the sort. A man able to do duty, and persistently refusing, is sentenced to solitary imprisonment on bread and water till he consents.[1]

---

[1] "sentenced to solitary imprisonment on bread and water till he consents" was added in the second edition to underline the power of the state. The first edition is more general and reads "cut off from all human society."

"The lowest grade of the officers of the industrial army, that of assistant foremen or lieutenants, is appointed out of men who have held their place for two years in the first class of the first grade. Where this leaves too large a range of choice, only the first group of this class are eligible. No one thus comes to the point of commanding men until he is about thirty years old. After a man becomes an officer, his rating of course no longer depends on the efficiency of his own work, but on that of his men. The foremen are appointed from among the assistant foremen, by the same exercise of discretion limited to a small eligible class. In the appointments to the still higher grades another principle is introduced, which it would take too much time to explain now.

"Of course such a system of grading as I have described would have been impracticable applied to the small industrial concerns of your day, in some of which there were hardly enough employees to have left one apiece for the classes. You must remember that, under the national organization of labor, all industries are carried on by great bodies of men, many of your farms or shops being combined as one. It is also owing solely to the vast scale on which each industry is organized, with coördinate establishments in every part of the country, that we are able by exchanges and transfers to fit every man so nearly with the sort of work he can do best.

"And now, Mr. West, I will leave it to you, on the bare outline of its features which I have given, if those who need special incentives to do their best are likely to lack them under our system. Does it not seem to you that men who found themselves obliged, whether they wished or not, to work, would under such a system be strongly impelled to do their best?"[1]

I replied that it seemed to me the incentives offered were, if any objection were to be made, too strong; that the pace set for the young men was too hot; and such, indeed, I would add with deference, still remains my opinion, now that by longer residence among you I have become better acquainted with the whole subject.

Dr. Leete, however, desired me to reflect, and I am ready to say that it is perhaps a sufficient reply to my objection, that the

---

[1] The sentence "Does it not seem to you…" was added in the second edition. It emphasizes the power of the state over the individual.

worker's livelihood is in no way dependent on his ranking, and anxiety for that never embitters his disappointments; that the working hours are short, the vacations regular, and that all emulation ceases at forty-five, with the attainment of middle life.

"There are two or three other points I ought to refer to," he added, "to prevent your getting mistaken impressions. In the first place, you must understand that this system of preferment given the more efficient workers over the less so, in no way contravenes the fundamental idea of our social system, that all who do their best are equally deserving, whether that best be great or small. I have shown that the system is arranged to encourage the weaker as well as the stronger with the hope of rising, while the fact that the stronger are selected for the leaders is in no way a reflection upon the weaker, but in the interest of the common weal.

"Do not imagine, either, because emulation is given free play as an incentive under our system, that we deem it a motive likely to appeal to the nobler sort of men, or worthy of them. Such as these find their motives within, not without, and measure their duty by their own endowments, not by those of others. So long as their achievement is proportioned to their powers, they would consider it preposterous to expect praise or blame because it chanced to be great or small. To such natures emulation appears philosophically absurd, and despicable in a moral aspect by its substitution of envy for admiration, and exultation for regret, in one's attitude toward the successes and the failures of others.

"But all men, even in the last year of the twentieth century, are not of this high order, and the incentives to endeavor requisite for those who are not must be of a sort adapted to their inferior natures. For these, then, emulation of the keenest edge is provided as a constant spur. Those who need this motive will feel it. Those who are above its influence do not need it.

"I should not fail to mention," resumed the doctor, "that for those too deficient in mental or bodily strength to be fairly graded with the main body of workers, we have a separate grade, unconnected with the others,—a sort of invalid corps, the members of which are provided with a light class of tasks fitted to their strength. All our sick in mind and body, all our deaf and dumb, and lame and blind and crippled, and even our insane, belong to this invalid corps, and bear its insignia. The strongest often do nearly a man's work, the feeblest, of course, nothing; but none who can do anything are willing quite to give up. In their lucid intervals, even our insane are eager to do what they can."

"That is a pretty idea of the invalid corps," I said. "Even a barbarian from the nineteenth century can appreciate that. It is a very graceful way of disguising charity, and must be grateful to the feelings of its recipients."

"Charity!" repeated Dr. Leete. "Did you suppose that we consider the incapable class we are talking of objects of charity?"

"Why, naturally," I said, "inasmuch as they are incapable of self-support."

But here the doctor took me up quickly.

"Who is capable of self-support?" he demanded. "There is no such thing in a civilized society as self-support. In a state of society so barbarous as not even to know family cooperation, each individual may possibly support himself, though even then for a part of his life only; but from the moment that men begin to live together, and constitute even the rudest sort of society, self-support becomes impossible. As men grow more civilized, and the subdivision of occupations and services is carried out, a complex mutual dependence becomes the universal rule. Every man, however solitary may seem his occupation, is a member of a vast industrial partnership, as large as the nation, as large as humanity. The necessity of mutual dependence should imply the duty and guarantee of mutual support; and that it did not in your day constituted the essential cruelty and unreason of your system."

"That may all be so," I replied, "but it does not touch the case of those who are unable to contribute anything to the product of industry."

"Surely I told you this morning, at least I thought I did," replied Dr. Leete, "that the right of a man to maintenance at the nation's table depends on the fact that he is a man, and not on the amount of health and strength he may have, so long as he does his best."

"You said so," I answered, "but I supposed the rule applied only to the workers of different ability. Does it also hold of those who can do nothing at all?"

"Are they not also men?"

"I am to understand, then, that the lame, the blind, the sick, and the impotent, are as well off as the most efficient, and have the same income?"

"Certainly," was the reply.

"The idea of charity on such a scale," I answered, "would have made our most enthusiastic philanthropists gasp."

"If you had a sick brother at home," replied Dr. Leete, "unable to work, would you feed him on less dainty food, and lodge and clothe him more poorly, than yourself? More likely far, you would give him the preference; nor would you think of calling it charity. Would not the word, in that connection, fill you with indignation?"

"Of course," I replied; "but the cases are not parallel. There is a sense, no doubt, in which all men are brothers; but this general sort of brotherhood is not to be compared, except for rhetorical purposes, to the brotherhood of blood, either as to its sentiment or its obligations."

"There speaks the nineteenth century!" exclaimed Dr. Leete. "Ah, Mr. West, there is no doubt as to the length of time that you slept. If I were to give you, in one sentence, a key to what may seem the mysteries of our civilization as compared with that of your age, I should say that it is the fact that the solidarity of the race and the brotherhood of man, which to you were but fine phrases, are, to our thinking and feeling, ties as real and as vital as physical fraternity.

"But even setting that consideration aside, I do not see why it so surprises you that those who cannot work are conceded the full right to live on the produce of those who can. Even in your day, the duty of military service for the protection of the nation, to which our industrial service corresponds, while obligatory on those able to discharge it, did not operate to deprive of the privileges of citizenship those who were unable. They stayed at home, and were protected by those who fought, and nobody questioned their right to be, or thought less of them. So, now, the requirement of industrial service from those able to render it does not operate to deprive of the privileges of citizenship, which now implies the citizen's maintenance, him who cannot work. The worker is not a citizen because he works, but works because he is a citizen. As you recognize the duty of the strong to fight for the weak, we, now that fighting is gone by, recognize his duty to work for him.

"A solution which leaves an unaccounted-for residuum is no solution at all; and our solution of the problem of human society would have been none at all had it left the lame, the sick, and the blind outside with the beasts, to fare as they might. Better far have left the strong and well unprovided for than these burdened ones, toward whom every heart must yearn, and for whom ease of mind and body should be provided, if for no others. Therefore it is, as I told you this morning, that the title of every man, woman, and child to the means of existence rests on no basis less plain, broad, and simple than the fact that they are fellows of one race—members of one human family. The only coin current is the image of God, and that is good for all we have.

"I think there is no feature of the civilization of your epoch so repugnant to modern ideas as the neglect with which you treated your dependent classes. Even if you had no pity, no feeling of brotherhood, how was it that you did not see that you were robbing the incapable class of their plain right in leaving them unprovided for?"

"I don't quite follow you there," I said. "I admit the claim of this class to our pity, but how could they who produced nothing claim a share of the product as a right?"

"How happened it," was Dr. Leete's reply, "that your workers were able to produce more than so many savages would have done? Was it not wholly on account of the heritage of the past knowledge and achievements of the race, the machinery of society, thousands of years in contriving, found by you ready-made to your hand? How did you come to be possessors of this knowledge and this machinery, which represent, nine parts to one contributed by yourself in the value of your product? You inherited it, did you not? And were not these others, these unfortunate and crippled brothers whom you cast out, joint inheritors, co-heirs with you? What did you do with their share? Did you not rob them when you put them off with crusts, who were entitled to sit with the heirs, and did you not add insult to robbery when you called the crusts charity?

"Ah, Mr. West," Dr. Leete continued, as I did not respond, "what I do not understand is, setting aside all considerations either of justice or brotherly feeling toward the crippled and defective, how the workers of your day could have had any heart for their work, knowing that their children, or grandchildren, if unfortunate, would be deprived of the comforts and even necessities of life. It is a mystery how men with children could favor a system under which they were rewarded beyond those less endowed with bodily strength or mental power. For, by the same discrimination by which the father profited, the son, for whom he would give his life, being perchance weaker than others, might be reduced to crusts and beggary. How men dared leave children behind them, I have never been able to understand."[1]

CHAPTER XIII.

AS Edith had promised he should do, Dr. Leete accompanied me to my bedroom when I retired, to instruct me as to the adjustment

---

[1] NOTE. Although in his talk on the previous evening Dr. Leete had emphasized the pains taken to enable every man to ascertain and follow his natural bent in choosing an occupation, it was not till I learned that the worker's income is the same in all occupations that I realized how absolutely he may be counted on to do so, and thus, by selecting the harness which sets most lightly on himself, find that in which he can pull best. The failure of my age in any systematic or effective way to develop and utilize the natural aptitudes of men for the industries and intellectual avocations was one of the great wastes, as well as one of the most common causes of unhappiness in that time. The vast majority of my contemporaries, though nominally free to do so, never really chose their occupations at all, but were forced by circumstances into work for which they were relatively inefficient, because not naturally fitted for it. The rich, in this respect, had little advantage over the poor. The latter, indeed, being generally deprived of education, had no opportunity even to ascertain the natural aptitudes they might have, and on account of their poverty were unable to develop them by cultivation even when ascertained. The liberal and technical professions, except by favorable accident, were shut to them, to their own great loss and that of the nation. On the other hand, the well-to-do, although they could command education and opportunity, were scarcely less hampered by social prejudice, which forbade them to pursue manual avocations, even when adapted to them, and destined them, whether fit or unfit, to the professions, thus wasting many an excellent handicraftsman. Mercenary considerations, tempting men to pursue money-making occupations for which they were unfit, instead of less remunerative employments for which they were fit, were responsible for another vast perversion of talent. All these things now are changed. Equal education and opportunity must needs bring to light whatever aptitudes a man has, and neither social prejudices nor mercenary considerations hamper him in the choice of his life work. [Bellamy's note]

of the musical telephone. He showed how, by turning a screw, the volume of the music could be made to fill the room, or die away to an echo so faint and far that one could scarcely be sure whether he heard or imagined it. If, of two persons side by side, one desired to listen to music and the other to sleep, it could be made audible to one and inaudible to another.

"I should strongly advise you to sleep if you can tonight, Mr. West, in preference to listening to the finest tunes in the world," the doctor said, after explaining these points. "In the trying experience you are just now passing through, sleep is a nerve tonic for which there is no substitute."

Mindful of what had happened to me that very morning, I promised to heed his counsel.

"Very well," he said, "then I will set the telephone at eight o'clock."

"What do you mean?" I asked.

He explained that, by a clockwork combination, a person could arrange to be awakened at any hour by the music.

It began to appear, as has since fully proved to be the case, that I had left my tendency to insomnia behind me with the other discomforts of existence in the nineteenth century; for though I took no sleeping draught this time, yet, as the night before, I had no sooner touched the pillow than I was asleep.

I dreamed that I sat on the throne of the Abencerrages in the banqueting hall of the Alhambra, feasting my lords and generals, who next day were to follow the crescent against the Christian dogs of Spain. The air, cooled by the spray of fountains, was heavy with the scent of flowers. A band of Nautch girls, round-limbed and luscious-lipped, danced with voluptuous grace to the music of brazen and stringed instruments. Looking up to the latticed galleries, one caught a gleam now and then from the eye of some beauty of the royal harem, looking down upon the assembled flower of Moorish chivalry. Louder and louder clashed the cymbals, wilder and wilder grew the strain, till the blood of the desert race could no longer resist the martial delirium, and the swart nobles leaped to their feet; a thousand scimetars were bared, and the cry, "Allah il Allah!" shook the hall and awoke me, to find it broad daylight, and the room tingling with the electric music of the "Turkish Reveille."[1]

At the breakfast-table, when I told my host of my morning's experience, I learned that it was not a mere chance that the piece of music which awakened me was a reveille. The airs played at one of the halls during the waking hours of the morning were always of an inspiring type.

"By the way," I said, "I have not thought to ask you anything about the state of Europe. Have the societies of the Old World also been remodeled?"

"Yes," replied Dr. Leete, "the great nations of Europe as well as Australia, Mexico, and parts of South America, are now organized industrially like the United States, which was the pioneer of the evolution. The peaceful relations of these nations are assured by a loose form of federal union of worldwide extent. An international council regulates the mutual intercourse and commerce of the members of the union and their joint policy toward the more backward races, which are gradually being educated up to civilized institutions. Complete autonomy within its own limits is enjoyed by every nation."

"How do you carry on commerce without money?" I said. "In trading with other nations, you must use some sort of money, although you dispense with it in the internal affairs of the nation."

"Oh, no; money is as superfluous in our foreign as in our internal relations. When foreign commerce was conducted by private enterprise, money was necessary to adjust it on account of the multifarious complexity of the transactions; but nowadays it is a function of the nations as units. There are thus only a dozen or so merchants in the world, and their business being supervised by the international council, a simple system of book accounts serves perfectly to regulate their dealings. Customs duties of every sort are of course superfluous. A nation simply does not import what its government does not think requisite for the general interest. Each nation has a bureau of foreign exchange, which manages its

---

[1] The Alhambra palace was built at Granada, Spain, by Moorish kings in the thirteenth century. In the East Indies Nautch girls are professional dancers. The "Turkish Reveille" was a popular piece by Th. Michaelis published in 1879.

trading. For example, the American bureau, estimating such and such quantities of French goods necessary to America for a given year, sends the order to the French bureau, which in turn sends its order to our bureau. The same is done mutually by all the nations."

"But how are the prices of foreign goods settled, since there is no competition?"

"The price at which one nation supplies another with goods," replied Dr. Leete, "must be that at which it supplies its own citizens. So you see there is no danger of misunderstanding. Of course no nation is theoretically bound to supply another with the product of its own labor, but it is for the interest of all to exchange some commodities. If a nation is regularly supplying another with certain goods, notice is required from either side of any important change in the relation."

"But what if a nation, having a monopoly of some natural product, should refuse to supply it to the others, or to one of them?"

"Such a case has never occurred, and could not without doing the refusing party vastly more harm than the others," replied Dr. Leete. "In the first place, no favoritism could be legally shown. The law requires that each nation shall deal with the others, in all respects, on exactly the same footing. Such a course as you suggest would cut off the nation adopting it from the remainder of the earth for all purposes whatever. The contingency is one that need not give us much anxiety."

"But," said I, "supposing a nation, having a natural monopoly in some product of which it exports more than it consumes, should put the price away up, and thus, without cutting off the supply, make a profit out of its neighbors' necessities? Its own citizens would of course have to pay the higher price on that commodity, but as a body would make more out of foreigners than they would be out of pocket themselves."

"When you come to know how prices of all commodities are determined nowadays, you will perceive how impossible it is that they could be altered, except with reference to the amount or arduousness of the work required respectively to produce them," was Dr. Leete's reply. "This principle is an international as well as a national guarantee; but even without it the sense of community of interest, international as well as national, and the conviction of the folly of selfishness, are too deep nowadays to render possible such a piece of sharp practice as you apprehend. You must understand that we all look forward to an eventual unification of the world as one nation. That, no doubt, will be the ultimate form of society, and will realize certain economic advantages over the present federal system of autonomous nations. Meanwhile, however, the present system works so nearly perfectly that we are quite content to leave to posterity the completion of the scheme. There are, indeed, some who hold that it never will be completed, on the ground that the federal plan is not merely a provisional solution of the problem of human society, but the best ultimate solution."

"How do you manage," I asked, "when the books of any two nations do not balance? Supposing we import more from France than we export to her."

"At the end of each year," replied the doctor, "the books of every nation are examined. If France is found in our debt, probably we are in the debt of some nation which owes France, and so on with all the nations. The balances that remain after the accounts have been cleared by the international council should not be large under our system. Whatever they may be, the council requires them to be settled every few years, and may require their settlement at any time if they are getting too large; for it is not intended that any nation shall run largely in debt to another, lest feelings unfavorable to amity should be engendered. To guard further against this, the international council inspects the commodities interchanged by the nations, to see that they are of perfect quality."

"But what are the balances finally settled with, seeing that you have no money?"

"In national staples; a basis of agreement as to what staples shall be accepted, and in what proportions, for settlement of accounts, being a preliminary to trade relations."

"Emigration is another point I want to ask you about," said I. "With every nation organized as a close industrial partnership, monopolizing all means of production in the country, the emigrant, even if he were permitted to land, would starve. I suppose there is no emigration nowadays."

"On the contrary, there is constant emigration, by which I

suppose you mean removal to foreign countries for permanent residence," replied Dr. Leete. "It is arranged on a simple international arrangement of indemnities. For example, if a man at twenty-one emigrates from England to America, England loses all the expense of his maintenance and education, and America gets a workman for nothing. America accordingly makes England an allowance. The same principle, varied to suit the case, applies generally. If the man is near the term of his labor when he emigrates, the country receiving him has the allowance. As to imbecile persons, it is deemed best that each nation should be responsible for its own, and the emigration of such must be under full guarantees of support by his own nation. Subject to these regulations, the right of any man to emigrate at any time is unrestricted."

"But how about mere pleasure trips; tours of observation? How can a stranger travel in a country whose people do not receive money, and are themselves supplied with the means of life on a basis not extended to him? His own credit card cannot, of course, be good in other lands. How does he pay his way?"

"An American credit card," replied Dr. Leete, "is just as good in Europe as American gold used to be, and on precisely the same condition, namely, that it be exchanged into the currency of the country you are traveling in. An American in Berlin takes his credit card to the local office of the international council, and receives in exchange for the whole or part of it a German credit card, the amount being charged against the United States in favor of Germany on the international account."

"Perhaps Mr. West would like to dine at the Elephant today," said Edith, as we left the table.

"That is the name we give to the general dining-house of our ward," explained her father. "Not only is our cooking done at the public kitchens, as I told you last night, but the service and quality of the meals are much more satisfactory if taken at the dining-house. The two minor meals of the day are usually taken at home, as not worth the trouble of going out; but it is general to go out to dine. We have not done so since you have been with us, from a notion that it would be better to wait till you had become a little more familiar with our ways. What do you think? Shall we take dinner at the dining-house today?"

I said that I should be very much pleased to do so.

Not long after, Edith came to me, smiling, and said: —

"Last night, as I was thinking what I could do to make you feel at home, until you came to be a little more used to us and our ways, an idea occurred to me. What would you say if I were to introduce you to some very nice people of your own times, whom I am sure you used to be well acquainted with?"

I replied, rather vaguely, that it would certainly be very agreeable, but I did not see how she was going to manage it.

"Come with me," was her smiling reply, "and see if I am not as good as my word."

My susceptibility to surprise had been pretty well exhausted by the numerous shocks it had received, but it was with some wonderment that I followed her into a room which I had not before entered. It was a small, cosy apartment, walled with cases filled with books.

"Here are your friends," said Edith, indicating one of the cases, and as my eye glanced over the names on the backs of the volumes, Shakespeare, Milton, Wordsworth, Shelley, Tennyson, Defoe, Dickens, Thackeray, Hugo, Hawthorne, Irving, and a score of other great writers of my time and all time, I understood her meaning. She had indeed made good her promise in a sense compared with which its literal fulfillment would have been a disappointment. She had introduced me to a circle of friends whom the century that had elapsed since last I communed with them had aged as little as it had myself. Their spirit was as high, their wit as keen, their laughter and their tears as contagious, as when their speech had whiled away the hours of a former century. Lonely I was not and could not be more, with this goodly companionship, however wide the gulf of years that gaped between me and my old life.

"You are glad I brought you here," exclaimed Edith, radiant, as she read in my face the success of her experiment. "It was a good idea, was it not, Mr. West? How stupid in me not to think of it before! I will leave you now with your old friends, for I know there will be no company for you like them just now; but remember you must not let old friends make you quite forget new ones!" and with that smiling caution she left me.

Attracted by the most familiar of the names before me, I laid my hand on a volume of Dickens, and sat down to read. He had been my prime favorite among the bookwriters of the century, —I mean the nineteenth century,—and a week had rarely passed in my old life during which I had not taken up some volume of his works to while away an idle hour. Any volume with which I had been familiar would have produced an extraordinary impression, read under my present circumstances, but my exceptional familiarity with Dickens, and his consequent power to call up the associations of my former life, gave to his writings an effect no others could have had, to intensify, by force of contrast, my appreciation of the strangeness of my present environment. However new and astonishing one's surroundings, the tendency is to become a part of them so soon that almost from the first the power to see them objectively and fully measure their strangeness, is lost. That power, already dulled in my case, the pages of Dickens restored by carrying me back through their associations to the standpoint of my former life. With a clearness which I had not been able before to attain, I saw now the past and present, like contrasting pictures, side by side.

The genius of the great novelist of the nineteenth century, like that of Homer, might indeed defy time; but the setting of his pathetic tales, the misery of the poor, the wrongs of power, the pitiless cruelty of the system of society, had passed away as utterly as Circe and the sirens, Charybdis and Cyclops.[1]

During the hour or two that I sat there with Dickens open before me, I did not actually read more than a couple of pages. Every paragraph, every phrase, brought up some new aspect of the world-transformation which had taken place, and led my

---

[1] All dangers encountered by Odysseus or Ulysses in his epic journey in Homer's *Odyssey*. Circe was a sorceress; the sirens were half women, half birds who lured sailors to their deaths; Charybdis was a dangerous whirlpool; and Cyclops was a one-eyed giant.

thoughts on long and widely ramifying excursions. As meditating thus in Dr. Leete's library I gradually attained a more clear and coherent idea of the prodigious spectacle which I had been so strangely enabled to view, I was filled with a deepening wonder at the seeming capriciousness of the fate that had given to one who so little deserved it, or seemed in any way set apart for it, the power alone among his contemporaries to stand upon the earth in this latter day. I had neither foreseen the new world nor toiled for it, as many about me had done regardless of the scorn of fools or the misconstruction of the good. Surely it would have been more in accordance with the fitness of things had one of those prophetic and strenuous souls been enabled to see the travail of his soul and be satisfied; he, for example, a thousand times rather than I, who, having beheld in a vision the world I looked on, sang of it in words that again and again, during these last wondrous days, had rung in my mind: —

For I dipt into the future, far as human eye could see,
Saw the vision of the world, and all the wonder that
    would be;

Till the wardrum throbbed no longer, and the battleflags
    were furled.
In the Parliament of man, the federation of the world.

Then the common sense of most shall hold a fretful
    realm in awe,
And the kindly earth shall slumber, lapt in universal law.

For I doubt not through the ages one increasing purpose
    runs,
And the thoughts of men are widened with the process
    of the suns.[1]

What though, in his old age, he momentarily lost faith in his own prediction, as prophets in their hours of depression and doubt

---

[1]   From Alfred, Lord Tennyson's "Locksley Hall" (1842).

generally do, the words had remained eternal testimony to the seer-ship of a poet's heart, the insight that is given to faith.

I was still in the library when some hours later Dr. Leete sought me there. "Edith told me of her idea," he said, "and I thought it an excellent one. I had a little curiosity what writer you would first turn to. Ah, Dickens! You admired him, then! That is where we moderns agree with you. Judged by our standards, he overtops all the writers of his age, not because his literary genius was highest, but because his great heart beat for the poor, because he made the cause of the victims of society his own, and devoted his pen to exposing its cruelties and shams. No man of his time did so much as he to turn men's minds to the wrong and wretchedness of the old order of things, and open their eyes to the necessity of the great change that was coming, although he himself did not clearly foresee it."

CHAPTER XIV.

A heavy rainstorm came up during the day, and I had concluded that the condition of the streets would be such that my hosts would have to give up the idea of going out to dinner, although the dining-hall I had understood to be quite near. I was much surprised when at the dinner hour the ladies appeared prepared to go out, but without either rubbers or umbrellas.

The mystery was explained when we found ourselves on the street, for a continuous waterproof covering had been let down so as to inclose the sidewalk and turn it into a well lighted and perfectly dry corridor, which was filled with a stream of ladies and gentlemen dressed for dinner. At the corners the entire open space was similarly roofed in. Edith Leete, with whom I walked, seemed much interested in learning what appeared to be entirely new to her, that in the stormy weather the streets of the Boston of my day had been impassable, except to persons protected by umbrellas, boots, and heavy clothing. "Were sidewalk coverings not used at all?" she asked. They were used, I explained, but in a scattered and utterly unsystematic way, being private enterprises.

She said to me that at the present time all the streets were provided against inclement weather in the manner I saw, the apparatus being rolled out of the way when it was unnecessary. She intimated that it would be considered an extraordinary imbecility to permit the weather to have any effect on the social movements of the people.

Dr. Leete, who was walking ahead, overhearing something of our talk, turned to say that the difference between the age of individualism and that of concert was well characterized by the fact that, in the nineteenth century, when it rained, the people of Boston put up three hundred thousand umbrellas over as many heads, and in the twentieth century they put up one umbrella over all the heads.

As we walked on, Edith said, "The private umbrella is father's favorite figure to illustrate the old way when everybody lived for himself and his family. There is a nineteenth century painting at the Art Gallery representing a crowd of people in the rain, each one holding his umbrella over himself and his wife, and giving his neighbors the drippings, which he claims must have been meant by the artist as a satire on his times."

We now entered a large building into which a stream of people was pouring. I could not see the front, owing to the awning, but, if in correspondence with the interior, which was even finer than the store I visited the day before, it would have been magnificent. My companion said that the sculptured group over the entrance was especially admired. Going up a grand staircase we walked some distance along a broad corridor with many doors opening upon it. At one of these, which bore my host's name, we turned in, and I found myself in an elegant dining-room containing a table for four. Windows opened on a courtyard where a fountain played to a great height and music made the air electric.

"You seem at home here," I said, as we seated ourselves at table, and Dr. Leete touched an annunciator.

"This is, in fact, a part of our house, slightly detached from the rest," he replied. "Every family in the ward has a room set apart in this great building for its permanent and exclusive use for a small annual rental. For transient guests and individuals there is accommodation on another floor. If we expect to dine here, we put in our orders the night before, selecting anything in market, according to the daily reports in the papers. The meal is as expensive or as simple as we please, though of course everything is vastly cheaper as well as better than it would be if prepared at home. There is actually nothing which our people take more interest in than the perfection of the catering and cooking done for them, and I admit that we are a little vain of the success that has been attained by this branch of the service. Ah, my dear Mr. West, though other aspects of your civilization were more tragical, I can imagine that none could have been more depressing than the poor dinners you had to eat, that is, all of you who had not great wealth."

"You would have found none of us disposed to disagree with you on that point," I said.

The waiter, a fine-looking young fellow, wearing a slightly distinctive uniform, now made his appearance. I observed him closely, as it was the first time I had been able to study particularly the bearing of one of the enlisted members of the industrial army. This young man, I knew from what I had been told, must be highly educated, and the equal, socially and in all respects, of those he served. But it was perfectly evident that to neither side was the situation in the slightest degree embarrassing. Dr. Leete addressed the young man in a tone devoid, of course, as any gentleman's would be, of superciliousness, but at the same time not in any way deprecatory, while the manner of the young man was simply that of a person intent on discharging correctly the task he was engaged in, equally without familiarity or obsequiousness. It was, in fact, the manner of a soldier on duty, but without the military stiffness. As the youth left the room, I said, "I cannot get over my wonder at seeing a young man like that serving so contentedly in a menial position."

"What is that word 'menial'? I never heard it," said Edith.

"It is obsolete now," remarked her father. "If I understand it rightly, it applied to persons who performed particularly disagreeable and unpleasant tasks for others, and carried with it an implication of contempt. Was it not so, Mr. West?"

"That is about it," I said. "Personal service, such as waiting on tables, was considered menial, and held in such contempt, in my day, that persons of culture and refinement would suffer hardship before condescending to it."

"What a strangely artificial idea," exclaimed Mrs. Leete, wonderingly.

"And yet these services had to be rendered," said Edith.

"Of course," I replied. "But we imposed them on the poor, and those who had no alternative but starvation."

"And increased the burden you imposed on them by adding your contempt," remarked Dr. Leete.

"I don't think I clearly understand," said Edith. "Do you mean that you permitted people to do things for you which you despised them for doing, or that you accepted services from them which you would have been unwilling to render them? You can't surely mean that, Mr. West?"

I was obliged to tell her that the fact was just as she had stated. Dr. Leete, however, came to my relief.

"To understand why Edith is surprised," he said, "you must know that nowadays it is an axiom of ethics that to accept a service from another which we would be unwilling to return in kind, if need were, is like borrowing with the intention of not repaying, while to enforce such a service by taking advantage of the poverty or necessity of a person would be an outrage like forcible robbery. It is the worst thing about any system which divides men, or allows them to be divided, into classes and castes, that it weakens the sense of a common humanity. Unequal distribution of wealth, and, still more effectually, unequal opportunities of education and culture, divided society in your day into classes which in many respects regarded each other as distinct races. There is not, after all, such a difference as might appear between our ways of looking at this question of service. Ladies and gentlemen of the cultured class in your day would no more have permitted persons of their own class to render them services they would scorn to return than we would permit anybody to do so. The poor and the uncultured, however, they looked upon as of another kind from themselves. The equal wealth and equal opportunities of culture which all persons now enjoy have simply made us all members of one class, which corresponds to the most fortunate class with you.

Until this equality of condition had come to pass, the idea of the solidarity of humanity, the brotherhood of all men, could never have become the real conviction and practical principle of action it is nowadays. In your day the same phrases were indeed used, but they were phrases merely."

"Do the waiters, also, volunteer?"

"No," replied Dr. Leete. "The waiters are young men in the unclassified grade of the industrial army who are assignable to all sorts of miscellaneous occupations not requiring special skill. Waiting on table is one of these, and every young recruit is given a taste of it. I myself served as a waiter for several months in this very dining-house some forty years ago. Once more you must remember that there is recognized no sort of difference between the dignity of the different sorts of work required by the nation. The individual is never regarded, nor regards himself, as the servant of those he serves, nor is he in any way dependent upon them. It is always the nation which he is serving. No difference is recognized between a waiter's functions and those of any other worker. The fact that his is a personal service is indifferent from our point of view. So is a doctor's. I should as soon expect our waiter today to look down on me because I served him as a doctor, as think of looking down on him because he serves me as a waiter."

After dinner my entertainers conducted me about the building, of which the extent, the magnificent architecture and richness of embellishment, astonished me. It seemed that it was not merely a dining-hall, but likewise a great pleasure-house and social rendezvous of the quarter, and no appliance of entertainment or recreation seemed lacking.

"You find illustrated here," said Dr. Leete, when I had expressed my admiration, "what I said to you in our first conversation, when you were looking out over the city, as to the splendor of our public and common life as compared with the simplicity of our private and home life, and the contrast which, in this respect, the twentieth bears to the nineteenth century. To save ourselves useless burdens, we have as little gear about us at home as is consistent with comfort, but the social side of our life is ornate and luxurious beyond anything the world ever knew before. All the industrial and professional guilds have clubhouses as extensive as this, as well as country, mountain, and seaside houses for sport and rest in vacations."[1]

CHAPTER XV.

WHEN, in the course of our tour of inspection, we came to the library, we succumbed to the temptation of the luxurious leather chairs with which it was furnished, and sat down in one of the booklined alcoves to rest and chat awhile.[2]

---

[1] NOTE. In the latter part of the nineteenth century it became a practice of needy young men at some of the colleges of the country to earn a little money for their term bills by serving as waiters on tables at hotels during the long summer vacation. It was claimed, in reply to critics who expressed the prejudices of the time in asserting that persons voluntarily following such an occupation could not be gentlemen, that they were entitled to praise for vindicating, by their example, the dignity of all honest and necessary labor. The use of this argument illustrates a common confusion in thought on the part of my former contemporaries. The business of waiting on tables was in no more need of defense than most of the other ways of getting a living in that day, but to talk of dignity attaching to labor of any sort under the system then prevailing was absurd. There is no way in which selling labor for the highest price it will fetch is more dignified than selling goods for what can be got. Both were commercial transactions to be judged by the commercial standard. By setting a price in money on his service, the worker accepted the money measure for it, and renounced all clear claim to be judged by any other. The sordid taint which this necessity imparted to the noblest and the highest sorts of service was bitterly resented by generous souls, but there was no evading it. There was no exemption, however transcendent the quality of one's service, from the necessity of haggling for its price in the marketplace. The physician must sell his healing and the apostle his preaching like the rest. The prophet, who had guessed the meaning of God, must dicker for the price of the revelation, and the poet hawk his visions in printers' row. If I were asked to name the most distinguishing felicity of this age, as compared to that in which I first saw the light, I should say that to me it seems to consist in the dignity you have given to labor by refusing to set a price upon it and abolishing the marketplace forever. By requiring of every man his best you have made God his taskmaster, and by making honor the sole reward of achievement you have imparted to all service the distinction peculiar in my day to the soldier's. [Bellamy's note]

[2] I cannot sufficiently celebrate the glorious liberty that reigns in the public libraries of the twentieth century as compared with the intolerable management of those of the nineteenth century, in which the books were jealously railed away from the people, and obtainable only at an expenditure of time and red tape calculated to discourage any ordinary taste for literature. [Bellamy's note]

"Edith tells me that you have been in the library all the morning," said Mrs. Leete. "Do you know, it seems to me, Mr. West, that you are the most enviable of mortals."

"I should like to know just why," I replied.

"Because the books of the last hundred years will be new to you," she answered. "You will have so much of the most absorbing literature to read as to leave you scarcely time for meals these five years to come. Ah, what would I give if I had not already read Berrian's novels."

"Or Nesmyth's, mamma," added Edith.

"Yes, or Oates' poems, or 'Past and Present,' or, 'In the Beginning,' or, -oh, I could name a dozen books, each worth a year of one's life," declared Mrs. Leete, enthusiastically.

"I judge, then, that there has been some notable literature produced in this century."

"Yes," said Dr. Leete. "It has been an era of unexampled intellectual splendor. Probably humanity never before passed through a moral and material evolution, at once so vast in its scope and brief in its time of accomplishment, as that from the old order to the new in the early part of this century. When men came to realize the greatness of the felicity which had befallen them, and that the change through which they had passed was not merely an improvement in details of their condition, but the rise of the race to a new plane of existence with an illimitable vista of progress, their minds were affected in all their faculties with a stimulus, of which the outburst of the mediaeval renaissance offers a suggestion but faint indeed. There ensued an era of mechanical invention, scientific discovery, art, musical and literary productiveness to which no previous age of the world offers anything comparable."

"By the way," said I, "talking of literature, how are books published now? Is that also done by the nation?"

"Certainly."

"But how do you manage it? Does the government publish everything that is brought it as a matter of course, at the public expense, or does it exercise a censorship and print only what it approves?"

"Neither way. The printing department has no censorial powers. It is bound to print all that is offered it, but prints it only on condition that the author defray the first cost out of his credit. He must pay for the privilege of the public ear, and if he has any message worth hearing we consider that he will be glad to do it. Of course, if incomes were unequal, as in the old times, this rule would enable only the rich to be authors, but the resources of citizens being equal, it merely measures the strength of the author's motive. The cost of an edition of an average book can be saved out of a year's credit by the practice of economy and some sacrifices. The book, on being published, is placed on sale by the nation."

"The author receiving a royalty on the sales as with us, I suppose," I suggested.

"Not as with you, certainly," replied Dr. Leete, "but nevertheless in one way. The price of every book is made up of the cost of its publication with a royalty for the author. The author fixes this royalty at any figure he pleases. Of course if he puts it unreasonably high it is his own loss, for the book will not sell. The amount of this royalty is set to his credit and he is discharged from other service to the nation for so long a period as this credit at the rate of allowance for the support of citizens shall suffice to support him. If his book be moderately successful, he has thus a furlough for several months, a year, two or three years, and if he in the mean time produces other successful work, the remission of service is extended so far as the sale of that may justify. An author of much acceptance succeeds in supporting himself by his pen during the entire period of service, and the degree of any writer's literary ability, as determined by the popular voice, is thus the measure of the opportunity given him to devote his time to literature. In this respect the outcome of our system is not very dissimilar to that of yours, but there are two notable differences. In the first place, the universally high level of education nowadays gives the popular verdict a conclusiveness on the real merit of literary work which in your day it was as far as possible from having. In the second place, there is no such thing now as favoritism of any sort to interfere with the recognition of true merit. Every author has precisely the same facilities for bringing his work before the popular tribunal. To judge from the complaints of the writers of your day, this absolute equality of opportunity would have been greatly prized."

"In the recognition of merit in other fields of original genius, such as music, art, invention, design," I said, "I suppose you follow a similar principle."

"Yes," he replied, "although the details differ. In art, for example, as in literature, the people are the sole judges. They vote upon the acceptance of statues and paintings for the public buildings, and their favorable verdict carries with it the artist's remission from other tasks to devote himself to his vocation. On copies of his work disposed of, he also derives the same advantage as the author on sales of his books. In all these lines of original genius the plan pursued is the same,—to offer a free field to aspirants, and as soon as exceptional talent is recognized to release it from all trammels and let it have free course. The remission of other service in these cases is not intended as a gift or reward, but as the means of obtaining more and higher service. Of course there are various literary, art, and scientific institutes to which membership comes to the famous and is greatly prized. The highest of all honors in the nation, higher than the presidency, which calls merely for good sense and devotion to duty, is the red ribbon awarded by the vote of the people to the great authors, artists, engineers, physicians, and inventors of the generation. Not over a certain number wear it at any one time, though every bright young fellow in the country loses innumerable nights' sleep dreaming of it. I even did myself."

"Just as if mamma and I would have thought any more of you with it," exclaimed Edith; "not that it isn't, of course, a very fine thing to have."

"You had no choice, my dear, but to take your father as you found him and make the best of him," Dr. Leete replied; "but as for your mother, there, she would never have had me if I had not assured her that I was bound to get the red ribbon or at least the blue."

On this extravagance Mrs. Leete's only comment was a smile.

"How about periodicals and newspapers?" I said. "I won't deny that your book publishing system is a considerable improvement on ours, both as to its tendency to encourage a real literary vocation, and, quite as important, to discourage mere scribblers; but I don't see how it can be made to apply to magazines and newspapers. It is very well to make a man pay for publishing a book, because the expense will be only occasional; but no man could afford the expense of publishing a newspaper every day in the year. It took the deep pockets of our private capitalists to do that, and often exhausted even them before the returns came in. If you have newspapers at all, they must, I fancy, be published by the government at the public expense, with government editors, reflecting government opinions. Now, if your system is so perfect that there is never anything to criticise in the conduct of affairs, this arrangement may answer. Otherwise I should think the lack of an independent unofficial medium for the expression of public opinion would have most unfortunate results. Confess, Dr. Leete, that a free newspaper press, with all that it implies, was a redeeming incident of the old system when capital was in private hands, and that you have to set off the loss of that against your gains in other respects."

"I am afraid I can't give you even that consolation," replied Dr. Leete, laughing. "In the first place, Mr. West, the newspaper press is by no means the only or, as we look at it, the best vehicle for serious criticism of public affairs. To us, the judgments of your newspapers on such themes seem generally to have been crude and flippant, as well as deeply tinctured with prejudice and bitterness. In so far as they may be taken as expressing public opinion, they give an unfavorable impression of the popular intelligence, while so far as they may have formed public opinion, the nation was not to be felicitated. Nowadays, when a citizen desires to make a serious impression upon the public mind as to any aspect of public affairs, he comes out with a book or pamphlet, published as other books are. But this is not because we lack newspapers and magazines, or that they lack the most absolute freedom. The newspaper press is organized so as to be a more perfect expression of public opinion than it possibly could be in your day, when private capital controlled and managed it primarily as a moneymaking business, and secondarily only as a mouthpiece for the people."

"But," said I, "if the government prints the papers at the public expense, how can it fail to control their policy? Who appoints the editors, if not the government?"

"The government does not pay the expense of the papers, nor appoint their editors, nor in any way exert the slightest influence on their policy," replied Dr. Leete. "The people who take the paper pay the expense of its publication, choose its editor, and remove him when unsatisfactory. You will scarcely say, I think, that such a newspaper press is not a free organ of popular opinion."

"Decidedly I shall not," I replied, "but how is it practicable?"

"Nothing could be simpler. Supposing some of my neighbors or myself think we ought to have a newspaper reflecting our opinions, and devoted especially to our locality, trade, or profession. We go about among the people till we get the names of such a number that their annual subscriptions will meet the cost of the paper, which is little or big according to the largeness of its constituency. The amount of the subscriptions marked off the credits of the citizens guarantees the nation against loss in publishing the paper, its business, you understand, being that of a publisher purely, with no option to refuse the duty required. The subscribers to the paper now elect somebody as editor, who, if he accepts the office, is discharged from other service during his incumbency. Instead of paying a salary to him, as in your day, the subscribers pay the nation an indemnity equal to the cost of his support for taking him away from the general service. He manages the paper just as one of your editors did, except that he has no counting-room to obey, or interests of private capital as against the public good to defend. At the end of the first year, the subscribers for the next either reëlect the former editor or choose any one else to his place. An able editor, of course, keeps his place indefinitely. As the subscription list enlarges, the funds of the paper increase, and it is improved by the securing of more and better contributors, just as your papers were."

"How is the staff of contributors recompensed, since they cannot be paid in money?"

"The editor settles with them the price of their wares. The amount is transferred to their individual credit from the guarantee credit of the paper, and a remission of service is granted the contributor for a length of time corresponding to the amount credited him, just as to other authors. As to magazines, the system is the same. Those interested in the prospectus of a new periodical pledge enough subscriptions to run it for a year; select their editor, who recompenses his contributors just as in the other case, the printing bureau furnishing the necessary force and material for publication, as a matter of course. When an editor's services are no longer desired, if he cannot earn the right to his time by other literary work, he simply resumes his place in the industrial army. I should add that, though ordinarily the editor is elected only at the end of the year, and as a rule is continued in office for a term of years, in case of any sudden change he should give to the tone of the paper, provision is made for taking the sense of the subscribers as to his removal at any time."

"However earnestly a man may long for leisure for purposes of study or meditation," I remarked, "he cannot get out of the harness, if I understand you rightly, except in these two ways you have mentioned. He must either by literary, artistic, or inventive productiveness indemnify the nation for the loss of his services, or must get a sufficient number of other people to contribute to such an indemnity."

"It is most certain," replied Dr. Leete, "that no able-bodied man nowadays can evade his share of work and live on the toil of others, whether he calls himself by the fine name of student or confesses to being simply lazy. At the same time our system is elastic enough to give free play to every instinct of human nature which does not aim at dominating others or living on the fruit of others' labor. There is not only the remission by indemnification but the remission by abnegation. Any man in his thirty-third year, his term of service being then half done, can obtain an honorable discharge from the army, provided he accepts for the rest of his life one half the rate of maintenance other citizens receive. It is quite possible to live on this amount, though one must forego the luxuries and elegancies of life, with some, perhaps, of its comforts."[1]

When the ladies retired that evening, Edith brought me a book and said: —

"If you should be wakeful tonight, Mr. West, you might be interested in looking over this story by Berrian. It is considered his masterpiece, and will at least give you an idea what the stories nowadays are like."

---

[1] The two paragraphs from "However earnestly..." to "of its comforts" were added in the second edition. They provide an important increase in the freedom of the individual.

I sat up in my room that night reading "Penthesilia"[1] till it grew gray in the east, and did not lay it down till I had finished it. And yet let no admirer of the great romancer of the twentieth century resent my saying that at the first reading what most impressed me was not so much what was in the book as what was left out of it. The storywriters of my day would have deemed the making of bricks without straw a light task compared with the construction of a romance from which should be excluded all effects drawn from the contrasts of wealth and poverty, education and ignorance, coarseness and refinement, high and low, all motives drawn from social pride and ambition, the desire of being richer or the fear of being poorer, together with sordid anxieties of any sort for one's self or others; a romance in which there should, indeed, be love galore, but love unfretted by artificial barriers created by differences of station or possessions, owning no other law but that of the heart. The reading of "Penthesilia" was of more value than almost any amount of explanation would have been in giving me something like a general impression of the social aspect of the twentieth century. The information Dr. Leete had imparted was indeed extensive as to facts, but they had affected my mind as so many separate impressions, which I had as yet succeeded but imperfectly in making cohere. Berrian put them together for me in a picture.

CHAPTER XVI.

NEXT morning I rose somewhat before the breakfast hour. As I descended the stairs, Edith stepped into the hall from the room which had been the scene of the morning interview between us described some chapters back.

"Ah!" she exclaimed, with a charmingly arch expression, "you thought to slip out unbeknown for another of those solitary morning rambles which have such nice effects on you. But you

---

[1]   Penthesilia was Queen of the Amazons who fought on the side of Troy and was killed by Achilles.

see I am up too early for you this time. You are fairly caught."

"You discredit the efficacy of your own cure," I said, "by supposing that such a ramble would now be attended with bad consequences."

"I am very glad to hear that," she said. "I was in here arranging some flowers for the breakfast table when I heard you come down, and fancied I detected something surreptitious in your step on the stairs."

"You did me injustice," I replied. "I had no idea of going out at all."

Despite her effort to convey an impression that my interception was purely accidental, I had at the time a dim suspicion of what I afterwards learned to be the fact, namely, that this sweet creature, in pursuance of her self-assumed guardianship over me, had risen for the last two or three mornings at an unheard-of hour, to insure against the possibility of my wandering off alone in case I should be affected as on the former occasion. Receiving permission to assist her in making up the breakfast bouquet, I followed her into the room from which she had emerged.

"Are you sure," she asked, "that you are quite done with those terrible sensations you had that morning?"

"I can't say that I do not have times of feeling decidedly queer," I replied, "moments when my personal identity seems an open question. It would be too much to expect after my experience that I should not have such sensations occasionally, but as for being carried entirely off my feet, as I was on the point of being that morning, I think the danger is past."

"I shall never forget how you looked that morning," she said.

"If you had merely saved my life," I continued, "I might, perhaps, find words to express my gratitude, but it was my reason you saved, and there are no words that would not belittle my debt to you." I spoke with emotion, and her eyes grew suddenly moist.

"It is too much to believe all this," she said, "but it is very delightful to hear you say it. What I did was very little. I was very much distressed for you, I know. Father never thinks anything ought to astonish us when it can be explained scientifically, as I suppose this long sleep of yours can be, but even to fancy myself in your place makes my head swim. I know that I could not have borne it at all."

"That would depend," I replied, "on whether an angel came to support you with her sympathy in the crisis of your condition, as one came to me." If my face at all expressed the feelings I had a right to have toward this sweet and lovely young girl, who had played so angelic a rôle toward me, its expression must have been very worshipful just then. The expression or the words, or both together, caused her now to drop her eyes with a charming blush.

"For the matter of that," I said, "if your experience has not been as startling as mine, it must have been rather overwhelming to see a man belonging to a strange century, and apparently a hundred years dead, raised to life."

"It seemed indeed strange beyond any describing at first," she said, "but when we began to put ourselves in your place, and realize[d] how much stranger it must seem to you, I fancy we forgot our own feelings a good deal, at least I know I did. It seemed then not so much astounding as interesting and touching beyond anything ever heard of before."

"But does it not come over you as astounding to sit at table with me, seeing who I am?"

"You must remember that you do not seem so strange to us as we must to you," she answered. "We belong to a future of which you could not form an idea, a generation of which you knew nothing until you saw us. But you belong to a generation of which our forefathers were a part. We know all about it; the names of many of its members are household words with us. We have made a study of your ways of living and thinking; nothing you say or do surprises us, while we say and do nothing which does not seem strange to you. So you see, Mr. West, that if you feel that you can, in time, get accustomed to us, you must not be surprised that from the first we have scarcely found you strange at all."

"I had not thought of it in that way," I replied. "There is indeed much in what you say. One can look back a thousand years easier than forward fifty. A century is not so very long a retrospect. I might have known your great-grand-parents. Possibly I did. Did they live in Boston?"

"I believe so."

"You are not sure, then?"

"Yes," she replied. "Now I think, they did."

"I had a very large circle of acquaintances in the city," I said. "It is not unlikely that I knew or knew of some of them. Perhaps I may have known them well. Wouldn't it be interesting if I should chance to be able to tell you all about your great-grandfather, for instance?"

"Very interesting."

"Do you know your genealogy well enough to tell me who your forbears were in the Boston of my day?"

"Oh, yes."

"Perhaps, then, you will some time tell me what some of their names were."

She was engrossed in arranging a troublesome spray of green, and did not reply at once. Steps upon the stairway indicated that the other members of the family were descending.

"Perhaps, some time," she said.

After breakfast, Dr. Leete suggested taking me to inspect the central warehouse and observe actually in operation the machinery of distribution, which Edith had described to me. As we walked away from the house I said, "It is now several days that I have been living in your household on a most extraordinary footing, or rather on none at all. I have not spoken of this aspect of my position before because there were so many other aspects yet more extraordinary. But now that I am beginning a little to feel my feet under me, and to realize that, however I came here, I am here, and must make the best of it, I must speak to you on this point."

"As for your being a guest in my house," replied Dr. Leete, "I pray you not to begin to be uneasy on that point, for I mean to keep you a long time yet. With all your modesty, you can but realize that such a guest as yourself is an acquisition not willingly to be parted with."

"Thanks, doctor," I said. "It would be absurd, certainly, for me to affect any oversensitiveness about accepting the temporary hospitality of one to whom I owe it that I am not still awaiting the end of the world in a living tomb. But if I am to be a permanent citizen of this century I must have some standing in it. Now, in my time a person more or less entering the world, however he got in, would not be noticed in the unorganized throng of men, and might make a place for himself anywhere he chose if he were strong enough. But nowadays everybody is a part of a system with a distinct place and function. I am outside the system, and don't see how I can get in; there seems no way to get in, except to be born in or to come in as an emigrant from some other system."

Dr. Leete laughed heartily.

"I admit," he said, "that our system is defective in lacking provision for cases like yours, but you see nobody anticipated additions to the world except by the usual process. You need, however, have no fear that we shall be unable to provide both a place and occupation for you in due time. You have as yet been brought in contact only with the members of my family, but you must not suppose that I have kept your secret. On the contrary, your case, even before your resuscitation, and vastly more since, has excited the profoundest interest in the nation. In view of your precarious nervous condition, it was thought best that I should take exclusive charge of you at first, and that you should, through me and my family, receive some general idea of the sort of world you had come back to before you began to make the acquaintance generally of its inhabitants. As to finding a function for you in society, there was no hesitation as to what that would be. Few of us have it in our power to confer so great a service on the nation as you will be able to when you leave my roof, which, however, you must not think of doing for a good time yet."

"What can I possibly do?" I asked. "Perhaps you imagine I have some trade, or art, or special skill. I assure you I have none whatever. I never earned a dollar in my life, or did an hour's work. I am strong, and might be a common laborer, but nothing more."

"If that were the most efficient service you were able to render the nation, you would find that avocation considered quite as respectable as any other," replied Dr. Leete; "but you can do something else better. You are easily the master of all our historians on questions relating to the social condition of the latter part of the nineteenth century, to us one of the most absorbingly interesting periods of history; and whenever in due time you have sufficiently familiarized yourself with our institutions, and are willing to teach us something concerning those of your day, you will find an historical lectureship in one of our colleges awaiting you."

"Very good! very good indeed," I said, much relieved by so practical a suggestion on a point which had begun to trouble me.

"If your people are really so much interested in the nineteenth century, there will indeed be an occupation ready made for me. I don't think there is anything else that I could possibly earn my salt at, but I certainly may claim without conceit to have some special qualifications for such a post as you describe."

CHAPTER XVII.

I FOUND the processes at the warehouse quite as interesting as Edith had described them, and became even enthusiastic over the truly remarkable illustration which is seen there of the prodigiously multiplied efficiency which perfect organization can give to labor. It is like a gigantic mill, into the hopper of which goods are being constantly poured by the train-load and ship-load, to issue at the other end in packages of pounds and ounces, yards and inches, pints and gallons, corresponding to the infinitely complex personal needs of half a million people. Dr. Leete, with the assistance of data furnished by me as to the way goods were sold in my day, figured out some astounding results in the way of the economies effected by the modern system.

As we set out homeward, I said: "After what I have seen today, together with what you have told me, and what I learned under Miss Leete's tutelage at the sample store, I have a tolerably clear idea of your system of distribution, and how it enables you to dispense with a circulating medium. But I should like very much to know something more about your system of production. You have told me in general how your industrial army is levied and organized, but who directs its efforts? What supreme authority determines what shall be done in every department, so that enough of everything is produced and yet no labor wasted? It seems to me that this must be a wonderfully complex and difficult function, requiring very unusual endowments."

"Does it indeed seem so to you?" responded Dr. Leete. "I assure you that it is nothing of the kind, but on the other hand so simple, and depending on principles so obvious and easily applied, that the functionaries at Washington to whom it is trusted require to be nothing more than men of fair abilities to discharge it to the entire satisfaction of the nation. The machine which they direct is indeed a vast one, but so logical in its principles and direct and simple in its workings, that it all but runs itself; and nobody but a fool could derange it, as I think you will agree after a few words of explanation. Since you already have a pretty good idea of the working of the distributive system, let us begin at that end. Even in your day statisticians were able to tell you the number of yards of cotton, velvet, woolen, the number of barrels of flour, potatoes, butter, number of pairs of shoes, hats, and umbrellas annually consumed by the nation. Owing to the fact that production was in private hands, and that there was no way of getting statistics of actual distribution, these figures were not exact, but they were nearly so. Now that every pin which is given out from a national warehouse is recorded, of course the figures of consumption for any week, month, or year, in the possession of the department of distribution at the end of that period, are precise. On these figures, allowing for tendencies to increase or decrease and for any special causes likely to affect demand, the estimates, say for a year ahead, are based. These estimates, with a proper margin for security, having been accepted by the general administration, the responsibility of the distributive department ceases until the goods are delivered to it. I speak of the estimates being furnished for an entire year ahead, but in reality they cover that much time only in case of the great staples for which the demand can be calculated on as steady. In the great majority of smaller industries for the product of which popular taste fluctuates, and novelty is frequently required, production is kept barely ahead of consumption, the distributive department furnishing frequent estimates based on the weekly state of demand.

"Now the entire field of productive and constructive industry is divided into ten great departments, each representing a group of allied industries, each particular industry being in turn represented by a subordinate bureau, which has a complete record of the plant and force under its control, of the present product, and means of increasing it. The estimates of the distributive department, after adoption by the administration, are sent as mandates to the ten great departments, which allot them to the subordinate bureaus representing the particular industries, and these set the men at work. Each bureau is responsible for the task given it, and this responsibility is enforced by departmental oversight and that of the administration; nor does the distributive department accept the product without its own inspection; while even if in the hands of the consumer an article turns out unfit, the system enables the fault to be traced back to the original workman. The production of the commodities for actual public consumption does not, of course, require by any means all the national force of workers. After the necessary contingents have been detailed for the various industries, the amount of labor left for other employment is expended in creating fixed capital, such as buildings, machinery, engineering works, and so forth."

"One point occurs to me," I said, "on which I should think there might be dissatisfaction. Where there is no opportunity for private enterprise, how is there any assurance that the claims of small minorities of the people to have articles produced, for which there is no wide demand, will be respected? An official decree at any moment may deprive them of the means of gratifying some special taste, merely because the majority does not share it."

"That would be tyranny indeed," replied Dr. Leete, "and you may be very sure that it does not happen with us, to whom liberty is as dear as equality or fraternity. As you come to know our system better, you will see that our officials are in fact, and not merely in name, the agents and servants of the people. The administration has no power to stop the production of any commodity for which there continues to be a demand. Suppose the demand for any article declines to such a point that its production becomes very costly. The price has to be raised in proportion, of course, but as long as the consumer cares to pay it, the production goes on. Again, suppose, an article not before produced is demanded. If the administration doubts the reality of the demand, a popular petition guaranteeing a certain basis of consumption compels it to produce the desired article. A government, or a majority, which should undertake to tell the people, or a minority, what they were to eat, drink, or wear, as I believe governments in America did in your day, would be regarded as a curious anachronism indeed. Possibly you had reasons for tolerating these infringements of personal independence, but we should not think them endurable. I am glad you raised this point, for it has given me a chance to show you how much more direct and efficient is the control over production exercised by the individual citizen now than it was in your day, when what you called private initiative prevailed, though it should have been called capitalist initiative, for the average private citizen had little enough share in it."

"You speak of raising the price of costly articles," I said. "How can prices be regulated in a country where there is no competition between buyers or sellers?"

"Just as they were with you," replied Dr. Leete. "You think that needs explaining," he added, as I looked incredulous, "but the explanation need not be long; the cost of the labor which produced it was recognized as the legitimate basis of the price of an article in your day, and so it is in ours. In your day, it was the difference in wages that made the difference in the cost of labor; now it is the relative number of hours constituting a day's work in different trades, the maintenance of the worker being equal in all cases. The cost of a man's work in a trade so difficult that in order to attract volunteers the hours have to be fixed at four a day is twice as great as that in a trade where the men work eight hours. The result as to the cost of labor, you see, is just the same as if the man working four hours were paid, under your system, twice the wages the other gets. This calculation applied to the labor employed in the various processes of a manufactured article gives its price relatively to other articles. Besides the cost of production and transportation, the factor of scarcity affects the prices of some commodities. As regards the great staples of life, of which an abundance can always be secured, scarcity is eliminated as a factor. There is always a large surplus kept on hand from which any fluctuations of demand or supply can be corrected, even in most cases of bad crops. The prices of the staples grow less year by year, but rarely, if ever, rise. There are, however, certain classes of articles permanently, and others temporarily, unequal to the demand, as, for example, fresh fish or dairy products in the latter category, and the products of high skill and rare materials in the other. All that can be done here is to equalize the inconvenience of the scarcity. This is done by temporarily raising the price if the scarcity be temporary, or fixing it high if it be permanent. High prices in your day meant restriction of the articles affected to the rich, but nowadays, when the means of all are the same, the effect is only that those to whom the articles seem most desirable are the ones who purchase them. Of course the nation, as any other caterer for the public needs must be, is frequently left with small lots of goods on its hands by changes in taste, unseasonable weather, and various other causes. These it has to dispose of at a sacrifice just as merchants often did in your day, charging up the loss to the expenses of the business. Owing, however, to the vast body of consumers to which such lots can be simultaneously offered, there is rarely any difficulty in getting rid of them at trifling loss. I have given you now some general notion of our system of production, as well as distribution. Do you find it as complex as you expected?"

I admitted that nothing could be much simpler.

"I am sure," said Dr. Leete, "that it is within the truth to say that the head of one of the myriad private businesses of your day, who had to maintain sleepless vigilance against the fluctuations of the market, the machinations of his rivals, and the failure of his debtors, had a far more trying task than the group of men at Washington who nowadays direct the industries of the entire nation. All this merely shows, my dear fellow, how much easier it is to do things the right way than the wrong. It is easier for a general up in a balloon, with perfect survey of the field, to manoeuvre a million men to victory than for a sergeant to manage a platoon in a thicket."

"The general of this army, including the flower of the manhood of the nation, must be the foremost man in the country, really greater even than the President of the United States," I said.

"He is the President of the United States," replied Dr. Leete, "or rather the most important function of the presidency is the headship of the industrial army."

"How is he chosen?" I asked

"I explained to you before," replied Dr. Leete, "when I was describing the force of the motive of emulation among all grades of the industrial army, that the line of promotion for the meritorious lies through three grades to the officer's grade, and thence up through the lieutenancies to the captaincy or foremanship, and superintendency or colonel's rank. Next, with an intervening grade in some of the larger trades, comes the general of the guild, under whose immediate control all the operations of the trade are conducted. This officer is at the head of the national bureau representing his trade, and is responsible for its work to the administration. The general of his guild holds a splendid position, and one which amply satisfies the ambition of most men, but above his rank, which may be compared—to follow the military analogies familiar to you—to that of a general of division or major-general, is that of the chiefs of the ten great departments, or groups of allied trades. The chiefs of these ten grand divisions of the industrial army may be compared to your commanders of army corps, or lieutenant-generals, each having from a dozen to a score of generals of separate guilds reporting to him. Above these ten great officers, who form his council, is the general-in-chief, who is the President of the United States.

"The general-in-chief of the industrial army must have passed through all the grades below him, from the common laborers up. Let us see how he rises. As I have told you, it is simply by the excellence of his record as a worker that one rises through the grades of the privates and becomes a candidate for a lieutenancy. Through the lieutenancies he rises to the colonelcy, or superintendent's position, by appointment from above, strictly limited to the candidates of the best records. The general of the guild appoints to the ranks under him, but he himself is not appointed, but chosen by suffrage."

"By suffrage!" I exclaimed. "Is not that ruinous to the discipline of the guild, by tempting the candidates to intrigue for the support of the workers under them?"

"So it would be, no doubt," replied Dr. Leete, "if the workers had any suffrage to exercise, or anything to say about the choice. But they have nothing. Just here comes in a peculiarity of our system. The general of the guild is chosen from among the superintendents by vote of the honorary members of the guild, that is, of those who have served their time in the guild and received their discharge. As you know, at the age of forty-five we are mustered out of the army of industry, and have the residue of life for the pursuit of our own improvement or recreation. Of course, however, the associations of our active lifetime retain a powerful hold on us. The companionships we formed then remain our companionships till the end of life. We always continue honorary members of our former guilds, and retain the keenest and most jealous interest in their welfare and repute in the hands of the following generation. In the clubs maintained by the honorary members of the several guilds, in which we meet socially, there are no topics of conversation so common as those which relate to these matters, and the young aspirants for guild leadership who can pass the criticism of us old fellows are likely to be pretty well equipped. Recognizing this fact, the nation entrusts to the honorary members of each guild the election of its general, and I venture to claim that no previous form of society could have developed a body of electors so ideally adapted to their office, as regards absolute impartiality, knowledge of the special qualifications and record of candidates, solicitude for the best result, and complete absence of self-interest.[1]

"Each of the ten lieutenant-generals or heads of departments is himself elected from among the generals of the guilds grouped as a department, by vote of the honorary members of the guilds thus grouped. Of course there is a tendency on the part of each guild to vote for its own general, but no guild of any group has nearly enough votes to elect a man not supported by most of the others. I assure you that these elections are exceedingly lively."

"The President, I suppose, is selected from among the ten heads of the great departments," I suggested.

"Precisely, but the heads of departments are not eligible to the presidency till they have been a certain number of years out of office. It is rarely that a man passes through all the grades to the headship of a department much before he is forty, and at the end of a five years' term he is usually forty-five. If more, he still serves through his term, and if less, he is nevertheless discharged from the industrial army at its termination. It would not do for him to return to the ranks. The interval before he is a candidate for the

---

[1]   Bellamy invokes the ancient tradition of deferring to the "elders" of a community for wisdom and decisions. During his lifetime the social movement was toward universal suffrage, but this did not happen until the U.S. Constitution was amended in 1920 to give women the vote.

presidency is intended to give time for him to recognize fully that he has returned into the general mass of the nation, and is identified with it rather than with the industrial army. Moreover, it is expected that he will employ this period in studying the general condition of the army, instead of that of the special group of guilds of which he was the head. From among the former heads of departments who may be eligible at the time, the President is elected by vote of all the men of the nation who are not connected with the industrial army."

"The army is not allowed to vote for President?"

"Certainly not. That would be perilous to its discipline, which it is the business of the President to maintain as the representative of the nation at large. His right hand for this purpose is the inspectorate, a highly important department of our system; to the inspectorate come all complaints or information as to defects in goods, insolence or inefficiency of officials, or dereliction of any sort in the public service. The inspectorate, however, does not wait for complaints. Not only is it on the alert to catch and sift every rumor of a fault in the service, but it is its business, by systematic and constant oversight and inspection of every branch of the army, to find out what is going wrong before anybody else does.[1] The President is usually not far from fifty when elected, and serves five years, forming an honorable exception to the rule of retirement at forty-five. At the end of his term of office, a national Congress is called to receive his report and approve or condemn it. If it is approved, Congress usually elects him to represent the nation for five years more in the international council. Congress, I should also say, passes on the reports of the outgoing heads of departments, and a disapproval renders any one of them ineligible for President. But it is rare, indeed, that the nation has occasion for other sentiments than those of gratitude toward its high officers. As to their ability, to have risen from the ranks, by tests so various and severe, to their positions, is proof in itself of extraordinary qualities, while as to faithfulness, our social system leaves them absolutely without any other motive than that of

---

[1] The passage about the Inspectorate, "His right hand..." to "anybody else does," was added in the second edition. It tends to emphasize the state's power to monitor individuals.

winning the esteem of their fellow citizens. Corruption is impossible in a society where there is neither poverty to be bribed nor wealth to bribe, while as to demagoguery or intrigue for office, the conditions of promotion render them out of the question."

"One point I do not quite understand," I said. "Are the members of the liberal professions eligible to the presidency? and if so, how are they ranked with those who pursue the industries proper?"

"They have no ranking with them," replied Dr. Leete. "The members of the technical professions, such as engineers and architects, have a ranking with the constructive guilds; but the members of the liberal professions, the doctors and teachers, as well as the artists and men of letters who obtain remissions of industrial service, do not belong to the industrial army. On this ground they vote for the President, but are not eligible to his office. One of its main duties being the control and discipline of the industrial army, it is essential that the President should have passed through all its grades to understand his business."

"That is reasonable," I said; "but if the doctors and teachers do not know enough of industry to be President, neither, I should think, can the President know enough of medicine and education to control those departments."

"No more does he," was the reply. "Except in the general way that he is responsible for the enforcement of the laws as to all classes, the President has nothing to do with the faculties of medicine and education, which are controlled by boards of regents of their own, in which the President is ex-officio chairman, and has the casting vote. These regents, who, of course, are responsible to Congress, are chosen by the honorary members of the guilds of education and medicine, the retired teachers and doctors of the country."

"Do you know," I said, "the method of electing officials by votes of the retired members of the guilds is nothing more than the application on a national scale of the plan of government by alumni, which we used to a slight extent occasionally in the management of our higher educational institutions."

"Did you, indeed?" exclaimed Dr. Leete, with animation. "That is quite new to me, and I fancy will be to most of us, and of much interest as well. There has been great discussion as to the germ of the idea, and we fancied that there was for once something new under the sun. Well! well! In your higher educational institutions! that is interesting indeed. You must tell me more of that."

"Truly, there is very little more to tell than I have told already," I replied. "If we had the germ of your idea, it was but as a germ."

CHAPTER XVIII.

THAT evening I sat up for some time after the ladies had retired, talking with Dr. Leete about the effect of the plan of exempting men from further service to the nation after the age of forty-five, a point brought up by his account of the part taken by the retired citizens in the government.

"At forty-five," said I, "a man still has ten years of good manual labor in him, and twice ten years of good intellectual service. To be superannuated at that age and laid on the shelf must be regarded rather as a hardship than a favor by men of energetic dispositions."

"My dear Mr. West," exclaimed Dr. Leete, beaming upon me, "you cannot have any idea of the piquancy your nineteenth century ideas have for us of this day, the rare quaintness of their effect. Know, O child of another race and yet the same, that the labor we have to render as our part in securing for the nation the means of a comfortable physical existence is by no means regarded as the most important, the most interesting, or the most dignified employment of our powers. We look upon it as a necessary duty to be discharged before we can fully devote ourselves to the higher exercise of our faculties, the intellectual and spiritual enjoyments and pursuits which alone mean life. Everything possible is indeed done by the just distribution of burdens, and by all manner of special attractions and incentives to relieve our labor of irksomeness, and, except in a comparative sense, it is not usually irksome, and is often inspiring. But it is not our labor, but the higher and larger activities which the performance of our task will leave us free to enter upon, that are considered the main business of existence.

"Of course not all, nor the majority, have those scientific, artistic, literary, or scholarly interests which make leisure the one thing valuable to their possessors. Many look upon the last half of life chiefly as a period for enjoyment of other sorts; for travel, for social relaxation in the company of their life-time friends; a time for the cultivation of all manner of personal idiosyncrasies and special tastes, and the pursuit of every imaginable form of recreation; in a word, a time for the leisurely and unperturbed appreciation of the good things of the world which they have helped to create. But whatever the differences between our individual tastes as to the use we shall put our leisure to, we all agree in looking forward to the date of our discharge as the time when we shall first enter upon the full enjoyment of our birth-right, the period when we shall first really attain our majority and become enfranchised from discipline and control, with the fee of our lives vested in ourselves. As eager boys in your day anticipated twenty-one, so men nowadays look forward to forty-five. At twenty-one we become men, but at forty-five we renew youth. Middle age and what you would have called old age are considered, rather than youth, the enviable time of life. Thanks to the better conditions of existence nowadays, and above all the freedom of every one from care, old age approaches many years later and has an aspect far more benign than in past times. Persons of average constitution usually live to eighty-five or ninety, and at forty-five we are physically and mentally younger, I fancy, than you were at thirty-five. It is a strange reflection that at forty-five, when we are just entering upon the most enjoyable period of life, you already began to think of growing old and to look backward. With you it was the forenoon, with us it is the afternoon, which is the brighter half of life."

After this I remember that our talk branched into the subject of popular sports and recreations at the present time as compared with those of the nineteenth century.

"In one respect," said Dr. Leete, "there is a marked difference. The professional sportsmen, which were such a curious feature of your day, we have nothing answering to, nor are the prizes for which our athletes contend money prizes, as with you. Our contests are always for glory only. The generous rivalry existing between the various guilds, and the loyalty of each worker to his own, afford a constant stimulation to all sorts of games and matches by sea and land, in which the young men take scarcely more interest than the honorary guildsmen who have served their time. The guild yacht races off Marblehead take place next week, and you will be able to judge for yourself of the popular enthusiasm which such events nowadays call out as compared with your day. The demand for '*panem et circenses*' preferred by the Roman populace is recognized nowadays as a wholly reasonable one.[1] If bread is the first necessity of life, recreation is a close second, and the nation caters for both. Americans of the nineteenth century were as unfortunate in lacking an adequate provision for the one sort of need as for the other. Even if the people of that period had enjoyed larger leisure, they would, I fancy, have often been at a loss how to pass it agreeably. We are never in that predicament."

CHAPTER XIX.

IN the course of an early morning constitutional I visited Charlestown. Among the changes, too numerous to attempt to indicate, which mark the lapse of a century in that quarter, I particularly noted the total disappearance of the old state prison.

"That went before my day, but I remember hearing about it," said Dr. Leete, when I alluded to the fact at the breakfast table. "We have no jails nowadays. All cases of atavism are treated in the hospitals."

"Of atavism!" I exclaimed, staring.

"Why, yes," replied Dr. Leete. "The idea of dealing punitively with those unfortunates was given up at least fifty years ago, and I think more."

"I don't quite understand you," I said. "Atavism in my day was a word applied to the cases of persons in whom some trait of a remote ancestor recurred in a noticeable manner. Am I to understand that crime is nowadays looked upon as the recurrence of an ancestral trait?"

---

[1]   From Juvenal's *Satires*: according to this view the Romans wanted bread and circuses (food and violent spectacles), although Bellamy here re-interprets the demand as a positive one.

"I beg your pardon," said Dr. Leete with a smile half humorous, half deprecating, "but since you have so explicitly asked the question, I am forced to say that the fact is precisely that."

After what I had already learned of the moral contrasts between the nineteenth and the twentieth centuries, it was doubtless absurd in me to begin to develop sensitiveness on the subject, and probably if Dr. Leete had not spoken with that apologetic air and Mrs. Leete and Edith shown a corresponding embarrassment, I should not have flushed, as I was conscious I did.

"I was not in much danger of being vain of my generation before," I said; "but, really"—

"This is your generation, Mr. West," interposed Edith. "It is the one in which you are living, you know, and it is only because we are alive now that we call it ours."

"Thank you. I will try to think of it so," I said, and as my eyes met hers their expression quite cured my senseless sensitiveness. "After all," I said, with a laugh, "I was brought up a Calvinist, and ought not to be startled to hear crime spoken of as an ancestral trait."[1]

"In point of fact," said Dr. Leete, "our use of the word is no reflection at all on your generation, if, begging Edith's pardon, we may call it yours, so far as seeming to imply that we think ourselves, apart from our circumstances, better than you were. In your day fully nineteen twentieths of the crime, using the word broadly to include all sorts of misdemeanors, resulted from the inequality in the possessions of individuals; want tempted the poor, lust of greater gains, or the desire to preserve former gains, tempted the well-to-do. Directly or indirectly, the desire for money, which then meant every good thing, was the motive of all this crime, the taproot of a

---

[1]   A reference to the doctrines of John Calvin (1509-64), especially the idea that human beings are naturally depraved. One of the best known features of Calvinism is the idea of "predestination," meaning that from the beginning of time some are among the "elect" and are destined to be saved while others are destined to be damned. The sense that he alone of his generation had been saved to see the new world is what sends Julian into his depression in Chapter XXVII, especially the idea that he is unworthy of this "election." An interesting twist on Calvinist gloominess is the doctrine that those who are successful economically must enjoy God's favour and be saved—see R.H. Tawney's *Religion and the Rise of Capitalism*, published in numerous editions since 1926.

vast poison growth, which the machinery of law, courts, and police could barely prevent from choking your civilization outright. When we made the nation the sole trustee of the wealth of the people, and guaranteed to all abundant maintenance, on the one hand abolishing want, and on the other checking the accumulation of riches, we cut this root, and the poison tree that overshadowed your society withered, like Jonah's gourd, in a day.[1] As for the comparatively small class of violent crimes against persons, unconnected with any idea of gain, they were almost wholly confined, even in your day, to the ignorant and bestial; and in these days, when education and good manners are not the monopoly of a few, but universal, such atrocities are scarcely ever heard of. You now see why the word "atavism" is used for crime. It is because nearly all forms of crime known to you are motiveless now, and when they appear can only be explained as the outcropping of ancestral traits. You used to call persons who stole, evidently without any rational motive, kleptomaniacs, and when the case was clear deemed it absurd to punish them as thieves. Your attitude toward the genuine kleptomaniac is precisely ours toward the victim of atavism, an attitude of compassion and firm but gentle restraint."

"Your courts must have an easy time of it," I observed. "With no private property to speak of, no disputes between citizens over business relations, no real estate to divide or debts to collect, there must be absolutely no civil business at all for them; and with no offenses against property, and mighty few of any sort to provide criminal cases, I should think you might almost do without judges and lawyers altogether."

"We do without the lawyers, certainly," was Dr. Leete's reply. "It would not seem reasonable to us, in a case where the only interest of the nation is to find out the truth, that persons should take part in the proceedings who had an acknowledged motive to color it."

"But who defends the accused?"

"If he is a criminal he needs no defense, for he pleads guilty in most instances," replied Dr. Leete. "The plea of the accused is

---

[1] Jonah's gourd: in Jonah 4:6 the plant that overshadows Jonah is a gift from God which shelters him, rather than a poison tree.

not a mere formality with us, as with you. It is usually the end of the case."

"You don't mean that the man who pleads not guilty is thereupon discharged?"

"No, I do not mean that. He is not accused on light grounds, and if he denies his guilt, must still be tried. But trials are few, for in most cases the guilty man pleads guilty. When he makes a false plea and is clearly proved guilty, his penalty is doubled. Falsehood is, however, so despised among us that few offenders would lie to save themselves."

"That is the most astounding thing you have yet told me," I exclaimed. "If lying has gone out of fashion, this is indeed the 'new heavens and the new earth wherein dwelleth righteousness,' which the prophet foretold."[1]

"Such is, in fact, the belief of some persons nowadays," was the doctor's answer. "They hold that we have entered upon the millennium, and the theory from their point of view does not lack plausibility. But as to your astonishment at finding that the world has outgrown lying, there is really no ground for it. Falsehood, even in your day, was not common between gentlemen and ladies, social equals. The lie of fear was the refuge of cowardice, and the lie of fraud the device of the cheat. The inequalities of men and the lust of acquisition offered a constant premium on lying at that time. Yet even then, the man who neither feared another nor desired to defraud him scorned falsehood. Because we are now all social equals, and no man either has anything to fear from another or can gain anything by deceiving him, the contempt of falsehood is so universal that it is rarely, as I told you, that even a criminal in other respects will be found willing to lie. When, however, a plea of not guilty is returned, the judge appoints two colleagues to state the opposite sides of the case. How far these men are from being like your hired advocates and prosecutors, determined to acquit or convict, may appear from the fact that unless both agree that the verdict found is just, the case is tried over, while anything like bias in the tone of either of the judges stating the case would be a shocking scandal."

---

[1] The prophecy of Isaiah 65:17 is echoed in the Book of Revelation 21:1.

"Do I understand," I said, "that it is a judge who states each side of the case as well as a judge who hears it?"

"Certainly. The judges take turns in serving on the bench and at the bar, and are expected to maintain the judicial temper equally whether in stating or deciding a case. The system is indeed in effect that of trial by three judges occupying different points of view as to the case. When they agree upon a verdict, we believe it to be as near to absolute truth as men well can come."

"You have given up the jury system, then?"

"It was well enough as a corrective in the days of hired advocates, and a bench sometimes venal, and often with a tenure that made it dependent, but is needless now. No conceivable motive but justice could actuate our judges."

"How are these magistrates selected?"

"They are an honorable exception to the rule which discharges all men from service at the age of forty-five. The President of the nation appoints the necessary judges year by year from the class reaching that age. The number appointed is, of course, exceedingly few, and the honor so high that it is held an offset to the additional term of service which follows, and though a judge's appointment may be declined, it rarely is. The term is five years, without eligibility to reappointment. The members of the Supreme Court, which is the guardian of the constitution, are selected from among the lower judges. When a vacancy in that court occurs, those of the lower judges, whose terms expire that year, select, as their last official act, the one of their colleagues left on the bench whom they deem fittest to fill it."

"There being no legal profession to serve as a school for judges," I said, "they must, of course, come directly from the law school to the bench."

"We have no such things as law schools," replied the doctor, smiling. "The law as a special science is obsolete. It was a system of casuistry which the elaborate artificiality of the old order of society absolutely required to interpret it, but only a few of the plainest and simplest legal maxims have any application to the existing state of the world. Everything touching the relations of men to one another is now simpler, beyond any comparison, than in your day. We should have no sort of use for the hairsplitting experts who presided and argued in your courts. You must not imagine, however, that we have any disrespect for those ancient worthies because we have no use for them. On the contrary, we entertain an unfeigned respect, amounting almost to awe, for the men who alone understood and were able to expound the interminable complexity of the rights of property, and the relations of commercial and personal dependence involved in your system. What, indeed, could possibly give a more powerful impression of the intricacy and artificiality of that system than the fact that it was necessary to set apart from other pursuits the cream of the intellect of every generation, in order to provide a body of pundits able to make it even vaguely intelligible to those whose fates it determined. The treatises of your great lawyers, the works of Blackstone and Chitty, of Story and Parsons, stand in our museums, side by side with the tomes of Duns Scotus and his fellow scholastics, as curious monuments of intellectual subtlety devoted to subjects equally remote from the interests of modern men.[1] Our judges are simply widely informed, judicious, and discreet men of ripe years.

"I should not fail to speak of one important function of the minor judges," added Dr. Leete. "This is to adjudicate all cases where a private of the industrial army makes a complaint of unfairness against an officer. All such questions are heard and settled without appeal by a single judge, three judges being required only in graver cases.[2] The efficiency of industry requires the strictest discipline in the army of labor, but the claim of the workman to just and considerate treatment is backed by the whole power of the nation. The officer commands and the private obeys, but no officer is so high that he would dare display an overbearing manner toward a workman of the lowest class. As for churl-

---

[1] Duns Scotus (1266-1308) became a symbol for overly subtle theology, and the word dunce comes from his name and the place of his birth in Scotland. Thus, the reference to famous legal theorists is not complimentary. However, Scotus was a serious philosopher associated with the idea that God fashioned each creature with a unique "haecceity" or particularity or "this-ness." (*Cambridge Dictionary of Philosophy* 2nd edition, 1999).

[2] In the first edition there is a passage allowing the individual to transfer if he does not like his foreman. This flexibility was removed in the second edition.

ishness or rudeness by an official of any sort, in his relations to the public, not one among minor offenses is more sure of a prompt penalty than this. Not only justice but civility is enforced by our judges in all sorts of intercourse. No value of service is accepted as a setoff to boorish or offensive manners."

It occurred to me, as Dr. Leete was speaking, that in all his talk I had heard much of the nation and nothing of the state governments. Had the organization of the nation as an industrial unit done away with the states? I asked.

"Necessarily," he replied. "The state governments would have interfered with the control and discipline of the industrial army, which, of course [was] required to be central and uniform. Even if the state governments had not become inconvenient for other reasons, they were rendered superfluous by the prodigious simplification in the task of government since your day. Almost the sole function of the administration now is that of directing the industries of the country. Most of the purposes for which governments formerly existed no longer remain to be subserved. We have no army or navy, and no military organization. We have no departments of state or treasury, no excise or revenue services, no taxes or tax collectors. The only function proper of government, as known to you, which still remains, is the judiciary and police system. I have already explained to you how simple is our judicial system as compared with your huge and complex machine. Of course the same absence of crime and temptation to it, which make the duties of judges so light, reduces the number and duties of the police to a minimum."

"But with no state legislatures, and Congress meeting only once in five years, how do you get your legislation done?"

"We have no legislation," replied Dr. Leete, "that is, next to none. It is rarely that Congress, even when it meets, considers any new laws of consequence, and then it only has power to commend them to the following Congress, lest anything be done hastily. If you will consider a moment, Mr. West, you will see that we have nothing to make laws about. The fundamental principles on which our society is founded settle for all time the strifes and misunderstandings which in your day called for legislation.

"Fully ninety-nine hundredths of the laws of that time

concerned the definition and protection of private property and the relations of buyers and sellers. There is neither private property, beyond personal belongings, now, nor buying and selling, and therefore the occasion of nearly all the legislation formerly necessary has passed away. Formerly, society was a pyramid poised on its apex. All the gravitations of human nature were constantly tending to topple it over, and it could be maintained upright, or rather upwrong (if you will pardon the feeble witticism), by an elaborate system of constantly renewed props and buttresses and guyropes in the form of laws. A central Congress and forty state legislatures, turning out some twenty thousand laws a year, could not make new props fast enough to take the place of those which were constantly breaking down or becoming ineffectual through some shifting of the strain. Now society rests on its base, and is in as little need of artificial supports as the everlasting hills."

"But you have at least municipal governments besides the one central authority?"

"Certainly, and they have important and extensive functions in looking out for the public comfort and recreation, and the improvement and embellishment of the villages and cities."

"But having no control over the labor of their people, or means of hiring it, how can they do anything?"

"Every town or city is conceded the right to retain, for its own public works, a certain proportion of the quota of labor its citizens contribute to the nation. This proportion, being assigned it as so much credit, can be applied in any way desired."

CHAPTER XX.

THAT afternoon Edith casually inquired if I had yet revisited the underground chamber in the garden in which I had been found.

"Not yet," I replied. "To be frank, I have shrunk thus far from doing so, lest the visit might revive old associations rather too strongly for my mental equilibrium."

"Ah, yes!" she said, "I can imagine that you have done well to stay away. I ought to have thought of that."

"No," I said, "I am glad you spoke of it. The danger, if there was any, existed only during the first day or two. Thanks to you, chiefly and always, I feel my footing now so firm in this new world, that if you will go with me to keep the ghosts off, I should really like to visit the place this afternoon."

Edith demurred at first, but, finding that I was in earnest, consented to accompany me. The rampart of earth thrown up from the excavation was visible among the trees from the house, and a few steps brought us to the spot. All remained as it was at the point when work was interrupted by the discovery of the tenant of the chamber, save that the door had been opened and the slab from the roof replaced. Descending the sloping sides of the excavation, we went in at the door and stood within the dimly-lighted room.

Everything was just as I had beheld it last on that evening one hundred and thirteen years previous, just before closing my eyes for that long sleep. I stood for some time silently looking about me. I saw that my companion was furtively regarding me with an expression of awed and sympathetic curiosity. I put out my hand to her and she placed hers in it, the soft fingers responding with a reassuring pressure to my clasp. Finally she whispered, "Had we not better go out now? You must not try yourself too far. Oh, how strange it must be to you!"

"On the contrary," I replied, "it does not seem strange; that is the strangest part of it."

"Not strange?" she echoed.

"Even so," I replied. "The emotions with which you evidently credit me, and which I anticipated would attend this visit, I simply do not feel. I realize all that these surroundings suggest, but without the agitation I expected. You can't be nearly as much surprised at this as I am myself. Ever since that terrible morning when you came to my help, I have tried to avoid thinking of my former life, just as I have avoided coming here, for fear of the agitating effects. I am for all the world like a man who has permitted an injured limb to lie motionless under the impression that it is exquisitely sensitive, and on trying to move it finds that it is paralyzed."

"Do you mean your memory is gone?"

"Not at all. I remember everything connected with my former life, but with a total lack of keen sensation. I remember it for clearness as if it had been but a day since then, but my feelings about what I remember are as faint as if to my consciousness, as well as in fact, a hundred years had intervened. Perhaps it is possible to explain this, too. The effect of change in surroundings is like that of lapse of time in making the past seem remote. When I first woke from that trance, my former life appeared as yesterday, but now, since I have learned to know my new surroundings, and to realize the prodigious changes that have transformed the world, I no longer find it hard, but very easy, to realize that I have slept a century. Can you conceive of such a thing as living a hundred years in four days? It really seems to me that I have done just that, and that it is this experience which has given so remote and unreal an appearance to my former life. Can you see how such a thing might be?"

"I can conceive it," replied Edith, meditatively, "and I think we ought all to be thankful that it is so, for it will save you much suffering, I am sure."

"Imagine," I said, in an effort to explain, as much to myself as to her, the strangeness of my mental condition, "that a man first heard of a bereavement many, many years, half a lifetime perhaps, after the event occurred. I fancy his feeling would be perhaps something as mine is. When I think of my friends in the world of that former day, and the sorrow they must have felt for me, it is with a pensive pity, rather than keen anguish, as of a sorrow long, long ago ended."

"You have told us nothing yet of your friends," said Edith. "Had you many to mourn you?"

"Thank God, I had very few relatives, none nearer than cousins," I replied. "But there was one, not a relative, but dearer to me than any kin of blood. She had your name. She was to have been my wife soon. Ah me!"

"Ah me!" sighed the Edith by my side. "Think of the heartache she must have had."

Something in the deep feeling of this gentle girl touched a chord in my benumbed heart. My eyes, before so dry, were flooded with the tears that had till now refused to come. When I had regained my composure, I saw that she too had been weeping freely.

"God bless your tender heart," I said. "Would you like to see her picture?"

A small locket with Edith Bartlett's picture, secured about my neck with a gold chain, had lain upon my breast all through that long sleep, and removing this I opened and gave it to my companion. She took it with eagerness, and after poring long over the sweet face, touched the picture with her lips.

"I know that she was good and lovely enough to well deserve your tears," she said; "but remember her heartache was over long ago, and she has been in heaven for nearly a century."

It was indeed so. Whatever her sorrow had once been, for nearly a century she had ceased to weep, and, my sudden passion spent, my own tears dried away. I had loved her very dearly in my other life, but it was a hundred years ago! I do not know but some may find in this confession evidence of lack of feeling, but I think, perhaps, that none can have had an experience sufficiently like mine to enable them to judge me. As we were about to leave the chamber, my eye rested upon the great iron safe which stood in one corner. Calling my companion's attention to it, I said:—

"This was my strong room as well as my sleeping room. In the safe yonder are several thousand dollars in gold, and any amount of securities. If I had known when I went to sleep that night just how long my nap would be, I should still have thought that the gold was a safe provision for my needs in any country or any century, however distant. That a time would ever come when it would lose its purchasing power,[1] I should have considered the wildest of fancies. Nevertheless, here I wake up to find myself among a people of whom a cartload of gold will not procure a loaf of bread."

As might be expected, I did not succeed in impressing Edith that there was anything remarkable in this fact. "Why in the world should it?" she merely asked.

---

[1] The OED suggests "purchasing power" was a recent expression in Bellamy's day (1876) but the notion that gold is useless for buying things is an old idea. In More's *Utopia* gold and silver are used for making prison chains and chamber pots.

CHAPTER XXI.

IT had been suggested by Dr. Leete that we should devote the next morning to an inspection of the schools and colleges of the city, with some attempt on his own part at an explanation of the educational system of the twentieth century.

"You will see," said he, as we set out after breakfast, "many very important differences between our methods of education and yours, but the main difference is that nowadays all persons equally have those opportunities of higher education which in your day only an infinitesimal portion of the population enjoyed. We should think we had gained nothing worth speaking of, in equalizing the physical comfort of men, without this educational equality."

"The cost must be very great," I said.

"If it took half the revenue of the nation, nobody would grudge it," replied Dr. Leete, "nor even if it took it all save a bare pittance. But in truth the expense of educating ten thousand youth is not ten nor five times that of educating one thousand. The principle which makes all operations on a large scale proportionally cheaper than on a small scale holds as to education also."

"College education was terribly expensive in my day," said I.

"If I have not been misinformed by our historians," Dr. Leete answered, "it was not college education but college dissipation and extravagance which cost so highly. The actual expense of your colleges appears to have been very low, and would have been far lower if their patronage had been greater. The higher education nowadays is as cheap as the lower, as all grades of teachers, like all other workers, receive the same support. We have simply added to the common school system of compulsory education, in vogue in Massachusetts a hundred years ago, a half dozen higher grades, carrying the youth to the age of twenty-one and giving him what you used to call the education of a gentleman, instead of turning him loose at fourteen or fifteen with no mental equipment beyond reading, writing, and the multiplication table."

"Setting aside the actual cost of these additional years of education," I replied, "we should not have thought we could afford the loss of time from industrial pursuits. Boys of the poorer classes usually went to work at sixteen or younger, and knew their trade at twenty."

"We should not concede you any gain even in material product by that plan," Dr. Leete replied. "The greater efficiency which education gives to all sorts of labor, except the rudest, makes up in a short period for the time lost in acquiring it."

"We should also have been afraid," said I, "that a high education, while it adapted men to the professions, would set them against manual labor of all sorts."

"That was the effect of high education in your day, I have read," replied the doctor; "and it was no wonder, for manual labor meant association with a rude, coarse, and ignorant class of people. There is no such class now. It was inevitable that such a feeling should exist then, for the further reason that all men receiving a high education were understood to be destined for the professions or for wealthy leisure, and such an education in one neither rich nor professional was a proof of disappointed aspirations, an evidence of failure, a badge of inferiority rather than superiority. Nowadays, of course, when the highest education is deemed necessary to fit a man merely to live, without any reference to the sort of work he may do, its possession conveys no such implication."

"After all," I remarked, "no amount of education can cure natural dullness or make up for original mental deficiencies. Unless the average natural mental capacity of men is much above its level in my day, a high education must be pretty nearly thrown away on a large element of the population. We used to hold that a certain amount of susceptibility to educational influences is required to make a mind worth cultivating, just as a certain natural fertility in soil is required if it is to repay tilling."

"Ah," said Dr. Leete, "I am glad you used that illustration, for it is just the one I would have chosen to set forth the modern view of education. You say that land so poor that the product will not repay the labor of tilling is not cultivated. Nevertheless, much land that does not begin to repay tilling by its product was cultivated in your day and is in ours. I refer to gardens, parks, lawns, and, in general, to pieces of land so situated that, were they left to grow up to weeds and briers, they would be eyesores and inconveniences to all about. They are therefore tilled, and though their product is little, there is yet no land that, in a wider sense, better repays cultivation. So it is with the men and women with whom we mingle in the relations of society, whose voices are always in our ears, whose behavior in innumerable ways affects our enjoyment, —who are, in fact, as much conditions of our lives as the air we breathe, or any of the physical elements on which we depend. If, indeed, we could not afford to educate everybody, we should choose the coarsest and dullest by nature, rather than the brightest, to receive what education we could give. The naturally refined and intellectual can better dispense with aids to culture than those less fortunate in natural endowments.

"To borrow a phrase which was often used in your day, we should not consider life worth living if we had to be surrounded by a population of ignorant, boorish, coarse, wholly uncultivated men and women, as was the plight of the few educated in your day. Is a man satisfied, merely because he is perfumed himself, to mingle with a malodorous crowd? Could he take more than a very limited satisfaction, even in a palatial apartment, if the windows on all four sides opened into stable yards? And yet just that was the situation of those considered most fortunate as to culture and refinement in your day. I know that the poor and ignorant envied the rich and cultured then; but to us the latter, living as they did, surrounded by squalor and brutishness, seem little better off than the former. The cultured man in your age was like one up to the neck in a nauseous bog solacing himself with a smelling bottle. You see, perhaps, now, how we look at this question of universal high education. No single thing is so important to every man as to have for neighbors intelligent, companionable persons. There is nothing, therefore, which the nation can do for him that will enhance so much his own happiness as to educate his neighbors. When it fails to do so, the value of his own education to him is reduced by half, and many of the tastes he has cultivated are made positive sources of pain.

"To educate some to the highest degree, and leave the mass wholly uncultivated, as you did, made the gap between them almost like that between different natural species, which have no means of communication. What could be more inhuman than this consequence of a partial enjoyment of education! Its universal and equal enjoyment leaves, indeed, the differences between men as to natural endowments as marked as in a state of nature, but the level of the lowest is vastly raised. Brutishness is eliminated. All have some inkling of the humanities, some appreciation of the things of the mind, and an admiration for the still higher culture they have fallen short of. They have become capable of receiving and imparting, in various degrees, but all in some measure, the pleasures and inspirations of a refined social life. The cultured society of the nineteenth century,—what did it consist of but here and there a few microscopic oases in a vast, unbroken wilderness? The proportion of individuals capable of intellectual sympathies or refined intercourse, to the mass of their contemporaries, used to be so infinitesimal as to be in any broad view of humanity scarcely worth mentioning. One generation of the world today represents a greater volume of intellectual life than any five centuries ever did before.

"There is still another point I should mention in stating the grounds on which nothing less than the universality of the best education could now be tolerated," continued Dr. Leete, "and that is, the interest of the coming generation in having educated parents. To put the matter in a nutshell, there are three main grounds on which our educational system rests: first, the right of every man to the completest education the nation can give him on his own account, as necessary to his enjoyment of himself; second, the right of his fellow-citizens to have him educated, as necessary to their enjoyment of his society; third, the right of the unborn to be guaranteed an intelligent and refined parentage."

I shall not describe in detail what I saw in the schools that day. Having taken but slight interest in educational matters in my former life, I could offer few comparisons of interest. Next to the fact of the universality of the higher as well as the lower education, I was most struck with the prominence given to physical culture, and the fact that proficiency in athletic feats and games as well as in scholarship had a place in the rating of the youth.

"The faculty of education," Dr. Leete explained, "is held to the same responsibility for the bodies as for the minds of its charges. The highest possible physical, as well as mental, development of every one is the double object of a curriculum which lasts from the age of six to that of twenty-one."

The magnificent health of the young people in the schools impressed me strongly. My previous observations, not only of the notable personal endowments of the family of my host, but of the people I had seen in my walks abroad, had already suggested the idea that there must have been something like a general improvement in the physical standard of the race since my day, and now, as I compared these stalwart young men and fresh, vigorous maidens with the young people I had seen in the schools of the nineteenth century, I was moved to impart my thought to Dr. Leete. He listened with great interest to what I said.

"Your testimony on this point," he declared, "is invaluable. We believe that there has been such an improvement as you speak of, but of course it could only be a matter of theory with us. It is an incident of your unique position that you alone in the world of today can speak with authority on this point. Your opinion, when you state it publicly, will, I assure you, make a profound sensation. For the rest it would be strange, certainly, if the race did not show an improvement. In your day, riches debauched one class with idleness of mind and body, while poverty sapped the vitality of the masses by overwork, bad food, and pestilent homes. The labor required of children, and the burdens laid on women, enfeebled the very springs of life. Instead of these maleficent circumstances, all now enjoy the most favorable conditions of physical life; the young are carefully nurtured and studiously cared for; the labor which is required of all is limited to the period of greatest bodily vigor, and is never excessive; care for one's self and one's family, anxiety as to livelihood, the strain of a ceaseless battle for life—all these influences, which once did so much to wreck the minds and bodies of men and women, are known no more. Certainly, an improvement of the species ought to follow such a change. In certain specific respects we know, indeed, that the improvement has taken place. Insanity, for instance, which in the nineteenth century was so terribly common a product of your insane mode of life, has almost disappeared, with its alternative, suicide."

CHAPTER XXII.

WE had made an appointment to meet the ladies at the dining-hall for dinner, after which, having some engagement, they left us sitting at table there, discussing our wine and cigars with a multitude of other matters.

"Doctor," said I, in the course of our talk, "morally speaking, your social system is one which I should be insensate not to admire in comparison with any previously in vogue in the world, and especially with that of my own most unhappy century. If I were to fall into a mesmeric sleep tonight as lasting as that other, and meanwhile the course of time were to take a turn backward instead of forward, and I were to wake up again in the nineteenth century, when I had told my friends what I had seen, they would every one admit that your world was a paradise of order, equity, and felicity. But they were a very practical people, my contemporaries, and after expressing their admiration for the moral beauty and material splendor of the system, they would presently begin to cipher and ask how you got the money to make everybody so happy; for certainly, to support the whole nation at a rate of comfort, and even luxury, such as I see around me, must involve vastly greater wealth than the nation produced in my day. Now, while I could explain to them pretty nearly everything else of the main features of your system, I should quite fail to answer this question, and failing there, they would tell me, for they were very close cipherers, that I had been dreaming; nor would they ever believe anything else. In my day, I know that the total annual product of the nation, although it might have been divided with absolute equality, would not have come to more than three or four hundred dollars per head, not very much more than enough to supply the necessities of life with few or any of its comforts. How is it that you have so much more?"

"That is a very pertinent question, Mr. West," replied Dr. Leete, "and I should not blame your friends, in the case you supposed, if they declared your story all moonshine, failing a satisfactory reply to it. It is a question which I cannot answer exhaustively at any one sitting, and as for the exact statistics to bear out my general statements, I shall have to refer you for them to books in my library, but it would certainly be a pity to leave you to be put to confusion by your old acquaintances, in case of the contingency you speak of, for lack of a few suggestions.

"Let us begin with a number of small items wherein we economize wealth as compared with you. We have no national, state, county, or municipal debts, or payments on their account. We have no sort of military or naval expenditures for men or materials, no army, navy, or militia. We have no revenue service, no swarm of tax assessors and collectors. As regards our judiciary, police, sheriffs, and jailers, the force which Massachusetts alone kept on foot in your day far more than suffices for the nation now. We have no criminal class preying upon the wealth of society as you had. The number of persons, more or less absolutely lost to the working force through physical disability, of the lame, sick, and debilitated, which constituted such a burden on the able-bodied in your day, now that all live under conditions of health and comfort, has shrunk to scarcely perceptible proportions, and with every generation is becoming more completely eliminated.

"Another item wherein we save is the disuse of money and the thousand occupations connected with financial operations of all sorts, whereby an army of men was formerly taken away from useful employments. Also consider that the waste of the very rich in your day on inordinate personal luxury has ceased, though, indeed, this item might easily be over-estimated. Again, consider that there are no idlers now, rich or poor,—no drones.

"A very important cause of former poverty was the vast waste of labor and materials which resulted from domestic washing and cooking, and the performing separately of innumerable other tasks to which we apply the cooperative plan.

"A larger economy than any of these—yes, of all together— is effected by the organization of our distributing system, by which the work done once by the merchants, traders, storekeepers, with their various grades of jobbers, wholesalers, retailers, agents, commercial travelers, and middlemen of all sorts, with an excessive waste of energy in needless transportation and interminable handlings, is performed by one-tenth the number of hands and an unnecessary turn of not one wheel. Something of what our distributing system is like you know. Our statisticians calculate that one eightieth part of our workers suffices for all the processes of distribution which in your day required one eighth of the population, so much being withdrawn from the force engaged in productive labor."

"I begin to see," I said, "where you get your greater wealth."

"I beg your pardon," replied Dr. Leete, "but you scarcely do as yet. The economies I have mentioned thus far, in the aggregate, considering the labor they would save directly and indirectly through saving of material, might possibly be equivalent to the addition to your annual production of wealth of one-half its former total. These items are, however, scarcely worth mentioning in comparison with other prodigious wastes, now saved, which resulted inevitably from leaving the industries of the nation to private enterprise. However great the economies your contemporaries might have devised in the consumption of products, and however marvelous the progress of mechanical invention, they could never have raised themselves out of the slough of poverty so long as they held to that system.

"No mode more wasteful for utilizing human energy could be devised, and for the credit of the human intellect it should be remembered that the system never was devised, but was merely a survival from the rude ages when the lack of social organization made any sort of cooperation impossible."

"I will readily admit," I said, "that our industrial system was ethically very bad, but as a mere wealth-making machine, apart from moral aspects, it seemed to us admirable."

"As I said," responded the doctor, "the subject is too large to discuss at length now, but if you are really interested to know the main criticisms which we moderns make on your industrial system as compared with our own, I can touch briefly on some of them.

"The wastes which resulted from leaving the conduct of industry to irresponsible individuals, wholly without mutual understanding or concert, were mainly four; first, the waste by mistaken undertakings; second, the waste from the competition and mutual hostility of those engaged in industry; third, the waste by periodical gluts and crises, with the consequent interruptions of industry; fourth, the waste from idle capital and labor, at all times. Any one of these four great leaks, were all the others stopped, would suffice to make the difference between wealth and poverty on the part of a nation.

"Take the waste by mistaken undertakings, to begin with. In your day the production and distribution of commodities being without concert or organization, there was no means of knowing just what demand there was for any class of products, or what was the rate of supply. Therefore, any enterprise by a private capitalist was always a doubtful experiment. The projector having no general view of the field of industry and consumption, such as our government has, could never be sure either what the people wanted, or what arrangements other capitalists were making to supply them. In view of this, we are not surprised to learn that the chances were considered several to one in favor of the failure of any given business enterprise, and that it was common for persons who at last succeeded in making a hit to have failed repeatedly. If a shoemaker, for every pair of shoes he succeeded in completing, spoiled the leather of four or five pair, besides losing the time spent on them, he would stand about the same chance of getting rich as your contemporaries did with their system of private enterprise, and its average of four or five failures to one success.

"The next of the great wastes was that from competition. The field of industry was a battlefield as wide as the world, in which the workers wasted, in assailing one another, energies which, if expended in concerted effort, as to-day, would have enriched all. As for mercy or quarter in this warfare, there was absolutely no suggestion of it. To deliberately enter a field of business and destroy the enterprises of those who had occupied it previously, in order to plant one's own enterprise on their ruins, was an achievement which never failed to command popular admiration. Nor is there any stretch of fancy in comparing this sort of struggle with actual warfare, so far as concerns the mental agony and physical suffering which attended the struggle, and the misery which overwhelmed the defeated and those dependent on them. Now nothing about your age is, at first sight, more astounding to a man of modern times than the fact that men engaged in the same industry, instead of fraternizing as comrades and co-laborers to a common end, should have regarded each other as rivals and enemies to be throttled and overthrown. This certainly seems like sheer madness, a scene from bedlam. But more closely regarded, it is seen to be no such thing. Your contemporaries, with their mutual throat-cutting, knew very well what they were at. The producers of the nineteenth century were not, like ours, working together for the maintenance of the community, but each solely for his own maintenance at the expense of the community. If, in working to this end, he at the same time increased the aggregate wealth, that was merely incidental. It was just as feasible and as common to increase one's private hoard by practices injurious to the general welfare. One's worst enemies were necessarily those of his own trade, for, under your plan of making private profit the motive of production, a scarcity of the article he produced was what each particular producer desired. It was for his interest that no more of it should be produced than he himself could produce. To secure this consummation as far as circumstances permitted, by killing off and discouraging those engaged in his line of industry, was his constant effort. When he had killed off all he could, his policy was to combine with those he could not kill, and convert their mutual warfare into a warfare upon the public at large by cornering the market, as I believe you used to call it, and putting up prices to the highest point people would stand before going without the goods. The day dream of the nineteenth century producer was to gain absolute control of the supply of some neces- sity of life, so that he might keep the public at the verge of starva- tion, and always command famine prices for what he supplied. This, Mr. West, is what was called in the nineteenth century a system of production. I will leave it to you if it does not seem, in some of its aspects, a great deal more like a system for preventing production. Some time when we have plenty of leisure I am going to ask you to sit down with me and try to make me comprehend, as I never yet could, though I have studied the matter a great deal, how such shrewd fellows as your contemporaries appear to have been in many respects ever came to entrust the business of providing for the community to a class whose interest it was to starve it. I assure you that the wonder with us is, not that the world did not get rich under such a system, but that it did not perish outright from want. This wonder increases as we go on to consider some of the other prodigious wastes that characterized it.

"Apart from the waste of labor and capital by misdirected industry, and that from the constant bloodletting of your industrial warfare, your system was liable to periodical convulsions, overwhelming alike the wise and unwise, the successful cutthroat as well as his victim. I refer to the business crises at intervals of five to ten years, which wrecked the industries of the nation, prostrating all weak enterprises and crippling the strongest, and were followed by long periods, often of many years, of so-called dull times, during which the capitalists slowly regathered their dissipated strength while the laboring classes starved and rioted. Then would ensue another brief season of prosperity, followed in turn by another crisis and the ensuing years of exhaustion. As commerce developed, making the nations mutually dependent, these crises became worldwide, while the obstinacy of the ensuing state of collapse increased with the area affected by the convulsions, and the consequent lack of rallying centres. In proportion as the industries of the world multiplied and became complex, and the volume of capital involved was increased, these business cataclysms became more frequent, till, in the latter part of the nineteenth century, there were two years of bad times to one of good, and the system of industry, never before so extended or so imposing, seemed in danger of collapsing by its own weight. After endless discussions, your economists appear by that time to have settled down to the despairing conclusion that there was no more possibility of preventing or controlling these crises than if they had been drouths or hurricanes. It only remained to endure them as necessary evils, and when they had passed over to build up again the shattered structure of industry, as dwellers in an earthquake country keep on rebuilding their cities on the same site.

"So far as considering the causes of the trouble inherent in their industrial system, your contemporaries were certainly correct. They were in its very basis, and must needs become more and more maleficent as the business fabric grew in size and complexity. One of these causes was the lack of any common control of the different industries, and the consequent impossibility of their orderly and coördinate development. It inevitably resulted from this lack that they were continually getting out of step with one another and out of relation with the demand.

"Of the latter there was no criterion such as organized distribution gives us, and the first notice that it had been exceeded in any group of industries was a crash of prices, bankruptcy of producers, stoppage of production, reduction of wages, or discharge of workmen. This process was constantly going on in many industries, even in what were called good times, but a crisis took place only when the industries affected were extensive. The markets then were glutted with goods, of which nobody wanted beyond a sufficiency at any price. The wages and profits of those making the glutted classes of goods being reduced or wholly stopped, their purchasing power as consumers of other classes of goods, of which there was no natural glut, was taken away, and, as a consequence, goods of which there was no natural glut became artificially glutted, till their prices also were broken down, and their makers thrown out of work and deprived of income. The crisis was by this time fairly under way, and nothing could check it till a nation's ransom had been wasted.

"A cause, also inherent in your system, which often produced and always terribly aggravated crises, was the machinery of money and credit. Money was essential when production was in many private hands, and buying and selling was necessary to secure what one wanted. It was, however, open to the obvious objection of substituting for food, clothing, and other things a merely conventional representative of them. The confusion of mind which this favored, between goods and their representative, led the way to the credit system and its prodigious illusions. Already accustomed to accept money for commodities, the people next accepted promises for money, and ceased to look at all behind the representative for the thing represented. Money was a sign of real commodities, but credit was but the sign of a sign. There was a natural limit to gold and silver, that is, money proper, but none to credit, and the result was that the volume of credit, that is, the promises of money, ceased to bear any ascertainable proportion to the money, still less to the commodities, actually in existence. Under such a system, frequent and periodical crises were necessitated by a law as absolute as that which brings to the ground a structure overhanging its centre of gravity. It was one of your fictions that the government and the banks authorized by it alone issued money; but everybody who gave a dollar's credit issued money to that extent, which was as good as any to swell the circulation till the next crises. The great extension of the credit system was a characteristic of the latter part of the nineteenth century, and accounts largely for the almost incessant business crises which marked that period. Perilous as credit was, you could not dispense with its use, for, lacking any national or other public organization of the capital of the country, it was the only means you had for concentrating and directing it upon industrial enterprises. It was in this way a most potent means for exaggerating the chief peril of the private enterprise system of industry by enabling particular industries to absorb disproportionate amounts of the disposable capital of the country, and thus prepare disaster. Business enterprises were always vastly in debt for advances of credit, both to one another and to the banks and capitalists, and the prompt withdrawal of this credit at the first sign of a crisis was generally the precipitating cause of it.

"It was the misfortune of your contemporaries that they had to cement their business fabric with a material which an accident might at any moment turn into an explosive. They were in the plight of a man building a house with dynamite for mortar, for credit can be compared with nothing else.

"If you would see how needless were these convulsions of business which I have been speaking of, and how entirely they resulted from leaving industry to private and unorganized management, just consider the working of our system. Overproduction in special lines, which was the great hobgoblin of your day, is impossible now, for by the connection between distribution and production supply is geared to demand like an engine to the governor which regulates its speed. Even suppose by an error of judgment an excessive production of some commodity. The consequent slackening or cessation of production in that line throws nobody out of employment. The suspended workers are at once found occupation in some other department of the vast workshop and lose only the time spent in changing, while, as for the glut, the business of the nation is large enough to carry any amount of product manufactured in excess of demand till the latter overtakes it. In such a case of overproduction, as I have supposed, there is not with us, as with you, any complex machinery to get out of order and magnify a thousand times the original mistake. Of course, having not even money, we still less have credit. All estimates deal directly with the real things, the flour, iron, wood, wool, and labor, of which money and credit were for you the very misleading representatives. In our calculations of cost there can be no mistakes. Out of the annual product the amount necessary for the support of the people is taken, and the requisite labor to produce the next year's consumption provided for. The residue of the material and labor represents what can be safely expended in improvements. If the crops are bad, the surplus for that year is less than usual, that is all. Except for slight occasional effects of such natural causes, there are no fluctuations of business; the material prosperity of the nation flows on uninterruptedly from generation to generation, like an ever broadening and deepening river.

"Your business crises, Mr. West," continued the doctor, "like either of the great wastes I mentioned before, were enough, alone, to have kept your noses to the grindstone forever; but I have still to speak of one other great cause of your poverty, and that was the idleness of a great part of your capital and labor. With us it is the business of the administration to keep in constant employment every ounce of available capital and labor in the country. In your day there was no general control of either capital or labor, and a large part of both failed to find employment. 'Capital,' you used to say, 'is naturally timid,' and it would certainly have been reckless if it had not been timid in an epoch when there was a large preponderance of probability that any particular business venture would end in failure. There was no time when, if security could have been guaranteed it, the amount of capital devoted to productive industry could not have been greatly increased. The proportion of it so employed underwent constant extraordinary fluctuations, according to the greater or less feeling of uncertainty as to the stability of the industrial situation, so that the output of the national industries greatly varied in different years. But for the same reason that the amount of capital employed at times of special insecurity was far less than at times of somewhat greater security, a very large proportion was never employed at all, because the hazard of business was always very great in the best of times.

"It should be also noted that the great amount of capital always seeking employment where tolerable safety could be insured terribly embittered the competition between capitalists when a promising opening presented itself. The idleness of capital, the result of its timidity, of course meant the idleness of labor in corresponding degree. Moreover, every change in the adjustments of business, every slightest alteration in the condition of commerce or manufactures, not to speak of the innumerable business failures that took place yearly, even in the best of times, were constantly throwing a multitude of men out of employment for periods of weeks or months, or even years. A great number of these seekers after employment were constantly traversing the country, becoming in time professional vagabonds, then criminals.[1] 'Give us work!' was the cry of an army of the unemployed at nearly all seasons, and in seasons of dullness in business this army swelled to a host so vast and desperate as to threaten the stability of the government. Could there conceivably be a more conclusive demonstration of the imbecility of the system of private enterprise as a method for enriching a nation than the fact that, in an age of such general poverty and want of everything, capitalists had to throttle one another to find a safe chance to invest their capital and workmen rioted and burned because they could find no work to do?

"Now, Mr. West," continued Dr. Leete, "I want you to bear in mind that these points of which I have been speaking indicate only negatively the advantages of the national organization of industry by showing certain fatal defects and prodigious imbecilities of the systems of private enterprise which are not found in it. These alone, you must admit, would pretty well explain why the nation is so much richer than in your day. But the larger half of our advantage over you, the positive side of it, I have yet barely spoken of. Supposing the system of private enterprise in industry were without any of the great leaks I have mentioned; that there were no waste on account of misdirected effort growing out of mistakes as to the demand, and inability to command a general view of the industrial field. Suppose, also, there were no neutralizing and duplicating of effort from competition. Suppose, also, there were no

---

[1] That society actually produces criminals and then punishes them is one of the abuses described in Book I of More's *Utopia*.

waste from business panics and crises through bankruptcy and long interruptions of industry, and also none from the idleness of capital and labor. Supposing these evils, which are essential to the conduct of industry by capital in private hands, could all be miraculously prevented, and the system yet retained; even then the superiority of the results attained by the modern industrial system of national control would remain overwhelming.

"You used to have some pretty large textile manufacturing establishments, even in your day, although not comparable with ours. No doubt you have visited these great mills in your time, covering acres of ground, employing thousands of hands, and combining under one roof, under one control, the hundred distinct processes between, say, the cotton bale and the bale of glossy calicoes. You have admired the vast economy of labor as of mechanical force resulting from the perfect interworking with the rest of every wheel and every hand. No doubt you have reflected how much less the same force of workers employed in that factory would accomplish if they were scattered, each man working independently. Would you think it an exaggeration to say that the utmost product of those workers, working thus apart, however amicable their relations might be, was increased not merely by a percentage, but many fold, when their efforts were organized under one control? Well now, Mr. West, the organization of the industry of the nation under a single control, so that all its processes interlock, has multiplied the total product over the utmost that could be done under the former system, even leaving out of account the four great wastes mentioned, in the same proportion that the product of those millworkers was increased by cooperation. The effectiveness of the working force of a nation, under the myriad-headed leadership of private capital, even if the leaders were not mutual enemies, as compared with that which it attains under a single head, may be likened to the military efficiency of a mob, or a horde of barbarians with a thousand petty chiefs, as compared with that of a disciplined army under one general—such a fighting machine, for example, as the German army in the time of Von Moltke."[1]

---

[1] Helmuth Von Moltke (1800–91) was Chief of the Prussian and German General Staff from 1858–88.

"After what you have told me," I said, "I do not so much wonder that the nation is richer now than then, but that you are not all Croesuses."[1]

"Well," replied Dr. Leete, "we are pretty well off. The rate at which we live is as luxurious as we could wish. The rivalry of ostentation, which in your day led to extravagance in no way conducive to comfort, finds no place, of course, in a society of people absolutely equal in resources, and our ambition stops at the surroundings which minister to the enjoyment of life. We might, indeed, have much larger incomes, individually, if we chose so to use the surplus of our product, but we prefer to expend it upon public works and pleasures in which all share, upon public halls and buildings, art galleries, bridges, statuary, means of transit, and the conveniences of our cities, great musical and theatrical exhibitions, and in providing on a vast scale for the recreations of the people. You have not begun to see how we live yet, Mr. West. At home we have comfort, but the splendor of our life is, on its social side, that which we share with our fellows. When you know more of it you will see where the money goes, as you used to say, and I think you will agree that we do well so to expend it."

"I suppose," observed Dr. Leete, as we strolled homeward from the dining hall, "that no reflection would have cut the men of your wealth-worshiping century more keenly than the suggestion that they did not know how to make money. Nevertheless, that is just the verdict history has passed on them. Their system of unorganized and antagonistic industries was as absurd economically as it was morally abominable. Selfishness was their only science, and in industrial production selfishness is suicide. Competition, which is the instinct of selfishness, is another word for dissipation of energy, while combination is the secret of efficient production; and not till the idea of increasing the individual hoard gives place to the idea of increasing the common stock can industrial combination be realized, and the acquisition of wealth really begin. Even if the principle of share and share alike for all men were not the only humane and rational basis for a society, we should still enforce it as economically expedient,

---

[1] Croesus was a very rich and powerful King of Lydia, 560–546 BC.

seeing that until the disintegrating influence of self-seeking is suppressed no true concert of industry is possible."

CHAPTER XXIII.

THAT evening, as I sat with Edith in the music room, listening to some pieces in the programme of that day which had attracted my notice, I took advantage of an interval in the music to say, "I have a question to ask you which I fear is rather indiscreet."

"I am quite sure it is not that," she replied, encouragingly.

"I am in the position of an eavesdropper," I continued, "who, having overheard a little of a matter not intended for him, though seeming to concern him, has the impudence to come to the speaker for the rest."

"An eavesdropper!" she repeated, looking puzzled.

"Yes," I said, "but an excusable one, as I think you will admit."

"This is very mysterious," she replied.

"Yes," said I, "so mysterious that often I have doubted whether I really overheard at all what I am going to ask you about, or only dreamed it. I want you to tell me. The matter is this: When I was coming out of that sleep of a century, the first impression of which I was conscious was of voices talking around me, voices that afterwards I recognized as your father's, your mother's, and your own. First, I remember your father's voice saying, 'He is going to open his eyes. He had better see but one person at first.' Then you said, if I did not dream it all, 'Promise me, then, that you will not tell him.' Your father seemed to hesitate about promising, but you insisted, and your mother interposing, he finally promised, and when I opened my eyes I saw only him."

I had been quite serious when I said that I was not sure that I had not dreamed the conversation I fancied I had overheard, so incomprehensible was it that these people should know anything of me, a contemporary of their great-grand-parents, which I did not know myself. But when I saw the effect of my words upon Edith, I knew that it was no dream, but another mystery, and a more puzzling one than any I had before encountered. For from the moment that the drift of my question became apparent, she showed indications of the most acute embarrassment. Her eyes, always so frank and direct in expression, had dropped in a panic before mine, while her face crimsoned from neck to forehead.

"Pardon me," I said, as soon as I had recovered from bewilderment at the extraordinary effect of my words. "It seems, then, that I was not dreaming. There is some secret, something about me, which you are withholding from me. Really, doesn't it seem a little hard that a person in my position should not be given all the information possible concerning himself?"

"It does not concern you—that is, not directly. It is not about you—exactly," she replied, scarcely audibly.

"But it concerns me in some way," I persisted. "It must be something that would interest me."

"I don't know even that," she replied, venturing a momentary glance at my face, furiously blushing, and yet with a quaint smile flickering about her lips which betrayed a certain perception of humor in the situation despite its embarrassment,—"I am not sure that it would even interest you."

"Your father would have told me," I insisted, with an accent of reproach. "It was you who forbade him. He thought I ought to know."

She did not reply. She was so entirely charming in her confusion that I was now prompted, as much by the desire to prolong the situation as by my original curiosity, to importune her further.

"Am I never to know? Will you never tell me?" I said.

"It depends," she answered, after a long pause.

"On what?" I persisted.

"Ah, you ask too much," she replied. Then, raising to mine a face which inscrutable eyes, flushed cheeks, and smiling lips combined to render perfectly bewitching, she added, "What should you think if I said that it depended on—yourself?"

"On myself?" I echoed. "How can that possibly be?"

"Mr. West, we are losing some charming music," was her only reply to this, and turning to the telephone, at a touch of her finger she set the air to swaying to the rhythm of an adagio. After that she took good care that the music should leave no opportunity for conversation. She kept her face averted from me, and pretended to be absorbed in the airs, but that it was a mere pretense the crimson tide standing at flood in her cheeks sufficiently betrayed.

When at length she suggested that I might have heard all I cared to, for that time, and we rose to leave the room, she came straight up to me and said, without raising her eyes, "Mr. West, you say I have been good to you. I have not been particularly so, but if you think I have, I want you to promise me that you will not try again to make me tell you this thing you have asked tonight, and that you will not try to find it out from any one else, my father or mother, for instance."

To such an appeal there was but one reply possible. "Forgive me for distressing you. Of course I will promise," I said. "I would never have asked you if I had fancied it could distress you. But do you blame me for being curious?"

"I do not blame you at all."

"And some time," I added, "if I do not tease you, you may tell me of your own accord. May I not hope so?"

"Perhaps," she murmured.

"Only perhaps?"

Looking up, she read my face with a quick, deep glance. "Yes," she said, "I think I may tell you—some time;" and so our conversation ended, for she gave me no chance to say anything more.

That night I don't think even Dr. Pillsbury could have put me to sleep, till toward morning at least. Mysteries had been my accustomed food for days now, but none had before confronted me at once so mysterious and so fascinating as this, the solution of which Edith Leete had forbidden me even to seek. It was a double mystery. How, in the first place, was it conceivable that she should know any secret about me, a stranger from a strange age? In the second place, even if she should know such a secret, how account for the agitating effect which the knowledge of it seemed to have upon her? There are puzzles so difficult that one cannot even get so far as a conjecture as to the solution, and this seemed one of them. I am usually of too practical a turn to waste time on such conundrums; but the difficulty of a riddle embodied in a beautiful young girl does not detract from its fascination. In general, no doubt, maidens' blushes may be safely assumed to tell the same tale to young men in all ages and races, but to give that interpretation to Edith's crimson cheeks would, considering my position and the length of time I had known her, and still more the fact that this mystery dated from before I had known her at all, be a piece of utter fatuity. And yet she was an angel, and I should not have been a young man if reason and common sense had been able quite to banish a roseate tinge from my dreams that night.

CHAPTER XXIV.

IN the morning I went down stairs early in the hope of seeing Edith alone. In this, however, I was disappointed. Not finding her in the house, I sought her in the garden, but she was not there. In the course of my wanderings I visited the underground chamber, and sat down there to rest. Upon the reading table in the chamber several periodicals and newspapers lay, and thinking that Dr. Leete might be interested in glancing over a Boston daily of 1887, I brought one of the papers with me into the house when I came.

At breakfast I met Edith. She blushed as she greeted me, but was perfectly self-possessed. As we sat at table, Dr. Leete amused himself with looking over the paper I had brought in. There was in it, as in all the newspapers of that date, a great deal about the labor troubles, strikes, lockouts, boycotts, the programmes of labor parties, and the wild threats of the anarchists.

"By the way," said I, as the doctor read aloud to us some of these items, "what part did the followers of the red flag take in the establishment of the new order of things? They were making considerable noise the last thing that I knew."

"They had nothing to do with it except to hinder it, of course," replied Dr. Leete. "They did that very effectually while they lasted, for their talk so disgusted people as to deprive the best considered projects for social reform of a hearing. The subsidizing of those fellows was one of the shrewdest moves of the opponents of reform."

"Subsidizing them!" I exclaimed in astonishment.

"Certainly," replied Dr. Leete. "No historical authority nowadays doubts that they were paid by the great monopolies to wave the red flag and talk about burning, sacking, and blowing people up, in order, by alarming the timid, to head off any real reforms. What astonishes me most is that you should have fallen into the trap so unsuspectingly."

"What are your grounds for believing that the red flag party was subsidized?" I inquired.

"Why simply because they must have seen that their course made a thousand enemies of their professed cause to one friend. Not to suppose that they were hired for the work is to credit them with an inconceivable folly.[1] In the United States, of all countries, no party could intelligently expect to carry its point without first winning over to its ideas a majority of the nation, as the national party eventually did."

"The national party!" I exclaimed. "That must have arisen after my day. I suppose it was one of the labor parties."

"Oh no!" replied the doctor. "The labor parties, as such, never could have accomplished anything on a large or permanent scale. For purposes of national scope, their basis as merely class organizations was too narrow. It was not till a rearrangement of the industrial and social system on a higher ethical basis, and for the more efficient production of wealth, was recognized as the interest, not of one class, but equally of all classes, of rich and poor, cultured and ignorant, old and young, weak and strong, men and women, that there was any prospect that it would be achieved. Then the national party arose to carry it out by political methods. It probably took that name because its aim was to nationalize the functions of production and distribution. Indeed, it could not well have had any other name, for its purpose was to realize the idea of the nation with a grandeur and completeness never before conceived, not as an association of men for certain merely political functions affecting their happiness only remotely and

---

[1] I fully admit the difficulty of accounting for the course of the anarchists on any other theory than that they were subsidized by the capitalists, but, at the same time, there is no doubt that the theory is wholly erroneous. It certainly was not held at the time by any one, though it may seem so obvious in the retrospect. [Bellamy's note]

superficially, but as a family, a vital union, a common life, a mighty heaven-touching tree[1] whose leaves are its people, fed from its veins, and feeding it in turn. The most patriotic of all possible parties, it sought to justify patriotism and raise it from an instinct to a rational devotion, by making the native land truly a father land, a father who kept the people alive and was not merely an idol for which they were expected to die."

CHAPTER XXV.

THE personality of Edith Leete had naturally impressed me strongly ever since I had come, in so strange a manner, to be an inmate of her father's house, and it was to be expected that after what had happened the night previous, I should be more than ever preoccupied with thoughts of her. From the first I had been struck with the air of serene frankness and ingenuous directness, more like that of a noble and innocent boy than any girl I had ever known, which characterized her. I was curious to know how far this charming quality might be peculiar to herself, and how far possibly a result of alterations in the social position of women which might have taken place since my time. Finding an opportunity that day, when alone with Dr. Leete, I turned the conversation in that direction.

"I suppose," I said, "that women nowadays, having been relieved of the burden of housework, have no employment but the cultivation of their charms and graces."

"So far as we men are concerned," replied Dr. Leete, "we should consider that they amply paid their way, to use one of your forms of expression, if they confined themselves to that occupation, but you may be very sure that they have quite too much spirit to consent to be mere beneficiaries of society, even as a return for ornamenting it. They did, indeed, welcome their riddance from housework, because that was not only exceptionally wearing in

---

[1] An allusion to Yggdrasil, the world tree of Scandinavian mythology that binds together heaven, earth and hell. *Brewer's Dictionary.*

itself, but also wasteful, in the extreme, of energy, as compared with the coöperative plan; but they accepted relief from that sort of work only that they might contribute in other and more effectual, as well as more agreeable, ways to the common weal. Our women, as well as our men, are members of the industrial army, and leave it only when maternal duties claim them. The result is that most women, at one time or another of their lives, serve industrially some five or ten or fifteen years, while those who have no children fill out the full term."

"A woman does not, then, necessarily leave the industrial service on marriage?" I queried.

"No more than a man," replied the doctor. "Why on earth should she? Married women have no housekeeping responsibilities now, you know, and a husband is not a baby that he should be cared for."

"It was thought one of the most grievous features of our civilization that we required so much toil from women," I said; "but it seems to me you get more out of them than we did."

Dr. Leete laughed. "Indeed we do, just as we do out of our men. Yet the women of this age are very happy, and those of the nineteenth century, unless contemporary references greatly mislead us, were very miserable. The reason that women nowadays are so much more efficient co-laborers with the men, and at the same time are so happy, is that, in regard to their work as well as men's, we follow the principle of providing every one the kind of occupation he or she is best adapted to. Women being inferior in strength to men, and further disqualified industrially in special ways, the kinds of occupation reserved for them, and the conditions under which they pursue them, have reference to these facts. The heavier sorts of work are everywhere reserved for men, the lighter occupations for women. Under no circumstances is a woman permitted to follow any employment not perfectly adapted, both as to kind and degree of labor, to her sex. Moreover, the hours of women's work are considerably shorter than those of men's, more frequent vacations are granted, and the most careful provision is made for rest when needed. The men of this day so well appreciate that they owe to the beauty and grace of women the chief zest of their lives and their main incentive to effort, that they permit them to work at all only because it is fully understood that a certain regular requirement of labor, of a sort adapted to their powers, is well for body and mind, during the period of maximum physical vigor. We believe that the magnificent health which distinguishes our women from those of your day, who seem to have been so generally sickly, is owing largely to the fact that all alike are furnished with healthful and inspiriting occupation."

"I understood you," I said, "that the women workers belong to the army of industry, but how can they be under the same system of ranking and discipline with the men, when the conditions of their labor are so different."

"They are under an entirely different discipline," replied Dr. Leete, "and constitute rather an allied force than an integral part of the army of the men. They have a woman general-in-chief and are under exclusively feminine régime. This general, as also the higher officers, is chosen by the body of women who have passed the time of service, in correspondence with the manner in which the chiefs of the masculine army and the President of the nation are elected. The general of the women's army sits in the cabinet of the President and has a veto on measures respecting women's work, pending appeals to Congress. I should have said, in speaking of the judiciary, that we have women on the bench, appointed by the general of the women, as well as men. Causes in which both parties are women are determined by women judges, and where a man and a woman are parties to a case, a judge of either sex must consent to the verdict."

"Womanhood seems to be organized as a sort of *imperium in imperio* in your system," I said.[1]

"To some extent," Dr. Leete replied; "but the inner *imperium* is one from which you will admit there is not likely to be much danger to the nation. The lack of some such recognition of the distinct individuality of the sexes was one of the innumerable defects of your society. The passional attraction between men and women has too often prevented a perception of the profound differences which make the members of each sex in many things

---

[1] imperium in imperio: authority within the authority.

strange to the other, and capable of sympathy only with their own.[1] It is in giving full play to the differences of sex rather than in seeking to obliterate them, as was apparently the effort of some reformers in your day, that the enjoyment of each by itself and the piquancy which each has for the other, are alike enhanced. In your day there was no career for women except in an unnatural rivalry with men. We have given them a world of their own, with its emulations, ambitions, and careers, and I assure you they are very happy in it. It seems to us that women were more than any other class the victims of your civilization. There is something which, even at this distance of time, penetrates one with pathos in the spectacle of their ennuied, undeveloped lives, stunted at marriage, their narrow horizon, bounded so often, physically, by the four walls of home, and morally by a petty circle of personal interests. I speak now, not of the poorer classes, who were generally worked to death, but also of the well-to-do and rich. From the great sorrows, as well as the petty frets of life, they had no refuge in the breezy outdoor world of human affairs, nor any interests save those of the family. Such an existence would have softened men's brains or driven them mad. All that is changed today. No woman is heard nowadays wishing she were a man, nor parents desiring boy rather than girl children. Our girls are as full of ambition for their careers as our boys. Marriage, when it comes, does not mean incarceration for them, nor does it separate them in any way from the larger interests of society, the bustling life of the world. Only when maternity fills a woman's mind with new interests does she withdraw from the world for a time. Afterwards, and at any time, she may return to her place among her comrades, nor need she ever lose touch with them. Women are a very happy race nowadays, as compared with what they ever were before in the world's history, and their power of giving happiness to men has been of course increased in proportion."

"I should imagine it possible," I said "that the interest which girls take in their careers as members of the industrial army and

---

[1] passional attraction: may be a reference to the theories of Charles Fourier (1772-1837) who described intentional communities called phalansteries where motivation would be based upon passional attractions rather than coercion.

candidates for its distinctions might have an effect to deter them from marriage."

Dr. Leete smiled. "Have no anxiety on that score, Mr. West," he replied. "The Creator took very good care that whatever other modifications the dispositions of men and women might with time take on, their attraction for each other should remain constant. The mere fact that in an age like yours, when the struggle for existence must have left people little time for other thoughts, and the future was so uncertain that to assume parental responsibilities must have often seemed like a criminal risk, there was even then marrying and giving in marriage, should be conclusive on this point. As for love nowadays, one of our authors says that the vacuum left in the minds of men and women by the absence of care for one's livelihood has been entirely taken up by the tender passion. That, however, I beg you to believe, is something of an exaggeration. For the rest, so far is marriage from being an interference with a woman's career, that the higher positions in the feminine army of industry are intrusted only to women who have been both wives and mothers, as they alone fully represent their sex."

"Are credit cards issued to the women just as to the men?"

"Certainly."

"The credits of the women, I suppose, are for smaller sums, owing to the frequent suspension of their labor on account of family responsibilities."

"Smaller!" exclaimed Dr, Leete, "oh, no! The maintenance of all our people is the same. There are no exceptions to that rule, but if any difference were made on account of the interruptions you speak of, it would be by making the woman's credit larger, not smaller. Can you think of any service constituting a stronger claim on the nation's gratitude than bearing and nursing the nation's children? According to our view, none deserve so well of the world as good parents. There is no task so unselfish, so necessarily without return, though the heart is well rewarded, as the nurture of the children who are to make the world for one another when we are gone."

"It would seem to follow, from what you have said, that wives are in no way dependent on their husbands for maintenance."

"Of course they are not," replied Dr. Leete, "nor children on their parents either, that is, for means of support, though of course they are for the offices of affection. The child's labor, when he grows up, will go to increase the common stock, not his parents', who will be dead, and therefore he is properly nurtured out of the common stock. The account of every person, man, woman, and child, you must understand, is always with the nation directly, and never through any intermediary, except, of course, that parents, to a certain extent, act for children as their guardians. You see that it is by virtue of the relation of individuals to the nation, of their membership in it, that they are entitled to, support; and this title is in no way connected with or affected by their relations to other individuals who are fellow members of the nation with them. That any person should be dependent for the means of support upon another would be shocking to the moral sense as well as indefensible on any rational social theory. What would become of personal liberty and dignity under such an arrangement? I am aware that you called yourselves free in the nineteenth century. The meaning of the word could not then, however, have been at all what it is at present, or you certainly would not have applied it to a society of which nearly every member was in a position of galling personal dependence upon others as to the very means of life, the poor upon the rich, or employed upon employer, women upon men, children upon parents. Instead of distributing the product of the nation directly to its members, which would seem the most natural and obvious method, it would actually appear that you had given your minds to devising a plan of hand to hand distribution, involving the maximum of personal humiliation to all classes of recipients.

"As regards the dependence of women upon men for support, which then was usual, of course natural attraction in case of marriages of love may often have made it endurable, though for spirited women I should fancy it must always have remained humiliating. What, then, must it have been in the innumerable cases where women, with or without the form of marriage, had to sell themselves to men to get their living? Even your contemporaries, callous as they were to most of the revolting aspects of their society, seem to have had an idea that this was not quite as it should be; but, it was still only for pity's sake that they deplored the lot of the women. It did not occur to them that it was robbery as well as cruelty when men seized for themselves the whole product of the world and left women to beg and wheedle for their share. Why—but bless me, Mr. West, I am really running on at a remarkable rate, just as if the robbery, the sorrow, and the shame which those poor women endured were not over a century since, or as if you were responsible for what you no doubt deplored as much as I do."

"I must bear my share of responsibility for the world as it then was," I replied. "All I can say in extenuation is that until the nation was ripe for the present system of organized production and distribution, no radical improvement in the position of woman was possible. The root of her disability, as you say, was her personal dependence upon man for her livelihood, and I can imagine no other mode of social organization than that you have adopted, which would have set woman free of man at the same time that it set men free of one another. I suppose, by the way, that so entire a change in the position of women cannot have taken place without affecting in marked ways the social relations of the sexes. That will be a very interesting study for me."

"The change you will observe," said Dr. Leete, "will chiefly be, I think, the entire frankness and unconstraint which now characterizes those relations, as compared with the artificiality which seems to have marked them in your time. The sexes now meet with the ease of perfect equals, suitors to each other for nothing but love. In your time the fact that women were dependent for support on men made the woman in reality the one chiefly benefited by marriage. This fact, so far as we can judge from contemporary records, appears to have been coarsely enough recognized among the lower classes, while among the more polished it was glossed over by a system of elaborate conventionalities which aimed to carry the precisely opposite meaning, namely, that the man was the party chiefly benefited. To keep up this convention it was essential that he should always seem the suitor. Nothing was therefore considered more shocking to the proprieties than that a woman should betray a fondness for a man before he had indicated a desire to marry her.

Why, we actually have in our libraries books, by authors of your day, written for no other purpose than to discuss the question whether, under any conceivable circumstances, a woman might, without discredit to her sex, reveal an unsolicited love. All this seems exquisitely absurd to us, and yet we know that, given your circumstances, the problem might have a serious side. When for a woman to proffer her love to a man was in effect to invite him to assume the burden of her support, it is easy to see that pride and delicacy might well have checked the promptings of the heart. When you go out into our society, Mr. West, you must be prepared to be often cross-questioned on this point by our young people, who are naturally much interested in this aspect of old-fashioned manners."[1]

"And so the girls of the twentieth century tell their love."

"If they choose" replied Dr. Leete. "There is no more pretense of a concealment of feeling on their part than on the part of their lovers. Coquetry would be as much despised in a girl as in a man. Affected coldness, which in your day rarely deceived a lover, would deceive him wholly now, for no one thinks of practicing it."

"One result which must follow from the independence of women I can see for myself," I said. "There can be no marriages now except those of inclination."

"That is a matter of course," replied Dr. Leete.

"Think of a world in which there are nothing but matches of pure love! Ah me, Dr. Leete, how far you are from being able to understand what an astonishing phenomenon such a world seems to a man of the nineteenth century!"

"I can, however, to some extent, imagine it," replied the doctor. "But the fact you celebrate, that there are nothing but love matches, means even more, perhaps, than you probably at first realize. It means that for the first time in human history the principle of sexual selection, with its tendency to preserve and transmit the better types of the race, and let the inferior types drop out, has

---

[1] I may say that Dr. Leete's warning has been fully justified by my experience. The amount and intensity of amusement which the young people of this day, and the young women especially, are able to extract from what they are pleased to call the oddities of courtship in the nineteenth century, appear unlimited. [Bellamy's note]

unhindered operation.[1] The necessities of poverty, the need of having a home, no longer tempt women to accept as the fathers of their children men whom they neither can love nor respect. Wealth and rank no longer divert attention from personal qualities. Gold no longer 'gilds the straitened forehead of the fool.'[2] The gifts of person, mind, and disposition; beauty, wit, eloquence, kindness, generosity, geniality, courage, are sure of transmission to posterity. Every generation is sifted through a little finer mesh than the last. The attributes that human nature admires are preserved, those that repel it are left behind. There are, of course, a great many women who with love must mingle admiration, and seek to wed greatly, but these not the less obey the same law, for to wed greatly now is not to marry men of fortune or title, but those who have risen above their fellows by the solidity or brilliance of their services to humanity. These form nowadays the only aristocracy with which alliance is distinction.

"You were speaking, a day or two ago, of the physical superiority of our people to your contemporaries. Perhaps more important than any of the causes I mentioned then as tending to race purification has been the effect of untrammeled sexual selection upon the quality of two or three successive generations. I believe that when you have made a fuller study of our people you will find in them not only a physical, but a mental and moral improvement. It would be strange if it were not so, for not only is one of the great laws of nature now freely working out the salvation of the race, but a profound moral sentiment has come to its support. Individualism, which in your day was the animating idea of society, not only was fatal to any vital sentiment of brotherhood and common interest among living men, but equally to any realization of the responsibility of the living for the generation to follow. To-day this sense of responsibility, practically unrecognized in all previous ages, has become one of the great ethical ideas of the race, reinforcing, with an intense conviction of duty, the natural impulse to seek in

---

[1]   Darwin's *Origin of Species* (1859) described both natural selection, how nature tends to favor certain characteristics which randomly appear, and sexual selection, which is the "struggle between the males for possession of the females" (Chapter IV).

[2]   The straitened or narrow forehead suggests inadequate brain development.

marriage the best and noblest of the other sex. The result is, that not all the encouragements and incentives of every sort which we have provided to develop industry, talent, genius, excellence of whatever kind, are comparable in their effect on our young men with the fact that our women sit aloft as judges of the race and reserve themselves to reward the winners. Of all the whips, and spurs, and baits, and prizes, there is none like the thought of the radiant faces which the laggards will find averted.

"Celibates nowadays are almost invariably men who have failed to acquit themselves creditably in the work of life. The woman must be a courageous one, with a very evil sort of courage, too, whom pity for one of these unfortunates should lead to defy the opinion of her generation—for otherwise she is free—so far as to accept him for a husband. I should add that, more exacting and difficult to resist than any other element in that opinion, she would find the sentiment of her own sex. Our women have risen to the full height of their responsibility as the wardens of the world to come, to whose keeping the keys of the future are confided.[1] Their feeling of duty in this respect amounts to a sense of religious consecration. It is a cult in which they educate their daughters from childhood."

After going to my room that night, I sat up late to read a romance of Berrian, handed me by Dr. Leete, the plot of which turned on a situation suggested by his last words, concerning the modern view of parental responsibility. A similar situation would almost certainly have been treated by a nineteenth-century romanticist so as to excite the morbid sympathy of the reader with the sentimental selfishness of the lovers, and his resentment toward the unwritten law which they outraged. I need not describe—for who has not read "Ruth Elton?"—how different is the course which Berrian takes, and with what tremendous effect he enforces the principle which he states: "Over the unborn our power is that of God, and our responsibility like His toward us. As we acquit ourselves toward them, so let Him deal with us."

---

[1] Keys are a symbol of power and authority, as with the keys of the Kingdom given to St. Peter (Matthew 16:19). In the nineteenth century keys were often associated with the womanly powers of the housekeeper; an example is Esther in Charles Dickens's *Bleak House* (1853).

CHAPTER XXVI.

I THINK if a person were ever excusable for losing track of the days of the week, the circumstances excused me. Indeed, if I had been told that the method of reckoning time had been wholly changed and the days were now counted in lots of five, ten, or fifteen instead of seven, I should have been in no way surprised after what I had already heard and seen of the twentieth century. The first time that any inquiry as to the days of the week occurred to me was the morning following the conversation related in the last chapter. At the breakfast table Dr. Leete asked me if I would care to hear a sermon.

"Is it Sunday, then?" I exclaimed.

"Yes," he replied. "It was on Friday, you see, when we made the lucky discovery of the buried chamber to which we owe your society this morning. It was on Saturday morning, soon after midnight, that you first awoke, and Sunday afternoon when you awoke the second time with faculties fully regained."

"So you still have Sundays and sermons," I said. "We had prophets who foretold that long before this time the world would have dispensed with both. I am very curious to know how the ecclesiastical systems fit in with the rest of your social arrangements. I suppose you have a sort of national church with official clergymen."

Dr. Leete laughed, and Mrs. Leete and Edith seemed greatly amused.

"Why, Mr. West," Edith said, "what odd people you must think us. You were quite done with national religious establishments in the nineteenth century, and did you fancy we had gone back to them?"

"But how can voluntary churches and an unofficial clerical profession be reconciled with national ownership of all buildings, and the industrial service required of all men?" I answered.

"The religious practices of the people have naturally changed considerably in a century," replied Dr. Leete; "but supposing them to have remained unchanged, our social system would accommodate them perfectly. The nation supplies any person or number of persons with buildings on guarantee of the rent, and they remain tenants while they pay it. As for the clergymen, if a number of persons wish the services of an individual for any particular end of their own, apart from the general service of the nation, they can always secure it, with that individual's own consent, of course, just as we secure the service of our editors, by contributing from their credit cards an indemnity to the nation for the loss of his services in general industry. This indemnity paid the nation for the individual answers to the salary in your day paid to the individual himself; and the various applications of this principle leave private initiative full play in all details to which national control is not applicable. Now, as to hearing a sermon to-day, if you wish to do so, you can either go to a church to hear it or stay at home."

"How am I to hear it if I stay at home?"

"Simply by accompanying us to the music room at the proper hour and selecting an easy chair. There are some who still prefer to hear sermons in church, but most of our preaching, like our musical performances, is not in public, but delivered in acoustically prepared chambers, connected by wire with subscribers' houses. If you prefer to go to a church I shall be glad to accompany you, but I really don't believe you are likely to hear anywhere a better discourse than you will at home. I see by the paper that Mr. Barton is to preach this morning, and he preaches only by telephone, and to audiences often reaching 150,000."

"The novelty of the experience of hearing a sermon under such circumstances would incline me to be one of Mr. Barton's hearers, if for no other reason," I said.

An hour or two later, as I sat reading in the library, Edith came for me, and I followed her to the music room, where Dr. and Mrs. Leete were waiting. We had not more than seated ourselves comfortably when the tinkle of a bell was heard, and a few moments after the voice of a man, at the pitch of ordinary conversation, addressed us, with an effect of proceeding from an invisible person in the room. This was what the voice said:—

MR. BARTON'S SERMON.

"We have had among us, during the past week, a critic from the nineteenth century, a living representative of the epoch of our great-grandparents. It would be strange if a fact so extraordinary had not somewhat strongly affected our imaginations. Perhaps most of us have been stimulated to some effort to realize the society of a century ago, and figure to ourselves what it must have been like to live then. In inviting you now to consider certain reflections upon this subject which have occurred to me, I presume that I shall rather follow than divert the course of your own thoughts."

Edith whispered something to her father at this point, to which he nodded assent and turned to me.

"Mr. West," he said, "Edith suggests that you may find it slightly embarrassing to listen to a discourse on the lines Mr. Barton is laying down, and if so, you need not be cheated out of a sermon. She will connect us with Mr. Sweetser's speaking room if you say so, and I can still promise you a very good discourse."

"No, no," I said. "Believe me, I would much rather hear what Mr. Barton has to say."

"As you please," replied my host.

When her father spoke to me Edith had touched a screw, and the voice of Mr. Barton had ceased abruptly. Now at another touch the room was once more filled with the earnest sympathetic tones which had already impressed me most favorably.

"I venture to assume that one effect has been common with us as a result of this effort at retrospection, and that it has been to leave us more than ever amazed at the stupendous change which one brief century has made in the material and moral conditions of humanity.

"Still, as regards the contrast between the poverty of the nation and the world in the nineteenth century and their wealth now, it is not greater, possibly, than had been before seen in human history, perhaps not greater, for example, than that between the poverty of this country during the earliest colonial period of the seventeenth century and the relatively great wealth it had attained at the close of the nineteenth, or between the England of William the Conqueror and that of Victoria.[1] Although the aggregate riches of a nation did not then, as now, afford any accurate criterion of the masses of its people, yet instances like these afford partial parallels for the merely material side of the contrast between the nineteenth and the twentieth centuries. It is when we contemplate the moral aspect of that contrast that we find ourselves in the presence of a phenomenon for which history offers no precedent, however far back we may cast our eye. One might almost be excused who should exclaim, 'Here, surely, is something like a miracle!' Nevertheless, when we give over idle wonder, and begin to examine the seeming prodigy critically, we find it no prodigy at all, much less a miracle. It is not necessary to suppose a moral new birth of humanity, or a wholesale destruction of the wicked and survival of the good, to account for the fact before us. It finds its simple and obvious explanation in the reaction of a changed environment upon human nature. It means merely that a form of society which was founded on the pseudo self-interest of selfishness, and appealed solely to the anti-social and brutal side of human nature, has been replaced by institutions based on the true self-interest of a rational unselfishness, and appealing to the social and generous instincts of men.

"My friends, if you would see men again the beasts of prey they seemed in the nineteenth century, all you have to do is to restore the old social and industrial system, which taught them to view their natural prey in their fellow-men, and find their gain in the loss of others. No doubt it seems to you that no necessity, however dire, would have tempted you to subsist on what superior skill or strength enabled you to wrest from others equally needy. But suppose it were not merely your own life that you were responsible for. I know well that there must have been many a man among our ancestors who, if it had been merely a question of his own life, would sooner have given it up than nourished it by bread snatched from others. But this he was not permitted to do. He had dear lives dependent on him. Men loved women in those days, as now. God knows how they dared be fathers, but they had babies as sweet, no doubt, to them as ours to us, whom they must feed, clothe,

---

[1]   William the Conqueror (1066–87) to Victoria (1837–1901).

educate. The gentlest creatures are fierce when they have young to provide for, and in that wolfish society the struggle for bread borrowed a peculiar desperation from the tenderest sentiments. For the sake of those dependent on him, a man might not choose, but must plunge into the foul fight, cheat, overreach, supplant, defraud, buy below worth and sell above, break down the business by which his neighbor fed his young ones, tempt men to buy what they ought not and to sell what they should not, grind his laborers, sweat his debtors, cozen his creditors. Though a man sought it carefully with tears, it was hard to find a way in which he could earn a living and provide for his family except by pressing in before some weaker rival and taking the food from his mouth. Even the ministers of religion were not exempt from this cruel necessity. While they warned their flocks against the love of money, regard for their families compelled them to keep an outlook for the pecuniary prizes of their calling. Poor fellows, theirs was indeed a trying business, preaching to men a generosity and unselfishness which they and everybody knew would, in the existing state of the world, reduce to poverty those who should practice them, laying down laws of conduct which the law of self-preservation compelled men to break. Looking on the inhuman spectacle of society, these worthy men bitterly bemoaned the depravity of human nature; as if angelic nature would not have been debauched in such a devil's school! Ah, my friends, believe me, it is not now in this happy age that humanity is proving the divinity within it. It was rather in those evil days when not even the fight for life with one another, the struggle for mere existence, in which mercy was folly, could wholly banish generosity and kindness from the earth.

"It is not hard to understand the desperation with which men and women, who under other conditions would have been full of gentleness and ruth, fought and tore each other in the scramble for gold, when we realize what it meant to miss it, what poverty was in that day. For the body it was hunger and thirst, torment by heat and frost, in sickness neglect, in health unremitting toil; for the moral nature it meant oppression, contempt, and the patient endurance of indignity, brutish associations from infancy, the loss of all the innocence of childhood, the grace of womanhood, the dignity of manhood; for the mind it meant the death of ignorance, the torpor of all those faculties which distinguish us from brutes, the reduction of life to a round of bodily functions.

"Ah, my friends, if such a fate as this were offered you and your children as the only alternative of success in the accumulation of wealth, how long do you fancy would you be in sinking to the moral level of your ancestors?

"Some two or three centuries ago an act of barbarity was committed in India, which, though the number of lives destroyed was but a few score, was attended by such peculiar horrors that its memory is likely to be perpetual. A number of English prisoners were shut up in a room containing not enough air to supply one-tenth their number. The unfortunates were gallant men, devoted comrades in service, but, as the agonies of suffocation began to take hold on them, they forgot all else, and became involved in a hideous struggle, each one for himself, and against all others, to force a way to one of the small apertures of the prison at which alone it was possible to get a breath of air. It was a struggle in which men became beasts, and the recital of its horrors by the few survivors so shocked our forefathers that for a century later we find it a stock reference in their literature as a typical illustration of the extreme possibilities of human misery, as shocking in its moral as its physical aspect. They could scarcely have anticipated that to us the Black Hole of Calcutta, with its press of maddened men tearing and trampling one another in the struggle to win a place at the breathing holes, would seem a striking type of the society of their age. It lacked something of being a complete type, however, for in the Calcutta Black Hole there were no tender women, no little children and old men and women, no cripples. They were at least all men, strong to bear, who suffered.[1]

"When we reflect that the ancient order of which I have been speaking was prevalent up to the end of the nineteenth century, while to us the new order which succeeded it already seems antique, even our parents having known no other, we cannot fail to be astounded at the suddenness with which a transition so profound beyond all previous experience of the race must have

---

[1] On 20 June 1756 the ruler of Bengal confined a large number of British prisoners in one small cell. Only a few escaped death by suffocation.

been effected. Some observation of the state of men's minds during the last quarter of the nineteenth century will, however, in great measure, dissipate this astonishment. Though general intelligence in the modern sense could not be said to exist in any community at that time, yet, as compared with previous generations, the one then on the stage was intelligent. The inevitable consequence of even this comparative degree of intelligence had been a perception of the evils of society, such as had never before been general. It is quite true that these evils had been even worse, much worse, in previous ages. It was the increased intelligence of the masses which made the difference, as the dawn reveals the squalor of surroundings which in the darkness may have seemed tolerable. The key-note of the literature of the period was one of compassion for the poor and unfortunate, and indignant outcry against the failure of the social machinery to ameliorate the miseries of men. It is plain from these outbursts that the moral hideousness of the spectacle about them was, at least by flashes, fully realized by the best of the men of that time, and that the lives of some of the more sensitive and generous hearted of them were rendered well-nigh unendurable by the intensity of their sympathies.

"Although the idea of the vital unity of the family of mankind, the reality of human brotherhood, was very far from being apprehended by them as the moral axiom it seems to us, yet it is a mistake to suppose that there was no feeling at all corresponding to it. I could read you passages of great beauty from some of their writers which show that the conception was clearly attained by a few, and no doubt vaguely by many more. Moreover, it must not be forgotten that the nineteenth century was in name Christian, and the fact that the entire commercial and industrial frame of society was the embodiment of the anti-Christian spirit must have had some weight, though I admit it was strangely little, with the nominal followers of Jesus Christ.

"When we inquire why it did not have more, why, in general, long after a vast majority of men had agreed as to the crying abuses of the existing social arrangement, they still tolerated it, or contented themselves with talking of petty reforms in it, we come upon an extraordinary fact. It was the sincere belief of even the best of men at that epoch that the only stable elements in human nature, on which a social system could be safely founded, were its worst propensities. They had been taught and believed that greed and self-seeking were all that held mankind together, and that all human associations would fall to pieces if anything were done to blunt the edge of these motives or curb their operation. In a word, they believed—even those who longed to believe otherwise—the exact reverse of what seems to us self-evident; they believed, that is, that the anti-social qualities of men, and not their social qualities, were what furnished the cohesive force of society. It seemed reasonable to them that men lived together solely for the purpose of overreaching and oppressing one another, and of being over-reached and oppressed, and that while a society that gave full scope to these propensities could stand, there would be little chance for one based on the idea of cooperation for the benefit of all. It seems absurd to expect any one to believe that convictions like these were ever seriously entertained by men; but that they were not only entertained by our great-grandfathers, but were responsible for the long delay in doing away with the ancient order, after a conviction of its intolerable abuses had become general, is as well established as any fact in history can be. Just here you will find the explanation of the profound pessimism of the literature of the last quarter of the nineteenth century, the note of melancholy in its poetry, and the cynicism of its humor.

"Feeling that the condition of the race was unendurable, they had no clear hope of anything better. They believed that the evolution of humanity had resulted in leading it into a *cul de sac,* and that there was no way of getting forward. The frame of men's minds at this time is strikingly illustrated by treatises which have come down to us, and may even now be consulted in our libraries by the curious, in which laborious arguments are pursued to prove that despite the evil plight of men, life was still, by some slight preponderance of considerations, probably better worth living than leaving. Despising themselves, they despised their Creator. There was a general decay of religious belief. Pale and watery gleams, from skies thickly veiled by doubt and dread, alone lighted up the chaos of earth. That men should doubt Him whose breath is in their nostrils, or dread the hands that moulded them, seems to us indeed a pitiable insanity; but we must remember that children who are brave by day have sometimes foolish fears at night. The dawn has come since then. It is very easy to believe in the fatherhood of God in the twentieth century.

"Briefly, as must needs be in a discourse of this character, I have adverted to some of the causes which had prepared men's minds for the change from the old to the new order, as well as some causes of the conservatism of despair which for a while held it back after the time was ripe. To wonder at the rapidity with which the change was completed after its possibility was first entertained is to forget the intoxicating effect of hope upon minds long accustomed to despair. The sunburst, after so long and dark a night, must needs have had a dazzling effect. From the moment men allowed themselves to believe that humanity after all had not been meant for a dwarf, that its squat stature was not the measure of its possible growth, but that it stood upon the verge of an avatar of limitless development, the reaction must needs have been overwhelming. It is evident that nothing was able to stand against the enthusiasm which the new faith inspired.

"Here, at last, men must have felt, was a cause compared with which the grandest of historic causes had been trivial. It was doubtless because it could have commanded millions of martyrs, that none were needed. The change of a dynasty in a petty kingdom of the old world often cost more lives than did the revolution which set the feet of the human race at last in the right way.

"Doubtless it ill beseems one to whom the boon of life in our resplendent age has been vouchsafed to wish his destiny other, and yet I have often thought that I would fain exchange my share in this serene and golden day for a place in that stormy epoch of transition, when heroes burst the barred gate of the future and revealed to the kindling gaze of a hopeless race, in place of the blank wall that had closed its path, a vista of progress whose end, for very excess of light, still dazzles us. Ah, my friends! who will say that to have lived then, when the weakest influence was a lever to whose touch the centuries trembled, was not worth a share even in this era of fruition?

"You know the story of that last, greatest, and most bloodless of revolutions. In the time of one generation men laid aside the social traditions and practices of barbarians, and assumed a social

order worthy of rational and human beings. Ceasing to be preda-
tory in their habits, they became co-workers, and found in fraternity, at once, the science of wealth and happiness. 'What shall I eat
and drink, and wherewithal shall I be clothed?' stated as a problem beginning and ending in self, had been an anxious and an
endless one. But when once it was conceived, not from the individual, but the fraternal standpoint, 'What shall we eat and drink,
and wherewithal shall we be clothed?'—its difficulties vanished.[1]

"Poverty with servitude had been the result, for the mass of
humanity, of attempting to solve the problem of maintenance from
the individual standpoint, but no sooner had the nation become
the sole capitalist and employer [that] not alone did plenty replace
poverty, but the last vestige of the serfdom of man to man disappeared from earth. Human slavery, so often vainly scotched, at last
was killed. The means of subsistence no longer doled out by men
to women, by employer to employed, by rich to poor, was distributed from a common stock as among children at the father's table.
It was impossible for a man any longer to use his fellow-men as
tools for his own profit. His esteem was the only sort of gain he
could thenceforth make out of him. There was no more either
arrogance or servility in the relations of human beings to one
another. For the first time since the creation every man stood up
straight before God. The fear of want and the lust of gain became
extinct motives when abundance was assured to all and immod-
erate possessions made impossible of attainment. There were no
more beggars nor almoners. Equity left charity without an occupation. The ten commandments became well-nigh obsolete in a
world where there was no temptation to theft, no occasion to lie
either for fear or favor, no room for envy where all were equal,
and little provocation to violence where men were disarmed of
power to injure one another. Humanity's ancient dream of liberty,
equality, fraternity, mocked by so many ages, at last was realized.

"As in the old society the generous, the just, the tender-hearted
had been placed at a disadvantage by the possession of those qualities, so in the new society the cold-hearted, the greedy, and

---

[1]   In Matthew 6:25–34 Jesus tells the disciples to set their hearts on the Kingdom of
    God and all earthly things will be given to them.

self-seeking found themselves out of joint with the world. Now that the conditions of life for the first time ceased to operate as a forcing process to develop the brutal qualities of human nature, and the premium which had heretofore encouraged selfishness was not only removed, but placed upon unselfishness, it was for the first time possible to see what unperverted human nature really was like. The depraved tendencies, which had previously overgrown and obscured the better to so large an extent, now withered like cellar fungi in the open air, and the nobler qualities showed a sudden luxuriance which turned cynics into panegyrists and for the first time in human history tempted mankind to fall in love with itself. Soon was fully revealed, what the divines and philosophers of the old world never would have believed, that human nature in its essential qualities is good, not bad, that men by their natural intention and structure are generous, not selfish, pitiful, not cruel, sympathetic, not arrogant, godlike in aspirations, instinct with divinest impulses of tenderness and self-sacrifice, images of God indeed, not the travesties upon Him they had seemed. The constant pressure, through numberless generations, of conditions of life which might have perverted angels, had not been able to essentially alter the natural nobility of the stock, and these conditions once removed, like a bent tree, it had sprung back to its normal uprightness.

"To put the whole matter in the nutshell of a parable, let me compare humanity in the olden time to a rosebush planted in a swamp, watered with black bog-water, breathing miasmatic fogs by day, and chilled with poison dews at night. Innumerable generations of gardeners had done their best to make it bloom, but beyond an occasional half-opened bud with a worm at the heart, their efforts had been unsuccessful. Many, indeed, claimed that the bush was no rosebush at all, but a noxious shrub, fit only to be uprooted and burned. The gardeners, for the most part, however, held that the bush belonged to the rose family, but had some ineradicable taint about it, which prevented the buds from coming out, and accounted for its generally sickly condition. There were a few, indeed, who maintained that the stock was good enough, that the trouble was in the bog, and that under more favorable conditions the plant might be expected to do better. But these persons were not regular gardeners, and being condemned by the latter as mere theorists and day dreamers, were, for the most part, so regarded by the people. Moreover, urged some eminent moral philosophers, even conceding for the sake of the argument that the bush might possibly do better elsewhere, it was a more valuable discipline for the buds to try to bloom in a bog than it would be under more favorable conditions. The buds that succeeded in opening might indeed be very rare, and the flowers pale and scentless, but they represented far more moral effort than if they had bloomed spontaneously in a garden.

"The regular gardeners and the moral philosophers had their way. The bush remained rooted in the bog, and the old course of treatment went on. Continually new varieties of forcing mixtures were applied to the roots, and more recipes than could be numbered, each declared by its advocates the best and only suitable preparation, were used to kill the vermin and remove the mildew. This went on a very long time. Occasionally some one claimed to observe a slight improvement in the appearance of the bush, but there were quite as many who declared that it did not look so well as it used to. On the whole there could not be said to be any marked change. Finally, during a period of general despondency as to the prospects of the bush where it was, the idea of transplanting it was again mooted, and this time found favor. 'Let us try it,' was the general voice. 'Perhaps it may thrive better elsewhere, and here it is certainly doubtful if it be worth cultivating longer.' So it came about that the rosebush of humanity was transplanted, and set in sweet, warm, dry earth, where the sun bathed it, the stars wooed it, and the south wind caressed it. Then it appeared that it was indeed a rosebush. The vermin and the mildew disappeared, and the bush was covered with most beautiful red roses, whose fragrance filled the world.

"It is a pledge of the destiny appointed for us that the Creator has set in our hearts an infinite standard of achievement, judged by which our past attainments seem always insignificant, and the goal never nearer. Had our forefathers conceived a state of society in which men should live together like brethren dwelling in unity, without strifes or envying, violence or overreaching, and where, at the price of a degree of labor not greater than health demands, in their chosen occupations, they should be wholly freed from care for the morrow and left with no more concern for their livelihood than trees which are watered by unfailing streams,—had they conceived such a condition, I say, it would have seemed to them nothing less than paradise. They would have confounded it with their idea of heaven, nor dreamed that there could possibly lie further beyond anything to be desired or striven for.

"But how is it with us who stand on this height which they gazed up to? Already we have well-nigh forgotten, except when it is especially called to our minds by some occasion like the present, that it was not always with men as it is now. It is a strain on our imaginations to conceive the social arrangements of our immediate ancestors. We find them grotesque. The solution of the problem of physical maintenance so as to banish care and crime, so far from seeming to us an ultimate attainment, appears but as a preliminary to anything like real human progress. We have but relieved ourselves of an impertinent and needless harassment which hindered our ancestors from undertaking the real ends of existence. We are merely stripped for the race; no more. We are like a child which has just learned to stand upright and to walk. It is a great event, from the child's point of view, when he first walks. Perhaps he fancies that there can be little beyond that achievement, but a year later he has forgotten that he could not always walk. His horizon did but widen when he rose, and enlarge as he moved. A great event indeed, in one sense, was his first step, but only as a beginning, not as the end. His true career was but then first entered on. The enfranchisement of humanity in the last century, from mental and physical absorption in working and scheming for the mere bodily necessities, may be regarded as a species of second birth of the race, without which its first birth to an existence that was but a burden would forever have remained unjustified, but whereby it is now abundantly vindicated. Since then, humanity has entered on a new phase of spiritual development, an evolution of higher faculties, the very existence of which in human nature our ancestors scarcely suspected. In place of the dreary hopelessness of the nineteenth century, its profound pessimism as to the future of humanity, the animating idea of the present age is an enthusiastic conception of the opportunities of our earthly existence, and the unbounded possibilities of human nature. The betterment of mankind from generation to generation, physically, mentally, morally, is recognized as the one great object supremely worthy of effort and of sacrifice. We believe the race for the first time to have entered on the realization of God's ideal of it, and each generation must now be a step upward.

"Do you ask what we look for when unnumbered generations shall have passed away? I answer, the way stretches far before us, but the end is lost in light. For twofold is the return of man to God 'who is our home,'[1] the return of the individual by the way of death, and the return of the race by the fulfilment of the evolution, when the divine secret hidden in the germ shall be perfectly unfolded. With a tear for the dark past, turn we then to the dazzling future, and, veiling our eyes, press forward. The long and weary winter of the race is ended. Its summer has begun. Humanity has burst the chrysalis. The heavens are before it."

CHAPTER XXVII.

I NEVER could tell just why, but Sunday afternoon during my old life had been a time when I was peculiarly subject to melancholy, when the color unaccountably faded out of all the aspects of life, and everything appeared pathetically uninteresting. The hours, which in general were wont to bear me easily on their wings, lost the power of flight, and toward the close of the day, drooping quite to earth, had fairly to be dragged along by main strength. Perhaps it was partly owing to the established association of ideas that, despite the utter change in my circumstances, I fell into a state of profound depression on the afternoon of this my first Sunday in the twentieth century.[2]

It was not, however, on the present occasion a depression without specific cause, the mere vague melancholy I have spoken

---

[1] The quotation is from William Wordsworth's "Ode: Intimations of Immortality": "But trailing clouds of glory do we come/From God, who is our home."

[2] Julian means his first full Sunday, since he had awakened the previous Sunday; see the opening of Chapter XXVI.

of, but a sentiment suggested and certainly quite justified by my position. The sermon of Mr. Barton, with its constant implication of the vast moral gap between the century to which I belonged and that in which I found myself, had had an effect strongly to accentuate my sense of loneliness in it. Considerately and philosophically as he had spoken, his words could scarcely have failed to leave upon my mind a strong impression of the mingled pity, curiosity, and aversion which I, as a representative of an abhorred epoch, must excite in all around me.

The extraordinary kindness with which I had been treated by Dr. Leete and his family, and especially the goodness of Edith, had hitherto prevented my fully realizing that their real sentiment toward me must necessarily be that of the whole generation to which they belonged. The recognition of this, as regarded Dr. Leete and his amiable wife, however painful, I might have endured, but the conviction that Edith must share their feeling was more than I could bear.

The crushing effect with which this belated perception of a fact so obvious came to me opened my eyes fully to something which perhaps the reader has already suspected, —I loved Edith.

Was it strange that I did? The affecting occasion on which our intimacy had begun, when her hands had drawn me out of the whirlpool of madness; the fact that her sympathy was the vital breath which had set me up in this new life and enabled me to support it; my habit of looking to her as the mediator between me and the world around in a sense that even her father was not,— these were circumstances that had predetermined a result which her remarkable loveliness of person and disposition would alone have accounted for. It was quite inevitable that she should have come to seem to me, in a sense quite different from the usual experience of lovers, the only woman in this world. Now that I had become suddenly sensible of the fatuity of the hopes I had begun to cherish, I suffered not merely what another lover might, but in addition a desolate loneliness, an utter forlornness, such as no other lover, however unhappy, could have felt.

My hosts evidently saw that I was depressed in spirits, and did their best to divert me. Edith especially, I could see, was distressed for me, but according to the usual perversity of lovers, having once been so mad as to dream of receiving something more from her, there was no longer any virtue for me in a kindness that I knew was only sympathy.

Toward nightfall, after secluding myself in my room most of the afternoon, I went into the garden to walk about. The day was overcast, with an autumnal flavor in the warm, still air. Finding myself near the excavation, I entered the subterranean chamber and sat down there. "This," I muttered to myself, "is the only home I have. Let me stay here, and not go forth any more." Seeking aid from the familiar surroundings, I endeavored to find a sad sort of consolation in reviving the past and summoning up the forms and faces that were about me in my former life. It was in vain. There was no longer any life in them. For nearly one hundred years the stars had been looking down on Edith Bartlett's grave, and the graves of all my generation.

The past was dead, crushed beneath a century's weight, and from the present I was shut out. There was no place for me anywhere. I was neither dead nor properly alive.

"Forgive me for following you."

I looked up. Edith stood in the door of the subterranean room, regarding me smilingly, but with eyes full of sympathetic distress.

"Send me away if I am intruding on you," she said; "but we saw that you were out of spirits, and you know you promised to let me know if that were so. You have not kept your word."

I rose and came to the door, trying to smile, but making, I fancy, rather sorry work of it, for the sight of her loveliness brought home to me the more poignantly the cause of my wretchedness.

"I was feeling a little lonely, that is all," I said. "Has it never occurred to you that my position is so much more utterly alone than any human being's ever was before that a new word is really needed to describe it?"

"Oh, you must not talk that way,—you must not let yourself feel that way,—you must not!" she exclaimed, with moistened eyes. "Are we not your friends? It is your own fault if you will not let us be. You need not be lonely."

"You are good to me beyond my power of understanding," I said, "but don't you suppose that I know it is pity merely, sweet pity, but pity only. I should be a fool not to know that I cannot seem to you as other men of your own generation do, but as some strange uncanny being, a stranded creature of an unknown sea, whose forlornness touches your compassion despite its grotesqueness. I have been so foolish, you were so kind, as to almost forget that this must needs be so, and to fancy I might in time become naturalized, as we used to say, in this age, so as to feel like one of you and to seem to you like the other men about you. But Mr. Barton's sermon taught me how vain such a fancy is, how great the gulf between us must seem to you."

"Oh that miserable sermon!" she exclaimed, fairly crying now in her sympathy, "I wanted you not to hear it. What does he know of you? He has read in old musty books about your times, that is all. What do you care about him, to let yourself be vexed by anything he said? Isn't it anything to you, that we who know you feel differently? Don't you care more about what we think of you than what he does who never saw you? Oh, Mr. West! you don't know, you can't think, how it makes me feel to see you so forlorn. I can't have it so. What can I say to you? How can I convince you how different our feeling for you is from what you think?"

As before, in that other crisis of my fate when she had come to me, she extended her hands towards me in a gesture of helpfulness, and, as then, I caught and held them in my own; her bosom heaved with strong emotion, and little tremors in the fingers which I clasped emphasized the depth of her feeling. In her face, pity contended in a sort of divine spite against the obstacles which reduced it to impotence. Womanly compassion surely never wore a guise more lovely.

Such beauty and such goodness quite melted me, and it seemed that the only fitting response I could make was to tell her just the truth. Of course I had not a spark of hope, but on the other hand I had no fear that she would be angry. She was too pitiful for that. So I said presently, "It is very ungrateful in me not to be satisfied with such kindness as you have shown me, and are showing me now. But are you so blind as not to see why they are not enough to make me happy? Don't you see that it is because I have been mad enough to love you?"

At my last words she blushed deeply and her eyes fell before mine, but she made no effort to withdraw her hands from my clasp. For some moments she stood so, panting a little. Then blushing deeper than ever, but with a dazzling smile, she looked up.

"Are you sure it is not you who are blind?" she said.

That was all, but it was enough, for it told me that, unaccountable, incredible as it was, this radiant daughter of a golden age had bestowed upon me not alone her pity, but her love. Still, I half believed I must be under some blissful hallucination even as I clasped her in my arms. "If I am beside myself," I cried, "let me remain so."

"It is I whom you must think beside myself," she panted, escaping from my arms when I had barely tasted the sweetness of her lips. "Oh! oh! what must you think of me almost to throw myself in the arms of one I have known but a week? I did not mean that you should find it out so soon, but I was so sorry for you I forgot what I was saying. No, no; you must not touch me again till you know who I am. After that, sir, you shall apologize to me very humbly for thinking, as I know you do, that I have been over quick to fall in love with you. After you know who I am, you will be bound to confess that it was nothing less than my duty to fall in love with you at first sight, and that no girl of proper feeling in my place could do otherwise."

As may be supposed, I would have been quite content to waive explanations, but Edith was resolute that there should be no more kisses until she had been vindicated from all suspicion of precipitancy in the bestowal of her affections, and I was fain to follow the lovely enigma into the house. Having come where her mother was, she blushingly whispered something in her ear and ran away, leaving us together.

It then appeared that, strange as my experience had been, I was now first to know what was perhaps its strangest feature. From Mrs. Leete I learned that Edith was the great-granddaughter of no other than my lost love, Edith Bartlett. After mourning me for fourteen years, she had made a marriage of esteem, and left a son who had been Mrs. Leete's father. Mrs. Leete had never seen her grandmother, but had heard much of her, and, when her daughter was born, gave her the name of Edith. This fact might have tended to increase the interest which the girl took, as she grew up, in all that concerned her ancestress, and especially the tragic story of the supposed death of the lover, whose wife she expected to be, in the conflagration of his house. It was a tale well calculated to touch the sympathy of a romantic girl, and the fact that the blood of the unfortunate heroine was in her own veins naturally heightened Edith's interest in it. A portrait of Edith Bartlett and some of her papers, including a packet of my own letters, were among the family heirlooms. The picture represented a very beautiful young woman about whom it was easy to imagine all manner of tender and romantic things. My letters gave Edith some material for forming a distinct idea of my personality, and both together sufficed to make the sad old story very real to her. She used to tell her parents, half jestingly, that she would never marry till she found a lover like Julian West, and there were none such nowadays.

Now all this, of course, was merely the daydreaming of a girl whose mind had never been taken up by a love affair of her own, and would have had no serious consequence but for the discovery that morning of the buried vault in her father's garden and the revelation of the identity of its inmate. For when the apparently lifeless form had been borne into the house, the face in the locket found upon the breast was instantly recognized as that of Edith Bartlett, and by that fact, taken in connection with the other circumstances, they knew that I was no other than Julian West. Even had there been no thought, as at first there was not, of my resuscitation, Mrs. Leete said she believed that this event would have affected her daughter in a critical and life-long manner. The presumption of some subtle ordering of destiny, involving her fate with mine, would under all circumstances have possessed an irresistible fascination for almost any woman.

Whether when I came back to life a few hours afterward, and from the first seemed to turn to her with a peculiar dependence and to find a special solace in her company, she had been too quick in giving her love at the first sign of mine, I could now, her mother said, judge for myself. If I thought so, I must remember that this, after all, was the twentieth and not the nineteenth century, and love was, no doubt, now quicker in growth, as well as franker in utterance than then.

From Mrs. Leete I went to Edith. When I found her, it was first of all to take her by both hands and stand a long time in rapt contemplation of her face. As I gazed, the memory of that other Edith, which had been affected as with a benumbing shock by the tremendous experience that had parted us, revived, and my heart was dissolved with tender and pitiful emotions, but also very blissful ones. For she who brought to me so poignantly the sense of my loss was to make that loss good. It was as if from her eyes Edith Bartlett looked into mine, and smiled consolation to me. My fate was not alone the strangest, but the most fortunate that ever befell a man. A double miracle had been wrought for me. I had not been stranded upon the shore of this strange world to find myself alone and companionless. My love, whom I had dreamed lost, had been reëmbodied for my consolation. When at last, in an ecstasy of gratitude and tenderness, I folded the lovely girl in my arms, the two Ediths were blended in my thought, nor have they ever since been clearly distinguished. I was not long in finding that on Edith's part there was a corresponding confusion of identities. Never, surely, was there between freshly united lovers a stranger talk than ours that afternoon. She seemed more anxious to have me speak of Edith Bartlett than of herself, of how I had loved her than how I loved herself, rewarding my fond words concerning another woman with tears and tender smiles and pressures of the hand.

"You must not love me too much for myself," she said. "I shall be very jealous for her. I shall not let you forget her. I am going to tell you something which you may think strange. Do you not believe that spirits sometimes come back to the world to fulfill some work that lay near their hearts? What if I were to tell you that I have sometimes thought that her spirit lives in me, that Edith Bartlett, not Edith Leete, is my real name. I cannot know it; of course none of us can know who we really are; but I can feel it. Can you wonder that I have such a feeling, seeing how my life was affected by her and by you, even before you came. So you see you need not trouble to love me at all, if only you are true to her. I shall not be likely to be jealous."

Dr. Leete had gone out that afternoon, and I did not have an interview with him till later. He was not, apparently, wholly unprepared for the intelligence I conveyed, and shook my hand heartily.

"Under any ordinary circumstances, Mr. West, I should say that this step had been taken on rather short acquaintance; but these are decidedly not ordinary circumstances. In fairness, perhaps I ought to tell you," he added, smilingly, "that while I cheerfully consent to the proposed arrangement, you must not feel too much indebted to me, as I judge my consent is a mere formality. From the moment the secret of the locket was out, it had to be, I fancy. Why, bless me, if Edith had not been there to redeem her great-grandmother's pledge, I really apprehend that Mrs. Leete's loyalty to me would have suffered a severe strain."

That evening the garden was bathed in moonlight, and till midnight Edith and I wandered to and fro there, trying to grow accustomed to our happiness.

"What should I have done if you had not cared for me?" she exclaimed. "I was afraid you were not going to. What should I have done then, when I felt I was consecrated to you! As soon as you came back to life, I was as sure as if she had told me that I was to be to you what she could not be, but that could only be if you would let me. Oh, how I wanted to tell you that morning, when you felt so terribly strange among us, who I was, but dared not open my lips about that, or let father or mother"—

"That must have been what you would not let your father tell me!" I exclaimed, referring to the conversation I had overheard as I came out of my trance.

"Of course it was," Edith laughed. "Did you only just guess that? Father being only a man, thought that it would make you feel among friends to tell you who we were. He did not think of me at all. But mother knew what I meant, and so I had my way. I could never have looked you in the face if you had known who I was. It would have been forcing myself on you quite too boldly. I am afraid you think I did that to-day, as it was. I am sure I did not mean to, for I know girls were expected to hide their feelings in your day, and I was dreadfully afraid of shocking you. Ah me, how hard it must have been for them to have always had to conceal their love like a fault. Why did they think it such a shame to love any one till they had been given permission? It is so odd to think of waiting for permission to fall in love. Was it because men in those days were angry when girls loved them? That is not the way women would feel, I am sure, or men either, I think, now. I don't understand it at all. That will be one of the curious things about the women of those days that you will have to explain to me. I don't believe Edith Bartlett was so foolish as the others."

After sundry ineffectual attempts at parting, she finally insisted that we must say good night. I was about to imprint upon her lips the positively last kiss, when she said, with an indescribable archness: —

"One thing troubles me. Are you sure that you quite forgive Edith Bartlett for marrying any one else? The books that have come down to us make out lovers of your time more jealous than fond, and that is what makes me ask. It would be a great relief to me if I could feel sure that you were not in the least jealous of my great-grandfather for marrying your sweetheart. May I tell my great-grandmother's picture when I go to my room that you quite forgive her for proving false to you?"

Will the reader believe it, this coquettish quip, whether the speaker herself had any idea of it or not, actually touched and with the touching cured a preposterous ache of something like jealousy which I had been vaguely conscious of ever since Mrs. Leete had told me of Edith Bartlett's marriage. Even while I had been holding Edith Bartlett's great-granddaughter in my arms, I had not, till this moment, so illogical are some of our feelings, distinctly realized that but for that marriage I could not have done so. The absurdity of this frame of mind could only be equalled by the abruptness with which it dissolved as Edith's roguish query cleared the fog from my perceptions. I laughed as I kissed her.

"You may assure her of my entire forgiveness," I said, "although if it had been any man but your great-grandfather whom she married, it would have been a very different matter."

On reaching my chamber that night I did not open the musical telephone that I might be lulled to sleep with soothing tunes, as had become my habit. For once my thoughts made better music than even twentieth century orchestras discourse, and it held me enchanted till well toward morning, when I fell asleep.

CHAPTER XXVIII.

"IT'S a little after the time you told me to wake you, sir. You did not come out of it as quick as common, sir."

The voice was the voice of my man Sawyer. I started bolt upright in bed and stared around. I was in my underground chamber. The mellow light of the lamp which always burned in the room when I occupied it illumined the familiar walls and furnishings. By my bedside, with the glass of sherry in his hand which Dr. Pillsbury prescribed on first rousing from a mesmeric sleep, by way of awakening the torpid physical functions, stood Sawyer.

"Better take this right off, sir," he said, as I stared blankly at him. "You look kind of flushed like, sir, and you need it."

I tossed off the liquor and began to realize what had happened to me. It was, of course, very plain. All that about the twentieth century had been a dream. I had but dreamed of that enlightened and care-free race of men and their ingeniously simple institutions, of the glorious new Boston with its domes and pinnacles, its gardens and fountains, and its universal reign of comfort. The amiable family which I had learned to know so well, my genial host and Mentor, Dr. Leete, his wife, and their daughter, the second and more beauteous Edith, my betrothed,—these, too, had been but figments of a vision.

For a considerable time I remained in the attitude in which this conviction had come over me, sitting up in bed gazing at vacancy, absorbed in recalling the scenes and incidents of my fantastic experience. Sawyer, alarmed at my looks, was meanwhile anxiously inquiring what was the matter with me. Roused at length by his importunities to a recognition of my surroundings, I pulled myself together with an effort and assured the faithful fellow that I was all right. "I have had an extraordinary dream, that's all, Sawyer," I said, "a most-ex-traor-dinary-dream."

I dressed in a mechanical way, feeling light-headed and oddly uncertain of myself, and sat down to the coffee and rolls which Sawyer was in the habit of providing for my refreshment before I left the house. The morning newspaper lay by the plate. I took it up, and my eye fell on the date, May 31, 1887. I had known, of course, from the moment I opened my eyes that my long and detailed experience in another century had been a dream, and yet it was startling to have it so conclusively demonstrated that the world was but a few hours older than when I had lain down to sleep.

Glancing at the table of contents at the head of the paper, which reviewed the news of the morning, I read the following summary:—

"FOREIGN AFFAIRS. —The impending war between France and Germany. The French Chambers asked for new military credits to meet Germany's increase of her army. Probability that all Europe will be involved in case of war.—Great suffering among the unemployed in London. They demand work. Monster demonstration to be made. The authorities uneasy.— Great strikes in Belgium. The government preparing to repress outbreaks. Shocking facts in regard to the employment of girls in Belgium coal mines. Wholesale evictions in Ireland.

"HOME AFFAIRS.—The epidemic of fraud unchecked. Embezzlement of half a million in New York.—Misappropriation of a trust fund by executors. Orphans left penniless.—Clever system of thefts by a bank teller; $50,000 gone.—The coal barons decide to advance the price of coal and reduce production.— Speculators engineering a great wheat corner at Chicago.—A clique forcing up the price of coffee.—Enormous land-grabs of Western syndicates.—Revelations of shocking corruption among Chicago officials. Systematic bribery.—The trials of the Boodle aldermen to go on at New York. —Large failures of business houses. Fears of a business crisis.—A large grist of burglaries and larcenies.—A woman murdered in cold blood for her money at New Haven. —A householder shot by a burglar in this city last night.—A man shoots himself in Worcester because he could not get work. A large family left destitute.—An aged couple in New Jersey commit suicide rather than go to the poor-house.— Pitiable destitution among the women wage-workers in the great cities.—Startling growth of illiteracy in Massachusetts. —More insane asylums wanted—Decoration Day addresses. Professor

Brown's oration on the moral grandeur of nineteenth century civilization."[1]

It was indeed the nineteenth century to which I had awaked; there could be no kind of doubt about that. Its complete microcosm this summary of the day's news had presented, even to that last unmistakable touch of fatuous self-complacency. Coming after such a damning indictment of the age as that one day's chronicle of world-wide bloodshed, greed, and tyranny, was a bit of cynicism worthy of Mephistopheles,[2] and yet of all whose eyes it had met this morning I was, perhaps, the only one who perceived the cynicism, and but yesterday I should have perceived it no more than the others. That strange dream it was which had made all the difference. For I know not how long, I forgot my surroundings after this, and was again in fancy moving in that vivid dream-world, in that glorious city, with its homes of simple comfort and its gorgeous public palaces. Around me were again faces unmarred by arrogance or servility, by envy or greed, by anxious care or feverish ambition, and stately forms of men and women who had never known fear of a fellow man or depended on his favor, but always, in the words of that sermon which still rang in my ears, had "stood up straight before God."

With a profound sigh and a sense of irreparable loss, not the less poignant that it was a loss of what had never really been, I roused at last from my reverie, and soon after left the house.

A dozen times between my door and Washington Street I had to stop and pull myself together, such power had been in that vision of the Boston of the future to make the real Boston strange. The squalor and malodorousness of the town struck me, from the moment I stood upon the street, as facts I had never before observed. But yesterday, moreover, it had seemed quite a matter of course that some of my fellow-citizens should wear silks, and others rags, that some should look well fed, and others hungry. Now on the contrary the glaring disparities in the dress and condition of

---

[1] A mixture of real and invented headlines. For example, the Boodle Aldermen took $22,000 each to vote for a railway franchise in 1884. www.progress.org/archive/hgjr17b

[2] Mephistopheles: a name for the devil.

the men and women who brushed each other on the sidewalks shocked me at every step, and yet more the entire indifference which the prosperous showed to the plight of the unfortunate. Were these human beings, who could behold the wretchedness of their fellows without so much as a change of countenance? And yet, all the while, I knew well that it was I who had changed, and not my contemporaries. I had dreamed of a city whose people fared all alike as children of one family and were one another's keepers in all things.

Another feature of the real Boston, which assumed the extraordinary effect of strangeness that marks familiar things seen in a new light, was the prevalence of advertising. There had been no personal advertising in the Boston of the twentieth century, because there was no need of any, but here the walls of the buildings, the windows, the broadsides of the newspapers in every hand, the very pavements, everything in fact in sight, save the sky, were covered with the appeals of individuals who sought, under innumerable pretexts, to attract the contributions of others to their support. However the wording might vary, the tenor of all these appeals was the same:—

"Help John Jones. Never mind the rest. They are frauds. I, John Jones, am the right one. Buy of me. Employ me. Visit me. Hear me, John Jones. Look at me. Make no mistake. John Jones is the man and nobody else. Let the rest starve, but for God's sake remember John Jones!"

Whether the pathos or the moral repulsiveness of the spectacle most impressed me, so suddenly become a stranger in my own city, I know not. Wretched men, I was moved to cry, who, because they will not learn to be helpers of one another, are doomed to be beggars of one another from the least to the greatest! This horrible babel[1] of shameless self-assertion and mutual depreciation, this stunning clamor of conflicting boasts, appeals, and adjurations, this stupendous system of brazen beggary, what was it all but the necessity of a society in which the opportunity to serve

---

[1] In Genesis 11 the people build a tower to the heavens and for their punishment are cast into confusion of languages. In histories of utopianism The Tower of Babel has been a symbol of human aspirations.

the world according to his gifts, instead of being secured to every man as the first object of social organization, had to be fought for!

I reached Washington Street at the busiest point, and there I stood and laughed aloud, to the scandal of the passers-by. For my life I could not have helped it, with such a mad humor was I moved at sight of the interminable rows of stores on either side, up and down the street so far as I could see, —scores of them, to make the spectacle more utterly preposterous, within a stone's throw devoted to selling the same sort of goods. Stores! stores! stores! miles of stores! ten thousand stores to distribute the goods needed by this one city, which in my dream had been supplied with all things from a single warehouse, as they were ordered through one great store in every quarter, where the buyer, without waste of time or labor, found under one roof the world's assortment in whatever line he desired. There the labor of distribution had been so slight as to add but a scarcely perceptible fraction to the cost of commodities to the user. The cost of production was virtually all he paid. But here the mere distribution of the goods, their handling alone, added a fourth, a third, a half and more, to the cost. All these ten thousand plants must be paid for, their rent, their staffs of superintendence, their platoons of salesmen, their ten thousand sets of accountants, jobbers, and business dependents, with all they spent in advertising themselves and fighting one another, and the consumers must do the paying. What a famous process for beggaring a nation!

Were these serious men I saw about me, or children, who did their business on such a plan? Could they be reasoning beings, who did not see the folly which, when the product is made and ready for use, wastes so much of it in getting it to the user? If people eat with a spoon that leaks half its contents between bowl and lip, are they not likely to go hungry?

I had passed through Washington Street thousands of times before and viewed the ways of those who sold merchandise, but my curiosity concerning them was as if I had never gone by their way before. I took wondering note of the show windows of the stores, filled with goods arranged with a wealth of pains and artistic device to attract the eye. I saw the throngs of ladies looking in, and the proprietors eagerly watching the effect of the bait. I went within and noted the hawk-eyed floor-walker watching for business, overlooking the clerks, keeping them up to their task of inducing the customers to buy, buy, buy, for money if they had it, for credit if they had it not, to buy what they wanted not, more than they wanted, what they could not afford. At times I momentarily lost the clue and was confused by the sight. Why this effort to induce people to buy? Surely that had nothing to do with the legitimate business of distributing products to those who needed them. Surely it was the sheerest waste to force upon people what they did not want, but what might be useful to another. The nation was so much the poorer for every such achievement. What were these clerks thinking of? Then I would remember that they were not acting as distributors like those in the store I had visited in the dream Boston. They were not serving the public interest, but their immediate personal interest, and it was nothing to them what the ultimate effect of their course on the general prosperity might be, if but they increased their own hoard, for these goods were their own, and the more they sold and the more they got for them, the greater their gain. The more wasteful the people were, the more articles they did not want which they could be induced to buy, the better for these sellers. To encourage prodigality was the express aim of the ten thousand stores of Boston.

Nor were these storekeepers and clerks a whit worse men than any others in Boston. They must earn a living and support their families, and how were they to find a trade to do it by which did not necessitate placing their individual interests before those of others and that of all? They could not be asked to starve while they waited for an order of things such as I had seen in my dream, in which the interest of each and that of all were identical. But, God in heaven! what wonder, under such a system as this about me— what wonder that the city was so shabby, and the people so meanly dressed, and so many of them ragged and hungry!

Some time after this it was that I drifted over into South Boston and found myself among the manufacturing establishments. I had been in this quarter of the city a hundred times before, just as I had been on Washington Street, but here, as well as there, I now first perceived the true significance of what I witnessed. Formerly I had taken pride in the fact that, by actual count, Boston had some four thousand independent manufacturing establishments; but in this very multiplicity and independence I recognized now the secret of the insignificant total product of their industry.

If Washington Street had been like a lane in Bedlam,[1] this was a spectacle as much more melancholy as production is a more vital function than distribution. For not only were these four thousand establishments not working in concert, and for that reason alone operating at prodigious disadvantage, but, as if this did not involve a sufficiently disastrous loss of power, they were using their utmost skill to frustrate one another's effort, praying by night and working by day for the destruction of one another's enterprises.

The roar and rattle of wheels and hammers resounding from every side was not the hum of a peaceful industry, but the clangor of swords wielded by foemen. These mills and shops were so many forts, each under its own flag, its guns trained on the mills and shops about it, and its sappers busy below, undermining them.

Within each one of these forts the strictest organization of industry was insisted on; the separate gangs worked under a single central authority. No interference and no duplicating of work were permitted. Each had his allotted task, and none were idle. By what hiatus in the logical faculty, by what lost link of reasoning, account, then, for the failure to recognize the necessity of applying the same principle to the organization of the national industries as a whole, to see that if lack of organization could impair the efficiency of a shop, it must have effects as much more disastrous in disabling the industries of the nation at large as the latter are vaster in volume and more complex in the relationship of their parts.

People would be prompt enough to ridicule an army in which there were neither companies, battalions, regiments, brigades, divisions, or army corps,—no unit of organization, in fact, larger than the corporal's squad, with no officer higher than a corporal, and all the corporals equal in authority. And yet just such an army were the manufacturing industries of nineteenth century Boston, an army of four thousand independent squads led by four thousand independent corporals, each with a separate plan of campaign.

---

[1] Bedlam: a contraction of St. Mary of Bethlehem, a London priory founded in 1247 which became a hospital for the insane.

Knots of idle men were to be seen here and there on every side, some idle because they could find no work at any price, others because they could not get what they thought a fair price.

I accosted some of the latter, and they told me their grievances. It was very little comfort I could give them. "I am sorry for you," I said. "You get little enough, certainly, and yet the wonder to me is, not that industries conducted as these are do not pay you living wages, but that they are able to pay you any wages at all."

Making my way back again after this to the peninsular city, toward three o'clock I stood on State Street, staring, as if I had never seen them before, at the banks and brokers' offices, and other financial institutions, of which there had been in the State Street of my vision no vestige. Business men, confidential clerks, and errand boys were thronging in and out of the banks, for it wanted but a few minutes of the closing hour. Opposite me was the bank where I did business, and presently I crossed the street, and, going in with the crowd, stood in a recess of the wall looking on at the army of clerks handling money, and the cues of depositors at the tellers' windows. An old gentleman whom I knew, a director of the bank, passing me and observing my contemplative attitude, stopped a moment.

"Interesting sight, isn't it, Mr. West," he said. "Wonderful piece of mechanism; I find it so myself. I like sometimes to stand and look on at it just as you are doing. It's a poem, sir, a poem, that's what I call it. Did you ever think, Mr. West, that the bank is the heart of the business system? From it and to it, in endless flux and reflux, the life blood goes. It is flowing in now. It will flow out again in the morning;" and pleased with his little conceit, the old man passed on smiling.

Yesterday I should have considered the simile apt enough, but since then I had visited a world incomparably more affluent than this, in which money was unknown and without conceivable use. I had learned that it had a use in the world around me only because the work of producing the nation's livelihood, instead of being regarded as the most strictly public and common of all concerns, and as such conducted by the nation, was abandoned to the hap-hazard efforts of individuals. This original mistake necessitated endless exchanges to bring about any sort of general distribution of products. These exchanges money effected —how equitably, might be seen in a walk from the tenement house districts to the Back Bay —at the cost of an army of men taken from productive labor to manage it, with constant ruinous breakdowns of its machinery, and a generally debauching influence on mankind which had justified its description, from ancient time, as the "root of all evil."[I]

Alas for the poor old bank director with his poem! He had mistaken the throbbing of an abscess for the beating of the heart. What he called "a wonderful piece of mechanism" was an imperfect device to remedy an unnecessary defect, the clumsy crutch of a self-made cripple.

After the banks had closed I wandered aimlessly about the business quarter for an hour or two, and later sat a while on one of the benches of the Common, finding an interest merely in watching the throngs that passed, such as one has in studying the populace of a foreign city, so strange since yesterday had my fellow citizens and their ways become to me. For thirty years I had lived among them, and yet I seemed to have never noted before how drawn and anxious were their faces, of the rich as of the poor, the refined, acute faces of the educated as well as the dull masks of the ignorant. And well it might be so, for I saw now, as never before I had seen so plainly, that each as he walked constantly turned to catch the whispers of a spectre at his ear, the spectre of Uncertainty. "Do your work never so well," the spectre was whispering,—"rise early and toil till late, rob cunningly or serve faithfully, you shall never know security. Rich you may be now and still come to poverty at last. Leave never so much wealth to your children, you cannot buy the assurance that your son may not be the servant of your servant, or that your daughter will not have to sell herself for bread."

A man passing by thrust an advertising card in my hand, which set forth the merits of some new scheme of life insurance. The incident reminded me of the only device, pathetic in its admission of the universal need it so poorly supplied, which offered these tired and hunted men and women even a partial protection from

---

[I]   In Timothy 6:10 it is "love of money" which is the "root of all evils."

uncertainty. By this means, those already well-to-do, I remembered, might purchase a precarious confidence that after their death their loved ones would not, for a while at least, be trampled under the feet of men. But this was all, and this was only for those who could pay well for it. What idea was possible to these wretched dwellers in the land of Ishmael,[1] where every man's hand was against each and the hand of each against every other, of true life insurance as I had seen it among the people of that dream land, each of whom, by virtue merely of his membership in the national family, was guaranteed against need of any sort, by a policy underwritten by one hundred million fellow countrymen.

Some time after this it was that I recall a glimpse of myself standing on the steps of a building on Tremont Street, looking at a military parade. A regiment was passing. It was the first sight in that dreary day which had inspired me with any other emotions than wondering pity and amazement. Here at last were order and reason, an exhibition of what intelligent coöperation can accomplish. The people who stood looking on with kindling faces, — could it be that the sight had for them no more than but a spectacular interest? Could they fail to see that it was their perfect concert of action, their organization under one control, which made these men the tremendous engine they were, able to vanquish a mob ten times as numerous? Seeing this so plainly, could they fail to compare the scientific manner in which the nation went to war with the unscientific manner in which it went to work? Would they not query since what time the killing of men had been a task so much more important than feeding and clothing them, that a trained army should be deemed alone adequate to the former, while the latter was left to a mob?

It was now toward nightfall, and the streets were thronged with the workers from the stores, the shops, and mills. Carried along with the stronger part of the current, I found myself, as it began to grow dark, in the midst of a scene of squalor and human degradation such as only the South Cove tenement district could present. I had seen the mad wasting of human labor; here I saw in direst shape the want that waste had bred.

---

[1] Genesis 16:12.

From the black doorways and windows of the rookeries on every side came gusts of fetid air. The streets and alleys reeked with the effluvia of a slave ship's between-decks. As I passed I had glimpses within of pale babies gasping out their lives amid sultry stenches, of hopeless-faced women deformed by hardship, retaining of womanhood no trait save weakness, while from the windows leered girls with brows of brass.[1] Like the starving bands of mongrel curs that infest the streets of Moslem towns, swarms of half-clad brutalized children filled the air with shrieks and curses as they fought and tumbled among the garbage that littered the courtyards.

There was nothing in all this that was new to me. Often had I passed through this part of the city and witnessed its sights with feelings of disgust mingled with a certain philosophical wonder at the extremities mortals will endure and still cling to life. But not alone as regarded the economical follies of this age, but equally as touched its moral abominations, scales had fallen from my eyes since that vision of another century. No more did I look upon the woeful dwellers in this Inferno with a callous curiosity as creatures scarcely human.[2] I saw in them my brothers and sisters, my parents, my children, flesh of my flesh, blood of my blood. The festering mass of human wretchedness about me offended not now my senses merely, but pierced my heart like a knife, so that I could not repress sighs and groans. I not only saw but felt in my body all that I saw.

Presently, too, as I observed the wretched beings about me more closely, I perceived that they were all quite dead. Their bodies were so many living sepulchres. On each brutal brow was plainly written the *hic jacet* of a soul dead within.[3]

As I looked, horror struck, from one death's head to another, I was affected by a singular hallucination. Like a wavering translucent spirit face superimposed upon each of these brutish masks I saw the ideal, the possible face that would have been the actual if mind and soul had lived. It was not till I was aware of

---

[1] Bold or brazen; see Isaiah 48:4.
[2] Inferno: a name for Hell, as in Dante's *Inferno*.
[3] hic jacet: "here lies…"—the first two words of the inscription on a tombstone.

these ghostly faces, and of the reproach that could not be gain-
said which was in their eyes, that the full piteousness of the ruin
that had been wrought was revealed to me. I was moved with
contrition as with a strong agony, for I had been one of those
who had endured that these things should be.

I had been one of those who, well knowing that they were, had
not desired to hear or be compelled to think much of them, but
had gone on as if they were not, seeking my own pleasure and
profit. Therefore now I found upon my garments the blood of this
great multitude of strangled souls of my brothers. The voice of
their blood cried out against me from the ground. Every stone of
the reeking pavements, every brick of the pestilential rookeries,
found a tongue and called after me as I fled: What hast thou done
with thy brother Abel?[1]

I have no clear recollection of anything after this till I found
myself standing on the carved stone steps of the magnificent home
of my betrothed in Commonwealth Avenue. Amid the tumult of
my thoughts that day, I had scarcely once thought of her, but now
obeying some unconscious impulse my feet had found the familiar way to her door. I was told that the family were at dinner, but
word was sent out that I should join them at table. Besides the
family, I found several guests present, all known to me. The table
glittered with plate and costly china. The ladies were sumptuously
dressed and wore the jewels of queens. The scene was one of costly
elegance and lavish luxury. The company was in excellent spirits,
and there was plentiful laughter and a running fire of jests.

To me it was as if, in wandering through the place of doom, my
blood turned to tears by its sights, and my spirit attuned to sorrow,
pity, and despair, I had happened in some glade upon a merry party
of roisterers. I sat in silence until Edith began to rally me upon my
sombre looks. What ailed me? The others presently joined in the
playful assault, and I became a target for quips and jests. Where had
I been, and what had I seen to make such a dull fellow of me?

"I have been in Golgotha,"[2] at last I answered. "I have seen

---

[1]   Cain took his brother into the country and killed him. God asked the question when
     Cain returned. (Genesis 4:9)
[2]   Golgotha (meaning "skull"): the place outside Jerusalem where Christ was crucified.

Humanity hanging on a cross! Do none of you know what sights the sun and stars look down on in this city, that you can think and talk of anything else? Do you not know that close to your doors a great multitude of men and women, flesh of your flesh, live lives that are one agony from birth to death? Listen! their dwellings are so near that if you hush your laughter you will hear their grievous voices, the piteous crying of the little ones that suckle poverty, the hoarse curses of men sodden in misery, turned half-way back to brutes, the chaffering of an army of women selling themselves for bread. With what have you stopped your ears that you do not hear these doleful sounds? For me, I can hear nothing else."

Silence followed my words. A passion of pity had shaken me as I spoke, but when I looked around upon the company, I saw that, far from being stirred as I was, their faces expressed a cold and hard astonishment, mingled in Edith's with extreme mortification, in her father's with anger. The ladies were exchanging scandalized looks, while one of the gentlemen had put up his eyeglass and was studying me with an air of scientific curiosity. When I saw that things which were to me so intolerable moved them not at all, that words that melted my heart to speak had only offended them with the speaker, I was at first stunned and then overcome with a desperate sickness and faintness at the heart. What hope was there for the wretched, for the world, if thoughtful men and tender women were not moved by things like these! Then I bethought myself that it must be because I had not spoken aright. No doubt I had put the case badly. They were angry because they thought I was berating them, when God knew I was merely thinking of the horror of the fact without any attempt to assign the responsibility for it.

I restrained my passion, and tried to speak calmly and logically that I might correct this impression. I told them that I had not meant to accuse them, as if they, or the rich in general, were responsible for the misery of the world. True indeed it was, that the superfluity which they wasted would, otherwise bestowed, relieve much bitter suffering. These costly viands, these rich wines, these gorgeous fabrics and glistening jewels represented the ransom of many lives. They were verily not without the guiltiness of those who waste in a land stricken with famine. Nevertheless, all the waste of all the rich, were it saved, would go but a little way to cure the poverty of the world. There was so little to divide that even if the rich went share and share with the poor, there would be but a common fare of crusts, albeit made very sweet then by brotherly love.

The folly of men, not their hard-heartedness, was the great cause of the world's poverty. It was not the crime of man, nor of any class of men, that made the race so miserable, but a hideous, ghastly mistake, a colossal world-darkening blunder. And then I showed them how four fifths of the labor of men was utterly wasted by the mutual warfare, the lack of organization and concert among the workers. Seeking to make the matter very plain, I instanced the case of arid lands where the soil yielded the means of life only by careful use of the watercourses for irrigation. I showed how in such countries it was counted the most important function of the government to see that the water was not wasted by the selfishness or ignorance of individuals, since otherwise there would be famine. To this end its use was strictly regulated and systematized, and individuals of their mere caprice were not permitted to dam it or divert it, or in any way to tamper with it.

The labor of men, I explained, was the fertilizing stream which alone rendered earth habitable. It was but a scanty stream at best, and its use required to be regulated by a system which expended every drop to the best advantage, if the world were to be supported in abundance. But how far from any system was the actual practice! Every man wasted the precious fluid as he wished, animated only by the equal motives of saving his own crop and spoiling his neighbor's, that his might sell the better. What with greed and what with spite some fields were flooded while others were parched, and half the water ran wholly to waste. In such a land, though a few by strength or cunning might win the means of luxury, the lot of the great mass must be poverty, and of the weak and ignorant bitter want and perennial famine.

Let but the famine-stricken nation assume the function it had neglected, and regulate for the common good the course of the life-giving stream, and the earth would bloom like one garden, and none of its children lack any good thing. I described the physical felicity, mental enlightenment, and moral elevation which would then attend the lives of all men. With fervency I spoke of that new world, blessed with plenty, purified by justice and sweetened by brotherly kindness, the world of which I had indeed but dreamed, but which might so easily be made real. But when I had expected now surely the faces around me to light up with emotions akin to mine, they grew ever more dark, angry, and scornful. Instead of enthusiasm, the ladies showed only aversion and dread, while the men interrupted me with shouts of reprobation and contempt. "Madman!" "Pestilent fellow!" "Fanatic!" "Enemy of society!" were some of their cries, and the one who had before taken his eyeglass to me exclaimed, "He says we are to have no more poor. Ha! ha!"

"Put the fellow out!" exclaimed the father of my betrothed, and at the signal the men sprang from their chairs and advanced upon me.

It seemed to me that my heart would burst with the anguish of finding that what was to me so plain and so all-important was to them meaningless, and that I was powerless to make it other. So hot had been my heart that I had thought to melt an iceberg with its glow, only to find at last the overmastering chill seizing my own vitals. It was not enmity that I felt toward them as they thronged me, but pity only, for them and for the world.

Although despairing, I could not give over. Still I strove with them. Tears poured from my eyes. In my vehemence I became inarticulate. I panted, I sobbed, I groaned, and immediately afterward found myself sitting upright in bed in my room in Dr. Leete's house, and the morning sun shining through the open window into my eyes. I was gasping. The tears were streaming down my face, and I quivered in every nerve.

As with an escaped convict who dreams that he has been recaptured and brought back to his dark and reeking dungeon, and opens his eyes to see the heaven's vault spread above him, so it was with me, as I realized that my return to the nineteenth century had been the dream, and my presence in the twentieth was the reality.

The cruel sights which I had witnessed in my vision, and could so well confirm from the experience of my former life, though they had, alas! once been, and must in the retrospect to the end of time move the compassionate to tears, were, God be thanked, forever gone by. Long ago oppressor and oppressed, prophet and scorner, had been dust. For generations, rich and poor had been forgotten words.

But in that moment, while yet I mused with unspeakable thankfulness upon the greatness of the world's salvation and my privilege in beholding it, there suddenly pierced me like a knife a pang of shame, remorse, and wondering self-reproach, that bowed my head upon my breast and made me wish the grave had hid me with my fellows from the sun. For I had been a man of that former time. What had I done to help on the deliverance whereat I now presumed to rejoice? I who had lived in those cruel, insensate days, what had I done to bring them to an end? I had been every whit as indifferent to the wretchedness of my brothers, as cynically incredulous of better things, as besotted a worshipper of Chaos and Old Night, as any of my fellows.[1] So far as my personal influence went, it had been exerted rather to hinder than to help forward the enfranchisement of the race which was even then preparing. What right had I to hail a salvation which reproached me, to rejoice in a day whose dawning I had mocked?

"Better for you, better for you," a voice within me rang, "had this evil dream been the reality, and this fair reality the dream; better your part pleading for crucified humanity with a scoffing generation, than here, drinking of wells you digged not, and eating of trees whose husbandmen you stoned;" and my spirit answered, "Better, truly."[2]

When at length I raised my bowed head and looked forth from the window, Edith, fresh as the morning, had come into the garden and was gathering flowers. I hastened to descend to her. Kneeling before her, with my face in the dust, I confessed with tears how little was my worth to breathe the air of this golden century, and how infinitely less to wear upon my breast its consummate flower. Fortunate is he who, with a case so desperate as mine, finds a judge so merciful.

---

[1] Chaos and Old Night: the formless and confused universe before creation.
[2] May be based on Isaiah 36:16 or Proverbs 5:15.

POSTSCRIPT.

THE RATE OF THE WORLD'S PROGRESS

To the Editor of the Boston Transcript. The Transcript of March 30, 1888, contained a review *of Looking Backward,* in response to which I beg to be allowed a word. The description to which the book is devoted, of the radically new social and industrial institutions and arrangements supposed to be enjoyed by the people of the United States in the twentieth century, is not objected to as depicting a degree of human felicity and moral development necessarily unattainable by the race, provided time enough had been allowed for its evolution from the present chaotic state of society. In failing to allow this, the reviewer thinks that the author has made an absurd mistake, which seriously detracts from the value of the book as a work of realistic imagination. Instead of placing the realization of the ideal social state a scant fifty years ahead, it is suggested that he should have made his figure seventy-five centuries. There is certainly a large discrepancy between seventy-five centuries and fifty years, and if the reviewer is correct in his estimate of the probable rate of human progress, the outlook of the world is decidedly discouraging. But is he right? I think not.

Looking Backward, although in form a fanciful romance, is intended, in all seriousness, as a forecast, in accordance with the principles of evolution, of the next stage in the industrial and social development of humanity, especially in this country; and no part of it is believed by the author to be better supported by the indications of probability than the implied prediction that the dawn of the new era is already near at hand, and that the full day will swiftly follow. Does this seem at first thought incredible, in view of the vastness of the changes presupposed? What is the teaching of history but that great national transformations, while ages in unnoticed preparation, when once inaugurated, are accomplished with a rapidity and resistless momentum proportioned to their magnitude, not limited by it?

In 1759, when Quebec fell, the might of England in America

seemed irresistible, and the vassalage of the colonies assured. Nevertheless, thirty years later, the first President of the American Republic was inaugurated. In 1849, after Novara, Italian prospects appeared as hopeless as at any time since the Middle Ages; yet only fifteen years after, Victor Emmanuel was crowned King of United Italy. In 1864, the fulfillment of the thousand-year dream of German unity was apparently as far off as ever. Seven years later it had been realized, and William had assumed at Versailles the Crown of Barbarossa. In 1832, the original Anti-slavery Society was formed in Boston by a few so-called visionaries. Thirty-eight years later, in 1870, the society disbanded, its programme fully carried out.

These precedents do not, of course, prove that any such industrial and social transformation as is outlined in *Looking Backward* is impending; but they do show that, when the moral and economical conditions for it are ripe, it may be expected to go forward with great rapidity. On no other stage are the scenes shifted with a swiftness so like magic as on the great stage of history when once the hour strikes. The question is not, then, how extensive the scene-shifting must be to set the stage for the new fraternal civilization, but whether there are any special indications that a social transformation is at hand. The causes that have been bringing it ever nearer have been at work from immemorial time. To the stream of tendency setting toward an ultimate realization of a form of society which, while vastly more efficient for material prosperity, should also satisfy and not outrage the moral instincts, every sigh of poverty, every tear of pity, every humane impulse, every generous enthusiasm, every true religious feeling, every act by which men have given effect to their mutual sympathy by drawing more closely together for any purpose, have contributed from the beginnings of civilization. That this long stream of influence, ever widening and deepening, is at last about to sweep away the barriers it has so long sapped, is at least one obvious interpretation of the present universal ferment of men's minds as to the imperfections of present social arrangements. Not only are the toilers of the world engaged in something like a world-wide insurrection, but true and humane men and women, of every degree, are in a mood of exasperation, verging on absolute revolt, against social conditions that reduce life to a brutal struggle for existence, mock every dictate of ethics and religion, and render well-nigh futile the efforts of philanthropy.

As an iceberg, floating southward from the frozen North, is gradually undermined by warmer seas, and, become at last unstable, churns the sea to yeast for miles around by the mighty rockings that portend its overturn, so the barbaric industrial and social system, which has come down to us from savage antiquity, undermined by the modern humane spirit, riddled by the criticism of economic science, is shaking the world with convulsions that presage its collapse.

All thoughtful men agree that the present aspect of society is portentous of great changes. The only question is, whether they will be for the better or the worse. Those who believe in man's essential nobleness lean to the former view, those who believe in his essential baseness to the latter. For my part, I hold to the former opinion. *Looking Backward* was written in the belief that the Golden Age lies before us and not behind us, and is not far away. Our children will surely see it, and we, too, who are already men and women, if we deserve it by our faith and by our works.

EDWARD BELLAMY.

Appendix A: Why and How Bellamy Wrote
Looking Backward

[These selections are from "Why I Wrote *Looking Backward*" (*The Nationalist*, May 1890) and "How I Wrote *Looking Backward*" (*The Ladies' Home Journal*, April 1894). They indicate Bellamy's process of writing and his motivation.]

I ACCEPT more readily the invitation to tell in The Nationalist how I came to write "Looking Backward" for the reason that it will afford an opportunity to clear up certain points on which inquiries have been frequently addressed to me. I never had, previous to the publication of the work, any affiliations with any class or sect of industrial or social reformers nor, to make my confession complete, any particular sympathy with undertakings of the sort. It is only just to myself to say, however, that this should not be taken to indicate any indifference to the miserable condition of the mass of humanity, seeing that it resulted rather from a perception all too clear of the depth and breadth of the social problem and a consequent skepticism as to the effectiveness of the proposed solutions which had come to my notice.

In undertaking to write "Looking Backward" I had, at the outset, no idea of attempting a serious contribution to the movement of social reform. The idea was of a mere literary fantasy, a fairy tale of social felicity. There was no thought of contriving a house which practical men might live in, but merely of hanging in mid-air, far out of reach of the sordid and material world of the present, a cloud-palace for an ideal humanity.

In order to secure plenty of elbow room for the fancy and prevent awkward collisions between the ideal structure and the hard facts of the real world, I fixed the date of the story in the year A. D. 3000. As to what might be in A. D. 3000 one man's opinion was as good as another's, and my fantasy of the social system of that day only required to be consistent with itself to defy criticism. Emboldened by the impunity my isolated position secured me, I was satisfied with nothing less than the whole earth for my social palace. In its present form the story is a romance of the ideal nation, but in its first form it was a romance of an ideal world. In the first draft of "Looking

Backward," though the immediate scene was laid in America (in Asheville, North Carolina, instead of Boston, by the way,) the United States was supposed to be merely an administrative province of the great World Nation, whose affairs were directed from the World Capital which was declared to be the city of Berne, in Switzerland. The action of the story was made to begin in the thirtieth century.

The opening scene was a grand parade of a departmental division of the industrial army on the occasion of the annual muster day when the young men coming of age that year were mustered into the national service and those who that year had reached the age of exemption were mustered out. That chapter always pleased me and it was with some regrets that I left it out of the final draft. The solemn pageantry of the great festival of the year, the impressive ceremonial of the oath of duty taken by the new recruits in presence of the world-standard, the formal return of the thanks of humanity to the veterans who received their honorable dismissal from service, the review and march past of the entire body of the local industrial forces, each battalion with its appropriate insignia, the triumphal arches, the garlanded streets, the banquets, the music, the open theatres and pleasure gardens, with all the features of a gala day sacred to the civic virtues and the enthusiasm of humanity, furnished materials for a picture exhilarating at least to the painter.

The idea of committing the duty of maintaining the community to an industrial army, precisely as the duty of protecting it is entrusted to a military army, was directly suggested to me by the grand object lesson of the organization of an entire people for national purposes presented by the military system of universal service for fixed and equal terms, which has been practically adopted by the nations of Europe and theoretically adopted everywhere else as the only just and only effectual plan of public defense on a great scale. What inference could possibly be more obvious and more unquestionable than the advisability of trying to see if a plan which was found to work so well for purposes of destruction might not be profitably applied to the business of production now in such shocking confusion. But while this idea had for some time been vaguely floating in my mind, for a year or two I think at least, I had been far from realizing all that was in it, and only thought then of utilizing it as an analogy to lend an effect of feasibility to the fancy sketch I had in hand. It was not till I began to work out the details of the scheme by way of explaining how the people of the thirtieth century disposed of the awkward problems of labor and avoided the evils of a classified society that I perceived the full potency of the instrument I was using and recognized in the modern military system not merely a rhetorical analogy for a national industrial service, but its prototype, furnishing at once a complete working model for its organization, an arsenal of patriotic and national motives and arguments for its animation, and the unanswerable demonstration of its feasibility drawn from the actual experience of whole nations organized and manoeuvred as armies.

Something in this way it was that, no thanks to myself, I stumbled over the destined corner-stone of the new social order. It scarcely needs to be said that having once apprehended it for what it was, it became a matter of pressing importance to me to show it in the same light to other people. This led to a complete recasting, both in form and purpose, of the book I was engaged upon. Instead of a mere fairy tale of social perfection, it became the vehicle of a definite scheme of industrial reorganization. The form of a romance was retained, although with some impatience, in the hope of inducing the more to give it at least a reading. Barely enough story was left to decently drape the skeleton of the argument and not enough, I fear, in spots, for even that purpose. A great deal of merely fanciful matter concerning the manners, customs, social and political institutions, mechanical contrivances, and so forth of the people of the thirtieth century, which had been intended for the book, was cut out for fear of diverting the attention of readers from the main theme. Instead of the year A. D. 3000, that of A. D. 2000 was fixed upon as the date of the story. Ten centuries had at first seemed to me none too much to allow for the evolution of anything like an ideal society, but with my new belief as to the part which the National organization of industry is to play in bringing in the good time coming, it appeared to me reasonable to suppose that by the year 2000 the order of things which we look forward to will already have become an exceedingly old story. This conviction as to the shortness of the time in which the hope of Nationalization is to be realized by the birth of the new, and the first true, nation, I wish to say, is one which every day's reflection and observation, since the publication of "Looking Backward," has tended to confirm.

The same clearer conviction as to the method by which this great change is to come about, which caused me to shorten so greatly my estimate of the time in which it was to be accomplished, necessitated the substitution of the conception of a separate national evolution for the original idea of a homogeneous world-wide social system. The year 3000 may, indeed, see something of that sort, but not the year 2000.

(Reprinted in *Edward Bellamy Speaks Again!* Chicago: The Peerage Press, 1937, 199–203)

UP TO the age of eighteen I had lived almost continually in a thriving village of New England, where there were no very rich and very few poor, and everybody who was willing to work was sure of a fair living. At that time I visited Europe and spent a year there in travel and study. It was in the great cities of England, Europe, and among the hovels of the peasantry that my eyes were first fully opened to the extent and consequences of man's inhumanity to man.

I well remember in those days of European travel how much more deeply that blue background of misery impressed me than the palaces and cathedrals in relief against it. I distinctly recall the innumerable debates, suggested by the piteous sights about us, which I had with a dear companion of my journey, as to the possibility of finding some great remedy for poverty, some plan for equalizing human conditions. Our discussions usually brought up against the same old stump: who would do the dirty work? We did not realize, as probably few do who lightly dismiss the subject of social reform with the same query, that its logic implies the condonation of all forms of slavery. Not until we all acknowledge the world's "dirty work" as our common and equal responsibility, shall we be in a position intelligently to consider, or have the disposition seriously to seek a just and reasonable way of distributing and adjusting the burden. So it was that I returned home, for the first time aroused to the existence and urgency of the social problem, but without as yet seeing any way out. Although it had required the sights of Europe to startle me to a vivid realization of the inferno of poverty beneath our civilization, my eyes having once been opened I had now no difficulty in recognizing in America, and even in my own comparatively prosperous village, the same conditions in course of progressive development.

The other day rummaging among old papers I was much interested by the discovery of some writings indicative of my state of mind at that period. If the reader will glance over the following extracts from the manuscript of an address which it appears I delivered before the Chicopee Falls Village Lyceum along in 1871 or 1872, he will probably admit that their youthful author was quite likely to attempt something in the line of "Looking Backward" if he only lived long enough. The subject of this address was "The Barbarism of Society," the barbarism being held to consist in and result from inequality in the distribution of wealth. From numerous equally radical expressions I excerpt these paragraphs: "The great reforms of the world have hitherto been political rather than social. In their progress classes privileged by title have been swept away, but classes privileged by wealth remain. A nominal aristocracy is ceasing to exist, but the actual aristocracy of wealth, the world over, is every day becoming more and more powerful. The idea that men can derive a right from birth or name to dispose of the destinies of their fellows is exploded, but the world thinks not yet of denying that gold confers a power upon its possessors to domineer over their equals and enforce from them a life's painful labors at the price of a bare subsistence. I would not have indignation blind my eyes or confuse my reason in the contemplation of this injustice, but I ask you what is the name of an institution by which men control the labor of other men, and out of the abundance created by that labor having doled out to the laborers such a pittance as may barely support life and sustain strength for added tasks, reserve to themselves the vast surplus for the support of a life of ease and splendor? This, gentlemen, is slavery; a slavery whose prison is the world, whose shackles and fetters are the unyielding frame of society, whose lash is hunger, whose taskmasters are those bodily necessities for whose supply the rich who hold the keys of the world's granaries must be appealed to, and the necks of the needy bowed to their yoke as the price of the boon of life...Consider a moment the condition of that class of society by whose unremitting toil the ascendancy of man over the material universe is maintained and his existence rendered possible on earth, remembering, also, that this class comprises the vast majority of the race. Born of parents whom brute passion impelled to the propagation of their kind; bred in penury and the utter lack of all those luxuries and amenities of life which go so far to make existence tolerable; their intellectual faculties neglected and an unnatural and forced development given to their basest instincts; their childhood, the sweet vacation of life, saddened and deadened by the pinching of poverty, and then, long before the immature frame could support the severity of labor, forced from the playground into the factory or field! Then begins the obscure, uninteresting drama of a laborer's life; an unending procession of toilsome days relieved by brief and rare holidays and harassed by constant anxiety lest he lose all he claims from the world—a place to labor. He feels, in some dumb, unreasoning way, oppressed by the frame of society, but it is too heavy for him to lift. The institutions that crush him down assume to his dulled brain the inevitable and irresistible aspect of natural laws. And so, with only that dim sense of injustice which no subtlety of reasoning, no array of argument can banish from the human soul when it feels itself oppressed, he bows his head to his fate.

"Let not any one falsely reply that I am dreaming of a happiness without toil, of abundance without labor. Labor is the necessary condition, not only of the abundance but of existence upon earth. I ask only that none labor beyond measure that others may be idle, that there be no more masters and no more slaves among men. Is this too much? Does any fearful soul exclaim, impossible, that this hope has been the dream of men in all ages, a shadowy and Utopian reverie of a divine fruition which the earth can never bear? That the few must revel and the many toil; the few waste, the many want; the few be masters, the many serve; the toilers of the earth be the poor and the idlers the rich, and that this must go on forever?

"Ah, no; has the world then dreamed in vain. Have the ardent longings of the lovers of men been toward an unattainable felicity? Are the aspirations after liberty, equality and happiness implanted in the very core of our hearts for nothing?

"Not so, for nothing that is unjust can be eternal and nothing that is just can be impossible."

Since I came across this echo of my youth and recalled the half-forgotten exercises of mind it testifies to, I have been wondering, not why I wrote "Looking Backward," but why I did not write it or try to twenty years ago.

Like most men, however, I was under the sordid and selfish necessity of solving the economic problem in its personal bearings before I could give much time to the cure of society in general. I had, like others, to fight my way to a place at the world's work-bench where I could make a living. For a dozen or fifteen years I followed journalism, doing in a desultory way, as opportunity offered, a good deal of magazine and book writing. In none of the writings of this period did I touch on the social question, but not the less all the while it was in mind, as a problem not by any means given up, how poverty might be abolished and the economic equality of all citizens of the republic be made as much a matter of course as their political equality. I had always the purpose, some time when

I had sufficient leisure, to give myself earnestly to the examination of this great problem, but meanwhile kept postponing it, giving my time and thoughts to easier tasks.

Possibly I never should have mustered up courage for an undertaking so difficult and indeed so presumptuous, but for events which gave the problem of life a new and more solemn meaning to me. I refer to the birth of my children...

According to my best recollection it was in the fall or winter of 1886 that I sat down to my desk with the definite purpose of trying to reason out a method of economic organization by which the republic might guarantee the livelihood and material welfare of its citizens on a basis of equality corresponding to and supplementing their political equality. There was no doubt in my mind that the proposed study should be in the form of a story. This was not merely because that was a treatment which would command greater popular attention than others. In adventuring in any new and difficult field of speculation I believe that the student often cannot do better than to use the literary form of fiction. Nothing outside of the exact sciences has to be so logical as the thread of a story, if it is to be acceptable. There is no such test of a false and absurd idea as trying to fit it into a story. You may make a sermon or an essay or a philosophical treatise as illogical as you please and no one know the difference, but all the world is a good critic of a story, for it has to conform to the laws of ordinary probability and commonly observed sequence, of which we are all judges.

The stories that I had written before "Looking Backward" were largely of one sort, namely, the working out of problems, that is to say, attempts to trace the logical consequences of certain assumed conditions. It was natural, therefore, that in this form the plan of "Looking Backward" should present itself to my mind. Given the United States, a republic based upon the equality of all men and conducted by their equal voice, what would the natural and logical way be by which to go about the work of guaranteeing an economic equality to its citizens corresponding with their political equality, but without the present unjust discrimination of sex? From the moment the problem first clearly presented itself to my mind in this way, the writing of the book was the simplest thing in the world...

(Reprinted in *Edward Bellamy Speaks Again!* Chicago: The Peerage Press, 1937, 217-28)

Appendix B: William Morris's review of Looking Backward *and Bellamy's review of* Morris's News from Nowhere, *plus periodical reviews of* Looking Backward

[When William Morris read *Looking Backward* he determined that he had to write a "counterblast." This took the form of a review in the journal *Commonweal* and ultimately a utopian novel of his own. Bellamy in turn reviewed Morris's utopia in the *New Nation*. The reviews are significant not only as utopian documents but as representative responses to the industrial age. The contrast between Bellamy's highly centralized and mechanized utopia and Morris's completely de-centralized utopia with its emphasis on hand-craft could hardly be more striking.]

We often hear it said that the signs of the spread of Socialism among English-speaking people are both abundant and striking. This is true; six or seven years ago the word Socialism was known in this country, but few even among the "educated" classes knew more about its meaning than Mr. Bradlaugh, Mr. Gladstone, or Admiral Maxse know now—i.e., nothing. Whereas at present it is fashionable for even West-end dinner-parties to affect an interest in and knowledge of it, which indicates a wide and deep public interest.[1] This interest is more obvious in literature perhaps than in anything else, quite outside the propagandist tracts issued by definitely Socialist societies. A certain tincture of Socialism, for instance (generally very watery), is almost a necessary ingredient nowadays in a novel which aims at being at once serious and life-like, while more serious treatment of the subject at the hands of non-Socialists is common enough. In short the golden haze of self-satisfaction and content with the best of all possible societies is rolling away before the sun-heat bred of misery and aspiration, and all people above the lowest level of intelligence (which I take to be low gambling and

---

[1]   Bradlaugh and Gladstone were well-known politicians; the "West end" of London
       was an "upscale" area.

statesmanship) are looking towards the new development, some timorously, some anxiously, some hopefully.

It seems clear to me [from] the reception which Mr. Bellamy's *Looking Backward* has received that there are a great many people who are hopeful in regard to Socialism. I am sure that ten years ago it would have been very little noticed, if at all; whereas now several editions have been sold in America, and it is attracting general attention in England, and to anyone not deeply interested in the social question it could not be at all an attractive book. It is true that it is cast into the form of a romance, but the author states very frankly in his preface that he has only given it this form as a sugar-coating to the pill, and the device of making a man wake up in a new world has now grown so common, and has been done with so much more care and art than Mr. Bellamy has used, that by itself this would have done little for it; it is the serious essay and not the slight envelope of romance which people have found interesting to them.

Since, therefore, both Socialists and non-Socialists have been so much impressed with the book, it seems to me necessary that the *Commonweal* should notice it. For it is a 'Utopia'. It purports to be written in the year 2000, and to describe the state of society at that period after a gradual and peaceable revolution has realized the Socialism which to us is but in the beginning of its militant period. It requires notice all the more because there is a certain danger in such books as this: a twofold danger; for there will be some temperaments to whom the answer given to the question, "How shall we live then?" will be pleasing and satisfactory, others to whom it will be displeasing and unsatisfactory. The danger to the first is that they will accept it with all its necessary errors and fallacies (which such a book *must* abound in) as conclusive statements of facts and rules of action, which will warp their efforts into futile directions. The danger to the second, if they are but enquirers or very young Socialists, is that they also accepting its speculations as facts will be inclined to say, "If *that* is Socialism, we won't help its advent, as it holds out no hope to us."

The only safe way of reading a utopia is to consider it as the expression of the temperament of its author. So looked at, Mr. Bellamy's utopia must be still called very interesting, as it is constructed with due economical knowledge, and with much adroitness; and of course his temperament is that of many thousands of people. This temperament may be called the unmixed modern one, unhistoric and unartistic; it makes its owner (if a Socialist) perfectly satisfied with modern civilization, if only the injustice, misery, and waste of class society could be got rid of; which half-change seems possible to him. The only ideal of life which such a man can see is that of the industrious *professional* middle-class men of to-day purified from their crime of complicity with the monopolist class, and become independent instead of being, as they now are, parasitical. It is not to be denied that if such an ideal could be realized, it would be a great improvement on the present society. But can it be realized? It means in fact the alteration of the machinery of life in such a way that all men shall be allowed to share in the fulness of that life, for the production and upholding of which the machinery was instituted. There are clear signs to show us that that very group whose life is thus put forward as an ideal for the future are condemning it in the present, and that they also demand a revolution. The pessimistic revolt of the latter end of this century led by John Ruskin[1] against the philistinism of the triumphant bourgeois, halting and stumbling as it necessarily was, shows that the change in the life of civilization had begun, before any one seriously believed in the possibility of altering its machinery.

It follows naturally from the author's satisfaction with the best part of modern life that he conceives of the change to Socialism as taking place without any breakdown of that life, or indeed disturbance of it, by means of the final development of the great private monopolies which are such a noteworthy feature of the present day. He supposes that these must necessarily be absorbed into one great monopoly which will include the whole people and be worked for its benefit by the whole people. It may be noted in passing that by this use of the word monopoly he shows unconsciously that he has his mind fixed firmly on the mere *machinery* of life: for clearly the only part of their system which the people would or could take over from the monopolists would be the machinery of organization, which monopoly is forced to use, but which is not an essential part of it. The essential of monopoly is, "I warm myself by the fire which you have made, and you (very much the plural) stay outside in the cold."

To go on. This hope of the development of the trusts and rings to which the competition for privilege has driven commerce, especially

---

[1] John Ruskin began in the 1840s as a writer of art criticism and by the 1860s was writing social and economic criticism, lamenting the de-humanizing effects of the industrial system. His artistic and social concerns came together in "The Nature of Gothic," his famous chapter on Gothic architecture in *The Stones of Venice* (1853).

in America, is the distinctive part of Mr. Bellamy's book; and it seems to me to be a somewhat dangerous hope to rest upon, too uncertain to be made a sheet-anchor of. It may be indeed the logical outcome of the most modern side of commercialism—*i.e.,* the outcome that *ought* to be; but then there is its historical outcome to be dealt with— *i.e.,* what *will* be; which I cannot help thinking may be after all, as far as this commercial development is concerned, the recurrence of breaks-up and re-formations of this kind of monopoly, under the influence of competition for privilege, or war for the division of plunder, till the flood comes and destroys them all. A far better hope to trust to is that men having once got it into their heads that true life implies free and equal life, and that is now possible of attainment, they will consciously strive for its attainment at any cost. The economical semi-fatalism of some Socialists is a deadening and discouraging view, and may easily become more so, if events at present unforeseen bring back the full tide of "commercial prosperity"; which is by no means unlikely to happen.

The great change having thus peaceably and fatalistically taken place, the author has to put forward this scheme of the organization of life; which is organized with a vengeance. His scheme may be described as State Communism, worked by the very extreme of national centralisation. The underlying vice in it is that the author cannot conceive, as aforesaid, of anything else than the *machinery* of society, and that, doubtless naturally, he reads in to the future of a society, which he tells us is unwastefully conducted, that terror of starvation, which is the necessary accompaniment of a society in which two-thirds or more of its labour-power *is* wasted: the result is that though he *tells* us that every man is free to choose his occupation and that work is no burden to anyone, the *impression* which he produces is that of a huge standing army, tightly drilled, compelled by some mysterious fate to unceasing anxiety for the production of wares to satisfy every caprice, however wasteful and absurd, that may cast up amongst them.

As an illustration it may be mentioned that everybody is to begin the serious work of production at the age of twenty-one, work three years as a labourer, and then choose his skilled occupation and work till he is forty-five, when he is to knock off his work and amuse himself (improve his mind, if he has one left him). Heavens! think of a man of forty-five changing all his habits suddenly and by compulsion! It is a small matter after this that the said persons past work should form a kind of aristocracy (how curiously old ideas cling) for the performance of certain judicial and political functions.

Mr. Bellamy's ideas of life are curiously limited; he has no idea beyond existence in a great city; his dwelling of man in the future is Boston (USA) beautified. In one passage, indeed, he mentions villages, but with unconscious simplicity shows that they do not come into his scheme of economical equality, but are mere servants of the great centres of civilization. This seems strange to some of us, who cannot help thinking that our experience ought to have taught us that such aggregations of population afford the worst possible form of dwelling-place, whatever the second-worst might be.

In short, a machine-life is the best which Mr. Bellamy can imagine for us on all sides; it is not to be wondered at then that his only idea of making labour tolerable is to decrease the amount of it by means of fresh and ever fresh developments of machinery. This view I know he will share with many Socialists with whom I might otherwise agree more than I can with him; but I think a word or two is due to this important side of the subject. Now surely this ideal of the great reduction of the hours of labour by the mere means of machinery is a futility. The human race has always put forth about as much energy as it could in given conditions of climate and the like, though that energy has had to struggle against the natural laziness of mankind: and the development of man's resources, which has given him greater power over nature, has driven him also into fresh desires and fresh demands on nature, and thus made his expenditure of energy much what it was before. I believe that this will be always so, and the multiplication of machinery will just—multiply machinery; I believe that the ideal of the future does not point to the lessening of men's energy by the reduction of *labour* to a minimum, but rather to the reduction of *pain in labour* to a minimum, so small that it will cease to be a pain; a gain to humanity which can only be dreamed of till men are even more completely equal than Mr. Bellamy's utopia would allow them to be, but which will most assuredly come about when men are really equal in condition; although it is probable that much of our so-called "refinement", our luxury—in short, our civilization—will have to be sacrificed to it. In this part of his scheme, therefore, Mr. Bellamy worries himself unnecessarily in seeking (with obvious failure) some incentive to labour to replace the fear of starvation, which is at present our only one, whereas it cannot be too often repeated that the true incentive to useful and happy labour is and must be pleasure in the work itself.

I think it necessary to state these objections to Mr. Bellamy's utopia, not because there is any need to quarrel with a man's vision of the future of society, which, as above said, must always be more or less personal to himself; but because this book, having produced a great impression on people who are really enquiring into Socialism, will be sure to be quoted as an authority for what Socialists believe, and that, therefore, it is necessary to point out that there are some Socialists who do not think that the problem of the organization of life and necessary labour can be dealt with by a huge national centralisation, working by a kind of magic for which no one feels himself responsible; that on the contrary it will be necessary for the unit of administration to be small enough for every citizen to feel himself responsible for its details, and be interested in them; that individual men cannot shuffle off the business of life on to the shoulders of an abstraction called the State, but must deal with it in conscious association with each other. That variety of life is as much an aim of a true Communism as equality of condition, and that nothing but an union of these two will bring about real freedom. That modern nationalities are mere artificial devices for the commercial war that we seek to put an end to, and will disappear with it. And, finally, that art, using that word in its widest and due signification, is not a mere adjunct of life which free and happy men can do without, but the necessary expression and indispensable instrument of human happiness.

On the other hand, it must be said that Mr. Bellamy has faced the difficulty of economical reconstruction with courage, though he does not see any other sides to the problem, such, *e.g.,* as the future of the family; that at any rate he sees the necessity for the equality of the reward of labour, which is such a stumbling-block for incomplete Socialists; and his criticism of the present monopolist system is forcible and fervid. Also up and down his pages there will be found satisfactory answers to many ordinary objections. The book is one to be read and considered seriously, but it should not be taken as the Socialist bible of reconstruction; a danger which perhaps it will not altogether escape, as incomplete systems impossible to be carried out but plausible on the surface are always attractive to people ripe for change, but not knowing clearly what their aim is.

(From Morris's review of *Looking Backward* in *Commonweal*, 22 June 1889, 194–95)

Perhaps the most distinguished of the many converts which socialism in England has made from among the cultured class is William Morris, author of "The Earthly Paradise," and one of the greatest of living poets. His "News From Nowhere," just published in this country by Roberts Brothers, is a setting forth in the form of a clever fiction of his ideal of the good time coming, and is exceedingly well worth reading. The tale is on this wise: After a heated discussion with his friends at the socialist league, the narrator goes home and to bed. When he wakes he is surprised to find it summer, whereas it was winter when he went to bed. On going forth he discovers that everything else is changed, and in fine that it is the England of the 20th century that he has awakened to. Then follows the story of a week's wanderings among the friendly people by whom he finds himself surrounded, his experience naturally consisting largely of questions and answers born of his surprise at what he sees about him and the surprise of those about him at his surprise. All the while he has a vague idea, just as one so often has in dreams, that he is dreaming, and it finally turns out that he was dreaming, and he awakes again much disgusted in this musty 19th century. This dream business is very cleverly managed, though of course it is merely the contrivance for getting the author's social ideas in objective form.

Mr. Morris appears to belong to the school of anarchistic rather than to the state socialists. That is to say, he believes that the present system of private capitalism once destroyed, voluntary co-operation, with little or no governmental administration, will be necessary to bring about the ideal social system. This is in strong contrast with the theory of nationalism, which holds that no amount of moral excellence or good feeling on the part of a community will enable them to dispense with a great deal of system in order so to co-ordinate their efforts as to obtain the best economic results. In the sense of a force to restrain and punish, governmental administration may no doubt be dispensed with in proportion as a better social system shall be introduced; but in no degree will any degree of moral improvement lessen the necessity of a strictly economic administration for the directing of the productive and distributive machinery. This is a distinction which anarchists too commonly overlook, when they argue against the necessity of government.

In Mr. Morris' ideal England there appears to be no central government, but merely an aggregation of communes or towns, each of which regulates its own affairs on a strictly democratic basis.

We are given no suggestion as to how any form of administration extending beyond town limits is conducted, as, for instance, the railroad system. We are told that manufacturing has been so much improved that the greatest fear of the people is that presently there will be no more work to do; but as to the industrial system, by which this result has been effected, Mr. Morris is provokingly silent, although nothing is more certain than that a great deal of system must have been required to produce the effect described.

Such glimpses as we are given of the business methods of the people pique our curiosity still further as to how they manage to make the ends meet. In the stores and markets everybody takes what he wants and as much of it as he wishes, and that is all there is about it. This is delightful, and we are not to be understood as saying that the plan under given conditions would be any more impossible than it now is for the community to maintain public roads and bridges for everybody to use at pleasure. We simply wish very much that Mr. Morris had told us more about the system. In Mr. Morris' England there appears to be no punishment for crime, not even homicide. It is found that society, being justly organized and artificial temptations to crime being absent, there is very little of it, and that the force of an absolutely united sentiment of public reprobation, together with his own conscience, is quite sufficient punishment for an offender. We believe that Mr. Morris is right in describing this order of things as a characteristic of the coming era of social improvement.

There is one sort of crime which Mr. Morris gives us slight hopes of ever getting rid of,—homicide growing out of love quarrels. If, indeed, the women are going to be so distracting lovely in the new age as Mr. Morris describes them, the men are scarcely to be blamed for losing their wits over them. Upon this theme he dwells with all a poet's enthusiasm. Upon the subject of education he has some very pregnant suggestions, though here too, as in the matter of economics, we wish he had been a little more definite. In one respect we regret to be obliged to make an issue with Mr. Morris. It is quite excusable for an Englishman to select England as the locality of his 20th century Eden; but we object to his describing America as being at that time so far behindhand in social progress as to be an object of pity.

(From "News from Nowhere" in *The New Nation,* 14 February 1891, 47)

[The following review, which appeared shortly after publication of *Looking Backward,* focused upon details of Bellamy's vision of the future.]

It is not because a topic has been often treated that it must be forever abandoned. The author of that very clever book, "Dr. Heidenoff's Process," has sufficient talent and ingenuity to take any salient idea and clothe and deck it with an ingenious manner, "Looking Backward" has something of an About fancy about it, inasmuch as Julian West, a Boston man, suffering from insomnia, goes to bed one night and wakes up, so he believes, just 113 years afterward. That doze was longer than the one forcedly taken by the French romancer's officer of Hussars who hibernated from the time of Napoleon the Great to that of Napoleon the Little.[1] Julian West sees a Boston reformed and Socialistically perfect. There may be a Beacon Street, but it does not exist for the elect alone. When you dine at the Elephant the waiter is a perfect gentleman swell and scholar. All Boston men have to be waiters. They make their début in that calling. No cooking is done at home. There is a general factory where the baked bean and the roast turkey are made quite perfect. You touch your electric button in the dining room of this gastronomic hash and ragout phalanstery, and you are served in a trice at the lowest possible cost. The newspaper business in the Boston A. D. 2000 does not differ much from that in vogue today. When people want a journal reflecting their opinions, or any trade or profession, they subscribe a certain amount and elect an editor. He is not hired, but elected. The book publishing is, however, peculiar. If a man must write a book he pays for its own printing. If it succeeds he gets a royalty, or percentage; or, if it don't succeed, that's an end of it. There are no mercenary publishers in this novel Boston. The music business is nicely managed in 2000. In a grand central building, provided with several hundreds of thousands of separate concert rooms, there are assembled musicians, who play night and day. In one room, may be, is performed the Wagnerian crash, in another are negro minstrels, with a banjo and bones. You work your telephone, and you hear just what you please. It's all done by means of tickets and a punch. You want a coat. It's so much. You present your ticket and a hole is cut in it. That's your debit. Your credit is the hours of work you

---

[1]   Edmond About's *L'homme à l'oreille cassée (The Man With The Broken Ear)* of 1862. About's hero also falls in love with a descendant of his sweetheart from 1813, but the Clementine of 1859 turns out to be his grand-daughter.

have done or are to do. There is no use for money in that blessed Boston of the future. Julian West had a delightful time. Just before he went to sleep, in 1887, he was going to marry Edith Bartlett, and in 2000 he still remembers her, but then there is another Edith—Edith Leeth [sic]—and the old Julian and the young Edith fall in love with one another. There has [sic] existed affinities à la Goethe between Julian and Edith Leeth, for the good reason that the early Edith, tired of waiting for the original Julian, married another fellow and the present Edith is the great-grand-daughter of Edith of the Boston of the Miocene period. Just before the marriage bells are to be sounded—if they did use such contrivances in a perfected Boston—Julian does really awake, and finds out that it has been only a dream. The whole business is elaborately well worked out, and Utopia neatly described.

("New Books," *The New-York Times,* 27 February 1888, 3)

[The following Canadian review of *Looking Backward* is highly favorable and shows how eagerly the religious themes of the novel were received.]

…We would warn readers of this notice that the author of this book is no visionary, and the society to the description of which this book is devoted is no imaginary and impossible thing. *Looking Backward,* although in form a fanciful romance, undertakes to give, in all seriousness, "a forecast in accordance with the principles of evolution of the next stage in the industrial and social development of humanity, especially in this country, and no part of it is believed by the author to be better supported by the indications of probability than the implied prediction that the dawn of the new era is already near at hand, and that the full day will swiftly follow."

We commend this book to ministers. During the month of August, and occasionally in other seasons, they can find time for a little light reading. There is nothing among recent fiction that will suit them as well as *Looking Backward.* We commend it all the more strongly because it may awaken in them an interest, or deepen interest already felt in the great social and economic problems so pressing to-day. Political Economy is coming to the front, and every minister of Christ should know something of its principles; and if this book will open any wise and reasonable minister's eyes to the enormities and barbaric inequalities of modern society, it will do much for the community in which he lives. The Church cannot pass by on the other side as she did before Christ came. She must study the great social problems. Christianity must vindicate her claim to Divine origin and her right to continued support, not by appeals to historic records or documents or creeds or confessions, but by showing her adaptability to present-day human needs. And when ministers of religion in increasing numbers become impressed with this truth, and turn again to their text-book—the Bible—they will find the true principles of political economy enunciated more clearly by Moses and by Christ than by Malthus, or Spencer, or Mill, or Rogers, or Cairnes, or Ashley. They will find, on studying history, that poverty and pauperism came not in obedience to God's laws, but in departure from simplicity of manners and in violations of Divine commands.

That the Golden Age lies so near at hand we do not say. But we believe it is coming, and that it is nearer by every worn-out lie, by every uttered truth, by every good law enacted and every good institution established, by every vanquished passion and lust and ambition and avarice and jealousy. We cannot dip far into the future, but the apocalyptic seer saw a new order of things, in which "there was no more sea," an end to "all the weary oar to all the weary wandering fields of barren foam."[1] What fools and barbarians we shall appear to those who, from that brighter day, will look backward upon the nineteenth century of the Christian era.

(From "Looking Backward" by J. A. M. *Knox College Monthly and Presbyterian Magazine*, Toronto, Ont, Canada. 10.4, 1889, 209-12)

[See Appendix G for an excerpt from Henry George's *Progress and Poverty*. The following is his view of *Looking Backward*.]

…my opinion is that "Looking Backward" is a castle in the air, with clouds for its foundation. Looked at from afar off by those who are weary of the heat and dust of daily life on the earth's surface, it seems exceedingly cool and tempting. How they might really like it if they were there is another matter. But no way of getting there is shown. "Looking Backward" is, in short, a popular presentation of the dream of state socialism, and in its failure to indicate any way

---

[1]   References to Tennyson's "Locksley Hall" and "The Lotos-Eaters."

of "getting there," does not differ from the more serious socialistic works which have supplied its suggestion.

Nevertheless, it is doing, and will do, great good. Reaching large numbers of people who would find it hard work to read anything more argumentative than a love story, it is breaking up in their minds the notion that things as they are are things as they must always be. To thousands and thousands of the men and women who read it, it has never before occurred to think of as possible a state of society in which stunting and embruting poverty should be unknown, and a whole people, not merely a favored few, should have leisure and opportunity to develop their finer tastes and higher powers. Such an idea is to those who first grasp it a revelation, and even if it is encumbered with all the wild impossibilities of state socialism, it is likely to do them permanent good, and to put many of them upon more careful inquiry.

The good that has been done by "Looking Backward" is indeed already evident in the formation of Nationalist clubs, the starting of periodicals like the Dawn of Boston, and the quickened impulse that has been given to thought on social subjects in circles that would have been hard to reach by anything less imaginative and more logical. That it is giving a strong impulse to socialism—the idea of effecting social improvement by governmental paternalism—is probably true. But socialism is far better than the contented acquiescence in suffering and wrong without thought of improvement in general conditions.

(Review of *Looking Backward* by Henry George in *The Standard*, New York, 31 August 1889, 1–2)

[Benjamin Tucker printed the following review in his anarchist journal *Liberty*. It objects primarily to what is seen as the coercive aspect of Bellamy's state.]

Mr. Edward Bellamy's book, "Looking Backward," in the form of a novel, portrays a social order akin to that advocated by the European State Socialists, but so largely impregnated with Christian communism that its large circulation may be readily accounted for among those who know that their aspirations for a better social state are not encouraged by the various religious denominations who are disinclined to look to this world for a practical goal in their race for happiness. The picture Mr. Bellamy draws is also captivating and plausible to the worker whose toil is unremunerative. An assurance that the family will always be provided for is more than he can get under the present social order, and he willingly listens to Mr. Bellamy's seductive schemes. The increasing discontent with existing conditions makes men eager to hear of a solution, and has also aided the circulation of Mr. Bellamy's book, even among the well-to-do, many of whom, he says, are riding in the stage coach without contributing to its progress, and who read that the toilers will upset the coach before the end of the journey.

The general idea pervading the work of Mr. Bellamy is that the social conditions of today are manifestly not in harmony with justice and equity. Without giving any of the details, it is supposed that one hundred years in the future a change in our industrial system has taken place, in which conditions appear that are a realization of what Mr. Bellamy considers the true relations of men to one another in the social state. The absence of the method by which so complete a change was effected is the weak feature of the book, as it is, in fact, the weakness of all the plans that have for their object the sudden transformation of one state of civilization to that of another so characteristic of the sentimental reformer of today…

We are in the habit of congratulating ourselves that the time has passed when a majority can dictate us as to what we shall do to be saved; but here is thrust upon us a system, which, while not concerning itself about our salvation in another world, compels us to mould ourselves to suit the majority's opinion about our salvation in this. We are not to buy and sell as buyer and seller wish, because "that would be inconsistent with the mutual benevolence and disinterestedness which should prevail between citizens, and the sense of community interests which supports our social system." We are all to have the same wages, although the term wages is repudiated, the hours of labor being regulated accordingly to offset the present natural law of supply and demand; still this law is made to do duty on special occasions. When volunteers fail to enter trades which the law of supply and demand has determined to be hazardous and uncongenial, the State resorts to a compulsory draft, and woe to the man who will not obey, because "a man able to do duty and persistently refusing is cut off from all human society"; this means that he is either imprisoned or outlawed.

("Beauties of Bellamism," *Liberty* 6.24. Boston, 25 January 1890, 7)

[The following is notice of "A French Opinion of 'Looking Backward.' Too Dull for Endurance."]

"Notwithstanding the apparent meaning of the title, 'Looking Backward,' is," M. Bentzon says, "simply a picture of the future, as an American of mediocre education may picture it," and he registers in honour of America Mr. Dudley Warner's emphatic protest that if he were allowed to choose as a place of residence between hell and Mr. Bellamy's America, he would choose the former without hesitation. The absence of art, literature, privacy, individuality in the pictured life, is more than the French critic can bear to contemplate. After following the fortunes of Julian West, up to the moment of his happy union with Edith, he takes leave of them in words which many of the unregenerate will echo: "Let them be happy if they can. The golden age promised to the hopes of the human race attracts us very little. To summarize it in a word, it is too industrial: it must end inevitably—the very doubtful taste of the public being the sole criterion in question[s] of art and literature—in the triumph of cheap bronze chromo-lithographs and newspaper novels. Perhaps it may suffice for new peoples—the Australians, for example; but we should always crave for a few essential refinements, without which this rich and rude pervert of positive progress would leave us indifferent. Would not a society which was without degrees, without passions, without contrasts of any sort, be terribly dull? Admitting that it could exist, would not some souls still regret the poetry of the suffering and heroism involved in the struggle between the strong will and the obstacles it has set itself to overcome, without which there is no triumph? . . If, however, the fate of the old world should be to follow with docility in the twentieth century the impulse of the chariot of equality which Mr. Bellamy substitutes for the old coach, it only remains for us to thank God that we have been born at a time when the world, however sick it may be, leaves still a little room for each man's individuality, and is something else besides a formidable industrial machine organized on the pattern of the German Army, with foremen in the place of generals."

Although this passage may be taken as representative of M. Bentzon's private opinions, the review is not, on the whole, unsympathetic, and will certainly serve Mr. Bellamy's purpose in causing his ideas to be discussed in a fresh circle.

(*The Review of Reviews* 2, 11. New York, November 1890, 457)

Appendix C: Excerpt from "The Religion of Solidarity"

["The Religion of Solidarity" was written in 1874 but not published until 1940. Bellamy said in 1887 that it constituted the "germ" of his philosophy of life and the basis for the great leap to brotherhood and sisterhood portrayed in *Looking Backward*. Also, in this germ may be seen the link between Edward Bellamy and the New England Transcendentalists of a previous generation.]

Seeing there is in every human being a soul common in nature with all other souls, but in a measure isolated by the conditions of individuality, it is easy to understand the origin of that cardinal motive of human life, which is a tendency and a striving to absorb or be absorbed in or united with other lives and all life. This passion for losing ourselves in others or for absorbing them into ourselves, which rebels against individuality as an impediment, is then the expression of the greatest law of solidarity. So long as the particle of this life of solidarity within us is hindered by individual conditions from merging with the rest, that is with the all, so long will desire and the pathos of its partial disappointment be an underlying fact of human nature. It is the operation of this law in great and low things, in the love of men for women, and for each other, for the race, for nature, and for those great ideas which are the symbols of solidarity, that has ever made up the web and woof of human passion. Love between individuals is the attraction between kindred particles, but the greatest of all loves, at once the most enthusiastic, the most sustaining, the most insatiable love of loves is that of an individual for his remnant, the universe. This is the love of God by whatever name men may choose to call it. The manner in which love asserts itself between individuals is illustrative of its genesis in the law of solidarity. It is the nature of our souls to fuse together, for they are one, but by the conditions of individuality, the particle in each one of us is, as it were, fenced about and shut into itself...

(*The Religion of Solidarity*. Ed. by Arthur E. Morgan. Yellow Springs, Ohio: Antioch Book Plate Company, 1940, 31-32)

Appendix D: Passages from Equality Showing Development of Bellamy's Utopian Ideas 1887–1897

[In the years between *Looking Backward* and *Equality* Bellamy thought deeply about his utopia and about the many comments and criticisms it evoked. As a result, the vision of *Equality* was different in several important ways. Among these are the following: (1) the provision in *Looking Backward* that shirkers of work could be imprisoned on bread and water was softened, and in *Equality* the anti-social are placed on reservations; (2) in *Looking Backward* Edith Leete seems like a typical Victorian young lady of the privileged class, whereas in the later novel Bellamy takes pains to indicate that women participate fully in all work; (3) *Looking Backward* identified utopia with a great city, whereas the Boston of *Equality* is much smaller than in the nineteenth century; (4) in *Looking Backward* the change was accomplished with absolutely no violence and although the transition in *Equality* is on the whole peaceful the portrait does include "considerable" violence. The fifth passage is included because of current interest in Bellamy's view of race relations. In *Looking Backward* itself, Julian West's servant Sawyer is presumably killed in the fire and there is no reference to blacks in the future society (although in the Postscript Bellamy refers to the defeat of slavery with strong approval). Here Bellamy rectifies the omission. His characterization of blacks as needing to be civilized up to white standards is certainly more controversial today than it would have been in Bellamy's day. His description of race separation as a bigoted local prejudice suggests his attitudes were on the whole very progressive ones.]

"Probably," I said, "you have sometimes eccentric persons—'crooked sticks' we used to call them—who refuse to adapt themselves to the social order on any terms or admit any such thing as social duty. If such a person should flatly refuse to render any sort of industrial or useful service on any terms, what would be done with him? No doubt there is a compulsory side to your system for dealing with such persons?"

"Not at all," replied the doctor. "If our system can not stand on its merits as the best possible arrangement for promoting the highest welfare of all, let it fall. As to the matter of industrial service, the law is simply that if any one shall refuse to do his or her part toward the maintenance of the social order he shall not be allowed to partake of its benefits. It would obviously not be fair to the rest that he should do so. But as to compelling him to work against his will by force, such an idea would be abhorrent to our people. The service of society is, above all, a service of honor, and all its associations are what you used to call chivalrous. Even as in your day soldiers would not serve with skulkers, but drummed cowards out of the camp, so would our workers refuse the companionship of persons openly seeking to evade their civic duty."

"But what do you do with such persons?"

"If an adult, being neither criminal nor insane, should deliberately and fixedly refuse to render his quota of service in any way, either in a chosen occupation or, on failure to choose, in an assigned one, he would be furnished with such a collection of seeds and tools as he might choose and turned loose on a reservation expressly prepared for such persons, corresponding a little perhaps with the reservations set apart for such Indians in your day as were unwilling to accept civilization. There he would be left to work out a better solution of the problem of existence than our society offers, if he could do so. We think we have the best possible social system, but if there is a better we want to know it, so that we may adopt it. We encourage the spirit of experiment."

"And are there really cases," I said, "of individuals who thus voluntarily abandon society in preference to fulfilling their social duty?"

"There have been such cases, though I do not know that there are any at the present time. But the provision for them exists."

(40–41)

"Talking of industrial service," I said, "reminds me of a question it has a dozen times occurred to me to ask you. I understand that everyone who is able to do so, women as well as men, serves the nation from twenty-one to forty-five years of age in some useful occupation; but so far as I have seen, although you are the picture of health and vigor, you have no employment, but are quite like young ladies of elegant leisure in my day, who spent their time sitting in the parlor and looking handsome. Of course, it is highly agreeable to me that you should be so free, but how, exactly, is so much leisure on your part squared with the universal obligation of service?"

Edith was greatly amused. "And so you thought I was shirking? Had it not occurred to you that there might probably be such things as vacations or furloughs in the industrial service, and that the rather unusual and interesting guest in our household might furnish a natural occasion for me to take an outing if I could get it?"

"And can you take your vacation when you please?"

"We can take a portion of it when we please, always subject, of course, to the needs of the service."

"But what do you do when you are at work—teach school, paint china, keep books for the Government, stand behind a counter in the public stores, or operate a typewriter or telegraph wire?"

"Does that list exhaust the number of women's occupations in your day?"

"Oh, no; those were only some of their lighter and pleasanter occupations. Women were also the scrubbers, the washers, the servants of all work. The most repulsive and humiliating kinds of drudgery were put off upon the women of the poorer class; but I suppose, of course, you do not do any such work."

"You may be sure that I do my part of whatever unpleasant things there are to do, and so does every one in the nation; but, indeed, we have long ago arranged affairs so that there is very little such work to do. But, tell me, were there no women in your day who were machinists, farmers, engineers, carpenters, iron workers, builders, engine drivers, or members of the other great crafts?"

"There were no women in such occupations. They were followed by men only."

"I suppose I knew that," she said; "I have read as much; but it is strange to talk with a man of the nineteenth century who is so much like a man of to-day and realize that the women were so different as to seem like another order of beings."

"But, really," said I, "I don't understand how in these respects the women can do very differently now unless they are physically much stronger. Most of these occupations you have just mentioned were too heavy for their strength, and for that reason, largely, were limited to men, as I should suppose they must still be."

"There is not a trade or occupation in the whole list," replied

Edith, "in which women do not take part. It is partly because we are physically much more vigorous than the poor creatures of your time that we do the sorts of work that were too heavy for them, but it is still more [on] account of the perfection of machinery. As we have grown stronger, all sorts of work have grown lighter. Almost no heavy work is done directly now; machines do all, and we only need to guide them, and the lighter the hand that guides, the better the work done. So you see that nowadays physical qualities have much less to do than mental with the choice of occupations. The mind is constantly getting nearer to the work, and father says some day we may be able to work by sheer will power directly and have no need of hands at all. It is said that there are actually more women than men in great machine works. My mother was first lieutenant in a great iron works. Some have a theory that the sense of power which one has in controlling giant engines appeals to women's sensibilities even more than to men's. [Following this, Edith reveals to Julian that she is thinking of becoming a farm worker for her occupation, that she and her mother have dressed in old-style dresses only to make Julian feel at home and that women generally wear trousers.]

(42-44)

"To do your contemporaries justice, they seemed themselves to realize that the swallowing up of the country by the city boded no good to civilization, and would apparently have been glad to find a cure for it, but they failed entirely to observe that, as it was a necessary effect of private capitalism, it could only be remedied by abolishing that."

"Just how," said I, "did the abolition of private capitalism and the substitution of a nationalized economic system operate to stop the growth of the cities?"

"By abolishing the need of markets for the exchange of labor and commodities," replied the doctor. "The facilities of exchange organized in the cities under the private capitalists were rendered wholly superfluous and impertinent by the national organization of production and distribution. The produce of the country was no longer handled by or distributed through the cities, except so far as produced or consumed there. The quality of goods furnished in all localities, and the measure of industrial service required of all, was the same. Economic equality having done away with rich and poor, the city ceased to be a place where greater luxury could be enjoyed or displayed than the country. The provision of employment and of maintenance on equal terms to all took away the advantages of locality as helps to livelihood. In a word, there was no longer any motive to lead a person to prefer city to country life, who did not like crowds for the sake of being crowded. Under these circumstances you will not find it strange that the growth of the cities ceased, and their depopulation began from the moment the effects of the Revolution became apparent."

"But you have cities yet!" I exclaimed.

"Certainly—that is, we have localities where population still remains denser than in other places. None of the great cities of your day have become extinct, but their populations are but small fractions of what they were."

"But Boston is certainly a far finer-looking city than in my day."

"All the modern cities are far finer and fairer in every way than their predecessors and infinitely fitter for human habitation, but in order to make them so it was necessary to get rid of their surplus population. There are in Boston to-day perhaps a quarter as many people as lived in the same limits in the Boston of your day, and that is simply because there were four times as many people within those limits as could be housed and furnished with environments consistent with the modern idea of healthful and agreeable living. New York, having been far worse crowded than Boston, has lost a still larger proportion of its former population. Were you to visit Manhattan Island I fancy your first impression would be that the Central Park of your day had been extended all the way from the Battery to Harlem River, though in fact the place is rather thickly built up according to modern notions, some two hundred and fifty thousand people living there among the groves and fountains."

"And you say this amazing depopulation took place at once after the Revolution?"

"It began then. The only way in which the vast populations of the old cities could be crowded into spaces so small was by packing them like sardines in tenement houses. As soon as it was settled that everybody must be provided with really and equally good habitations, it followed that the cities must lose the greater part of their population. These had to be provided with dwellings in the country. Of course, so vast a work could not be accomplished instantly, but it proceeded with all possible speed. In addition to the exodus of people from the cities because there was no room for them to live decently, there was also a great outflow of others who, now there had ceased to be any economic advantages in city life, were attracted by the natural charms of the country; so that you may easily see that it was one of the great tasks of the first decade after the Revolution to provide homes elsewhere for those who desired to leave the cities. The tendency countryward continued until the cities having been emptied of their excess of people, it was possible to make radical changes in their arrangements. A large proportion of the old buildings and all the unsightly, lofty, and inartistic ones were cleared away and replaced with structures of the low, broad, roomy style adapted to the new ways of living. Parks, gardens, and roomy spaces were multiplied on every hand and the system of transit so modified as to get rid of the noise and dust, and finally, in a word, the city of your day was changed into the modern city. Having thus been made as pleasant places to live in as was the country itself, the outflow of population from the cities ceased and an equilibrium became established."

(293–95)

"You must not fail to bear in mind that the great Revolution, as it came in America, was not a revolution at all in the political sense in which all former revolutions in the popular interest had been. In all these instances the people, after making up their minds what they wanted changed, had to overthrow the Government and seize the power in order to change it. But in a democratic state like America the Revolution was practically done when the people had made up their minds that it was for their interest. There was no one to dispute their power and right to do their will when once resolved on it. The Revolution as regards America and in other countries, in proportion as their governments were popular, was more like the trial of a case in court than a revolution of the traditional blood-and-thunder sort. The court was the people, and the only way that either contestant could win was by convincing the court, from which there was no appeal.

"So far as the stage properties of the traditional revolution were concerned, plots, conspiracies, powder-smoke, blood and thunder, any one of the ten thousand squabbles in the medieval, Italian, and Flemish towns, furnishes far more material to the romancer or playwright than did the great Revolution in America."

"Am I to understand that there [were] actually no violent doings in connection with this great transformation?"

"There were a great number of minor disturbances and collisions, involving in the aggregate a considerable amount of violence and bloodshed, but there was nothing like the war with pitched lines which the early reformers looked for. Many a petty dispute, causeless and resultless, between nameless kings in the past, too small for historical mention, has cost far more violence and bloodshed than, so far as America is concerned, did the greatest of all revolutions."

"And did the European nations fare as well when they passed through the same crisis?"

"The conditions of none of them were so favorable to peaceful social revolution as were those of the United States, and the experience of most was longer and harder, but it may be said that in the case of none of the European peoples were the direful apprehensions of blood and slaughter justified which the earlier reformers seem to have entertained. All over the world the Revolution was, as to its main factors, a triumph of moral forces."

(346–47)

"In my day," I said, "a peculiar complication of the social problem in America was the existence in the Southern States of many millions of recently freed negro slaves, but partially as yet equal to the responsibility of freedom. I should be interested to know just how the new order adapted itself to the condition of the colored race in the South."

"It proved," replied the doctor, "the prompt solution of a problem which otherwise might have continued indefinitely to plague the American people. The population of recent slaves was in need of some sort of industrial regimen, at once firm and benevolent, administered under conditions which should meanwhile tend to educate, refine, and elevate its members. These conditions the new order met with ideal perfection. The centralized discipline of the national industrial army, depending for its enforcement not so much on force as on the inability of any one to subsist outside of the system of which it was a part, furnished just the sort of a control— gentle yet resistless—which was needed by the recently emancipated bondsman. On the other hand, the universal education and the refinements and amenities of life which came with the economic welfare presently brought to all alike by the new order, meant for the colored race even more as a civilizing agent than it did to the white population which relatively had been further advanced."

"There would have been in some parts," I remarked, "a strong prejudice on the part of the white population against any system which compelled a closer commingling of the races."

"So we read, but there was absolutely nothing in the new system to offend that prejudice. It related entirely to economic organization, and had nothing more to do then than it has now with social relations. Even for industrial purposes the new system involved no more commingling of races than the old had done. It was perfectly consistent with any degree of race separation in industry which the most bigoted local prejudices might demand."

(364–65; passages from Equality.
Toronto: George N. Morang, 1897)

Appendix E: A Victorian "Angel In the House"—Emma Bellamy

[The following portrait of Emma Bellamy, by Fanny M. Johnson, appeared as "Unknown Wives of Well-Known Men. XIX—Mrs. Edward Bellamy." *The Ladies' Home Journal* vol. IX, No. 8, Philadelphia: July 1892, p. 1. It is one of a series of portraits including Mrs. Edison, Mrs. Barnum, and Mrs. Gladstone. It is an excellent illustration of the stock Victorian notion of wife and mother as moral influence. In *Looking Backward* Bellamy reflects this view of women to some extent, but in other ways (such as equality of income for both sexes) he goes far beyond this conventional view.]

In her husband's work and aims, Mrs. Bellamy is an earnest believer and hearty sympathizer. "I am often asked," she says, "whether Mr. Bellamy seriously believed in the theories of 'Looking Backward,' or whether it was written merely for effect. I know he was, and is, thoroughly in earnest in all he has written and done. He is far more sanguine than I, but yet I feel that the ends which he and his friends are working for will be brought about, and that much sooner than people can now believe."

Such is the theory and belief of this gentle woman, into whose calm life the accident of fame has wrought little change. Wholly without ostentation or pretense, she keeps on in the quiet round of her home duties, a type of the many wives and mothers to whom loyalty and love for husband and children stand first, but whose influence is beyond all reckoning in keeping the standards of a community pure, and its home life sweet.

Appendix F: A Response to Looking Backward *by Charlotte Perkins Gilman*

[Charlotte Perkins Gilman (1860-1935) is known to many as the author of a chilling short story called "The Yellow Wallpaper" and of the feminist utopia *Herland* (1915). In *The New Nation* of 14 March 1891 (when she was Charlotte Perkins Stetson) she published a poem which satirized the notion of economic competition and supported the central thrust of *Looking Backward* to economic co-operation.]

THE SURVIVAL OF THE FITTEST.

In northern zones the ranging bear
Protects himself with fat and hair.
Where snow is deep and ice is stark,
And half the year is cold and dark,
He still survives a clime like that
By growing fur, by growing fat.
These traits, O Bear, which thou transmittest
Prove the survival of the fittest!

To polar regions waste and wan
Comes the encroaching race of man.
A puny, feeble, little lubber –
He had no fur, he had no blubber.
The scornful bear sat down at ease
To see the stranger starve and freeze;
But lo! The stranger slew the bear,
And ate his fat, and wore his hair!
These deeds, O Man! which thou committest,
Prove the survival of the fittest!

In modern times the millionaire
Protects himself as did the bear.
Where Poverty and Hunger are,
He counts his bullion by the car.
Where thousands suffer, still he thrives,

And after death his Will survives.
The wealth, O Croesus! thou transmittest,
Proves the survival of the fittest!

But lo! some people, odd and funny,
Some men without a cent of money,
The simple, common Human Race,—
Chose to improve their dwelling place!
They had no use for Millionaires;
They calmly said the world was theirs;
They were so wise – so strong – so many –
The Millionaire? –There wasn't any!
These deeds, O Man, which thou committest,
Prove the survival of the fittest!

Appendix G: "The True Remedy" from Henry George's Progress and Poverty (1879)

[Henry George (1839-97) was another famous utopian economist of Bellamy's era. His *Progress and Poverty* generated the same kind of wide interest as *Looking Backward*, and sold millions of copies.]

We have traced the unequal distribution of wealth which is the curse and menace of modern civilization to the institution of private property in land. We have seen that so long as this institution exists no increase in productive power can permanently benefit the masses; but, on the contrary, must tend still further to depress their condition. We have examined all the remedies, short of the abolition of private property in land, which are currently relied on or proposed for the relief of poverty and the better distribution of wealth, and have found them all inefficacious or impracticable.

There is but one way to remove an evil—and that is, to remove its cause. Poverty deepens as wealth increases, and wages are forced down while productive power grows, because land, which is the source of all wealth and the field of all labor, is monopolized. To extirpate poverty, to make wages what justice commands they should be, the full earnings of the laborer, we must therefore substitute for the individual ownership of land a common ownership. Nothing else will go to the cause of the evil—in nothing else is there the slightest hope.

This, then, is the remedy for the unjust and unequal distribution of wealth apparent in modern civilization, and for all the evils which flow from it:

We must make land common property.

We have reached this conclusion by an examination in which every step has been proved and secured. In the chain of reasoning no link is wanting and no link is weak. Deduction and induction have brought us to the same truth—that the unequal ownership of land necessitates the unequal distribution of wealth. And as in the nature of things unequal ownership of land is inseparable from the recognition of individual property in land, it necessarily follows that the only remedy for the unjust distribution of wealth is in making land common property.

But this is a truth which, in the present state of society, will arouse the most bitter antagonism, and must fight its way, inch by inch. It will be necessary, therefore, to meet the objections of those who, even when driven to admit this truth, will declare that it cannot be practically applied.

In doing this we shall bring our previous reasoning to a new and crucial test. Just as we try addition by subtraction and multiplication by division, so may we, by testing the sufficiency of the remedy, prove the correctness of our conclusions as to the cause of the evil.

The laws of the universe are harmonious. And if the remedy to which we have been led is the true one, it must be consistent with justice; it must be practicable of application; it must accord with the tendencies of social development and must harmonize with other reforms.

All this I propose to show. I propose to meet all practical objections that can be raised; and to show that this simple measure is not only easy of application; but that it is a sufficient remedy for all the evils which, as modern progress goes on, arise from the greater and greater inequality in the distribution of wealth—that it will substitute equality for inequality, plenty for want, justice for injustice, social strength for social weakness, and will open the way to grander and nobler advances of civilization...

(*The Complete Works of Henry George,* vol 1. Garden City, New York: Doubleday, Page & Co., 1911. 326-28)

Appendix H: Excerpts from A Traveler From Altruria by William Dean Howells

[William Dean Howells (1837–1920) was a prolific author of fiction, drama, poetry and criticism. *A Traveler From Altruria* (1894) is a reverse utopia in the sense that the utopian visits America rather than the other way around. The excerpts given here set the stage and discuss work and neighborliness (showing the influence of William Morris), the appearance of the country and the economic system (in which there are strong parallels with Bellamy). The gulf between Mr. Homos and his listeners makes for some lively exchanges.]

I said, "Gentlemen, I wish to introduce my friend, Mr. Homos," and then I presented them severally to him by name. We all sat down, and I explained: "Mr. Homos is from Altruria. He is visiting our country for the first time, and is greatly interested in the working of our institutions. He has been asking me some rather hard questions about certain phases of our civilization; and the fact is that I have launched him upon you because I don't feel quite able to cope with him."

They all laughed civilly at this sally of mine, but the professor asked, with a sarcasm that I thought hardly merited, "What point in our polity can be obscured to the author of 'Glove and Gauntlet' and 'Airs and Graces'?"

They all laughed again, not so civilly, I felt, and then the banker asked my friend, "Is it long since you left Altruria?"

"It seems a great while ago," the Altrurian answered, "but it is really only a few weeks."

"You came by way of England, I suppose?"

"Yes; there is no direct line to America," said the Altrurian.

"That seems rather odd," I ventured, with some patriotic grudge.

"Oh, the English have direct lines everywhere," the banker instructed me.

"The tariff has killed our shipbuilding," said the professor. No one took up this firebrand, and the professor added, "Your name is Greek, isn't it, Mr. Homos?"

"Yes; we are of one of the early Hellenic families," said the Altrurian.

"And do you think," asked the lawyer, who, like most lawyers, was a lover of romance, and was well read in legendary lore especially, "that there is any reason for supposing that Altruria is identical with the fabled Atlantis?"

"No, I can't say that I do. We have no traditions of a submergence of the continent, and there are only the usual evidences of a glacial epoch which you find everywhere, to support such a theory. Besides, our civilization is strictly Christian, and dates back to no earlier period than that of the first Christian commune after Christ. It is a matter of history with us that one of these communists, when they were dispersed, brought the gospel to our continent; he was cast away on our eastern coast on his way to Britain."

"Yes, we know that," the minister intervened, "but it is perfectly astonishing that an island so large as Altruria should have been lost to the knowledge of the rest of the world ever since the beginning of our era. You would hardly think that there was a space of the ocean's surface a mile square which had not been traversed by a thousand keels since Columbus sailed westward."

(46–48)

The Altrurian seemed to be sensible of the kindly skepticism which persisted in our reception of his statements, after all we had read of Altruria. He smiled indulgently, and said: "You mustn't imagine that work in Altruria is the same as it is here. As we all work, the amount that each one need do is very little, a few hours each day at the most, so that every man and woman has abundant leisure and perfect spirits for the higher pleasures which the education of their whole youth has fitted them to enjoy. If you can understand a state of things where the sciences and arts and letters are cultivated for their own sake, and not as a means of livelihood"—

"No," said the lawyer, smiling, "I'm afraid we can't conceive of that. We consider the pinch of poverty the highest incentive that a man can have."

(80–81)

The Altrurian looked around at all our faces, and no doubt read our eager curiosity in them. He smiled, and said… "I do not think you will find anything so remarkable in our civilization, if you will conceive of it as the outgrowth of the neighborly instinct. In fact, neighborliness is the essence of Altrurianism. If you will imagine having the same feeling toward all," he explained to Mrs. Makely, "as you have toward your next door neighbor"—

"My next door neighbor!" she cried. "But I don't *know* the people next door! We live in a large apartment house, some forty families, and I assure you I do not know a soul among them."

He looked at her with a puzzled air, and she continued, "Sometimes it *does* seem rather hard. One day the people on the same landing with us, lost one of their children, and I should never have been a whit the wiser, if my cook hadn't happened to mention it. The servants all know each other; they meet in the back elevator, and get acquainted. I don't encourage it. You can't tell what kind of families they belong to."

"But surely," the Altrurian persisted, "you have friends in the city whom you think of as your neighbors?"

"No, I can't say that I have," said Mrs. Makely. "I have my visiting list, but I shouldn't think of anybody on *that* as a neighbor."

The Altrurian looked so blank and baffled that I could hardly help laughing. "Then I should not know how to explain Altruria to you, I'm afraid."

"Well," she returned lightly, "if it's anything like neighborliness, as I've seen it in small places, deliver me from it! I like being independent. That's why I like the city. You're let alone."

(185–86)

"As soon as we were freed from the necessity of preying upon one another, we found that *there was no hurry*. The good work would wait to be well done; and one of the earliest effects of the Evolution was the disuse of the swift trains which had traversed the continent, night and day, that one man might overreach another, or make haste to undersell his rival, or seize some advantage of him, or plot some profit to his loss. Nine-tenths of the railroads, which in the old time had ruinously competed, and then in the hands of the Accumulation had been united to impoverish and oppress the people, fell into disuse. The commonwealth operated the few lines that were necessary for the collection of materials and the distribution of manufactures, and for pleasure travel and the affairs of state: but the roads that had been built to invest capital, or parallel other roads, or 'make work,' as it was called, or to develop resources, or boom localities, were suffered to fall into ruin; the rails were stripped from the landscape, which they had bound as with shackles, and the road-beds became highways for the use of kindly neighborhoods, or nature recovered them wholly and hid the memory of their former abuse in grass and flowers and wild vines. The ugly towns that they had forced into being, as Frankenstein was fashioned, from the materials of the charnel, and that had no life in or from the good of the community, soon tumbled into decay. The administration used parts of them in the construction of the villages in which the Altrurians now mostly live; but generally these towns were built of materials so fraudulent, in form so vile, that it was judged best to burn them. In this way their sites were at once purified and obliterated.

(279–81)

"We have totally eliminated chance from our economic life. There is still a chance that a man will be tall or short, in Altruria, that he will be strong or weak, well or ill, gay or grave, happy or unhappy in love, but none that he will be rich or poor, busy or idle, live splendidly or meanly. These stupid and vulgar accidents of human contrivance cannot befall us; but I shall not be able to tell you just how or why, or to detail the process of eliminating chance. I may say, however, that it began with the nationalization of telegraphs, expresses, railroads, mines and all large industries operated by stock companies. This at once struck a fatal blow at the speculation in values, real and unreal, and at the stock exchange, or bourse; we had our own name for that gambler's paradise, or gambler's hell, whose baleful influence penetrated every branch of business.

"There were still business fluctuations, as long as we had business, but they were on a smaller and smaller scale, and with the final lapse of business they necessarily vanished; all economic chance vanished. The founders of the common-wealth understood perfectly that business was the sterile activity of the function interposed between the demand and the supply; that it was nothing structural; and they intended its extinction, and expected it from the moment that money was abolished."

"This is all pretty tiresome," said the professor, to our immediate party. "I don't see why we oblige ourselves to listen to that fellow's stuff. As if a civilized state could exist for a day without money or business."

(307–08. William Dean Howells. *A Traveler From Altruria.*
New York: Harper & Brothers, 1894)

Appendix I: An Excerpt on Education from
William Morris's News from Nowhere *(1890)*

[Partly in reaction to Bellamy's highly systematic approach to education Morris's approach is almost entirely dependent on the child's curiosity: he or she will pick up a book or ask someone when ready. The same radical difference is apparent in the two approaches to work and government. Note also the anticipation of W. D. Howells's *Altruria* as quoted above, that life in utopia offers "time to grow."]

"I want an extra word or two about your ideas of education; although I gathered from Dick that you let your children run wild and didn't teach them anything; and in short, that you have so refined your education, that now you have none."

"Then you gathered left-handed," quoth he. "But of course I understand your point of view about education, which is that of times past, when 'the struggle for life,' as men used to phrase it (i.e., the struggle for a slave's rations on one side, and for a bouncing share of the slaveholders' privilege on the other), pinched 'education' for most people into a niggardly dole of not very accurate information; something to be swallowed by the beginner in the art of living whether he liked it or not, and was hungry for it or not: and which had been chewed and digested over and over again by people who didn't care about it."

I stopped the old man's rising wrath by a laugh, and said: "Well, *you* were not taught that way, at any rate, so you may let your anger run off you a little."

"True, true," said he, smiling. "I thank you for correcting my ill-temper: I always fancy myself as living in any period of which we may be speaking. But, however, to put it in a cooler way: you expected to see children thrust into schools when they had reached an age conventionally supposed to be the due age, whatever their varying faculties and dispositions might be, and when there, with like disregard to facts to be subjected to a certain conventional course of 'learning.' My friend, can't you see that such a proceeding means ignoring the fact of *growth*, bodily and mental? No one could come out of such a mill uninjured; and those only would avoid being crushed by it who would have the spirit of rebellion strong in them. Fortunately most children have had that at all times, or I do not know that we should ever have reached our present position. Now you see what it all comes to. In the old times all this was the result of *poverty*. In the nineteenth century, society was so miserably poor, owing to the systematised robbery on which it was founded, that real education was impossible for anybody. The whole theory of their so-called education was that it was necessary to shove a little information into a child, even if it were by means of torture, and accompanied by twaddle which it was well known was of no use, or else he would lack information lifelong: the hurry of poverty forbade anything else. All that is past; we are no longer hurried, and the information lies ready to each one's hand when his own inclinations impel him to seek it. In this as in other matters we have become wealthy: we can afford to give ourselves time to grow."

"Yes," said I, "but suppose the child, youth, man, never wants the information, never grows in the direction you might hope him to do: suppose, for instance, he objects to learning arithmetic or mathematics; you can't force him when he *is* grown; can't you force him while he is growing, and oughtn't you to do so?"

"Well," said he, "were you forced to learn arithmetic and mathematics?"

"A little," said I.

"And how old are you now?"

"Say fifty-six," said I.

"And how much arithmetic and mathematics do you know now?" quoth the old man, smiling rather mockingly.

Said I: "None whatever, I am sorry to say."

Hammond laughed quietly, but made no other comment on my admission, and I dropped the subject of education, perceiving him to be hopeless on that side.

(*The Collected Works of William Morris*, Vol XVI. London: Longmans Green and Company, 1912, 63-65)

Further Reading

Bibliography

Griffith, Nancy Snell. *Edward Bellamy: A Bibliography*. Metuchen, N.J.: Scarecrow, 1986. [A selected version of this reference appears in Patai, cited below.]

Widdicombe, Richard Toby. *Edward Bellamy: An Annotated Bibliography of Secondary Criticism*. New York and London: Garland Publishing, 1988.

About Bellamy and *Looking Backward*

Auerbach, Jonathan. "'The Nation Organized': Utopian Impotence in Edward Bellamy's *Looking Backward.*" *American Literary History* 6:1 (1994) 24–47.

Bowman, Sylvia E., ed. *Edward Bellamy Abroad: An American Prophet's Influence*. New York: Twayne Publishers, 1962.

———. *Edward Bellamy*. Boston: Twayne Publishers, 1986.

Connor, George E. "The Awakening of Edward Bellamy: *Looking Backward* at Religious Influence." *Utopian Studies* 11:1 (2000) 38–50.

Dentith, Simon. "Imagination and Inversion in Nineteenth-Century Utopian Writing". *Anticipations. Essays on Early Science Fiction and Its Precursors*. Ed. David Seed. Liverpool: Syracuse University Press, 1995, 137–52.

"Edward Bellamy. Hopes and Dreams." Video. Executive Producer Beth Curley. WGBY TV/WGBY Educational Foundation. Springfield, Mass., 1988. Available from the Edward Bellamy Memorial Association, 91–93 Church Street, Chicopee MA 01020.

Halewood, W.H. "Catching Up With Edward Bellamy." *University of Toronto Quarterly* 63:3 (Spring 1994) 451–61.

Hall, Richard A.S. "The Religious Ethics of Edward Bellamy and Jonathan Edwards." *Utopian Studies* 8:2 (1997) 13–31.

Hartman, Matthew. "Utopian Evolution: The Sentimental Critique of Social Darwinism in Bellamy and Pierce." *Utopian Studies* 10:1 (1999) 26–41.

Levitas, Ruth. "Who Holds the Hose: Domestic Labour in the Work of Bellamy, Gilman and Morris." *Utopian Studies* 6:1 (1995) 65–84.

Lipow, Arthur. *Authoritarian Socialism in America: Edward Bellamy and the Nationalist Movement.* Berkeley: University of California Press, 1982.

McClay, Wilfred M. "Edward Bellamy and the Politics of Meaning." *The American Scholar* 64:2 (Spring 1994) 264–71.

Morgan, Arthur E. *Edward Bellamy.* New York: Columbia University Press, 1944.

Mullin, John R. "Edward Bellamy's Ambivalence: Can Utopia Be Urban?" *Utopian Studies* 11:1 (2000) 51–65.

Patai, Daphne, ed. *Looking Backward, 1988–1888. Essays on Edward Bellamy.* Amherst: University of Massachusetts Press, 1988.

Roemer, Kenneth M. *Utopian Audiences. How Readers Locate Nowhere.* Amherst: University of Massachusetts Press, forthcoming.

Thomas, John L. *Alternative America. Henry George, Edward Bellamy, Henry Demarest Lloyd and the Adversary Tradition.* Cambridge, Mass.: Harvard University Press, 1983.

Toth, Csaba. "When The Future Was Ours To See: Edward Bellamy, Utopian Politics and the Project of Modernity." *Studies in Language and Culture,* 2 (July 2001).

Widdicombe, Richard Toby and Preiser, Hank. *Edward Bellamy: His Legacy for a New Millennium.* Edwin Mellen Press, forthcoming.

Williams, Nicholas M. "The Limits of Spacialized Form: Visibility and Obscurity in Edward Bellamy's *Looking Backward.*" *Utopian Studies* 10:2 (1999) 25–39.

Zauderer, Naomi B. "Charlotte Perkins Gilman's *Moving the Mountain*: A Response to *Looking Backward.*" *Utopian Studies* 3:1 (1992) 53–69.

Utopian Scholarship

Manuel, Frank E. and Fritzie P. *Utopian Thought In The Western World.* Cambridge, Mass.: Harvard University Press, 1979.

Pfaelzer, Jean. *The Utopian Novel in America, 1886–1896: The Politics of Form.* Pittsburgh: University of Pittsburgh Press, 1984.

Roemer, Kenneth M. *The Obsolete Necessity. America in Utopian Writings, 1888–1900.* Ashland, Ohio: Kent State University Press, 1976.

Sargent, Lyman Tower. *British and American Utopian Literature, 1516–1985: An Annotated, Chronological Bibliography.* New York: Garland, 1988.

————, ed. *Utopian Studies.* The journal of the Society for Utopian Studies includes wide-ranging articles on utopian literature and thought, and on Edward Bellamy.

———— et al. *Utopia. The Search for the Ideal Society in the Western World.*

New York: New York Public Library and Oxford University Press, 2000.

Tod, Ian and Wheeler, Michael. *Utopia*. New York, Harmony Books, 1978.